Bernhard Tauchnitz

The Works of William Shakespeare

From the text of Alexander Dyce's complete in seven volumes, vol. VII

Bernhard Tauchnitz

The Works of William Shakespeare
From the text of Alexander Dyce's complete in seven volumes, vol. VII

ISBN/EAN: 9783742857279

Manufactured in Europe, USA, Canada, Australia, Japa

Cover: Foto ©Andreas Hilbeck / pixelio.de

Manufactured and distributed by brebook publishing software
(www.brebook.com)

Bernhard Tauchnitz

The Works of William Shakespeare

THE WORKS

OF

WILLIAM SHAKESPEARE

FROM THE TEXT OF THE

REV. ALEXANDER DYCE'S

SECOND EDITION.

COMPLETE IN SEVEN VOLUMES.

VOL. VII.

LEIPZIG

BERNHARD TAUCHNITZ

1868.

CONTENTS

OF VOLUME VII.

——

——

PERICLES.

DRAMATIS PERSONÆ.

ANTIOCHUS, king of Antioch.	Marshal.
PERICLES, prince of Tyre.	A Pander.
HELICANUS, } two lords of Tyre.	BOULT, his servant.
ESCANES,	
SIMONIDES, king of Pentapolis.	
CLEON, governor of Tharsus.	The Daughter of Antiochus.
LYSIMACHUS, governor of Myti-	DIONYZA, wife to Cleon.
lene.	THAISA, daughter to Simonides.
CERIMON, a lord of Ephesus.	MARINA, daughter to Pericles and
THALIARD, a lord of Antioch.	Thaisa.
PHILEMON, servant to Cerimon.	LYCHORIDA, nurse to Marina.
LEONINE, servant to Dionyza.	A Bawd.

Lords, Ladies, Knights, Gentlemen, Sailors, Pirates, Fishermen,
and Messengers.

DIANA.

GOWER, as Chorus.

SCENE — *dispersedly in various countries.*

ACT I.

Enter GOWER.

Before the palace of Antioch.

To sing a song that old was sung,
From ashes ancient Gower is come;
Assuming man's infirmities,
To glad your ear and please your eyes.
It hath been sung at festivals,
On ember-eves and holy-ales;

And lords and ladies in their lives
Have read it for restoratives:
The purchase is to make men glorious;
Et bonum quo antiquius, eo melius.
If you, born in these latter times,
When wit's more ripe, accept my rhymes,
And that to hear an old man sing
May to your wishes pleasure bring,
I life would wish, and that I might
Waste it for you, like taper-light. —
This Antioch, then, Antiochus the Great
Built up, this city, for his chiefest seat;
The fairest in all Syria, —
I tell you what mine authors say:
This king unto him took a fere,
Who died and left a female heir,
So buxom, blithe, and full of face,
As heaven had lent her all his grace;
With whom the father liking took,
And her to incest did provoke: —
Bad child; worse father! to entice his own
To evil should be done by none:
But custom what they did begin
Was with long use account no sin.
The beauty of this sinful dame
Made many princes thither frame,
To seek her as a bed-fellow,
In marriage-pleasures play-fellow:
Which to prevent he made a law, —
To keep her still, and men in awe, —
That whoso ask'd her for his wife,
His riddle told not, lost his life:
So for her many a wight did die,
As yon grim looks do testify.
What now ensues, to the judgment of your eye
I give, my cause who best can justify.

[*Exit.*

SCENE I. *Antioch. A room in the palace.*

Enter ANTIOCHUS, PERICLES, *and* Attendants.

Ant. Young prince of Tyre, you have at large receiv'd
The danger of the task you undertake.

Per. I have, Antiochus, and, with a soul
Embolden'd with the glory of her praise,
Think death no hazard in this enterprise.

Ant. Bring in our daughter, clothèd like a bride,
For the embracements even of Jove himself;
At whose conception, till Lucina reign'd,
Nature this dowry gave, to glad her presence,
The senate-house of planets all did sit,
To knit in her their best perfections.

Music. Enter the Daughter of Antiochus.

Per. See where she comes, apparell'd like the spring,
Graces her subjects, and her thoughts the king
Of every virtue gives renown to men!
Her face the book of praises, where is read
Nothing but curious pleasures, as from thence
Sorrow were ever raz'd, and testy wrath
Could never be her mild companion.
You gods that made me man, and sway in love,
That have inflam'd desire in my breast
To taste the fruit of yon celestial tree,
Or die in the adventure, be my helps,
As I am son and servant to your will,
To compass such a boundless happiness!

Ant. Prince Pericles, —

Per. That would be son to great Antiochus.

Ant. Before thee stands this fair Hesperides,
With golden fruit, but dangerous to be touch'd;
For death-like dragons here affright thee hard:
Her face, like heaven, enticeth thee to view
Her countless glory, which desert must gain;
And which, without desert, because thine eye

1*

Presumes to reach, all thy whole heap must die.
Yon sometime famous princes, like thyself,
Drawn by report, adventurous by desire,
Tell thee, with speechless tongues and semblance pale,
That, without covering, save yon field of stars,
Here they stand martyrs, slain in Cupid's wars;
And with dead cheeks advise thee to desist
For going on death's net, whom none resist.

    Per. Antiochus, I thank thee, who hath taught
My frail mortality to know itself,
And by those fearful objects to prepare
This body, like to them, to what I must;
For death remember'd should be like a mirror,
Who tells us life 's but breath, to trust it error.
I'll make my will, then; and, as sick men do,
Who know the world, see heaven, but, feeling woe,
Gripe not at earthly joys, as erst they did;
So I bequeath a happy peace to you
And all good men, as every prince should do;
My riches to the earth from whence they came; —
But my unspotted fire of love to you.

                                    [*To the Daughter of Antiochus.*
Thus ready for the way of life or death,
I wait the sharpest blow.

    Ant. Scorning advice, — read the conclusion, then:
Which read and not expounded, 'tis decreed,
As these before thee, thou thyself shalt bleed.

    Daugh. Of all say'd yet, mayst thou prove prosperous!
Of all say'd yet, I wish thee happiness!

    Per. Like a bold champion, I assume the lists,
Nor ask advice of any other thought
But faithfulness and courage.   [*Reads the riddle.*

      "*I am no viper, yet I feed*
        On mother's flesh which did me breed.
        I sought a husband, in which labour
        I found that kindness in a father:

> *He's father, son, and husband mild;*
> *I mother, wife, and yet his child.*
> *How they may be, and yet in two,*
> *As you will live, resolve it you."*

Sharp physic is the last: but, O you powers
That give heaven countless eyes to view men's acts,
Why cloud they not their sights perpetually,
If this be true, which makes me pale to read it? —
Fair glass of light, I lov'd you, and could still,
                    . [*Takes hold of the hand of the Princess.*
Were not this glorious casket stor'd with ill:
But I must tell you, — now my thoughts revolt;
For he's no man on whom perfections wait
That, knowing sin within, will touch the gate.
You're a fair viol, and your sense the strings;
Who, finger'd to make man his lawful music,
Would draw heaven down, and all the gods, to hearken;
But being play'd upon before your time,
Hell only danceth at so harsh a chime.
Good sooth, I care not for you.
    Ant. Prince Pericles, touch not, upon thy life,
For that's an article within our law,
As dangerous as the rest. Your time's expir'd:
Either expound now, or receive your sentence.
    Per. Great king,
Few love to hear the sins they love to act;
'Twould braid yourself too near for me to tell it.
Who has a book of all that monarchs do,
He's more secure to keep it shut than shown:
For vice repeated is like the wandering wind,
Blows dust in others' eyes, to spread itself;
And yet the end of all is bought thus dear,
The breath is gone, and the sore eyes see clear
To stop the air would hurt them. The blind mole casts
Copp'd hills towards heaven, to tell the earth is throng'd
By man's oppression; and the poor worm doth die for't.

Kings are earth's gods; in vice their law's their will;
And if Jove stray, who dares say Jove doth ill?
It is enough you know; and it is fit;
What being more known grows worse, to smother it.
All love the womb that their first being bred,
Then give my tongue like leave to love my head.

    Ant. [*aside*] Heaven, that I had thy head! he has found
        the meaning:
But I will gloze with him. — Young prince of Tyre,
Though by the tenour of our strict edict,
Your exposition misinterpreting,
We might proceed to cancel of your days;
Yet hope, succeeding from so fair a tree
As your fair self, doth tune us otherwise:
Forty days longer we do respite you;
If by which time our secret be undone,
This mercy shows we'll joy in such a son:
And until then your entertain shall be
As doth befit our honour and your worth.

                  [*Exeunt all except Pericles.*

    Per. How courtesy would seem to cover sin,
When what is done is like an hypocrite,
The which is good in nothing but in sight!
If it be true that I interpret false,
Then were it certain you were not so bad
As with foul incest to abuse your soul;
Where now you're both a father and a son
By your untimely claspings with your child, —
Which pleasure fits an husband, not a father;
And she an eater of her mother's flesh
By the defiling of her parent's bed;
And both like serpents are, who though they feed
On sweetest flowers, yet they poison breed.
Antioch, farewell! for wisdom sees, those men
Blush not in actions blacker than the night,
Will shun no course to keep them from the light.
One sin, I know, another doth provoke;

Murder's as near to lust as flame to smoke:
Poison and treason are the hands of sin,
Ay, and the targets, to put off the shame:
Then, lest my life be cropp'd to keep you clear,
By flight I'll shun the danger which I fear.   [*Exit.*

Re-enter ANTIOCHUS.

    Ant. He hath found the meaning, for the which we mean
To have his head.
He must not live to trumpet forth my infamy,
Nor tell the world Antiochus doth sin
In such a loathèd manner;
And therefore instantly this prince must die;
For by his fall my honour must keep high. —
Who attends us there?

Enter THALIARD.

    Thal.   Doth your highness call?
    Ant. Thaliard,
You're of our chamber, and our mind partakes
Her private actions to your secrecy:
And for your faithfulness we will advance you.
Thaliard, behold, here's poison, and here's gold;
We hate the prince of Tyre, and thou must kill him:
It fits thee not to ask the reason why,
Because we bid it. Say, is it done?
    Thal.   My lord,
'Tis done.
    Ant. Enough.

Enter a Messenger.

Let your breath cool yourself, telling your haste.
    Mess. My lord, Prince Pericles is fled.   [*Exit.*
    Ant.   As thou
Wilt live, fly after; and, like an arrow shot
From a well-experienc'd archer, hits the mark
His eye doth level at, so thou ne'er return
Unless thou say "Prince Pericles is dead."

Thal. My lord,
If I can get him within my pistol's length,
I'll make him sure enough: so, farewell to your highness.
    Ant. Thaliard, adieu! [*Exit Thal.*] Till Pericles be dead
My heart can lend no succour to my head.   [*Exit.*

SCENE II. *Tyre. A room in the palace.*

Enter PERICLES.

Per. [*to those without*] Let none disturb us. — Why should
      this charge of thoughts,
The sad companion, dull-ey'd melancholy,
Be my so-us'd a guest as not an hour,
In the day's glorious walk or peaceful night, —
The tomb where grief should sleep, — can breed me quiet?
Here pleasures court mine eyes, and mine eyes shun them,
And danger, which I fear'd, 's at Antioch,
Whose aim seems far too short to hit me here:
Yet neither pleasure's art can joy my spirits,
Nor yet the other's distance comfort me.
Then it is thus: the passions of the mind,
That have their first conception by mis-dread,
Have after-nourishment and life by care;
And what was first but fear what might be done,
Grows elder now, and cares it be not done.
And so with me: — the great Antiochus —
'Gainst whom I am too little to contend, —
Since he's so great can make his will his act —
Will think me speaking, though I swear to silence;
Nor boots it me to say I honour him,
If he suspect I may dishonour him:
And what may make him blush in being known,
He'll stop the course by which it might be known;
With hostile forces he'll o'erspread the land,
And with th' ostent of war will look so huge,
Amazement shall drive courage from the state;
Our men be vanquish'd ere they do resist,

And subjects punish'd that ne'er thought offence:
Which care of them, not pity of myself, —
Who am no more but as the tops of trees,
Which fence the roots they grow by, and defend them, —
Makes both my body pine and soul to languish,
And punish that before that he would punish.

Enter HELICANUS *and other* Lords.

First Lord.   Joy and all comfort in your sacred breast!
Sec. Lord.   And keep your mind, till you return to us,
Peaceful and comfortable!
Hel.   Peace, peace, and give experience tongue.
They do abuse the king that flatter him:
For flattery is the bellows blows up sin;
The thing the which is flatter'd, but a spark,
To which that blast gives heat and stronger glowing;
Whereas reproof, obedient, and in order,
Fits kings, as they are men, for they may err.
When Signior Sooth here does proclaim a peace,
He flatters you, makes war upon your life.
Prince, pardon me, or strike me, if you please;
I cannot be much lower than my knees.
Per.   All leave us else; but let your cares o'erlook
What shipping and what lading's in our haven,
And then return to us. [*Exeunt Lords.*] Helicanus, thou
Hast movèd us: what seest thou in our looks?
Hel.   An angry brow, dread lord.
Per.   If there be such a dart in princes' frowns,
How durst thy tongue move anger to our face?
Hel.   How dare the plants look up to heaven, from whence
They have their nourishment?
Per.   Thou know'st I've power
To take thy life from thee.
Hel. [*kneeling*]   I've ground the axe myself;
Do you but strike the blow.
Per.   Rise, prithee, rise.
Sit down: thou art no flatterer:

I thank thee for it; and heaven forbid
That kings should let their ears hear their faults chid!
Fit counsellor and servant for a prince,
Who by thy wisdom mak'st a prince thy servant,
What wouldst thou have me do?

  Hel.   To bear with patience
Such griefs as you yourself do lay upon yourself.

  Per. Thou speak'st like a physician, Helicanus,
That minister'st a potion unto me
That thou wouldst tremble to receive thyself.
Attend me, then: I went to Antioch,
Where, as thou know'st, against the face of death,
I sought the purchase of a glorious beauty,
From whence an issue I might propagate,
Are arms to princes, and bring joys to subjects.
Her face was to mine eye beyond all wonder;
The rest — hark in thine ear — as black as incest:
Which by my knowledge found, the sinful father
Seem'd not to strike, but smooth: but thou know'st this,
'Tis time to fear when tyrants seem to kiss.
Which fear so grew in me, I hither fled,
Under the covering of a careful night,
Who seem'd my good protector; and, being here,
Bethought me what was past, what might succeed
I knew him tyrannous; and tyrants' fears
Decrease not, but grow faster than their years:
And should he doubt it, — as no doubt he doth, —
That I should open to the listening air
How many worthy princes' bloods were shed,
To keep his bed of blackness unlaid ope, —
To lop that doubt, he'll fill this land with arms,
And make pretence of wrong that I have done him;
When all, for mine, if I may call't offence,
Must feel war's blow, who spares not innocence:
Which love to all, — of which thyself art one,
Who now reprov'st me for it, —

  Hel.   Alas, sir!

Per. Drew sleep out of mine eyes, blood from my cheeks,
Musings into my mind, with thousand doubts
How I might stop this tempest, ere it came;
And finding little comfort to relieve them,
I thought it princely charity to grieve them.

Hel. Well, my lord, since you've given me leave to speak,
Freely will I speak. Antiochus you fear,
And justly too, I think, you fear the tyrant,
Who either by public war or private treason
Will take away your life.
Therefore, my lord, go travel for a while,
Till that his rage and auger be forgot,
Or till the Destinies do cut his thread of life.
Your rule direct to any; if to me,
Day serves not light more faithful than I'll be.

Per. I do not doubt thy faith;
But should he wrong my liberties in my absence?

Hel. We'll mingle our bloods together in the earth,
From whence we had our being and our birth.

Per. Tyre, I now look from thee, then, and to Tharsus
Intend my travel, where I'll hear from thee;
And by whose letters I'll dispose myself.
The care I had and have of subjects' good
On thee I lay, whose wisdom's strength can bear it.
I'll take thy word for faith, not ask thine oath:
Who shuns not to break one will sure crack both:
But in our orbs we'll live so round and safe,
That time of both this truth shall ne'er convince,
Thou show'dst a subject's shine, I a true prince.   [*Exeunt.*

SCENE III. *Tyre. An ante-chamber in the palace.*

Enter THALIARD.

Thal. So, this is Tyre, and this the court. Here must I
kill King Pericles; and if I do it not, I am sure to be hanged
at home: 'tis dangerous. — Well, I perceive he was a wise
fellow and had good discretion, that, being bid to ask what

he would of the king, desired he might know none of his
secrets: now do I see he had some reason for 't; for if a king
bid a man be a villain, he's bound by the indenture of his
oath to be one. — Hush! here come the lords of Tyre.

Enter HELICANUS, ESCANES, *and other* Lords.

    Hel. You shall not need, my fellow peers of Tyre,
Further to question me of your king's departure:
His seal'd commission, left in trust with me,
Doth speak sufficiently he's gone to travel.
    Thal. [aside] How! the king gone!
    Hel. If further yet you will be satisfied,
Why, as it were unlicens'd of your loves,
He would depart, I'll give some light unto you.
Being at Antioch, —
    Thal. [aside]   What from Antioch?
    Hel. Royal Antiochus — on what cause I know not —
Took some displeasure at him, — at least he judg'd so;
And doubting lest that he had err'd or sinn'd,
To show his sorrow, he'd correct himself;
So puts himself unto the shipman's toil,
With whom each minute threatens life or death.
    Thal. [aside] Well, I perceive
I shall not be hang'd now, although I would;
But since he's gone, the king's ears it must please, —
He scap'd the land, to perish at the seas.
I'll present myself. — Peace to the lords of Tyre!
    Hel. Lord Thaliard from Antiochus is welcome.
    Thal. From him I come
With message unto princely Pericles;
But since my landing I have understood
Your lord has betook himself to unknown travels,
My message must return from whence it came.
    Hel. We have no reason to desire it,
Commended to our master, not to us:
Yet, ere you shall depart, this we desire, —
As friends to Antioch, we may feast in Tyre.   [*Exeunt.*

SCENE IV. *Tharsus.   A room in the* Governor's *house.*

Enter CLEON, DIONYZA, *and* Attendants.

Cle. My Dionyza, shall we rest us here,
And by relating tales of others' griefs,
See if 'twill teach us to forget our own?

Dio.   That were to blow at fire in hope to quench it;
For who digs hills because they do aspire
Throws down one mountain to cast up a higher.
O my distressèd lord, even such our griefs are;
Here they're but felt, and seen with mischief's eyes,
But like to groves, being topp'd, they higher rise.

Cle. O Dionyza,
Who wanteth food, and will not say he wants it,
Or can conceal his hunger till he famish?
Our tongues and sorrows do sound deep our woes
Into the air; our eyes do weep, till lungs
Fetch breath that may proclaim them louder; that,
If heaven slumber while their creatures want,
They may awake their helps to comfort them:
I'll, then, discourse our woes, felt several years,
And, wanting breath to speak, help me with tears.

Dio. I'll do my best, sir.

Cle. This Tharsus, o'er which I have the government,
A city on whom Plenty held full hand,
For Riches strew'd herself even in the streets;
Whose towers bore heads so high they kiss'd the clouds,
And strangers ne'er beheld but wonder'd at;
Whose men and dames so jetted and adorn'd,
Like one another's glass to trim them by:
Their tables were stor'd full, to glad the sight,
And not so much to feed on as delight;
All poverty was scorn'd, and pride so great,
The name of help grew odious to repeat.

Dio. O, 'tis too true.

Cle. But see what heaven can do! By this our change,
Those mouths who but of late, earth, sea, and air,

Were all too little to content and please,
Although they gave their creatures in abundance,
As houses are defil'd for want of use,
They are now starv'd for want of exercise:
Those palates who, not yet two summers younger,
Must have inventions to delight the taste,
Would now be glad of bread, and beg for it:
Those mothers who, to nousle up their babes,
Thought naught too curious, are ready now
To eat those little darlings whom they lov'd.
So sharp are hunger's teeth, that man and wife
Draw lots who first shall die to lengthen life:
Here stands a lord, and there a lady weeping;
Here many sink, yet those which see them fall
Have scarce strength left to give them burial.
Is not this true?

Dio. Our cheeks and hollow eyes do witness it.

Cle. O, let those cities that of Plenty's cup
And her prosperities so largely taste,
With their superfluous riots, hear these tears!
The misery of Tharsus may be theirs.

Enter a Lord.

Lord. Where's the lord governor?

Cle. Here.
Speak out thy sorrows which thou bring'st in haste,
For comfort is too far for us t' expect.

Lord. We have descried, upon our neighbouring shore,
A portly sail of ships make hitherward.

Cle. I thought as much.
One sorrow never comes but brings an heir,
That may succeed as his inheritor;
And so in ours: some neighbouring nation,
Taking advantage of our misery,
Hath stuff'd these hollow vessels with their power,
To beat us down, the which are down already;

And make a conquest of unhappy me,
Whereas no glory's got to overcome.
    Lord. That's the least fear; for, by the semblance
Of their white flags display'd, they bring us peace,
And come to us as favourers, not as foes.
    Cle. Thou speak'st like him's untutor'd to repeat:
Who makes the fairest show means most deceit.
But bring they what they will and what they can,
What need we fear?
The ground's the lowest, and we're half-way there.
Go tell their general we attend him here,
To know for what he comes, and whence he comes,
And what he craves.
    Lord. I go, my lord.   [*Exit.*
    Cle. Welcome is peace, if he on peace consist;
If wars, we are unable to resist.

Enter PERICLES *with* Attendants.

    Per. Lord governor, for so we hear you are,
Let not our ships and number of our men
Be, like a beacon fir'd, t' amaze your eyes.
We've heard your miseries as far as Tyre,
And seen the desolation of your streets:
Nor come we to add sorrow to your tears,
But to relieve them of their heavy load;
And these our ships, you happily may think
Are like the Trojan horse was stuff'd within
With bloody veins, expecting overthrow,
Are stor'd with corn to make your needy bread,
And give them life whom hunger starv'd half dead.
    All. The gods of Greece protect you!
And we'll pray for you.
    Per.   Rise, I pray you, rise:
We do not look for reverence, but for love,
And harbourage for ourself, our ships, and men.
    Cle. The which when any shall not gratify,
Or pay you with unthankfulness in thought,

Be it our wives, our children, or ourselves,
The curse of heaven and men succeed their evils!
Till when, — the which I hope shall ne'er be seen, —
Your grace is welcome to our town and us.
    Per. Which welcome we'll accept; feast here awhile,
Until our stars that frown lend us a smile.   [*Exeunt.*

ACT II.

Enter Gower.

    Gow. Here have you seen a mighty king
His child, I wis, to incest bring;
A better prince, and benign lord,
That will prove awful both in deed and word.
Be quiet, then, as men should be,
Till he hath pass'd necessity.
I'll show you those in troubles reign,
Losing a mite, a mountain gain.
The good in conversation —
To whom I give my benison —
Is still at Tharsus, where each man
Thinks all is writ he spoken can;
And, to remember what he does,
Build his statue to make him glorious:
But tidings to the contrary
Are brought your eyes; what need speak I?

Dumb-Show.

Enter, from one side, Pericles, *talking with* Cleon; *their Trains with them. Enter, from the other side, a* Gentleman, *with a letter to* Pericles; *who shows the letter to* Cleon; *then gives thé* Messenger *a reward, and knights him. Exeunt severally* Pericles *and* Cleon, *with their Trains.*

Good Helicane, that stay'd at home,
Not to eat honey like a drone
From others' labours; for though he strive

To killen bad, keep good alive;
And to fulfil his prince' desire,
Sends word of all that haps in Tyre:
How 'Thaliard came full bent with sin
And hid intent to murder him;
And that in Tharsus was not best
Longer for him to make his rest.
He, doing so, put forth to seas,
Where when men been, there's seldom ease;
For now the wind begins to blow;
Thunder above, and deeps below,
Make such unquiet, that the ship
Should house him safe is wreck'd and split;
And he, good prince, having all lost,
By waves from coast to coast is tost:
All perishen of man, of pelf,
Ne aught escapen but himself;
Till fortune, tir'd with doing bad,
Threw him ashore, to give him glad:
And here he comes. What shall be next,
Pardon old Gower, — this longs the text.   [*Exit.*

SCENE I. *Pentapolis.* *An open place by the sea-side.*

Enter PERICLES, *wet.*

Per. Yet cease your ire, you angry stars of heaven!
Wind, rain, and thunder, remember, earthly man
Is but a substance that must yield to you;
And I, as fits my nature, do obey you:
Alas, the sea hath cast me on the rocks,
Wash'd me from shore to shore, and left me breath
Nothing to think on but ensuing death:
Let it suffice the greatness of your powers
To have bereft a prince of all his fortunes;
And having thrown him from your watery grave,
Here to have death in peace is all he'll crave.

Enter three Fishermen.

First Fish. What, ho, Pilch!

Sec. Fish. Ho, come and bring away the nets!

First Fish. What, Patch-breech, I say!

Third Fish. What say you, master?

First Fish. Look how thou stirrest now! come away, or I'll fetch thee with a wanion.

Third Fish. Faith, master, I am thinking of the poor men that were cast away before us even now.

First Fish. Alas, poor souls, it grieved my heart to hear what pitiful cries they made to us to help them, when, well-a-day, we could scarce help ourselves.

Third Fish. Nay, master, said not I as much when I saw the porpus, how he bounced and tumbled? they say they're half-fish, half-flesh: a plague on them, they ne'er come but I look to be washed. Master, I marvel how the fishes live in the sea.

First Fish. Why, as men do a-land, — the great ones eat up the little ones: I can compare our rich misers to nothing so fitly as to a whale; 'a plays and tumbles, driving the poor fry before him, and at last devours them all at a mouthful: such whales have I heard on o' the land, who never leave gaping till they've swallowed the whole parish, church, steeple, bells, and all.

Per. [*aside*] A pretty moral.

Third Fish. But, master, if I had been the sexton, I would have been that day in the belfry.

Sec. Fish. Why, man?

Third Fish. Because he should have swallowed me too: and when I had been in his belly, I would have kept such a jangling of the bells, that he should never have left, till he cast bells, steeple, church, and parish, up again. But if the good King Simonides were of my mind, —

Per. [*aside*] Simonides!

Third Fish. He would purge the land of these drones, that rob the bee of her honey.

Per. [*aside*] How from the finny subject of the sea

These fishers tell th' infirmities of men;
And from their watery empire recollect
All that may men approve or men detect! —
Peace be at your labour, honest fishermen.

Sec. Fish. Honest! good fellow, what's that? If it be a day fits you, search out of the calendar, and nobody look after it.

Per. May see the sea hath cast upon your coast.

Sec. Fish. What a drunken knave was the sea to cast thee in our way!

Per. A man whom both the waters and the wind,
In that vast tennis-court, have made the ball
For them to play upon, entreats you pity him;
He asks of you, that never us'd to beg.

First Fish. No, friend, cannot you beg? Here's them in our country of Greece gets more with begging than we can do with working.

Sec. Fish. Canst thou catch any fishes, then?

Per. I never practis'd it.

Sec. Fish. Nay, then thou wilt starve, sure; for here's nothing to be got now-a-days, unless thou canst fish for't.

Per. What I have been I have forgot to know;
But what I am, want teaches me to think on:
A man throng'd up with cold: my veins are chill,
And have no more of life than may suffice
To give my tongue that heat to ask your help;
Which if you shall refuse, when I am dead,
For that I am a man, pray see me buried.

First Fish. Die quoth-a? Now gods forbid! I have a gown here; come, put it on; keep thee warm. Now, afore me, a handsome fellow! Come, thou shalt go home, and we'll have flesh for holidays, fish for fasting-days, and moreo'er puddings and flap-jacks; and thou shalt be welcome.

Per. I thank you, sir.

Sec. Fish. Hark you, my friend, — you said you could not beg.

Per. I did but crave.

Sec. Fish. But crave! Then I'll turn craver too, and so I shall scape whipping.

Per. Why, are all your beggars whipped, then?

Sec. Fish. O, not all, my friend, not all; for if all your beggars were whipped, I would wish no better office than to be beadle. — But, master, I'll go draw up the net.

[*Exit with Third Fisherman.*

Per. [*aside*] How well this honest mirth becomes their labour!

First Fish. Hark you, sir, — do you know where ye are?

Per. Not well.

First Fish. Why, I'll tell you: this is called Pentapolis, and our king the good Simonides.

Per. The good King Simonides, do you call him?

First Fish. Ay, sir; and he deserves so to be called for his peaceable reign and good government.

Per. He is a happy king, since he gains from his subjects the name of good by his government. How far is his court distant from this shore?

First Fish. Marry, sir, half a day's journey: and I'll tell you, he hath a fair daughter, and to-morrow is her birth-day; and there are princes and knights come from all parts of the world to just and tourney for her love.

Per. Were my fortunes equal to my desires, I could wish to make one there.

First Fish. O, sir, things must be as they may; and what a man cannot get, he may lawfully deal for — his wife's soul.

Re-enter Second *and* Third Fishermen, *drawing up a net.*

Sec. Fish. Help, master, help! here's a fish hangs in the net, like a poor man's right in the law; 'twill hardly come out. Ha! bots on't, 'tis come at last, and 'tis turned to a rusty armour.

Per. An armour, friends! I pray you, let me see it. — Thanks, fortune, yet, that, after all my crosses, Thou giv'st me somewhat to repair myself; And though it was mine own, part of my heritage,

Which my dead father did bequeath to me,
With this strict charge, even as he left his life,
"Keep it, my Pericles; it hath been a shield
'Twixt me and death;" — and pointed to this brace; —
"For that it sav'd me, keep it; in like necessity —
The which the gods protect thee from! — 't may defend thee."
It kept where I kept, I so dearly lov'd it;
Till the rough seas, that spare not any man,
Took it in rage, though calm'd have given 't again:
I thank thee for't; my shipwreck now's no ill,
Since I have here my father's gift in 's will.
    First Fish.   What mean you, sir?
    Per.   To beg of you, kind friends, this coat of worth,
For it was sometime target to a king;
I know it by this mark. He lov'd me dearly,
And for his sake I wish the having of it;
And that you'd guide me to your sovereign's court,
Where with it I may appear a gentleman;
And if that ever my low fortunes better,
I'll pay your bounties; till then rest your debtor.
    First Fish.   Why, wilt thou tourney for the lady?
    Per.   I'll show the virtue I have borne in arms.
    First Fish.   Why, do ye take it, and the gods give thee
good on't!
    Sec. Fish.   Ay, but hark you, my friend; 'twas we that
made up this garment through the rough seams of the waters:
there are certain condolements, certain vails. I hope, sir, if
you thrive, you'll remember from whence you had it.
    Per.   Believe 't, I will.
By your furtherance I am cloth'd in steel;
And, spite of all the rapture of the sea,
This jewel holds his building on my arm:
Unto the value I will mount myself
Upon a courser, whose delightful steps
Shall make the gazer joy to see him tread. —
Only, my friends, I yet am unprovided
Of a pair of bases.

Sec. Fish. We'll sure provide thee: thou shalt have my best gown to make thee a pair: and I'll bring thee to the court myself.

Per. Then honour be but a goal to my will,
This day I'll rise, or else add ill to ill.   [*Exeunt.*

SCENE II. *The same. A public way or platform leading to the lists. A pavilion by the side of it for the reception of the King, Princess, Lords, &c.*

Enter SIMONIDES, THAISA, Lords, *and* Attendants.

Sim. Are the knights ready to begin the triumph?
First Lord. They are, my liege;
And stay your coming to present themselves.

Sim. Return them, we are ready; and our daughter,
In honour of whose birth these triumphs are,
Sits here, like beauty's child, whom nature gat
For men to see, and seeing wonder at.   [*Exit a Lord.*

Thai. It pleaseth you, my royal father, to express
My commendations great, whose merit's less.

Sim. It's fit it should be so; for princes are
A model, which heaven makes like to itself:
As jewels lose their glory if neglected,
So princes their renown if not respected.
'Tis now your honour, daughter, to explain
The labour of each knight in his device.

Thai. Which, to preserve mine honour, I'll perform.

Enter a Knight; *he passes over, and his* Squire *presents his shield to the* Princess.

Sim. Who is the first that doth prefer himself?
Thai. A knight of Sparta, my renownèd father;
And the device he bears upon his shield
Is a black Æthiop reaching at the sun;
The word, *Lux tua vita mihi.*

Sim. He loves you well that holds his life of you.
          [*The Second Knight passes over.*
Who is the second that presents himself?

Thai. A prince of Macedon, my royal father;
And the device he bears upon his shield
Is an arm'd knight that's conquer'd by a lady;
The motto thus, in Spanish, *Piu por dulzura que por fuerza.*
[*The Third Knight passes over.*

Sim. And what's the third?
Thai.   The third of Antioch;
And his device, a wreath of chivalry;
The word, *Me pompæ provexit apex.*
[*The Fourth Knight passes over.*

Sim. What is the fourth?
Thai. A burning torch that's turnèd upside down;
The word, *Quod me alit, me extinguit.*
Sim. Which shows that beauty hath his power and will,
Which can as well inflame as it can kill.
[*The Fifth Knight passes over.*

Thai. The fifth, an hand environèd with clouds,
Holding out gold that's by the touchstone tried;
The motto thus, *Sic spectanda fides.*
[*The Sixth Knight (Pericles) passes over.*

Sim. And what's
The sixth and last, the which the knight himself
With such a graceful courtesy deliver'd?
Thai. He seems to be a stranger; but his present is
A wither'd branch, that's only green at top;
The motto, *In hac spe vivo.*
Sim. A pretty moral;
From the dejected state wherein he is,
He hopes by you his fortunes yet may flourish.
First Lord. He had need mean better than his outward show
Can any way speak in his just commend;
For, by his rusty outside, he appears
T' have practis'd more the whipstock than the lance.
Sec. Lord. He well may be a stranger, for he comes
To an honour'd triumph strangely furnishèd.
Third Lord. And on set purpose let his armour rust
Until this day, to scour it in the dust.

Sim. Opinion's but a fool, that makes us scan
The outward habit by the inward man.
But stay, the knights are coming: we'll withdraw
Into the gallery.   [*Exeunt.*
     [*Great shouts within, all crying* "The mean knight!"

SCENE III. *The same. A hall of state; a banquet prepared.*

Enter SIMONIDES, THAISA, Ladies, Lords, Knights, *and*
Attendants.

  Sim. Knights,
To say you're welcome were superfluous.
To place upon the volume of your deeds,
As in a title-page, your worth in arms,
Were more than you expect, or more than's fit,
Since every worth in show commends itself.
Prepare for mirth, for mirth becomes a feast:
You are princes and my guests.
  Thai. But you, my knight and guest;
To whom this wreath of victory I give,
And crown you king of this day's happiness.
  Per. 'Tis more by fortune, lady, than by merit.
  Sim. Call it by what you will, the day is yours;
And here, I hope, is none that envies it.
In framing an artist, art hath thus decreed,
To make some good, but others to exceed;
And you're her labour'd scholar.—Come, queen o'the feast,—
For, daughter, so you are, — here take your place:
Marshal the rest, as they deserve their grace.
  Knights. We're honour'd much by good Simonides.
  Sim. Your presence glads our days: honour we love;
For who hates honour hates the gods above.
  Marshal. Sir, yonder is your place.
  Per.   Some other is more fit.
  First Knight. Contend not, sir; for we are gentlemen
That neither in our hearts nor outward eyes
Envy the great nor do the low despise.

Per.   You are right courteous knights.

Sim.   Sit, sir, sit. —
By Jove, I wonder, that is king of thoughts,
These cates resist me, he not thought upon.

Thai.   By Juno, that is queen
Of marriage, all viands that I eat
Do seem unsavoury, wishing him my meat.
Sure, he's a gallant gentleman.

Sim.   He's but a country gentleman;
Has done no more than other knights have done;
Has broken a staff or so; so let it pass.

Thai.   To me he seems like diamond to glass.

Per.   Yon king's to me like to my father's picture,
Which tells me in that glory once he was;
Had princes sit, like stars, about his throne,
And he the sun, for them to reverence;
None that beheld him, but, like lesser lights,
Did vail their crowns to his supremacy:
Where now his son's like glow-worm in the night,
The which hath fire in darkness, none in light:
Whereby I see that Time's the king of men,
For he's their parent, and he is their grave,
And gives them what he will, not what they crave.

Sim.   What, are you merry, knights?

First Knight.   Who can be other in this royal presence?

Sim.   Here, with a cup that's stor'd unto the brim, —
As you do love, fill to your mistress' lips, —
We drink this health to you.

Knights.   We thank your grace.

Sim.   Yet pause awhile:
Yon knight doth sit too melancholy,
As if the entertainment in our court
Had not a show might countervail his worth.
Note it not you, Thaisa?

Thai.   What is it
To me, my father?

Sim.   O, attend, my daughter:

Princes, in this, should live like gods above,
Who freely give to every one that comes
To honour them:
And princes not doing so are like to gnats,
Which make a sound, but kill'd are wonder'd at.
Therefore to make his entertain more sweet,
Here, say we drink this standing-bowl of wine to him.
   Thai. Alas, my father, it befits not me
Unto a stranger knight to be so bold:
He may my proffer take for an offence,
Since men take women's gifts for impudence.
   Sim. How!
Do as I bid you, or you'll move me else.
   Thai. [*aside*] Now, by the gods, he could not please me
          better.
   Sim. And furthermore tell him, we desire to know of him,
Of whence he is, his name and parentage.
   Thai. The king my father, sir, has drunk to you.
   Per. I thank him.
   Thai. Wishing it so much blood unto your life.
   Per. I thank both him and you, and pledge him freely.
   Thai. And further he desires to know of you,
Of whence you are, your name and parentage.
   Per. A gentleman of Tyre, — my name, Pericles;
My education been in arts and arms; —
Who, looking for adventures in the world,
Was by the rough seas reft of ships and men,
And, after shipwreck, driven upon this shore.
   Thai. He thanks your grace; names himself Pericles,
A gentleman of Tyre,
Who only by misfortune of the seas
Bereft of ships and men, cast on this shore.
   Sim. Now, by the gods, I pity his misfortune,
And will awake him from his melancholy. —
Come, gentlemen, we sit too long on trifles,
And waste the time, which looks for other revels.
Even in your armours, as you are address'd,

Will very well become a soldier's dance.
I will not have excuse, with saying this
Loud music is too harsh for ladies' heads,
Since they love men in arms as well as beds.
                              [*The Knights dance.*
So, this was well ask'd, 'twas so well perform'd. —
Come, sir;
Here is a lady that wants breathing too:
And I have heard, you knights of Tyre
Are excellent in making ladies trip;
And that their measures are as excellent.
   Per.   In those that practise them they are, my lord.
   Sim.   O, that's as much as you would be denied
Of your fair courtesy.   [*The Knights and Ladies dance.*
                    Unclasp, unclasp:
Thanks, gentlemen, to all; all have done well,
[*To Pericles*] But you the best. — Pages and lights, to conduct
These knights unto their several lodgings! — [*To Pericles*]
              Yours, sir,
We've given order to be next our own.
   Per.   I am at your grace's pleasure.
   Sim.   Princes, it is too late to talk of love;
And that's the mark I know you level at:
Therefore each one betake him to his rest;
To-morrow all for speeding do their best.   [*Exeunt.*

SCENE IV.   *Tyre.   A room in the* Governor's *house.*

Enter HELICANUS *and* ESCANES.

   Hel.   No, Escanes; know this of me, —
Antiochus from incest liv'd not free:
For which, the most high gods not minding longer
To withhold the vengeance that they had in store,
Due to this heinous capital offence,
Even in the height and pride of all his glory,
When he was seated in a chariot
Of an inestimable value, and his daughter with him,

A fire from heaven came, and shrivell'd up
'Their bodies, even to loathing; for they so stunk,
That all those eyes ador'd them ere their fall
Scorn now their hand should give them burial.

 Esca. 'Twas very strange.

 Hel.   And yet but justice; for though
This king were great, his greatness was no guard
To bar heaven's shaft, but sin had his reward.

 Esca. 'Tis very true.

Enter two or three Lords.

 First Lord. See, not a man in private conference
Or council has respect with him but he.

 Sec. Lord. It shall no longer grieve without reproof.

 Third Lord. And curs'd be he that will not second it.

 First Lord. Follow me, then. — Lord Helicane, a word.

 Hel. With me? and welcome: — happy day, my lords.

 First Lord. Know that our griefs are risen to the top,
And now at length they overflow their banks.

 Hel. Your griefs! for what? wrong not the prince you
    love.

 First Lord. Wrong not yourself, then, noble Helicane;
But if the prince do live, let us salute him,
Or know what ground's made happy by his breath.
If in the world he live, we'll seek him out;
If in his grave he rest, we'll find him there;
And be resolv'd he lives to govern us,
Or dead, gives cause to mourn his funeral,
And leaves us to our free election.

 Sec. Lord. Whose death's indeed the strongest in our
    censure:
And knowing this kingdom, if without a head, —
Like goodly buildings left without a roof, —
Will soon to ruin fall, your noble self,
That best know'st how to rule and how to reign,
We thus submit unto, — our sovereign.

 All. Live, noble Helicane!

Hel. For honour's cause, forbear your suffrages:
If that you love Prince Pericles, forbear.
Take I your wish, I leap into the seas,
Where's hourly trouble for a minute's ease.
A twelvemonth longer, let me entreat you
To forbear the absence of your king;
If in which time expir'd, he not return,
I shall with agèd patience bear your yoke.
But if I cannot win you to this love,
Go search like nobles, like noble subjects,
And in your search spend your adventurous worth;
Whom if you find, and win unto return,
You shall like diamonds sit about his crown.

First Lord. To wisdom he's a fool that will not yield;
And since Lord Helicane enjoineth us,
We with our travels will endeavour it.

Hel. Then you love us, we you, and we'll clasp hands:
When peers thus knit, a kingdom ever stands.   [*Exeunt.*

SCENE V. *Pentapolis. A room in the palace.*

Enter SIMONIDES, *reading a letter: the* Knights *meet him.*

First Knight. Good morrow to the good Simonides.

Sim. Knights, from my daughter this I let you know,
That for this twelvemonth she'll not undertake
A married life.
Her reason to herself is only known,
Which yet from her by no means can I get.

Sec. Knight. May we not get access to her, my lord?

Sim. Faith, by no means; she hath so strictly tied her
To her chamber, that it is impossible.
One twelve moons more she'll wear Diana's livery;
This by the eye of Cynthia hath she vow'd,
And on her virgin honour will not break it.

Third Knight. Loth to bid farewell, we take our leaves.
                                          [*Exeunt Knights.*

Sim. So,

They're well dispatch'd; now to my daughter's letter:
She tells me here, she'll wed the stranger knight
Or never more to view nor day nor light.
'Tis well, mistress; your choice agrees with mine;
I like that well: — nay, how absolute she's in't,
Not minding whether I dislike or no!
Well, I do commend her choice;
And will no longer have it be delay'd. —
Soft! here he comes: I must dissemble it.

Enter PERICLES.

Per. All fortune to the good Simonides!
Sim. To you as much, sir! I'm beholding to you
For your sweet music this last night: I do
Protest my ears were never better fed
With such delightful pleasing harmony.
Per. It is your grace's pleasure to commend;
Not my desert.
Sim.   Sir, you are music's master.
Per. The worst of all her scholars, my good lord.
Sim. Let me ask you one thing:
What do you think of my daughter, sir?
Per. A most virtuous princess.
Sim. And she is fair too, is she not?
Per. As a fair day in summer, — wondrous fair.
Sim. Sir, my daughter thinks very well of you;
Ay, so well, that you must be her master,
And she will be your scholar: therefore look to it.
Per. I am unworthy for her schoolmaster.
Sim. She thinks not so; peruse this writing else.
Per. [*aside*] What's here?
A letter, that she loves the knight of Tyre!
'Tis the king's subtilty to have my life. —
O, seek not to entrap me, gracious lord,
A stranger and distressèd gentleman,
That never aim'd so high to love your daughter,
But bent all offices to honour her.

Sim. Thou hast bewitch'd my daughter, and thou art
A villain.

Per. By the gods, I have not:
Never did thought of mine levy offence;
Nor never did my actions yet commence
A deed might gain her love or your displeasure.

Sim. Traitor, thou liest.

Per.   Traitor!

Sim.   Ay, traitor.

Per. Even in his throat — unless it be the king —
That calls me traitor, I return the lie.

Sim. [*aside*] Now, by the gods, I do applaud his courage.

Per. My actions are as noble as my thoughts,
That never relish'd of a base descent.
I came unto your court for honour's cause,
And not to be a rebel to her state;
And he that otherwise accounts of me,
This sword shall prove he's honour's enemy.

Sim. No?
Here comes my daughter, she can witness it!

Enter THAISA.

Per. Then, as you are as virtuous as fair,
Resolve your angry father, if my tongue
Did e'er solicit, or my hand subscribe
To any syllable that made love to you.

Thai. Why, sir, say if you had,
Who takes offence at that would make me glad?

Sim. Yea, mistress, are you so peremptory? —
[*Aside*] I am glad on't with all my heart. —
I'll tame you; I'll bring you in subjection.
Will you, not having my consent,
Bestow your love and your affections
Upon a stranger? — [*aside*] who, for aught I know,
May be — nor can I think the contrary —
As great in blood as I myself. —
Therefore hear you, mistress; either frame

Your will to mine, — and you, sir, hear you,
Either be rul'd by me, or I will make you —
Man and wife: —
Nay, come, your hands and lips must seal it too;
And being join'd, I'll thus your hopes destroy; —
And for a further grief, — God give you joy! —
What, are you both pleas'd?

Thai.   Yes, — if you love me, sir.
Per.   Even as my life, or blood that fosters it.
Sim.   What, are you both agreed?
Both.   Yes, if't please your majesty.
Sim.   It pleaseth me so well, that I will see you wed;
And then with what haste you can get you to bed.   [*Exeunt.*

ACT III.

Enter GOWER.

Gow.   Now sleep yslakèd hath the rout;
No din but snores the house about,
Made louder by the o'er-fed breast
Of this most pompous marriage-feast.
The cat, with eyne of burning coal,
Now couches fore the mouse's hole;
And crickets sing at th' oven's mouth,
Aye the blither for their drouth.
Hymen hath brought the bride to bed,
Where, by the loss of maidenhead,
A babe is moulded. — Be attent,
And time that is so briefly spent
With your fine fancies quaintly eche:
What's dumb in show I'll plain with speech.

DUMB-SHOW.

Enter, from one side, PERICLES *and* SIMONIDES *with* Attendants; *a* Messenger *meets them, kneels, and gives* PERICLES *a
letter: he shows it to* SIMONIDES; *the Lords kneel to* PERICLES.
Then enter THAISA *with child, and* LYCHORIDA.   SIMONIDES *shows*

his daughter the letter; she rejoices: she and PERICLES *take leave
of her father, and depart with* LYCHORIDA *and their* Attendants.
Then exeunt SIMONIDES *and the rest.*

By many a dern and painful perch
Of Pericles the careful search,
By the four opposing coigns
Which the world together joins,
Is made with all due diligence
That horse and sail and high expense
Can stead the quest. At last from Tyre —
Fame answering the most strange inquire —
To the court of King Simonides
Are letters brought, the tenour these: —
Antiochus and his daughter dead;
The men of Tyrus on the head
Of Helicanus would set on
The crown of Tyre, but he will none:
The mutiny he there hastes t' oppress;
Says to 'em, if King Pericles
Come not home in twice six moons,
He, obedient to their dooms,
Will take the crown. The sum of this,
Brought hither to Pentapolis,
Yravishèd the regions round,
And every one with claps can sound,
"Our heir-apparent is a king!
Who dream'd, who thought of such a thing?"
Brief, he must hence depart to Tyre:
His queen with child makes her desire —
Which who shall cross? — along to go: —
Omit we all their dole and woe: —
Lychorida, her nurse, she takes,
And so to sea. Their vessel shakes
On Neptune's billow; half the flood
Hath their keel cut: but fortune's mood
Varies again; the grisly north
Disgorges such a tempest forth,

That, as a duck for life that dives,
So up and down the poor ship drives:
The lady shrieks, and, well-a-near,
Does fall in travail with her fear:
And what ensues in this fell storm
Shall for itself itself perform.
I nill relate, action may
Conveniently the rest convey;
Which might not what by me is told.
In your imagination hold
This stage the ship, upon whose deck
The sea-tost Pericles appears to speak.   [*Exit.*

Scene I.

Enter Pericles, *on shipboard.*

Per.   Thou god of this great vast, rebuke these surges,
Which wash both heaven and hell; and thou, that hast
Upon the winds command, bind them in brass,
Having recall'd them from the deep!   O, still
Thy deafening, dreadful thunders; gently quench
Thy nimble, sulphurous flashes! — O, how, Lychorida,
How does my queen? — Thou stormest venomously;
Wilt thou spit all thyself? — The seaman's whistle
Is as a whisper in the ears of death,
Unheard. — Lychorida! — Lucina, O
Divinest patroness, and midwife gentle
To those that cry by night, convey thy deity
Aboard our dancing boat; make swift the pangs
Of my queen's travail!

Enter Lychorida, *with an Infant.*

Now, Lychorida!

Lyc.   Here is a thing too young for such a place,
Who, if it had conceit, would die, as I
Am like to do: take in your arms this piece
Of your dead queen.

Per.   How, how, Lychorida!

Lyc. Patience, good sir; do not assist the storm.
Here's all that is left living of your queen, —
A little daughter: for the sake of it,
Be manly, and take comfort.

Per.　　　　　　　　　O you gods!
Why do you make us love your goodly gifts,
And snatch them straight away? We here below
Recall not what we give, and therein may
Vie honour with you.

Lyc.　　　　　　　　Patience, good sir,
Even for this charge.

Per.　　　　　　　Now, mild may be thy life!
For a more blusterous birth had never babe:
Quiet and gentle thy conditions! for
Thou art the rudeliest welcome to this world
That e'er was prince's child. Happy what follows!
Thou hast as chiding a nativity
As fire, air, water, earth, and heaven can make,
To herald thee from the womb: even at the first
Thy loss is more than can thy portage quit,
With all thou canst find here. — Now, the good gods
Throw their best eyes upon't!

Enter two Sailors.

First Sail. What courage, sir? God save you!

Per. Courage enough: I do not fear the flaw;
It hath done to me the worst. Yet, for the love
Of this poor infant, this fresh-new seafarer,
I would it would be quiet.

First Sail. Slack the bolins there! — Thou wilt not, wilt
thou? Blow, and split thyself.

Sec. Sail. But sea-room, an the brine and cloudy billow
kiss the moon, I care not.

First Sail. Sir, your queen must overboard: the sea
works high, the wind is loud, and will not lie till the ship be
cleared of the dead.

Per. That's your superstition.

First Sail. Pardon us, sir; with us at sea it hath been
still observed; and we are strong in custom. Therefore
briefly yield her; for she must overboard straight.

Per. As you think meet. — Most wretched queen!

Lyc. Here she lies, sir.

Per. A terrible childbed hast thou had, my dear;
No light, no fire: th' unfriendly elements
Forgot thee utterly; nor have I time
To give thee hallow'd to thy grave, but straight
Must cast thee, scarcely coffin'd, in the ooze;
Where, for a monument upon thy bones,
And aye-remaining lamps, the belching whale
And humming water must o'erwhelm thy corpse,
Lying with simple shells. — O Lychorida,
Bid Nestor bring me spices, ink and paper,
My casket and my jewels; and bid Nicander
Bring me the satin coffer: lay the babe
Upon the pillow: hie thee, whiles I say
A priestly farewell to her: suddenly, woman.

[Exit Lychorida.

Sec. Sail. Sir, we have a chest beneath the hatches,
caulked and bitumed ready.

Per. I thank thee. — Mariner, say what coast is this?

Sec. Sail. We are near Tharsus.

Per. Thither, gentle mariner,
Alter thy course for Tyre. When canst thou reach it?

Sec. Sail. By break of day, if the wind cease.

Per. O, make for Tharsus! —
There will I visit Cleon, for the babe
Cannot hold out to Tyrus: there I'll leave it
At careful nursing. — Go thy ways, good mariner:
I'll bring the body presently. *[Exeunt.*

SCENE II. *Ephesus. A room in* CERIMON'S *house.*

Enter CERIMON, *a Servant, and some Persons who have been
shipwrecked.*

Cer. Philemon, ho!

Enter PHILEMON.

Phil.   Doth my lord call?

Cer.   Get fire and meat for these poor men:
'T has been a turbulent and stormy night.

Serv.   I've been in many; but such a night as this,
Till now, I ne'er endur'd.

Cer.   Your master will be dead ere you return;
There's nothing can be minister'd to nature
That can recover him. — [*To Philemon*] Give this to the
            pothecary,
And tell me how it works.   [*Exeunt all except Cerimon.*

Enter two Gentlemen.

First Gent.   Good morrow.

Sec. Gent.   Good morrow to your lordship.

Cer.   Gentlemen,
Why do you stir so early?

First Gent.   Sir,
Our lodgings, standing bleak upon the sea,
Shook as the earth did quake;
The very principals did seem to rend,   .
And all to-topple: pure surprise and fear
Made me to quit the house.

Sec. Gent.   That is the cause we trouble you so early;
'Tis not our husbandry.

Cer.   O, you say well.

First Gent.   But I much marvel that your lordship, having
Rich tire about you, should at these early hours
Shake off the golden slumber of repose.
'Tis most strange,
Nature should be so conversant with pain,
Being thereto not compell'd.

Cer.   I held it ever,
Virtue and cunning were endowments greater
Than nobleness and riches: careless heirs
May the two latter darken and expend;
But immortality attends the former,

Making a man a god. 'Tis known, I ever
Have studied physic, through which secret art,
By turning o'er authorities, I have —
Together with my practice — made familiar
To me and to my aid the blest infusions
That dwell in vegetives, in metals, stones;
And I can speak of the disturbances
That nature works, and of her cures; which doth give me
A more content in course of true delight
Than to be thirsty after tottering honour,
Or tie my treasure up in silken bags,
To please the fool and death.

    Sec. Gent. Your honour has through Ephesus pour'd forth
Your charity, and hundreds call themselves
Your creatures, who by you have been restor'd:
And not your knowledge, your personal pain, but even
Your purse, still open, hath built Lord Cerimon
Such strong renown as time shall never raze.

       Enter two or three Servants *with a chest.*

    First Serv. So; lift there.
    Cer.   What is that?
    First Serv.   Sir, even now
Did the sea toss upon our shore this chest:
'Tis of some wreck.
    Cer.   Set 't down, let's look upon 't.
    Sec. Gent. 'Tis like a coffin, sir.
    Cer.   Whate'er it be,
'Tis wondrous heavy. Wrench it open straight:
If the sea's stomach be o'ercharged with gold,
'Tis a good constraint of fortune it belches upon us.
    Sec. Gent. 'Tis so, my lord.
    Cer.   How close 'tis caulk'd and bitum'd! —
Did the sea cast it up?
    First Serv. I never saw so huge a billow, sir,
As toss'd it upon shore.
    Cer.   Wrench it open;
Soft! — it smells most sweetly in my sense.

Sec. Gent.　A delicate odour.

Cer.　As ever hit my nostril. — So, up with it. —
O you most potent gods! what's here? a corse!

First Gent.　Most strange!

Cer.　Shrouded in cloth of state; balm'd and entreasur'd
With full bags of spices! A passport too! —
Apollo, perfect me in the characters!　　[*Reads from a scroll.*

> "Here I give to understand, —
> If e'er this coffin drive a-land, —
> I, King Pericles, have lost
> This queen, worth all our mundane cost.
> Who finds her, give her burying;
> She was the daughter of a king:
> Besides this treasure for a fee,
> The gods requite his charity!"

If thou liv'st, Pericles, thou hast a heart
That even cracks for woe! — This chanc'd to-night.

Sec. Gent.　Most likely, sir.

Cer.　　　　　　　　　Nay, certainly to-night;
For look how fresh she looks! — They were too rough
That threw her in the sea. — Make a fire within:
Fetch hither all my boxes in my closet. —　　[*Exit a Servant.*
Death may usurp on nature many hours,
And yet the fire of life kindle again
The o'erpress'd spirits. I heard of an Egyptian
That had nine hours lien dead,
Who was by good appliances recover'd.

Re-enter a Servant, *with boxes, napkins, and fire.*

Well said, well said; the fire and cloths. —
The rough and woful music that we have,
Cause it to sound, beseech you.
The viol once more: — how thou stirr'st, thou block! —
The music there! — I pray you, give her air. —
Gentlemen, this queen will live: nature awakes;
A warmth breathes out of her: she hath not been

Entranc'd above five hours: see how she gins
To blow into life's flower again!

First Gent.   The heavens,
Through you, increase our wonder, and set up
Your fame for ever.

Cer.   ,   She's alive; behold,
Her eyelids, cases to those heavenly jewels
Which Pericles hath lost, begin to part
Their fringes of bright gold; the diamonds
Of a most praisèd water do appear,
To make the world twice rich. — O, live, and make
Us weep to hear your fate, fair creature,
Rare as you seem to be!   [*She moves.*

Thai.   O dear Diana,
Where am I? Where's my lord? What world is this?

Sec. Gent. Is not this strange?

First Gent.   Most rare.

Cer.   Hush, my gentle neighbours!
Lend me your hands; to the next chamber bear her.
Get linen: now this matter must be look'd to,
For her relapse is mortal. Come, come;
And Æsculapius guide us!   [*Exeunt, carrying out Thaisa.*

SCENE III. *Tharsus. A room in the* Governor's *house.*

Enter PERICLES, CLEON, DIONYZA, *and* LYCHORIDA *with* MARINA
in her arms.

Per. Most honour'd Cleon, I must needs be gone;
My twelve months are expir'd, and Tyrus stands
In a litigious peace. You, and your lady,
Take from my heart all thankfulness! The gods
Make up the rest upon you!

Cle. Your shafts of fortune, though they hurt you mor-
          tally,
Yet glance full wanderingly on us.

Dion.   O your sweet queen!

That the strict Fates had pleas'd you had brought her hither,
T' have bless'd mine eyes with her!
    Per.   We cannot but obey
The powers above us. Could I rage and roar
As doth the sea she lies in, yet the end
Must be as 'tis. My gentle babe Marina, — whom,
For she was born at sea, I've nam'd so, — here
I charge your charity withal, leaving her
The infant of your care; beseeching you
To give her princely training, that she may be
Manner'd as she is born.
    Cle.   Fear not, my lord, but think
Your grace, that fed my country with your corn, —
For which the people's prayers still fall upon you, —
Must in your child be thought on. If neglection
Should therein make me vile, the common body,
By you reliev'd, would force me to my duty:
But if to that my nature need a spur,
The gods revenge it upon me and mine,
To the end of generation!
    Per.   I believe you;
Your honour and your goodness teach me to't,
Without your vows. — Till she be married, madam,
By bright Diana, whom we honour, all
Unscissar'd shall this hair of mine remain,
Though I show ill in't. So I take my leave.
Good madam, make me blessèd in your care
In bringing up my child.
    Dion.   I've one myself,
Who shall not be more dear to my respect
Than yours, my lord.
    Per.   Madam, my thanks and prayers.
    Cle. We'll bring your grace e'en to the edge o' the shore,
Then give you up to the mask'd Neptune and
The gentlest winds of heaven.
    Per.   I will embrace
Your offer. Come, dearest madam. — O, no tears,

Lychorida, no tears:
Look to your little mistress, on whose grace
You may depend hereafter. — Come, my lord.   [*Exeunt.*

SCENE IV. *Ephesus. A room in* CERIMON'S *house.*

Enter CERIMON *and* THAISA.

Cer. Madam, this letter, and some certain jewels,
Lay with you in your coffer: which are now
At your command. Know you the character?
Thai. It is my lord's.
That I was shipp'd at sea, I well remember,
Even on my eaning time; but whether there
Deliver'd, by the holy gods,
I cannot rightly say. But since King Pericles,
My wedded lord, I ne'er shall see again,
A vestal livery will I take me to,
And never more have joy.
Cer. Madam, if this you purpose as ye speak,
Diana's temple is not distant far,
Where you may abide till your date expire.
Moreover, if you please, a niece of mine
Shall there attend you.
Thai. My recompense is thanks, that's all;
Yet my good will is great, though the gift small.   [*Exeunt.*

ACT IV.

Enter GOWER.

Gow. Imagine Pericles arriv'd at Tyre,
Welcom'd and settled to his own desire.
His woful queen we leave at Ephesus,
Unto Diana there a votaress.
Now to Marina bend your mind,
Whom our fast-growing scene must find
At Tharsus, and by Cleon train'd
In music, letters; who hath gain'd

Of education all the grace,
Which makes her both the heart and place
Of general wonder. But, alack,
That monster envy, oft the wrack
Of earnèd praise, Marina's life
Seeks to take off by treason's knife.
And in this kind hath our Cleon
One daughter, and a wench full grown,
Even ripe for marriage-rite; this maid
Hight Philoten: and it is said
For certain in our story, she
Would ever with Marina be:
Be't when she weav'd the sleided silk
With fingers long, small, white as milk;
Or when she would with sharp neeld wound
The cambric, which she made more sound
By hurting it; or when to the lute
She sung, and made the night-bird mute,
That still records with moan; or when
She would with rich and constant pen
Vail to her mistress Dian; still
This Philoten contends in skill
With absolute Marina: so
With the dove of Paphos might the crow
Vie feathers white. Marina gets
All praises, which are paid as debts,
And not as given. This so darks
In Philoten all graceful marks,
That Cleon's wife, with envy rare,
A present murderer does prepare
For good Marina, that her daughter
Might stand peerless by this slaughter.
The sooner her vile thoughts to stead,
Lychorida, our nurse, is dead:
And cursèd Dionyza hath
The pregnant instrument of wrath
Prest for this blow. Th' unborn event

I do commend to your content:
Only I carry wingèd time
Post on the lame feet of my rhyme;
Which never could I so convey,
Unless your thoughts went on my way. —
Dionyza does appear,
With Leonine, a murderer. [*Exit.*

SCENE I. *Tharsus. An open place near the sea-shore.*

Enter DIONYZA *and* LEONINE.

Dion. Thy oath remember; thou hast sworn to do't:
'Tis but a blow, which never shall be known.
Thou canst not do a thing in the world so soon,
To yield thee so much profit. Let not conscience,
Which is but cold, inflaming love in thy bosom,
Inflame too nicely; nor let pity, which
Even women have cast off, melt thee, but be
A soldier to thy purpose.

Leon. I'll do't; but yet she is a goodly creature.

Dion. The fitter, then, the gods should have her. — Here
She comes weeping for her only mistress' death. —
Thou art resolv'd?

Leon. I am resolv'd.

Enter MARINA, *with a basket of flowers.*

Mar. No, I will rob Tellus of her weed,
To strew thy green with flowers; the yellows, blues,
The purple violets, and marigolds,
Shall, as a carpet, hang upon thy grave,
While summer-days do last. — Ay me! poor maid,
Born in a tempest, when my mother died,
This world to me is like a lasting storm,
Whirring me from my friends.

Dion. How now, Marina! why do you keep alone?
How chance my daughter is not with you? Do not
Consume your blood with sorrowing: you have

A nurse of me. Lord, how your favour 's chang'd
With this unprofitable woe! Come,
Give me your flowers, ere the sea mar it.
Walk with Leonine; the air is quick there,
And it pierces and sharpens the stomach. — Come,
Leonine, take her by the arm, walk with her.

　Mar.　　No, I pray you;
I'll not bereave you of your servant.

　Dion.　　　　　　　　　　Come, come;
I love the king your father, and yourself,
With more than foreign heart. We every day
Expect him here: when he shall come, and find
Our paragon to all reports thus blasted,
He will repent the breadth of his great voyage;
Blame both my lord and me, that we have taken
No care to your best courses. Go, I pray you,
Walk, and be cheerful once again; reserve
That excellent complexion, which did steal
The eyes of young and old. Care not for me;
I can go home alone.

　Mar.　　　　　　Well, I will go;
But yet I've no desire to it.

　Dion.　　　　　　　　Come, come,
I know 'tis good for you. —
Walk half an hour, Leonine, at the least:
Remember what I've said.

　Leon.　　　　　　I warrant you, madam.

　Dion.　I'll leave you, my sweet lady, for a while:
Pray, walk softly, do not heat your blood:
What! I must have a care of you.

　Mar.　　　　　　　　My thanks, sweet madam. —
　　　　　　　　　　　　　　　　[*Exit Dionyza.*

Is this wind westerly that blows?

　Leon.　　　　　　　　South-west.

　Mar. When I was born, the wind was north.

　Leon.　　　　　　　　　　Was't so?

　Mar. My father, as nurse said, did never fear,

But cried "Good seamen!" to the sailors, galling
His kingly hands, haling ropes;
And, clasping to the mast, endur'd a sea
That almost burst the deck.

    Leon. When was this?

    Mar. When I was born:
Never was waves nor wind more violent;
And from the ladder-tackle washes off
A canvas-climber. "Ha!" says one, "wilt out?"
And with a dropping industry they skip
From stem to stern: the boatswain whistles, and
The master calls, and trebles their confusion.

    Leon. Come, say your prayers.

    Mar. What mean you?

    Leon. If you require a little space for prayer,
I grant it: pray; but be not tedious, for
The gods are quick of ear, and I am sworn
To do my work with haste.

    Mar.   Why will you kill me?

    Leon. To satisfy my lady.

    Mar. Why would she have me kill'd?
Now, as I can remember, by my troth,
I never did her hurt in all my life:
I never spake bad word, nor did ill turn
To any living creature: believe me, la,
I never kill'd a mouse, nor hurt a fly:
I trod upon a worm once 'gainst my will,
But I wept for it. How have I offended,
Wherein my death might yield her any profit,
Or my life imply her any danger?

    Leon. My commission
Is not to reason of the deed, but do it.

    Mar. You will not do't for all the world, I hope.
You are well-favour'd, and your looks foreshow
You have a gentle heart. I saw you lately,
When you caught hurt in parting two that fought:
Good sooth, it show'd well in you: do so now:

Your lady seeks my life; come you between,
And save poor me, the weaker.
    Leon.   I am sworn,
And will dispatch.

       Enter Pirates, *whilst* MARINA *is struggling.*

    First Pirate. Hold, villain!   [*Leonine runs away.*
    Sec. Pirate. A prize! a prize!
    Third Pirate. Half-part, mates, half-part. Come, let's
have her aboard suddenly.   [*Exeunt Pirates with Marina.*

           Re-enter LEONINE.

    Leon. These roguing thieves serve the great pirate Valdes;
And they have seiz'd Marina. Let her go:
There's no hope she'll return. I'll swear she's dead,
And thrown into the sea. — But I'll see further:
Perhaps they will but please themselves upon her,
Not carry her aboard. If she remain,
Whom they have ravish'd must by me be slain.   [*Exit.*

    SCENE II. *Mytilene. A room in a brothel.*

      Enter Pander, Bawd, *and* BOULT.

    Pand. Boult, —
    Boult. Sir?
    Pand. Search the market narrowly; Mytilene is full of
gallants. We lost too much money this mart by being too
wenchless.
    Bawd. We were never so much out of creatures. We
have but poor three, and they can do no more than they can
do; and with continual action are even as good as rotten.
    Pand. Therefore let's have fresh ones, whate'er we pay
for them. If there be not a conscience to be used in every
trade, we shall never prosper.
    Bawd. Thou sayest true: 'tis not our bringing up of poor
bastards, — as, I think, I have brought up some eleven, —
    Boult. Ay, to eleven; and brought them down again. —
But shall I search the market?

Bawd. What else, man? The stuff we have, a strong wind will blow it to pieces, they are so pitifully sodden.

Pand. Thou sayest true; they're too unwholesome, o' conscience. The poor Transylvanian is dead, that lay with the little baggage.

Boult. Ay, she quickly pooped him; she made him roast-meat for worms. — But I'll go search the market. [*Exit.*

Pand. Three or four thousand chequins were as pretty a proportion to live quietly, and so give over.

Bawd. Why to give over, I pray you? is it a shame to get when we are old?

Pand. O, our credit comes not in like the commodity, nor the commodity wages not with the danger: therefore, if in our youths we could pick up some pretty estate, 'twere not amiss to keep our door hatched. Besides, the sore terms we stand upon with the gods will be strong with us for giving over.

Bawd. Come, other sorts offend as well as we.

Pand. As well as we! ay, and better too; we offend worse. Neither is our profession any trade; it's no calling. — But here comes Boult.

Re-enter BOULT, *with* MARINA *and the* Pirates.

Boult. [*to Marina*] Come your ways. — My masters, you say she's a virgin?

First Pirate. O, sir, we doubt it not.

Boult. Master, I have gone through for this piece, you see: if you like her, so; if not, I have lost my earnest.

Bawd. Boult, has she any qualities?

Boult. She has a good face, speaks well, and has excellent good clothes: there's no further necessity of qualities can make her be refused.

Bawd. What's her price, Boult?

Boult. I cannot be bated one doit of a thousand pieces.

Pand. Well, follow me, my masters, you shall have your money presently. — Wife, take her in; instruct her what she has to do, that she may not be raw in her entertainment.

[*Exeunt Pander and Pirates.*

Bawd. Boult, take you the marks of her, — the colour of her hair, complexion, height, age, with warrant of her virginity; and cry, "He that will give most shall have her first." Such a maidenhead were no cheap thing, if men were as they have been. Get this done as I command you.

Boult. Performance shall follow.　　　　　　　　　[*Exit.*

Mar. Alack that Leonine was so slack, so slow! He should have struck, not spoke; or that these pirates — Not enough barbarous — had not o'erboard thrown me For to seek my mother!

Bawd. Why lament you, pretty one?

Mar. That I am pretty.

Bawd. Come, the gods have done their part in you.

Mar. I accuse them not.

Bawd. You are light into my hands, where you are like to live.

Mar. The more my fault To scape his hands where I was like to die.

Bawd. Ay, and you shall live in pleasure.

Mar. No.

Bawd. Yes, indeed shall you, and taste gentlemen of all fashions: you shall fare well; you shall have the difference of all complexions. What! do you stop your ears?

Mar. Are you a woman?

Bawd. What would you have me be, an I be not a woman?

Mar. An honest woman, or not a woman.

Bawd. Marry, whip thee, gosling: I think I shall have something to do with you. Come, you're a young foolish sapling, and must be bowed as I would have you.

Mar. The gods defend me!

Bawd. If it please the gods to defend you by men, then men must comfort you, men must feed you, men must stir you up. — Boult's returned.

Re-enter BOULT.

Now, sir, hast thou cried her through the market?

Boult. I have cried her almost to the number of her hairs; I have drawn her picture with my voice.

Bawd. And I prithee tell me, how dost thou find the inclination of the people, especially of the younger sort?

Boult. Faith, they listened to me as they would have
hearkened to their father's testament. There was a Spa-
niard's mouth so watered, that he went to bed to her very
description.

Bawd. We shall have him here to-morrow with his best
ruff on.

Boult. To-night, to-night. But, mistress, do you know
the French knight that cowers i' the hams?

Bawd. Who, Monsieur Veroles?

Boult. Ay: he offered to cut a caper at the proclamation;
but he made a groan at it, and swore he would see her to-
morrow.

Bawd. Well, well; as for him, he brought his disease
hither: here he does but repair it. I know he will come in
our shadow, to scatter his crowns in the sun.

Boult. Well, if we had of every nation a traveller, we
should lodge them with this sign.

Bawd. [to *Mar.*] Pray you, come hither awhile. You
have fortunes coming upon you. Mark me: you must seem
to do that fearfully which you commit willingly; to despise profit where you have most gain. To weep that you
live as you do makes pity in your lovers: seldom but that
pity begets you a good opinion, and that opinion a mere
profit.

Mar. I understand you not.

Boult. O, take her home, mistress, take her home:
these blushes of hers must be quenched with some present
practice.

Bawd. Thou sayest true, i'faith, so they must; for your
bride goes to that with shame which is her way to go with
warrant.

Boult. Faith, some do, and some do not. But, mistress,
if I have bargained for the joint, —

Bawd. Thou mayst cut a morsel off the spit.

Boult. I may so.

Bawd. Who should deny it? — Come, young one, I like
the manner of your garments well.

Boult. Ay, by my faith, they shall not be changed yet.

Bawd. Boult, spend thou that in the town: report what
a sojourner we have; you'll lose nothing by custom. When
nature framed this piece, she meant thee a good turn; therefore say what a paragon she is, and thou hast the harvest out
of thine own report.

Boult. I warrant you, mistress, thunder shall not so
awake the beds of eels as my giving out her beauty stir up
the lewdly-inclined. I'll bring home some to-night.

Bawd. Come your ways; follow me.

Mar. If fires be hot, knives sharp, or waters deep,
Untied I still my virgin knot will keep.
Diana, aid my purpose!

Bawd. What have we to do with Diana? Pray you, will
you go with us?　　　　　　　　　　　　　　*[Exeunt.*

SCENE III. *Tharsus. A room in the* Governor's *house.*

Enter CLEON *and* DIONYZA.

Dion. Why, are you foolish? Can it be undone?

Cle. O Dionyza, such a piece of slaughter
The sun and moon ne'er look'd upon!

Dion.　　　　　　　　　　　　　I think
You'll turn a child again.

Cle. Were I chief lord of all this spacious world,
I'd give it to undo the deed. — O lady,
Much less in blood than virtue, yet a princess
To equal any single crown o' th' earth
I' the justice of compare! — O villain Leonine!
Whom thou hast poison'd too:
If thou hadst drunk to him, 't had been a kindness
Becoming well thy fact: what canst thou say
When noble Pericles shall demand his child?

Dion. That she is dead. Nurses are not the Fates,
To foster it, nor ever to preserve.

4*

She died at night; I'll say so. Who can cross it?
Unless you play the pious innocent,
And for an honest attribute cry out
"She died by foul play."

   Cle.   O, go to. Well, well,
Of all the faults beneath the heavens, the gods
Do like this worst.

   Dion.   Be one of those that think
The petty wrens of Tharsus will fly hence,
And open this to Pericles. I do shame
To think of what a noble strain you are,
And of how coward a spirit.

   Cle.   To such proceeding
Who ever but his approbation added,
Though not his prime consent, he did not flow
From honourable sources.

   Dion.   Be 't so, then:
Yet none does know, but you, how she came dead,
Nor none can know now, Leonine being gone.
She did distain my child, and stood between
Her and her fortunes: none would look on her,
But cast their gazes on Marina's face;
Whilst ours was blurted at, and held a malkin,
Not worth the time of day. It pierc'd me thorough;
And though you call my course unnatural,
You not your child well loving, yet I find
It greets me as an enterprise of kindness
Perform'd to our sole daughter.

   Cle.   Heavens forgive it!

   Dion. And as for Pericles,
What should he say? We wept after her hearse,
And yet we mourn: her monument
Is almost finish'd, and her epitaphs
In glittering golden characters express
A general praise to her, and care in us
At whose expense 'tis done.

   Cle.   Thou'rt like the harpy,

Which, to betray, dost, with thine angel's face,
Seize with thine eagle's talons.

    Dion. You are like one that superstitiously
Doth swear to the gods that winter kills the flies:
But yet I know you'll do as I advise.   [*Exeunt.*

   Enter GOWER, *before the monument of* MARINA *at Tharsus.*

    Gow. Thus time we waste, and longest leagues make
        short;
Sail seas in cockles, have an wish but for 't;
Making — to take your imagination —
From bourn to bourn, region to region.
By you being pardon'd, we commit no crime
To use one language in each several clime
Where our scenes seem to live. I do beseech you
To learn of me, who stand i' the gaps to teach you,
The stages of our story. Pericles
Is now again thwarting the wayward seas,
Attended on by many a lord and knight,
To see his daughter, all his life's delight.
Old Escanes, whom Helicanus late
Advanc'd in time to great and high estate,
Is left to govern. Bear you it in mind,
Old Helicanus goes along behind.
Well-sailing ships and bounteous winds have brought
This king to Tharsus — think his pilot thought;
So with his steerage shall your thoughts grow on —
To fetch his daughter home, who first is gone.
Like motes and shadows see them move awhile;
Your ears unto your eyes I'll reconcile.

DUMB-SHOW.

Enter, from one side, PERICLES *with his Train; from the other,*
CLEON *and* DIONYZA. CLEON *shows* PERICLES *the tomb of* MARINA;
whereat PERICLES *makes lamentation, puts on sackcloth, and in*
a mighty passion departs. Then exeunt CLEON *and* DIONYZA.

See how belief may suffer by foul show!
This borrow'd passion stands for true old woe;

And Pericles, in sorrow all devour'd,
With sighs shot through and biggest tears o'ershower'd,
Leaves Tharsus, and again embarks.   He swears
Never to wash his face, nor cut his hairs:
He puts on sackcloth, and to sea.   He bears
A tempest, which his mortal vessel tears,
And yet he rides it out.   Now please you wit
The epitaph is for Marina writ
By wicked Dionyza.

                [Reads the inscription on Marina's monument.

"*The fairest, sweet'st, and best lies here,*
 Who wither'd in her spring of year.
 She was of Tyrus the king's daughter,
 On whom foul death hath made this slaughter;
 Marina was she call'd; and at her birth,
 Thetis, being proud, swallow'd some part o' th' earth:
 Therefore the earth, fearing to be o'erflow'd,
 Hath Thetis' birth-child on the heavens bestow'd:
 Wherefore she does — and swears she'll never stint —
 Make raging battery upon shores of flint."
No visor doth become black villany
So well as soft and tender flattery.
Let Pericles believe his daughter's dead,
And bear his courses to be order'd
By Lady Fortune; while our scene must play
His daughter's woe and heavy well-a-day
In her unholy service.   Patience, then,
And think you now are all in Mytilen.

                                    [Exit.

SCENE IV.   *Mytilene.   A street before the brothel.*

Enter, from the brothel, two Gentlemen.

First Gent.   Did you ever hear the like?

Sec. Gent.   No, nor never shall do in such a place as this,
she being once gone.

First Gent.   But to have divinity preached there! did you
ever dream of such a thing?

Sec. Gent. No, no. Come, I am for no more bawdy-houses: — shall's go hear the vestals sing?

First Gent. I'll do any thing now that is virtuous; but I am out of the road of rutting for ever.   [*Exeunt.*

SCENE V. *The same. A room in the brothel.*

Enter Pander, Bawd, *and* BOULT.

Pand. Well, I had rather than twice the worth of her she had ne'er come here.

Bawd. Fie, fie upon her! she's able to freeze the god Priapus, and undo a whole generation. We must either get her ravished, or be rid of her. When she should do for clients her fitment, and do me the kindness of our profession, she has me her quirks, her reasons, her master reasons, her prayers, her knees; that she would make a puritan of the devil, if he should cheapen a kiss of her.

Boult. Faith, I must ravish her, or she'll disfurnish us of all our cavaliers, and make all our swearers priests.

Pand. Now, the pox upon her green-sickness for me!

Bawd. Faith, there's no way to be rid on't but by the way to the pox. — Here comes the Lord Lysimachus disguised.

Boult. We should have both lord and lown, if the peevish baggage would but give way to customers.

Enter LYSIMACHUS.

Lys. How now! How a dozen of virginities?

Bawd. Now, the gods to-bless your honour!

Boult. I am glad to see your honour in good health.

Lys. You may so; 'tis the better for you that your resorters stand upon sound legs. How now, wholesome iniquity! Have you that a man may deal withal, and defy the surgeon?

Bawd. We have here one, sir, if she would — but there never came her like in Mytilene.

Lys. If she'd do the deed of darkness, thou wouldst say.

Bawd. Your honour knows what 'tis to say well enough.

Lys. Well, call forth, call forth.

Boult. For flesh and blood, sir, white and red, you shall see a rose; and she were a rose indeed, if she had but —

Lys. What, prithee?

Boult. O, sir, I can be modest.

Lys. That dignifies the renown of a bawd, no less than it gives a good report to a number to be chaste. · [*Exit Boult.*

Bawd. Here comes that which grows to the stalk, — never plucked yet, I can assure you.

Re-enter BOULT *with* MARINA.

Is she not a fair creature?

Lys. Faith, she would serve after a long voyage at sea. Well, there's for you: — leave us.

Bawd. I beseech your honour, give me leave: a word, and I'll have done presently.

Lys. I beseech you, do.

Bawd. [*to Marina*] First, I would have you note, this is an honourable man.

Mar. I desire to find him so, that I may worthily note him.

Bawd. Next, he's the governor of this country, and a man whom I am bound to.

Mar. If he govern the country, you are bound to him indeed; but how honourable he is in that, I know not.

Bawd. Pray you, without any more virginal fencing, will you use him kindly? He will line your apron with gold.

Mar. What he will do graciously, I will thankfully receive.

Lys. Ha' you done?

Bawd. My lord, she's not paced yet: you must take some pains to work her to your manage. — Come, we will leave his honour and her together. — Go thy ways.

[*Exeunt Bawd, Pander, and Boult.*

Lys. Now, pretty one, how long have you been at this trade?

Mar. What trade, sir?

Lys. Why, I cannot name't but I shall offend.

Mar. I cannot be offended with my trade. Please you
to name it.

Lys. How long have you been of this profession?

Mar. E'er since I can remember.

Lys. Did you go to't so young? Were you a gamester
at five or at seven?

Mar. Earlier too, sir, if now I be one.

Lys. Why, the house you dwell in proclaims you to be a
creature of sale.

Mar. Do you know this house to be a place of such resort, and will come into 't? I hear say you are of honourable
parts, and are the governor of this place.

Lys. Why, hath your principal made known unto you
who I am?

Mar. Who is my principal?

Lys. Why, your herb-woman; she that sets seeds and
roots of shame and iniquity. O, you have heard something
of my power, and so stand aloof for more serious wooing. But
I protest to thee, pretty one, my authority shall not see thee,
or else look friendly upon thee. Come, bring me to some
private place: come, come.

Mar. If you were born to honour, show it now;
If put upon you, make the judgment good
That thought you worthy of it.

Lys. How's this? how's this? — Some more; — be sage.

Mar.   For me,
That am a maid, though most ungentle fortune
Have plac'd me in this sty, where, since I came,
Diseases have been sold dearer than physic, —
O, that the gods
Would set me free from this unhallow'd place,
Though they did change me to the meanest bird
That flies i' the purer air!

Lys.   I did not think
Thou couldst have spoke so well; ne'er dream'd thou couldst.
Had I brought hither a corrupted mind,
Thy speech had alter'd it. Hold, here's gold for thee:

Persever in that clear way thou goest,
And the gods strengthen thee!
 Mar.   The good gods preserve you!
 Lys. For me, be you thoughten
That I came with no ill intent; for to me
The very doors and windows savour vilely.
Fare thee well. Thou art a piece of virtue, and
I doubt not but thy training hath been noble. —
Hold, here's more gold for thee. —
A curse upon him, die he like a thief,
That robs thee of thy goodness! If thou dost
Hear from me, it shall be for thy good.

Re-enter BOULT.

 Boult. I beseech your honour, one piece for me.
 Lys. Avaunt, thou damnèd doorkeeper!
Your house, but for this virgin that doth prop it,
Would sink, and overwhelm you. Away!   [*Exit.*
 Boult. How's this? We must take another course with
you. If your peevish chastity, which is not worth a break-
fast in the cheapest country under the cope, shall undo a
whole household, let me be gelded like a spaniel. Come
your ways.
 Mar. Whither would you have me?
 Boult. I must have your maidenhead taken off, or the
common hangman shall execute it. Come your ways. We'll
have no more gentlemen driven away. Come your ways,
I say.

Re-enter Bawd.

 Bawd. How now! what's the matter?
 Boult. Worse and worse, mistress; she has here spoken
holy words to the Lord Lysimachus.
 Bawd. O abominable!
 Boult. She makes our profession as it were to stink afore
the face of the gods.
 Bawd. Marry, hang her up for ever!
 Boult. The nobleman would have dealt with her like a

nobleman, and she sent him away as cold as a snowball;
saying his prayers too.

Bawd. Boult, take her away; use her at thy pleasure:
crack the glass of her virginity, and make the rest malleable.

Boult. An if she were a thornier piece of ground than she
is, she shall be ploughed.

Mar. Hark, hark, you gods!

Bawd. She conjures: away with her! Would she had
never come within my doors! — Marry, hang you! — She's
born to undo us. — Will you not go the way of women-kind?
Marry, come up, my dish of chastity with rosemary and bays!

                                                                [Exit.

Boult. Come, mistress; come your ways with me.

Mar. Whither wilt thou have me?

Boult. To take from you the jewel you hold so dear.

Mar. Prithee, tell me one thing first.

Boult. Come now, your one thing.

Mar. What canst thou wish thine enemy to be?

Boult. Why, I could wish him to be my master, or rather,
my mistress.

Mar. Neither of these are so bad as thou art,
Since they do better thee in their command.
Thou hold'st a place, for which the pained'st fiend
Of hell would not in reputation change:
Thou art the damnèd doorkeeper to every
Coistrel that comes inquiring for his Tib;
To the choleric fisting of every rogue
Thy ear is liable; thy food is such
As hath been belch'd on by infected lungs.

Boult. What would you have me do? go to the wars,
would you? where a man may serve seven years for the loss
of a leg, and have not money enough in the end to buy him
a wooden one?

Mar. Do any thing but this thou doest. Empty
Old receptacles, or common shores, of filth;
Serve by indenture to the common hangman:
Any of these ways are yet better than this;

For what thou professest, a baboon, could he speak,
Would own a name too dear. — O, that the gods
Would safely from this place deliver me! —
Here, here's gold for thee.
If that thy master would gain by me,
Proclaim that I can sing, weave, sew, and dance,
With other virtues, which I'll keep from boast;
And I will undertake all these to teach.
I doubt not but this populous city will
Yield many scholars.

Boult. But can you teach all this you speak of?

Mar. Prove that I cannot, take me home again,
And prostitute me to the basest groom
That doth frequent your house.

Boult. Well, I will see what I can do for thee: if I can
place thee, I will.

Mar. But amongst honest women.

Boult. Faith, my acquaintance lies little amongst them.
But since my master and mistress have bought you, there's
no going but by their consent: therefore I will make them
acquainted with your purpose, and I doubt not but I shall
find them tractable enough. Come, I'll do for thee what I
can; come your ways.

ACT V.

Enter GOWER.

Gow. Marina thus the brothel scapes, and chances
Into an honest house, our story says.
She sings like one immortal, and she dances
As goddess-like to her admirèd lays;
Deep clerks she dumbs; and with her neeld composes
Nature's own shape, of bud, bird, branch, or berry,
That even her art sisters the natural roses;
Her inkle, silk, twin with the rubied cherry:
That pupils lacks she none of noble race,
Who pour their bounty on her; and her gain

She gives the cursèd bawd.   Here we her place;
And to her father turn our thoughts again,
Where we left him, on the sea.   We there him lost:
Whence, driven before the winds, he is arriv'd
Here where his daughter dwells; and on this coast
Suppose him now at anchor.   The city striv'd
God Neptune's annual feast to keep: from whence
Lysimachus our Tyrian ship espies,
His banners sable, trimm'd with rich expense;
And to him in his barge with fervour hies.
In your supposing once more put your sight
Of heavy Pericles; think this his bark:
Where what is done in action, more, if might,
Shall be discover'd; please you, sit, and hark.   [*Exit.*

SCENE I.   *On board* PERICLES' *ship, off Mytilene.   A pavilion on
deck, with a curtain before it;* PERICLES *within it, reclined on a
couch.   A barge lying beside the Tyrian vessel.*

Enter two Sailors, *one belonging to the Tyrian vessel, the other
to the barge; to them* HELICANUS.

   Tyr. Sail. [*to the Sailor of Mytilene*] Where is Lord Heli-
      cane? he can resolve you.
O, here he is. —
Sir, there's a barge put off from Mytilene,
And in it is Lysimachus the governor,
Who craves to come aboard.   What is your will?

   Hel.   That he have his.   Call up some gentlemen.

   Tyr. Sail.   Ho, gentlemen! my lord calls.

          Enter two or three Gentlemen.

   First Gent.   Doth your lordship call?

   Hel. Gentlemen, there's some of worth would come aboard:
I pray ye, greet them fairly.
         [*The Gentlemen and the two Sailors descend, and
           go on board the barge. .*

Enter, from thence, LYSIMACHUS *and Lords, with the* Gentlemen
and the two Sailors.

   Tyr. Sail. Sir,
This is the man that can, in aught you would,
Resolve you.
   Lys. Hail, reverend sir! the gods preserve you!
   Hel. And you, sir, to outlive the age I am,
And die as I would do.
   Lys.   You wish me well.
Being on shore, honouring of Neptune's triumphs,
Seeing this goodly vessel ride before us,
I made to it, to know of whence you are.
   Hel. First, what is your place?
   Lys.   I am the governor
Of this place you lie before.
   Hel. Sir,
Our vessel is of Tyre, in it the king;
A man who for this three months hath not spoken
To any one, nor taken sustenance
But to prorogue his grief.
   Lys. Upon what ground is his distemperature?
   Hel. 'Twould be too tedious to repeat;
But the main grief springs from the loss
Of a belovèd daughter and a wife.
   Lys. May we not see him?
   Hel. You may;
But bootless is your sight, — he will not speak
To any.
   Lys. Yet let me obtain my wish.
   Hel. Behold him [*Draws the curtain, and discovers Pericles*].
       This was a goodly person,
Till the disaster that, one mortal night,
Drove him to this.
   Lys. Sir king, all hail! the gods preserve you!
Hail, royal sir!
   Hel. It is in vain; he will not speak to you.
   First Lord. Sir,

We have a maid in Mytilen, I durst wager,
Would win some words of him.
    Lys.   'Tis well bethought.
She, questionless, with her sweet harmony
And other chosen attractions, would allure,
And make a battery through his deafen'd parts,
Which now are midway stopp'd:
She is all happy as the fairest of all,
And, with her fellow maids, is now upon
The leafy shelter that abuts against
The island's side.   [*Whispers First Lord; who goes off in
                         the barge of Lysimachus.*

    Hel. Sure, all's effectless; yet nothing we'll omit
That bears recovery's name. But, since your kindness
We have stretch'd thus far, let us beseech you
That for our gold we may provision have,
Wherein we are not destitute for want,
But weary for the staleness.
    Lys.   O, sir, a courtesy
Which if we should deny, the most just gods
For every graff would send a caterpillar,
And so afflict our province. — Yet once more
Let me entreat to know at large the cause
Of your king's sorrow.
    Hel.   Sit, sir; I will recount it to you: —
But, see, I am prevented.

    Re-enter, from the barge, First Lord, *with* MARINA *and a
                 young* Lady.

    Lys.   O, here is
The lady that I sent for. — Welcome, fair one! —
Is't not a goodly presence?
    Hel.   She's a gallant lady.
    Lys. She's such a one, that, were I well assur'd
Came of a gentle kind and noble stock,
I'd wish no better choice, and think me rarely wed. —
Fair one, all goodness that consists in bounty

Expect even here, where is a kingly patient:
If that thy prosperous-artificial feat
Can draw him but to answer thee in aught,
Thy sacred physic shall receive such pay
As thy desires can wish.

    Mar.   Sir, I will use
My utmost skill in his recovery,
Provided
That none but I and my companion maid
Be suffer'd to come near him.

    Lys.   Come, let 's leave her;
And the gods make her prosperous!   [*Marina sings.*

    Lys. Mark'd he your music?

    Mar.   No, nor look'd on us.

    Lys. See, she will speak to him.

    Mar. Hail, sir! my lord, lend ear.

    Per. Hum, ha!

    Mar. I am a maid,
My lord, that ne'er before invited eyes,
But have been gaz'd on like a comet: she speaks,
My lord, that, may be, hath endur'd a grief
Might equal yours, if both were justly weigh'd.
Though wayward fortune did malign my state,
My derivation was from ancestors
Who stood equivalent with mighty kings:
But time hath rooted out my parentage,
And to the world and awkward casualties
Bound me in servitude. — [*Aside*] I will desist;
But there is something glows upon my cheek,
And whispers in mine ear, "Go not till he speak."

    Per. My fortunes — parentage — good parentage —
To equal mine! — was it not thus? what say you?

    Mar. I said, my lord, if you did know my parentage,
You would not do me violence.

    Per. I do think so. — Pray you, turn your eyes upon me.
You are like something that — What countrywoman?
Here of these shores?

Mar.   No, nor of any shores:
Yet I was mortally brought forth, and am
No other than I appear.
   Per.   I'm great with woe, and shall deliver weeping.
My dearest wife was like this maid, and such a one
My daughter might have been: my queen's square brows;
Her stature to an inch; as wand-like straight;
As silver-voic'd; her eyes as jewel-like,
And cas'd as richly; in pace another Juno;
Who starves the ears she feeds, and makes them hungry,
The more she gives them speech. — Where do you live?
   Mar.   Where I am but a stranger: from the deck
You may discern the place.
   Per.   Where were you bred?
And how achiev'd you these endowments, which
You make more rich to owe?
   Mar.   If I should tell my history, it would seem
Like lies disdain'd in the reporting.
   Per.   Prithee, speak:
Falseness cannot come from thee; for thou look'st
Modest as Justice, and thou seem'st a palace
For the crown'd Truth to dwell in: I'll believe thee,
And make my senses credit thy relation
To points that seem impossible; for thou look'st
Like one I lov'd indeed.   What were thy friends?
Didst thou not say, when I did push thee back, —
Which was when I perceiv'd thee, — that thou cam'st
From good descending?
   Mar.   So indeed I did.
   Per.   Report thy parentage.   I think thou said'st
Thou hadst been toss'd from wrong to injury,
And that thou thought'st thy griefs might equal mine,
If both were open'd.
   Mar.   Some such thing
I said, and said no more but what my thoughts
Did warrant me was likely.
   Per.   Tell thy story;

Shakespeare. VII.   5

If thine consider'd prove the thousandth part
Of my endurance, thou'rt a man, and I
Have suffer'd like a girl: yet thou dost look
Like Patience gazing on kings' graves, and smiling
Extremity out of act. What were thy friends?
How lost thou them? Thy name, my most kind virgin?
Recount, I do beseech thee: come, sit by me.

    Mar. My name is Marina.

    Per.   O, I am mock'd,
And thou by some incensèd god sent hither
To make the world to laugh at me.

    Mar.   Patience, good sir,
Or here I'll cease.

    Per.   Nay, I'll be patient.
Thou little know'st how thou dost startle me,
To call thyself Marina.

    Mar.   The name
Was given me by one that had some power, —
My father, and a king.

    Per.   How! a king's daughter?
And call'd Marina?

    Mar.   You said you would believe me;
But, not to be a troubler of your peace,
I will end here.

    Per.   But are you flesh and blood?
Have you a working pulse? and are no fairy?
Motion! — Well; speak on. Where were you born?
And wherefore call'd Marina?

    Mar.   Call'd Marina
For I was born at sea.

    Per.   At sea! what mother?

    Mar. My mother was the daughter of a king;
Who died the very minute I was born,
As my good nurse Lychorida hath oft
Deliver'd weeping.

    Per.   O, stop there a little! —
[*Aside*] This is the rarest dream that e'er dull sleep

Did mock sad fools withal: this cannot be:
My daughter's buried. — Well: — where were you bred?
I'll hear you more, to the bottom of your story,
And never interrupt you.

    Mar.   You'll scarce believe me;
'Twere best I did give o'er.

    Per. I will believe you by the syllable
Of what you shall deliver. Yet, give me leave: —
How came you in these parts? where were you bred?

    Mar. The king my father did in Tharsus leave me;
Till cruel Cleon, with his wicked wife,
Did seek to murder me: and having woo'd
A villain to attempt it, who having drawn to do't,
A crew of pirates came and rescu'd me;
Brought me to Mytilene. But, good sir,
Whither will you have me? Why do you weep? It may be,
You think me an impostor: no, good faith;
I am the daughter to King Pericles,
If good King Pericles be.

    Per. Ho, Helicanus!

    Hel. Calls my lord?

    Per. Thou art a grave and noble counsellor,
Most wise in general: tell me, if thou canst,
What this maid is, or what is like to be,
That thus hath made me weep?

    Hel.   I know not; but
Here is the regent, sir, of Mytilene
Speaks nobly of her.

    Lys.   She would never tell
Her parentage; being demanded that,
She would sit still and weep.

    Per. O Helicanus, strike me, honour'd sir;
Give me a gash, put me to present pain;
Lest this great sea of joys rushing upon me
O'erbear the shores of my mortality,
And drown me with their sweetness. — O, come hither,
Thou that begett'st him that did thee beget;

                        5*

Thou that wast born at sea, buried at Tharsus,
And found at sea again! — O Helicanus,
Down on thy knees, thank th' holy gods as loud
As thunder threatens us: this is Marina. —
What was thy mother's name? tell me but that,
For truth can never be confirm'd enough,
Though doubts did ever sleep.

    Mar.   First, sir, I pray,
What is your title?

    Per. I'm Pericles of Tyre: but tell me now
My drown'd queen's name, — as in the rest you said
Thou hast been godlike perfect, —
The heir of kingdoms, and another like
To Pericles thy father.

    Mar. Is it no more to be your daughter than
To say my mother's name was Thaisa?
Thaisa was my mother, who did end
The minute I began.

    Per. Now, blessing on thee! rise; thou art my child. —
Give me fresh garments. — Mine own, Helicanus, —
She is not dead at Tharsus, as she should have been,
By savage Cleon: she shall tell thee all;
When thou shalt kneel, and justify in knowledge
She is thy very princess. — Who is this?

    Hel. Sir, 'tis the governor of Mytilene,
Who, hearing of your melancholy state,
Did come to see you.

    Per.   I embrace you, sir.
Give me my robes. — I'm wild in my beholding. —
O heavens bless my girl! — But, hark, what music? —
Tell Helicanus, my Marina, tell him
O'er, point by point, for yet he seems to doubt,
How sure you are my daughter. — But, what music?

    Hel. My lord, I hear none.

    Per. None!
The music of the spheres! — List, my Marina.

    Lys. It is not good to cross him; give him way.

Per.   Rar'st sounds! Do ye not hear?

Lys.   My lord, I hear.
                                                    [*Music.*

Per.   Most heavenly music!
It nips me unto listening, and thick slumber
Hangs upon mine eyes: let me rest.   [*Sleeps.*
    Lys.   A pillow for his head: —
So, leave him all. — Well, my companion friends,
If this but answer to my just belief,
I'll well remember you.   [*Exeunt all except Pericles.*

DIANA *appears.*

Dia.   My temple stands in Ephesus: hie thee thither,
And do upon mine altar sacrifice.
There, when my maiden priests are met together,
Before the people all,
Reveal how thou at sea didst lose thy wife:
To mourn thy crosses, with thy daughter's, call,
And give them repetition to the life.
Or perform my bidding, or thou liv'st in woe;
Do it, and happy; by my silver bow!
Awake, and tell thy dream.   [*Disappears.*
    Per.   Celestial Dian, goddess argentine,
I will obey thee. — Helicanus!

Re-enter HELICANUS, LYSIMACHUS, MARINA, &c.

Hel.   Sir?
    Per.   My purpose was for Tharsus, there to strike
Th' inhospitable Cleon; but I am
For other service first: toward Ephesus
Turn our blown sails; eftsoons I'll tell thee why. —
[*To Lysimachus*] Shall we refresh us, sir, upon your shore,
And give you gold for such provision
As our intents will need?
    Lys.   Sir,
With all my heart; and, when you come ashore,
I have another suit.

Per.   You shall prevail,
Were it to woo my daughter; for it seems
You have been noble towards her.
    Lys.   Sir, lend me your arm.
    Per. Come, my Marina.   [*Exeunt.*

    Enter GOWER, *before the temple of* DIANA *at Ephesus.*

      Gow. Now our sands are almost run;
More a little, and then dumb.
This, my last boon, give me, —
For such kindness must relieve me,
That you aptly will suppose
What pageantry, what feats, what shows,
What minstrelsy, and pretty din,
The regent made in Mytilin,
To greet the king. So he thriv'd,
That he is promis'd to be wiv'd
To fair Marina; but in no wise
Till he had done his sacrifice,
As Dian bade: whereto being bound,
The interim, pray you, all confound.
In feather'd briefness sails are fill'd,
And wishes fall out as they're will'd.
At Ephesus, the temple see,
Our king, and all his company.
That can he hither come so soon,
Is by your fancies' thankful doom.   [*Exit.*

SCENE II. *The temple of* DIANA *at Ephesus;* THAISA *standing
near the altar, as high priestess; a number of Virgins on each
side;* CERIMON *and other Inhabitants of Ephesus attending.*

Enter PERICLES, *with his Train;* LYSIMACHUS, HELICANUS, MA-
RINA, *and a* Lady.

    Per. Hail, Dian! to perform thy just command,
I here confess myself the king of Tyre;
Who, frighted from my country, did wed

At Pentapolis the fair Thaisa.
At sea in childbed died she, but brought forth
A maid-child call'd Marina; who, O goddess,
Wears yet thy silver livery. She at Tharsus
Was nurs'd with Cleon; who at fourteen years
He sought to murder: but her better stars
Brought her to Mytilene; 'gainst whose shore
Riding, her fortunes-brought the maid aboard us,
Where, by her own most clear remembrance, she
Made known herself my daughter.

   Thai.   Voice and favour! —
You are, you are — O royal Pericles! —   [*Faints.*

   Per. What means the nun? she dies! help, gentlemen!

   Cer. Noble sir,
If you have told Diana's altar true,
This is your wife.

   Per.   Reverend appearer, no;
I threw her o'erboard with these very arms.

   Cer. Upon this coast, I warrant you.

   Per.   'Tis most certain.

   Cer. Look to the lady; — O, she's but o'erjoy'd. —
Early in blustering morn this lady was
Thrown upon this shore. I op'd the coffin,
Found there rich jewels; recover'd her, and plac'd her
Here in Diana's temple.

   Per.   May we see them?

   Cer. Great sir, they shall be brought you to my house,
Whither I invite you. — Look, Thaisa is
Recover'd.

   Thai. O, let me look!
If he be none of mine, my sanctity
Will to my sense bend no licentious ear,
But curb it, spite of seeing. — O, my lord,
Are you not Pericles? Like him you speak,
Like him you are: did you not name a tempest,
A birth, and death?

   Per.   The voice of dead Thaisa!

Thai.   That Thaisa am I, supposèd dead
And drown'd.

Per.   Immortal Dian!

Thai.   Now I know you better. —
When we with tears parted Pentapolis,
The king my father gave you such a ring.   [*Shows a ring.*

Per.   This, this: no more, you gods! your present kind-
    · ness
Makes my past miseries sport: you shall do well,
That on the touching of her lips I may
Melt, and no more be seen. — O, come, be buried
A second time within these arms.

Mar.   My heart
Leaps to be gone into my mother's bosom.

                              [*Kneels to Thaisa.*

Per.   Look, who kneels here! Flesh of thy flesh, Thaisa;
Thy burden at the sea, and call'd Marina
For she was yielded there.

Thai.   Bless'd, and mine own!

Hel.   Hail, madam, and my queen!

Thai.   I know you not.

Per.   You've heard me say, when I did fly from Tyre,
I left behind an ancient substitute:
Can you remember what I call'd the man?
I've nam'd him oft.

Thai.   'Twas Helicanus then.

Per.   Still confirmation:
Embrace him, dear Thaisa; this is he.
Now do I long to hear how you were found;
How possibly preserv'd; and who to thank,
Besides the gods, for this great miracle.

Thai.   Lord Cerimon, my lord; this is the man,
Through whom the gods have shown their power, that can
From first to last resolve you.

Per.   Reverend sir,
The gods can have no mortal officer

More like a god than you.   Will you deliver
How this dead queen re-lives?
    Cer.   I will, my lord.
Beseech you, first go with me to my house,
Where shall be shown you all was found with her;
How she came placèd here in the temple;
No needful thing omitted.
    Per.   Pure Dian, bless thee for thy vision!   I
Will offer night-oblations to thee. — Thaisa,
This prince, the fair-betrothèd of your daughter,
Shall marry her at Pentapolis. — And now,
This ornament
Makes me look dismal will I clip to form;
And what this fourteen years no razor touch'd,
To grace thy marriage-day, I'll beautify.
    Thai.   Lord Cerimon hath letters of good credit, sir,
My father's dead.
    Per.   Heavens make a star of him!   Yet there, my queen,
We'll celebrate their nuptials, and ourselves
Will in that kingdom spend our following days:
Our son and daughter shall in Tyrus reign. —
Lord Cerimon, we do our longing stay
To hear the rest untold: sir, lead's the way.   [*Exeunt.*

Enter GOWER.

    Gow.   In Antiochus and his daughter you have heard
Of monstrous lust the due and just reward:
In Pericles, his queen and daughter, seen,
Although assail'd with fortune fierce and keen,
Virtue preserv'd from fell destruction's blast,
Led on by heaven, and crown'd with joy at last:
In Helicanus may you well descry
A figure of truth, of faith, of loyalty:
In reverend Cerimon there well appears
The worth that learnèd charity aye wears:
For wicked Cleon and his wife, when fame
Had spread their cursèd deed, and honour'd name

Of Pericles, to rage the city turn,
That him and his they in his palace burn;
The gods for murder seemèd so content
To punish them, — although not done, but meant
So, on your patience evermore attending,
New joy wait on you!   Here our play has ending.

                                        [*Exit.*

THE TEMPEST.

DRAMATIS PERSONÆ.

ALONSO, King of Naples.
FERDINAND, his son.
SEBASTIAN, brother to Alonso.
PROSPERO, the rightful Duke of Milan.
ANTONIO, his brother, the usurping Duke of Milan.
GONZALO, an honest old counsellor.
ADRIAN, } lords.
FRANCISCO, }
TRINCULO, a jester.
STEPHANO, a drunken butler.

Master of a ship, Boatswain, and Mariners.

CALIBAN, a savage and deformed slave.

MIRANDA, daughter to Prospero.

ARIEL, an airy spirit.
IRIS,
CERES,
JUNO, } presented by spirits.
Nymphs,
Reapers,

Other Spirits attending on Prospero.

SCENE — *On board a ship at sea; afterwards various parts of an island.*

ACT I.

SCENE I. *On board a ship at sea: a storm, with thunder and lightning.*

Enter Master *and* Boatswain *severally.*

Mast. Boatswain!

Boats. Here, master: what cheer?

Mast. Good, speak to the mariners: fall to't yarely, or we run ourselves a-ground: bestir, bestir.   [*Exit.*

Enter Mariners.

Boats. Heigh, my hearts! cheerly, cheerly, my hearts! yare, yare! Take in the topsail! Tend to the master's

whistle! [*Exeunt Mariners.*] — Blow, till thou burst thy wind,
if room enough!

Enter ALONSO, SEBASTIAN, ANTONIO, FERDINAND, GONZALO,
and others.

Alon. Good boatswain, have care. Where's the master?
Play the men.

Boats. I pray now, keep below.

Ant. Where is the master, boatswain?

Boats. Do you not hear him? You mar our labour: keep
your cabins: you do assist the storm.

Gon. Nay, good, be patient.

Boats. When the sea is. Hence! What care these roarers
for the name of king? To cabin: silence! trouble us not.

Gon. Good, yet remember whom thou hast aboard.

Boats. None that I more love than myself. You are a
counsellor; — if I can command these elements to silence,
and work the peace of the present, we will not hand a rope
more; use your authority: if you cannot, give thanks you
have lived so long, and make yourself ready in your cabin
for the mischance of the hour, if it so hap. — Cheerly, good
hearts! — Out of our way, I say.   [*Exit.*

Gon. I have great comfort from this fellow: methinks he
hath no drowning-mark upon him; his complexion is perfect
gallows. Stand fast, good Fate, to his hanging! make the
rope of his destiny our cable, for our own doth little advantage! If he be not born to be hanged, our case is miserable.
                    [*Exeunt.*

Re-enter Boatswain.

Boats. Down with the topmast! yare; lower, lower!
Bring her to try with main-course! [*A cry within.*] A plague
upon this howling! they are louder than the weather or our
office.

Re-enter SEBASTIAN, ANTONIO, *and* GONZALO.

Yet again! what do you here? Shall we give o'er, and
drown? Have you a mind to sink?

Seb. A pox o' your throat, you bawling, blasphemous, incharitable dog!

Boats. Work you, then.

Ant. Hang, cur, hang! you whoreson, insolent noise-maker, we are less afraid to be drowned than thou art.

Gon. I'll warrant him for drowning; though the ship were no stronger than a nutshell, and as leaky as an unstanched wench.

Boats. Lay her a-hold, a-hold! set her two courses! off to sea again; lay her off!

Re-enter Mariners *wet.*

Mariners. All lost! to prayers, to prayers! all lost!
[*Exeunt.*

Boats. What, must our mouths be cold?

Gon. The king and prince at prayers! let's assist them, For our case is as theirs.

Seb.   I'm out of patience.

Ant. We are merely cheated of our lives by drunkards:— This wide-chapp'd rascal,—would thou mightst lie drowning, The washing of ten tides!

Gon.   He'll be hang'd yet,
Though every drop of water swear against it,
And gape at wid'st to glut him.
[*A confused noise within,*—"Mercy on us!"— "We split, we split!"—"Farewell, my wife and children!"— "Farewell, brother!"—"We split, we split, we split!"]
[*Exit Boatswain.*

Ant. Let's all sink with the king.   [*Exit.*

Seb.   Let's take leave of him.
[*Exit.*

Gon. Now would I give a thousand furlongs of sea for an acre of barren ground,—ling, heath, broom, furze, any thing. The wills above be done! but I would fain die a dry death.   [*Exit.*

SCENE II. *The island: before the cell of* PROSPERO.

Enter PROSPERO *and* MIRANDA.

Mir.   If by your art, my dearest father, you have
Put the wild waters in this roar, allay them.
The sky, it seems, would pour down stinking pitch,
But that the sea, mounting to the welkin's cheek,
Dashes the fire out.   O, I have suffer'd
With those that I saw suffer! a brave vessel,
Who had, no doubt, some noble creatures in her,
Dash'd all to pieces.   O, the cry did knock
Against my very heart! Poor souls, they perish'd!
Had I been any god of power, I would
Have sunk the sea within the earth, or e'er
It should the good ship so have swallow'd, and
The fraughting souls within her.

    Pros.   Be collected;
No more amazement: tell your piteous heart
There's no harm done.

    Mir.   O, woe the day!

    Pros.   No harm.
I have done nothing but in care of thee, —
Of thee, my dear one, thee, my daughter, — who
Art ignorant of what thou art, naught knowing
Of whence I am, nor that I am more better
Than Prospero, master of a full poor cell,
And thy no greater father.

    Mir.   More to know
Did never meddle with my thoughts.

    Pros.   'Tis time
I should inform thee further.   Lend thy hand,
And pluck my magic garment from me. — So:

                        [*Lays down his robe.*
Lie there, my art. — Wipe thou thine eyes; have comfort.
The direful spectacle of the wreck, which touch'd
The very virtue of compassion in thee,
I have with such prevision in mine art

So safely order'd, that there is no soul —
No, not so much perdition as an hair
Betid to any creature in the vessel
Which thou heard'st cry, which thou saw'st sink. Sit down;
For thou must now know further.

  Mir.   You have often
Begun to tell me what I am; but stopp'd,
And left me to a bootless inquisition,
Concluding, "Stay, not yet."

  Pros.   The hour's now come;
The very minute bids thee ope thine ear:
Obey, and be attentive. Canst thou remember
A time before we came unto this cell?
I do not think thou canst, for then thou wast not
Out three years old.

  Mir.   Certainly, sir, I can.

  Pros. By what? by any other house or person?
Of any thing the image tell me that
Hath kept with thy remembrance.

  Mir.   'Tis far off,
And rather like a dream than an assurance
That my remembrance warrants. Had I not
Four or five women once that tended me?

  Pros. Thou hadst, and more, Miranda. But how is it
That this lives in thy mind? What see'st thou else
In the dark backward and abysm of time?
If thou remember'st aught ere thou cam'st here,
How thou cam'st here thou mayst.

  Mir.   But that I do not.

  Pros. Twelve year since, Miranda, twelve year since,
Thy father was the Duke of Milan, and
A prince of power.

  Mir.   Sir, are not you my father?

  Pros. Thy mother was a piece of virtue, and
She said thou wast my daughter; and thy father
Was Duke of Milan; thou his only heir,
A princess, — no worse issu'd.

Mir.   O the heavens!
What foul play had we, that we came from thence?
Or blessèd was't we did?
  Pros.   Both, both, my girl:
By foul play, as thou say'st, were we heav'd thence;
But blessedly holp hither.
  Mir. .   O, my heart bleeds
To think o' the teen that I have turn'd you to,
Which is from my remembrance! Please you, further.
  Pros. My brother, and thy uncle, call'd Antonio, —
I pray thee, mark me, — that a brother should
Be so perfidious! — he whom, next thyself,
Of all the world I lov'd, and to him put
The manage of my state; as, at that time,
Through all the signiories it was the first,
And Prospero the prime duke; being so reputed
In dignity, and for the liberal arts
Without a parallel: those being all my study,
The government I cast upon my brother,
And to my state grew stranger, being transported
And rapt in secret studies. Thy false uncle —
Dost thou attend me?
  Mir.   Sir, most heedfully.
  Pros. Being once perfected how to grant suits,
How to deny them, who t' advance, and who
To trash for over-topping, — new-created
The creatures that were mine, I say, or chang'd 'em,
Or else new-form'd 'em; having both the key
Of officer and office, set all hearts i' the state
To what tune pleas'd his ear; that now he was
The ivy which had hid my princely trunk,
And suck'd my verdure out on't. Thou attend'st not.
  Mir. O, good sir, I do.
  Pros.   I pray thee, mark me.
I, thus neglecting worldly ends, all dedicated
To closeness, and the bettering of my mind
With that which, but by being so retir'd,

O'er-priz'd all popular rate, in my false brother
Awak'd an evil nature; and my trust,
Like a good parent, did beget of him
A falsehood, in its contrary as great
As my trust was; which had indeed no limit, .
A confidence sans bound. He being thus lorded,
Not only with what my revenue yielded,
But what my power might else exact, — like one
Who having into truth, by telling of it,
Made such a sinner of his memory,
To credit his own lie, — he did believe
He was indeed the duke; out o' the substitution,
And executing th' outward face of royalty,
With all prerogative: — hence his ambition growing, —
Dost thou hear?

    Mir.　　　　Your tale, sir, would cure deafness.

    Pros. To have no screen between this part he play'd
And him he play'd it for, he needs will be
Absolute Milan. Me, poor man, my library
Was dukedom large enough: of temporal royalties
He thinks me now incapable; confederates —
So dry he was for sway — with the King of Naples
To give him annual tribute, do him homage,
Subject his coronet to his crown, and bend
The dukedom, yet unbow'd, — alas, poor Milan! —
To most ignoble stooping.

    Mir. .　　　　　O the heavens!

    Pros. Mark his condition, and th' event; then tell me
If this might be a brother.

    Mir. .　　　　I should sin
To think but nobly of my grandmother:
Good wombs have borne bad sons.

    Pros.　　　　　Now the condition.
This King of Naples, being an enemy
To me inveterate, hearkens my brother's suit;
Which was, that he, in lieu o' the premises, —
Of homage, and I know not how much tribute, —

Should presently extirpate me and mine
Out of the dukedom, and confer fair Milan,
With all the honours, on my brother: whereon,
A treacherous army levied, one midnight
Fated to the practice, did Antonio open
The gates of Milan; and, i' the dead of darkness,
The ministers for the purpose hurried thence
Me and thy crying self.

    Mir.   Alack, for pity!
I, not remembering how I cried on't then,
Will cry it o'er again: it is a hint
That wrings mine eyes to't.

    Pros.   Hear a little further,
And then I'll bring thee to the present business
Which now 's upon 's; without the which, this story
Were most impertinent.

    Mir.   Wherefore did they not
That hour destroy us?

    Pros.   Well demanded, wench:
My tale provokes that question. Dear, they durst not, —
So dear the love my people bore me, — nor set
A mark so bloody on the business; but
With colours fairer painted their foul ends.
In few, they hurried us aboard a bark,
Bore us some leagues to sea; where they prepar'd
A rotten carcass of a boat, not rigg'd,
Nor tackle, sail, nor mast; the very rats
Instinctively had quit it: there they hoist us,
To cry to the sea that roar'd to us; to sigh
To the winds, whose pity, sighing back again,
Did us but loving wrong.

    Mir.   Alack, what trouble
Was I then to you!

    Pros.   O, a cherubin
Thou wast that did preserve me! Thou didst smile,
Infusèd with a fortitude from heaven,
When I have deck'd the sea with drops full salt,

Under my burden groan'd; which rais'd in me
An undergoing stomach, to bear up
Against what should ensue.

 Mir.   How came we ashore?

 Pros. By Providence divine.
Some food we had, and some fresh water, that
A noble Neapolitan, Gonzalo,
Out of his charity, — who being then appointed
Master of this design, — did give us; with
Rich garments, linens, stuffs, and necessaries,
Which since have steaded much; so, of his gentleness,
Knowing I lov'd my books, he furnish'd me,
From mine own library, with volumes that
I prize above my dukedom.

 Mir.   Would I might
But ever see that man!

 Pros.   Now I arise: —
Sit still, and hear the last of our sea-sorrow.
Here in this island we arriv'd; and here
Have I, thy schoolmaster, made thee more profit
Than other princess' can, that have more time
For vainer hours, and tutors not so careful.

 Mir. Heavens thank you for't! And now, I pray you, sir, —
For still 'tis beating in my mind, — your reason
For raising this sea-storm?

 Pros.   Know thus far forth.
By accident most strange, bountiful Fortune —
Now my dear lady — hath mine enemies
Brought to this shore; and by my prescience
I find my zenith doth depend upon
A most auspicious star, whose influence
If now I court not, but omit, my fortunes
Will ever after droop. Here cease more questions:
Thou art inclin'd to sleep; 'tis a good dulness,
And give it way: — I know thou canst not choose. —

           [*Miranda sleeps.*

         6*

Come away, servant, come! I'm ready now:
Approach, my Ariel; come!

Enter ARIEL.

Ari. All hail, great master! grave sir, hail! I come
To answer thy best pleasure; be't to fly,
To swim, to dive into the fire, to ride
On the curl'd clouds, — to thy strong bidding task
Ariel and all his quality.
  Pros.   Hast thou, spirit,
Perform'd to point the tempest that I bade thee?
  Ari. To every article.
I boarded the king's ship; now on the beak,
Now in the waist, the deck, in every cabin,
I flam'd amazement: sometime I'd divide,
And burn in many places; on the topmast,
The yards, and bowsprit, would I flame distinctly,
Then meet, and join. Jove's lightnings, the precursors
O' the dreadful thunder-claps, more momentary
And sight-outrunning were not: the fire, and cracks
Of sulphurous roaring, the most mighty Neptune
Seem'd to besiege, and make his bold waves tremble,
Yea, his dread trident shake.
  Pros.   My brave spirit!
Who was so firm, so constant, that this coil
Would not infect his reason?
  Ari.   Not a soul
But felt a fever of the mad, and play'd
Some tricks of desperation. All but mariners
Plung'd in the foaming brine, and quit the vessel,
Then all a-fire with me: the king's son, Ferdinand,
With hair up-staring, — then like reeds, not hair, —
Was the first man that leap'd; cried, "Hell is empty,
And all the devils are here."
  Pros.   Why, that's my spirit!
But was not this nigh shore?
  Ari.   Close by, my master.

Pros. But are they, Ariel, safe?

Ari.   Not a hair perish'd;
On their sustaining garments not a blemish,
But fresher than before: and, as thou bad'st me,
In troops I have dispers'd them 'bout the isle.
The king's son have I landed by himself;
Whom I left cooling of the air with sighs
In an odd angle of the isle, and sitting,
His arms in this sad knot.

Pros.   Of the king's ship
The mariners, say how thou hast dispos'd,
And all the rest o' the fleet.

Ari.   Safely in harbour
Is the king's ship; in the deep nook, where once
Thou call'dst me up at midnight to fetch dew
From the still-vex'd Bermoothes, there she's hid:
The mariners all under hatches stow'd;
Who, with a charm join'd to their suffer'd labour,
I've left asleep: and for the rest o' the fleet,
Which I dispers'd, they all have met again,
And are upon the Mediterranean flote,
Bound sadly home for Naples;
Supposing that they saw the king's ship wreck'd,
And his great person perish.

Pros.   Ariel, thy charge
Exactly is perform'd: but there's more work.
What is the time o' the day?

Ari.   Past the mid season.

Pros. At least two glasses. The time 'twixt six and now
Must by us both be spent most preciously.

Ari. Is there more toil? Since thou dost give me pains,
Let me remember thee what thou hast promis'd,
Which is not yet perform'd me.

Pros.   How now, moody!
What is't thou canst demand?

Ari.   My liberty.

Pros. Before the time be out? no more!

Ari.   I prithee,
Remember I have done thee worthy service;
T'old thee no lies, made no mistakings, serv'd
Without or grudge or grumblings: thou didst promise
To bate me a full year.
     Pros.   Dost thou forget
From what a torment I did free thee?
     Ari.   No.
     Pros. Thou dost; and think'st it much to tread the ooze
Of the salt deep,
To run upon the sharp wind of the north,
To do me business in the veins o' th' earth
When it is bak'd with frost.
     Ari.   I do not, sir.
     Pros. Thou liest, malignant thing! Hast thou forgot
The foul witch Sycorax, who with age and envy
Was grown into a hoop? hast thou forgot her?
     Ari. No, sir.
     Pros.   Thou hast. Where was she born? speak;
               tell me.
     Ari. Sir, in Argier.
     Pros.   O, was she so? I must
Once in a month recount what thou hast been,
Which thou forgett'st. This damn'd witch Sycorax,
For mischiefs manifold, and sorceries terrible
To enter human hearing, from Argier,
Thou know'st, was banish'd: for one thing she did
They would not take her life. Is not this true?
     Ari. Ay, sir.
     Pros. This blue-ey'd hag was hither brought with child,
And here was left by the sailors. Thou, my slave,
As thou report'st thyself, wast then her servant;
And, for thou wast a spirit too delicate
To act her earthy and abhorr'd commands,
Refusing her grand hests, she did confine thee,
By help of her more potent ministers,
· And in her most unmitigable rage,

Into a cloven pine; within which rift
Imprison'd, thou didst painfully remain
A dozen years; within which space she died,
And left thee there; where thou didst vent thy groans
As fast as mill-wheels strike.   Then was this island —
Save for the son that she did litter here,
A freckled whelp hag-born — not honour'd with
A human shape.
    Ari.   Yes, Caliban her son.
    Pros.   Dull thing, I say so; he, that Caliban,
Whom now I keep in service.   Thou best know'st
What torment I did find thee in; thy groans
Did make wolves howl, and penetrate the breasts
Of ever-angry bears: it was a torment
To lay upon the damn'd, which Sycorax
Could not again undo: it was mine art,
When I arriv'd and heard thee, that made gape
The pine, and let thee out.
    Ari.   I thank thee, master.
    Pros.   If thou more murmur'st, I will rend an oak,
And peg thee in his knotty entrails, till
Thou'st howl'd away twelve winters.
    Ari.   Pardon, master:
I will be correspondent to command,
And do my spriting gently.
    Pros.   Do so; and after two days
I will discharge thee.
    Ari.   That's my noble master!
What shall I do? say what; what shall I do?
    Pros.   Go make thyself like to a nymph o' the sea:
Be subject to no sight but mine; invisible
To every eyeball else.   Go take this shape,
And hither come in't: hence with diligence!   [*Exit Ariel.*
Awake, dear heart, awake! thou hast slept well;
Awake!
    Mir. [*waking*] The strangeness of your story put
Heaviness in me.

Pros.   Shake it off. Come on;
We'll visit Caliban my slave, who never
Yields us kind answer.
 Mir.   'Tis a villain, sir,
I do not love to look on.
 Pros.   But, as 'tis,
We cannot miss him: he does make our fire,
Fetch in our wood; and serves in offices
That profit us. — What, ho! slave! Caliban!
Thou earth, thou! speak.
 Cal. [*within*]   There's wood enough within.
 Pros. Come forth, I say! there's other business for thee:
Come, thou tortoise! when?

Re-enter ARIEL *like a water-nymph.*

Fine apparition! My quaint Ariel,
Hark in thine ear.
 Ari.   My lord, it shall be done.   [*Exit.*
 Pros. Thou poisonous slave, got by the devil himself
Upon thy wicked dam, come forth!

Enter CALIBAN.

 Cal. As wicked dew as e'er my mother brush'd
With raven's feather from unwholesome fen
Drop on you both! a south-west blow on ye,
And blister you all o'er!
 Pros. For this, be sure, to-night thou shalt have cramps,
Side-stitches that shall pen thy breath up; urchins
Shall, for that vast of night that they may work,
All exercise on thee; thou shalt be pinch'd
As thick as honeycomb, each pinch more stinging
Than bees that made 'em.
 Cal.   I must eat my dinner.
This island's mine, by Sycorax my mother,
Which thou tak'st from me. When thou cam'st here first,
Thou strok'dst me, and mad'st much of me; wouldst give me
Water with berries in't; and teach me how

To name the bigger light, and how the less,
That burn by day and night: and then I lov'd thee,
And show'd thee all the qualities o' th' isle,
The fresh springs, brine-pits, barren place and fertile: —
Cursèd be I that did so! All the charms
Of Sycorax, toads, beetles, bats, light on you!
For I am all the subjects that you have,
Which first was mine own king: and here you sty me
In this hard rock, whiles you do keep from me
The rest o' th' island.

    Pros.   Thou most lying slave,
Whom stripes may move, not kindness! I have us'd thee,
Filth as thou art, with human care; and lodg'd thee
In mine own cell, till thou didst seek to violate
The honour of my child.

    Cal. O ho, O ho! — would 't had been done!
Thou didst prevent me; I had peopled else
This isle with Calibans.

    Pros.   Abhorrèd slave,
Which any print of godness wilt not take,
Being capable of all ill! I pitied thee,
Took pains to make thee speak, taught thee each hour
One thing or other: when thou didst not, savage,
Know thine own meaning, but wouldst gabble like
A thing most brutish, I endow'd thy purposes
With words that made them known. But thy vile race,
Though thou didst learn, had that in't which good natures
Could not abide to be with; therefore wast thou
Deservedly confin'd into this rock,
Who hadst deserv'd more than a prison.

    Cal. You taught me language; and my profit on't
Is, I know how to curse. The red plague rid you
For learning me your language!

    Pros.   Hag-seed, hence!
Fetch us in fuel; and be quick, thou'rt best,
To answer other business. Shrugg'st thou, malice?
If thou neglect'st, or dost unwillingly

What I command, I'll rack thee with old cramps,
Fill all thy bones with achès, make thee roar,
That beasts shall tremble at thy din.

    Cal.   No, pray thee. —
[*Aside*] I must obey: his art is of such power,
It would control my dam's god, Setebos,
And make a vassal of him.

    Pros.   So, slave; hence! [*Exit Caliban.*

Re-enter ARIEL, *invisible, playing and singing;* FERDINAND
                   following.

ARIEL'S *song.*

Come unto these yellow sands,
   And then take hands:
Court'sied when you have and kiss'd, —
   The wild waves whist, —
Foot it featly here and there;
And, sweet sprites, the burden bear.
   Hark, hark!
     [*Burden, dispersedly, within.* Bow, wow.]
   The watch-dogs bark:
     [*Burden, dispersedly, within.* Bow, wow.]
   Hark, hark! I hear
The strain of strutting chanticleer
   Cry, Cock-a-diddle-dow.

    Fer. Where should this music be? i' th' air or th' earth?
It sounds no more: — and, sure, it waits upon
Some god o' th' island. Sitting on a bank,
Weeping again the king my father's wreck,
This music crept by me upon the waters,
Allaying both their fury and my passion
With its sweet air: thence I have follow'd it,
Or it hath drawn me rather: — but 'tis gone.
No, it begins again.

ARIEL *sings.*

Full fathom five thy father lies;
　Of his bones are coral made;
Those are pearls that were his eyes;
　Nothing of him that doth fade
But doth suffer a sea-change
Into something rich and strange.
Sea-nymphs hourly ring his knell:
　　　　　[*Burden, within.* Ding-dong.]
Hark! now I hear them, — Ding-dong, bell.

Fer. The ditty does remember my drown'd father: —
This is no mortal business, nor no sound
That the earth owes: — I hear it now above me.

Pros. The fringèd curtains of thine eye advance,
And say what thou see'st yond.

Mir.　　　　　　　What is't? a spirit?
Lord, how it looks about! Believe me, sir,
It carries a brave form: — but 'tis a spirit.

Pros. No, wench; it eats, and sleeps, and hath such senses
As we have, such. This gallant which thou see'st
Was in the wreck; and, but he's something stain'd
With grief, that's beauty's canker, thou mightst call him
A goodly person: he hath lost his fellows,
And strays about to find 'em.

Mir.　　　　　　　I might call him
A thing divine; for nothing natural
I ever saw so noble.

Pros. [*aside*]　　It goes on, I see,
As my soul prompts it. — Spirit, fine spirit! I'll free thee
Within two days for this.

Fer.　　　　　　Most sure, the goddess
On whom these airs attend! — Vouchsafe my prayer
May know if you remain upon this island;
And that you will some good instruction give
How I may bear me here: my prime request,

Which I do last pronounce, is, — O you wonder! —
If you be maid or no?
  Mir.   No wonder, sir;
But certainly a maid.
    Fer.   My language! heavens! —
I am the best of them that speak this speech,
Were I but where 'tis spoken.
    Pros.   How! the best!
What wert thou, if the King of Naples heard thee?
    Fer. A single thing, as I am now, that wonders
To hear thee speak of Naples. He does hear me;
And that he does I weep: myself am Naples;
Who with mine eyes, ne'er since at ebb, beheld
The king my father wreck'd.
    Mir.   Alack, for mercy!
    Fer. Yes, faith, and all his lords; the Duke of Milan
And his brave son being twain.
    Pros. [*aside*]   The Duke of Milan
And his more braver daughter could control thee,
If now 'twere fit to do't. — At the first sight
They have chang'd eyes. — Delicate Ariel,
I'll set thee free for this! — A word, good sir;
I fear you've done yourself some wrong: a word.
    Mir. Why speaks my father so ungently? This
Is the third man that e'er I saw; the first
That e'er I sigh'd for: pity move my father
To be inclin'd my way!
    Fer.   O, if a virgin,
And your affection not gone forth, I'll make you
The queen of Naples.
    Pros.   Soft, sir! one word more. —
[*Aside*] They 're both in either's powers: but this swift busi-
          ness
I must uneasy make, lest too light winning
Make the prize light. — One word more; I charge thee
That thou attend me: thou dost here usurp
The name thou ow'st not; and hast put thyself

Upon this island as a spy, to win it
From me, the lord on't.

    Fer.   No, as I'm a man.

    Mir. There's nothing ill can dwell in such a temple:
If the ill spirit have so fair a house,
Good things will strive to dwell with't.

    Pros.   Follow me. —   [*To Fer.*
Speak not you for him; he's a traitor. — Come;
I'll manacle thy neck and feet together:
Sea-water shalt thou drink; thy food shall be
The fresh-brook muscles, wither'd roots, and husks
Wherein the acorn cradled. Follow.

    Fer.   No;
I will resist such entertainment till
Mine enemy has more power.

             [*Draws, and is charmed from moving.*

    Mir.   O dear father,
Make not too rash a trial of him, for
He's gentle, and not fearful.

    Pros.   What, I say,
My fool my tutor! — Put thy sword up, traitor;
Who mak'st a show, but dar'st not strike, thy conscience
Is so possess'd with guilt: come from thy ward;
For I can here disarm thee with this stick,
And make thy weapon drop.

    Mir.   Beseech you, father! —

    Pros. Hence! hang not on my garments.

    Mir.   Sir, have pity;
I'll be his surety.

    Pros.   Silence! one word more
Shall make me chide thee, if not hate thee. What,
An advocate for an impostor! hush!
Thou think'st there are no more such shapes as he,
Having seen but him and Caliban: foolish wench!
To the most of men this is a Caliban,
And they to him are angels.

    Mir.   My affections

Are, then, most humble; I have no ambition
To see a goodlier man.

    Pros.   Come on; obey: [*To Fer.*
Thy nerves are in their infancy again,
And have no vigour in them.

    Fer.   So they are:
My spirits, as in a dream, are all bound up.
My father's loss, the weakness which I feel,
The wreck of all my friends, nor this man's threats
To whom I am subdu'd, are but light to me,
Might I but through my prison once a-day
Behold this maid: all corners else o' th' earth
Let liberty make use of; space enough
Have I in such a prison.

    Pros. [*aside*]   It works. — Come on. —   [*To Fer.*
Thou hast done well, fine Ariel! — Follow me. —   [*To Fer.*
Hark what thou else shalt do me.   [*To Ariel.*

    Mir.   Be of comfort;
My father's of a better nature, sir,
Than he appears by speech: this is unwonted
Which now came from him.

    Pros.   Thou shalt be as free
As mountain winds: but then exactly do
All points of my command.

    Ari.   To the syllable.

    Pros. Come, follow. — Speak not for him.   [*Exeunt.*

ACT II.

Scene I.   *Another part of the island.*

Enter Alonso, Sebastian, Antonio, Gonzalo, Adrian,
Francisco, *and others.*

    Gon. Beseech you, sir, be merry; you have cause —
So have we all — of joy; for our escape
Is much beyond our loss. Our hint of woe

Is common; every day some sailor's wife,
The master of some merchant, and the merchant,
Have just our theme of woe: but for the miracle,
I mean our preservation, few in millions
Can speak like us: then wisely, good sir, weigh
Our sorrow with our comfort.

  Alon.   Prithee, peace.

  Seb. He receives comfort like cold porridge.

  Ant. The visitor will not give him o'er so.

  Seb. Look, he's winding up the watch of his wit; by and
by it will strike.

  Gon. Sir, —

  Seb. One: — tell.

  Gon. When every grief is entertain'd that's offer'd,
Comes to the entertainer —

  Seb. A dollar.

  Gon. Dolour comes to him, indeed: you have spoken
truer than you purposed.

  Seb. You have taken it wiselier than I meant you should.

  Gon. Therefore, my lord, —

  Ant. Fie, what a spendthrift is he of his tongue!

  Alon. I prithee, spare.

  Gon.   Well, I have done: but yet, —

  Seb. He will be talking.

  Ant. Which, of he or Adrian, for a good wager, first
begins to crow?

  Seb. The old cock.

  Ant. The cockerel.

  Seb. Done! The wager?

  Ant. A laughter.

  Seb. A match!

  Adr. Though this island seem to be desert, —

  Seb. Ha, ha, ha! — So, you're paid.

  Adr. Uninhabitable, and almost inaccessible, —

  Seb. Yet, —

  Adr. Yet, —

  Ant. He could not miss't.

Adr. It must needs be of subtle, tender, and delicate temperance.

Ant. Temperance was a delicate wench.

Seb. Ay, and a subtle; as he most learnedly delivered.

Adr. The air breathes upon us here most sweetly.

Seb. As if it had lungs, and rotten ones.

Ant. Or as 'twere perfumed by a fen.

Gon. Here is every thing advantageous to life.

Ant. True; save means to live.

Seb. Of that there's none, or little.

Gon. How lush and lusty the grass looks! how green!

Ant. The ground, indeed, is tawny.

Seb. With an eye of green in't.

Ant. He misses not much.

Seb. No; he doth but mistake the truth totally.

Gon. But the rarity of it is, — which is indeed almost beyond credit, —

Seb. As many vouched rarities are.

Gon. That our garments, being, as they were, drenched in the sea, hold, notwithstanding, their freshness and gloss, being rather new-dyed than stained with salt water.

Ant. If but one of his pockets could speak, would it not say he lies?

Seb. Ay, or very falsely pocket up his report.

Gon. Methinks our garments are now as fresh as when we put them on first in Afric, at the marriage of the king's fair daughter Claribel to the King of Tunis.

Seb. 'Twas a sweet marriage, and we prosper well in our return.

Adr. Tunis was never graced before with such a paragon to their queen.

Gon. Not since widow Dido's time.

Ant. Widow! a pox o' that! How came that widow in? widow Dido!

Seb. What if he had said "widower Æneas" too? Good Lord, how you take it!

Adr. Widow Dido, said you? you make me study of that:
she was of Carthage, not of Tunis.

Gon. This Tunis, sir, was Carthage.

Adr. Carthage!

Gon. I assure you, Carthage.

Ant. His word is more than the miraculous harp.

Seb. He hath raised the wall, and houses too.

Ant. What impossible matter will he make easy next?

Seb. I think he will carry this island home in his pocket,
and give it his son for an apple.

Ant. And, sowing the kernels of it in the sea, bring forth
more islands.

Alon. Ay!

Ant. Why, in good time.

Gon. Sir, we were talking that our garments seem now
as fresh as when we were at Tunis at the marriage of your
daughter, who is now queen.

Ant. And the rarest that e'er came there.

Seb. Bate, I beseech you, widow Dido.

Ant. O, widow Dido; ay, widow Dido.

Gon. Is not, sir, my doublet as fresh as the first day I
wore it? I mean, in a sort.

Ant. That sort was well fished for.

Gon. When I wore it at your daughter's marriage?

Alon. You cram these words into mine ears against
The stomach of my sense. Would I had never
Married my daughter there! for, coming thence,
My son is lost; and, in my rate, she too,
Who is so far from Italy remov'd,
I ne'er again shall see her. O thou mine heir
Of Naples and of Milan, what strange fish
Hath made his meal on thee?

Fran.   Sir, he may live:
I saw him beat the surges under him,
And ride upon their backs; he trod the water,
Whose enmity he flung aside, and breasted
The surge most swoln that met him; his bold head

'Bove the contentious waves he kept, and oar'd
Himself with his good arms in lusty stroke
To the shore, that o'er his wave-worn basis bow'd,
As stooping to relieve him: I not doubt
He came alive to land.
  Alon.   No, no, he's gone.
  Seb. Sir, you may thank yourself for this great loss
That would not bless our Europe with your daughter,
But rather lose her to an African;
Where she, at least, is banish'd from your eye,
Who hath cause to wet the grief on't.
  Alon.   Prithee, peace.
  Seb. You were kneel'd to, and impórtun'd otherwise,
By all of us; and the fair soul herself
Weigh'd, between loathness and obedience, at
Which end o' the beam she'd bow. We've lost your son,
I fear, for ever: Milan and Naples have
More widows in them of this business' making
Than we bring men to comfort them: the fault's
Your own.
  Alon. So is the dear'st o' the loss.
  Gon.   My lord Sebastian,
The truth you speak doth lack some gentleness,
And time to speak it in: you rub the sore,
When you should bring the plaster.
  Seb.   Very well.
  Ant. And most chirurgeonly.
  Gon. It is foul weather in us all, good sir,
When you are cloudy.
  Seb.   Foul weather!
  Ant.   Very foul.
  Gon. Had I plantation of this isle, my lord, —
  Ant. He'd sow't with nettle-seed.
  Seb   Or docks, or mallows.
  Gon. And were the king on't, what would I do?
  Seb. Scape being drunk for want of wine.
  Gon. I' the commonwealth I would by contraries

Execute all things; for no kind of traffic
Would I admit; no name of magistrate;
Letters should not be known; riches, poverty,
And use of service, none; contract, succession,
Bourn, bound of land, tilth, vineyard, none; ·
No use of metal, corn, or wine, or oil;
No occupation; all men idle, all;
And women too, — but innocent and pure;
No sovereignty, —

 Seb.   Yet he would be king on't.
 Ant. The latter end of his commonwealth forgets the
beginning.

 Gon. All things in common nature should produce
Without sweat or endeavour: treason, felony,
Sword, pike, knife, gun, or need of any engine,
Would I not have; but nature should bring forth,
Of its own kind, all foison, all abundance,
To feed my innocent people.

 Seb. : No marrying 'mong his subjects?
 Ant. None, man; all idle, — whores and knaves.
 Gon. I would with such perfection govern, sir,
T' excel the golden age.

 Seb.   Save his majesty!
 Ant. Long live Gonzalo!
 Gon.   And, — do you mark me, sir?—
 Alon. Prithee, no more: thou dost talk nothing to me.
 Gon. I do well believe your highness; and did it to mi-
nister occasion to these gentlemen, who are of such sensible
and nimble lungs that they always use to laugh at nothing.
 Ant. 'Twas you we laughed at.
 Gon. Who in this kind of merry fooling am nothing to
you: so you may continue, and laugh at nothing still.
 Ant. What a blow was there given!
 Seb. An it had not fallen flat-long.
 Gon. You are gentlemen of brave mettle; you would lift
the moon out of her sphere, if she would continue in it five
weeks without changing. ·

           7*

Enter ARIEL, *invisible; solemn music playing.*

Seb.　We would so, and then go a bat-fowling.

Ant.　Nay, good my lord, be not angry.

Gon.　No, I warrant you; I will not adventure my discretion so weakly.　Will you laugh me asleep, for I am very heavy?

Ant.　Go sleep, and hear us.

　　　　　　　　　　[*All sleep except Alon., Seb., and Ant.*

Alon.　What, all so soon asleep! I wish mine eyes
Would, with themselves, shut up my thoughts: I find
They are inclin'd to do so.

Seb.　　　　　　　　Please you, sir,
Do not omit the heavy offer of it:
It seldom visits sorrow; when it doth,
It is a comforter.

Ant.　　　　　　We two, my lord,
Will guard your person while you take your rest,
And watch your safety.

Alon.　　　　　　Thank you. — Wondrous heavy.

　　　　　　　　　　[*Alonso sleeps. Exit Ariel.*

Seb.　What a strange drowsiness possesses them!

Ant.　It is the quality o' the climate.

Seb.　　　　　　　　　　Why
Doth it not, then, our eyelids sink? I find not
Myself dispos'd to sleep.

Ant.　　　　　　　　Nor I; my spirits are nimble.
They fell together all, as by consent;
They dropp'd, as by a thunder-stroke.　What might,
Worthy Sebastian, — O, what might? — No more: —
And yet methinks I see it in thy face,
What thou shouldst be: th' occasion speaks thee; and
My strong imagination sees a crown
Dropping upon thy head.

Seb.　　　　　　What, art thou waking?

Ant.　Do you not hear me speak?

Seb.　　　　　　　　　I do; and surely
It is a sleepy language, and thou speak'st

Out of thy sleep. What is it thou didst say?
This is a strange repose, to be asleep
With eyes wide open; standing, speaking, moving,
And yet so fast asleep.

  Ant.   Noble Sebastian,
Thou lett'st thy fortune sleep, — die, rather; wink'st
Whiles thou art waking.

  Seb.   Thou dost snore distinctly;
There's meaning in thy snores.

  Ant. I am more serious than my custom: you
Must be so too, if heed me; which to do
Trebles thee o'er.

  Seb.   Well, I am standing water.

  Ant. I'll teach you how to flow.

  Seb.   Do so: to ebb
Hereditary sloth instructs me.

  Ant.   O,
If you but knew how you the purpose cherish
Whiles thus you mock it! how, in stripping it,
You more invest it! Ebbing men, indeed,
Most often do so near the bottom run
By their own fear or sloth.

  Seb.   Prithee, say on:
The setting of thine eye and cheek proclaim
A matter from thee; and a birth, indeed,
Which throes thee much to yield.

  Ant.   Thus, sir:
Although this lord of weak remembrance, this, —
Who shall be of as little memory
When he is earth'd, — hath here almost persuaded, —
For he's a spirit of persuasion, only
Professes to persuade, — the king his son's alive, —
'Tis as impossible that he's undrown'd
As he that sleeps here swims.

  Seb.   I have no hope
That he's undrown'd.

  Ant.   O, out of that no hope,

What great hope have you! no hope, that way, is
Another way so high a hope that even
Ambition cannot pierce a wink beyond,
But doubts discovery there. Will you grant with me
That Ferdinand is drown'd?

    Seb. He's gone.

    Ant. Then, tell me,
Who's the next heir of Naples?

    Seb. Claribel.

    Ant. She that is queen of Tunis; she that dwells
Ten leagues beyond man's life; she that from Naples
Can have no note, unless the sun were post, —
The man-i'-the-moon's too slow, — till new-born chins
Be rough and razorable; she from whom
We all were sea-swallow'd, though some cast again;
And, by that destiny, to perform an act
Whereof what's past is prologue; what to come,
In yours and my discharge.

    Seb. What stuff is this! — How say you?
'Tis true, my brother's daughter's queen of Tunis;
So is she heir of Naples; 'twixt which regions
There is some space.

    Ant. A space whose every cubit
Seems to cry out, "How shall that Claribel
Measure us back to Naples? Keep in Tunis,
And let Sebastian wake!" — Say, this were death
That now hath seiz'd them; why, they were no worse
Than now they are. There be that can rule Naples
As well as he that sleeps; lords that can prate
As amply and unnecessarily
As this Gonzalo; I myself could make
A chough of as deep chat. O, that you bore
The mind that I do! what a sleep were this
For your advancement! Do you understand me?

    Seb. Methinks I do.

    Ant. And how does your content
Tender your own good fortune?

Seb.   I remember
You did supplant your brother Prospero.
    Ant.   True:
And look how well my garments sit upon me;
Much feater than before: my brother's servants
Were then my fellows; now they are my men.
  · *Seb.* But, for your conscience, —
    Ant. Ay, sir; and where lies that? if 'twere a kibe,
'Twould put me to my slipper: but I feel not
This deity in my bosom: twenty consciences,
That stand 'twixt me and Milan, candied be they,
And melt, ere they molest! Here lies your brother,
No better than the earth he lies upon,   ·
If he were that which now he's like, that's dead;
Whom I, with this obedient steel, three inches of it,
Can lay to bed for ever; whiles you, doing thus,
To the perpetual wink for aye might put
This ancient morsel, this Sir Prudence, who
Should not upbraid our course. For all the rest,
They'll take suggestion as a cat laps milk;
They'll tell the clock to any business that
We say befits the hour.
    Seb.   Thy case, dear friend,
Shall be my precedent; as thou gott'st Milan,
I'll come by Naples. Draw thy sword: one stroke
Shall free thee from the tribute which thou pay'st;
And I the king shall love thee.
    Ant.   Draw together;
And when I rear my hand, do you the like,
·To fall it on Gonzalo.
    Seb.   O, but one word. [*They converse apart.*

         Music. Re-enter ARIEL, *invisible.*

  Ari. My master through his art foresees the danger
That you, his friend, are in; and sends me forth, —
·For else his project dies, — to keep thee living.
                             [*Sings in Gonzalo's ear.*

While you here do snoring lie,
Open-ey'd conspiracy
   His time doth take.
If of life you keep a care,
Shake off slumber, and beware:
   Awake, Awake!

Ant.   Then let us both be sudden.
Gon. [*waking*]   Now, good angels
Preserve the king! — [*To Seb. and Ant.*] Why, how now! —
     [*To Alon.*] Ho, awake! —
[*To Seb. and Ant.*] Why are you drawn? wherefore this ghastly
   looking?
Alon. [*waking*] What's the matter?
Seb.   Whiles we stood here securing your repose,
Even now, we heard a hollow burst of bellowing
Like bulls, or rather lions: did't not wake you?
It struck mine ear most terribly.
Alon.   I heard nothing.
Ant.   O, 'twas a din to fright a monster's ear,
To make an earthquake! sure, it was the roar
Of a whole herd of lions.
Alon.   Heard you this, Gonzalo?
Gon.   Upon mine honour, sir, I heard a humming,
And that a strange one too, which did awake me:
I shak'd you, sir, and cried: as mine eyes open'd,
I saw their weapons drawn: — there was a noise,
That's verity. 'Tis best we stand upon our guard,
Or that we quit this place: let's draw our weapons.
Alon. Lead off this ground; and let's make further search
For my poor son.
Gon.   Heavens keep him from these beasts!
For he is, sure, i' th' island.
Alon.   Lead away. [*Exit with the others.*
Ari.   Prospero my lord shall know what I have done: —
So, king, go safely on to seek thy son.   [*Exit.*

SCENE II. *Another part of the island.*

Enter CALIBAN *with a burden of wood. A noise of thunder heard.*

Cal. All the infections that the sun sucks up
from bogs, fens, flats, on Prosper fall, and make him
by inch-meal a disease! His spirits hear me,
and yet I needs must curse. But they'll nor pinch,
fright me with urchin-shows, pitch me i' the mire,
nor lead me, like a firebrand, in the dark
out of my way, unless he bid 'em: but
for every trifle are they set upon me;
sometime like apes, that mow and chatter at me,
and after bite me; then like hedgehogs, which..
lie tumbling in my barefoot way, and mount
their pricks at my footfall; sometime am I
all wound with adders, who with cloven tongues
do hiss me into madness. — Lo, now, lo!
here comes a spirit of his; and to torment me
for bringing wood in slowly. I'll fall flat;
perchance he will not mind me.

Enter TRINCULO.

Trin. Here's neither bush nor shrub, to bear off any
weather at all, and another storm brewing; I hear it sing i'
the wind: yond same black cloud, yond huge one, looks like a
foul bombard that would shed his liquor. If it should thunder
as it did before, I know not where to hide my head: yond
same cloud cannot choose but fall by pailfuls. — What have
we here? a man or a fish? dead or alive? A fish: he smells
like a fish; a very ancient and fish-like smell; a kind of, not
of the newest, Poor-John. A strange fish! Were I in England now, as once I was, and had but this fish painted, not a
holiday fool there but would give a piece of silver: there
would this monster make a man; any strange beast there
makes a man: when they will not give a doit to relieve a lame
beggar, they will lay out ten to see a dead Indian. Legged
like a man! and his fins like arms! Warm, o' my troth! I

do now let loose my opinion, hold it no longer, — this is no
fish, but an islander, that hath lately suffered by a thunderbolt.
[*Thunder.*] Alas, the storm is come again! my best way is to
creep under his gaberdine; there is no other shelter here-
about: misery acquaints a man with strange bedfellows. I
will here shroud till the dregs of the storm be past.
                                   [*Creeps under Caliban's garment.*

Enter STEPHANO, *singing; a bottle in his hand.*

Ste. *I shall no more to sea, to sea,*
          Here shall I die a-shore, —

This is a very scurvy tune to sing at a man's funeral: well,
here's my comfort.   [*Drinks.*

          The master, the swabber, the boatswain, and I,
                  The gunner, and his mate,
          Lov'd Mall, Meg, and Marian, and Margery,
              But none of us car'd for Kate;
              For she had a tongue with a tang,
              Would cry to a sailor, Go hang!
          She lov'd not the savour of tar nor of pitch;
          Yet a tailor might scratch her where'er she did itch.
              Then, to sea, boys, and let her go hang!

This is a scurvy tune too: but here's my comfort.   [*Drinks.*
  Cal. Do not torment me: — O!
  Ste. What's the matter? Have we devils here? Do you
put tricks upon 's with savages and men of Inde, ha? I have
not scaped drowning, to be afeard now of your four legs; for
it hath been said, As proper a man as ever went on four legs
cannot make him give ground; and it shall be said so again,
while Stephano breathes at's nostrils.
  Cal. The spirit torments me: — O!
  Ste. This is some monster of the isle with four legs, who
hath got, as I take it, an ague. Where the devil should he
learn our language? I will give him some relief, if it be but
for that. If I can recover him, and keep him tame, and get

to Naples with him, he's a present for any emperor that ever
trod on neat's-leather.

Cal. Do not torment me, prithee;
I'll bring my wood home faster.

Ste. He's in his fit now, and does not talk after the wisest.
He shall taste of my bottle: if he have never drunk wine
afore, it will go near to remove his fit. If I can recover him,
and keep him tame, I will not take too much for him; he shall
pay for him that hath him, and that soundly.

Cal. Thou dost me yet but little hurt;
Thou wilt anon, I know it by thy trembling:
Now Prosper works upon thee.

Ste. Come on your ways; open your mouth; here is that
which will give language to you, cat: open your mouth; this
will shake your shaking, I can tell you, and that soundly
[*Gives Cal. drink*]: you cannot tell who's your friend: open
your chaps again [*Gives Cal. drink*].

Trin. I should know that voice: it should be — but he is
drowned; and these are devils: — O, defend me!

Ste. Four legs and two voices, — a most delicate monster!
His forward voice, now, is to speak well of his friend; his
backward voice is to utter foul speeches and to detract. If all
the wine in my bottle will recover him, I will help his ague. —
[*Gives Cal. drink.*] Come, — Amen! I will pour some in thy
other mouth.

Trin. Stephano! —

Ste. Doth thy other mouth call me? — Mercy, mercy!
This is a devil, and no monster: I will leave him; I have no
long spoon.

Trin. Stephano! — if thou beest Stephano, touch me, and
speak to me; for I am Trinculo, — be not afeard, — thy
good friend Trinculo.

Ste. If thou beest Trinculo, come forth: I'll pull thee
by the lesser legs: if any be Trinculo's legs, these are they.
[*Draws Trin. out by the legs from under Caliban's garment.*] —
Thou art very Trinculo indeed! How camest thou to be the
siege of this moon-calf? can he vent Trinculos?

Trin. I took him to be killed with a thunder-stroke. — But art thou not drowned, Stephano? I hope, now, thou art not drowned. Is the storm overblown? I hid me under the dead moon-calf's gaberdine for fear of the storm. And art thou living, Stephano? O Stephano, two Neapolitans scaped!

Ste. Prithee, do not turn me about; my stomach is not constant.

Cal. [aside] These be fine things, an if they be not sprites. That's a brave god, and bears celestial liquor:
I will kneel to him.

Ste. How didst thou scape? How camest thou hither? swear, by this bottle, how thou camest hither. I escaped upon a butt of sack, which the sailors heaved o'erboard, by this bottle! which I made of the bark of a tree with mine own hands, since I was cast ashore.

Cal. I'll swear, upon that bottle, to be thy
True subject; for the liquor is not earthly.

Ste. Here; swear, then, how thou escapedst.

Trin. Swam ashore, man, like a duck: I can swim like a duck, I'll be sworn.

Ste. Here, kiss the book [*Gives Trin. drink*]. Though thou canst swim like a duck, thou art made like a goose.

Trin. O Stephano, hast any more of this?

Ste. The whole butt, man: my cellar is in a rock by the sea-side, where my wine is hid. — How now, moon-calf! how does thine ague?

Cal. Hast thou not dropp'd from heaven?

Ste. Out o' the moon, I do assure thee: I was the man-i'-the-moon when time was.

Cal. I've seen thee in her, and I do adore thee:
My mistress show'd me thee, and thy dog, and thy bush.

Ste. Come, swear to that; kiss the book: — I will furnish it anon with new contents: — swear. [*Gives Cal. drink.*

Trin. By this good light, this is a very shallow monster!
— I afeard of him! — a very weak monster: — the man-i'-the-

moon!—a most poor credulous monster!—Well drawn, monster, in good sooth.

Cal. I'll show thee every fertile inch o' th' island;
And I'll kiss thy foot: I prithee, be my god.

Trin. By this light, a most perfidious and drunken monster! when 's god 's asleep, he'll rob his bottle.

Cal. I 'll kiss thy foot; I 'll swear myself thy subject.

Ste. Come on, then; down, and swear.

Trin. I shall laugh myself to death at this puppy-headed monster: a most scurvy monster! I could find in my heart to beat him, —

Ste. Come, kiss.   {*Gives Cal. drink.*

Trin. But that the poor monster's in drink: an abominable monster!

Cal. I'll show thee the best springs; I'll pluck thee berries;
I'll fish for thee, and get thee wood enough.
A plague upon the tyrant that I serve!
I'll bear him no more sticks, but follow thee,
Thou wondrous man.

Trin. A most ridiculous monster, to make a wonder of a poor drunkard!

Cal. I prithee, let me bring thee where crabs grow;
And I with my long nails will dig thee pig-nuts;
Show thee a jay's nest, and instruct thee how
To snare the nimble marmoset; I'll bring thee
To clustering filberts, and sometimes I'll get thee
Young scamels from the rock. Wilt thou go with me?

Ste. I prithee now, lead the way, without any more talking. — Trinculo, the king and all our company else being drowned, we will inherit here. Here, bear my bottle: fellow Trinculo, we'll fill him by and by again.

Cal. Farewell, master; farewell, farewell! [*Sings drunkenly.*

Trin. A howling monster; a drunken monster!

> *Cal.   No more dams I'll make for fish;*
> *Nor fetch in firing*
> *At requiring;*

> *Nor scrape trencher, nor wash dish:*
> *'Ban, 'Ban, Ca—Caliban*
> *Has a new master — Get a new man.*

Freedom, hey-day! hey-day, freedom! freedom, hey-day;
freedom!

Ste.   O brave monster! lead the way.   [*Exeunt.*

ACT III.

Scene I.   *Before* Prospero's *cell.*

Enter Ferdinand, *bearing a log.*

Fer.   There be some sports are painful, and their labour
Delight in them sets off: some kinds of baseness
Are nobly undergone; and most poor matters
Point to rich ends.   This my mean task would be
As heavy to me as 'tis odious, but
The mistress which I serve quickens what's dead,
And makes my labours pleasures: O, she is
Ten times more gentle than her father's crabbed, —
And he's compos'd of harshness!   I must remove
Some thousands of these logs, and pile them up,
Upon a sore injunction: my sweet mistress
Weeps when she sees me work; and says such baseness
Had never like executor.   I forget:
But these sweet thoughts do even refresh my labour;
Most busiless when I do it.

Enter Miranda; *and* Prospero *behind.*

Mir.   Alas, now, pray you,
Work not so hard: I would the lightning had
Burnt up those logs that you're enjoin'd to pile!
Pray, set it down, and rest you: when this burns,
'Twill weep for having wearied you.   My father
Is hard at study; pray, now, rest yourself:
He's safe for these three hours.

Fer.   O most dear mistress,

The sun will set before I shall discharge
What I must strive to do.
  Mir.   If you'll sit down,
I'll bear your logs the while: pray, give me that;
I'll carry 't to the pile.
  Fer.   No, precious creature;
I had rather crack my sinews, break my back,
Than you should such dishonour undergo,
While I sit lazy by.
  Mir.   It would become me
As well as it does you: and I should do it
With much more ease; for my good will is to it,
And yours 'tis 'gainst.
  Pros. [*aside*] Poor worm, thou art infected!
This visitation shows it.
  Mir.   You look wearily.
  Fer. No, noble mistress; 'tis fresh morning with me
When you are by at night. I do beseech you,—
Chiefly that I might set it in my prayers, —
What is your name?
  Mir.   Miranda: — O my father,
I've broke your hest to say so!
  Fer.   Admir'd Miranda!
Indeed the top of admiration; worth
What's dearest to the world! Full many a lady
I've ey'd with best regard; and many a time
The harmony of their tongues hath into bondage
Brought my too diligent ear: for several virtues
Have I lik'd several women; never any
With so full soul, but some defect in her
Did quarrel with the noblest grace she ow'd,
And put it to the foil: but you, O you,
So perfect and so peerless, are created
Of every creature's best!
  Mir.   I do not know
One of my sex; no woman's face remember,
Save, from my glass, mine own; nor have I seen

More that I may call men, than you, good friend,
And my dear father: how features are abroad,
I'm skilless of; but, by my modesty, —
The jewel in my dower, — I would not wish
Any companion in the world but you;
Nor can imagination form a shape,
Besides yourself, to like of.   But I prattle
Something too wildly, and my father's precepts
I therein do forget.
    Fer.   I am, in my condition,
A prince, Miranda; I do think, a king, —
I would not so! — and would no more endure
This wooden slavery than to suffer tamely
The flesh-fly blow my mouth.   Hear my soul speak:
The very instant that I saw you, did
My heart fly to your service; there resides,
To make me slave to it; and for your sake
Am I this patient log-man.
    Mir.   Do you love me?
    Fer. O heaven, O earth, bear witness to this sound,
And crown what I profess with kind event,
If I speak true! if hollowly, invert
What best is boded me to mischief!   I,
Beyond all limit of what else i' the world,
Do love, prize, honour you.
    Mir.   I am a fool
To weep at what I'm glad of.
    Pros. [*aside*]   Fair encounter
Of two most rare affections!   Heavens rain grace
On that which breeds between 'em!
    Fer.   Wherefore weep you?
    Mir. At mine unworthiness, that dare not offer
What I desire to give; and much less take
What I shall die to want.   But this is trifling:
And all the more it seeks to hide itself,
The bigger bulk it shows.   Hence, bashful cunning!
And prompt me, plain and holy innocence!

I am your wife, if you will marry me;
If not, I'll die your maid: to be your fellow
You may deny me; but I'll be your servant,
Whether you will or no.

Fer. My mistress, dearest;
And I thus humble ever.

Mir. My husband, then?

Fer. Ay, with a heart as willing
As bondage e'er of freedom: here's my hand.

Mir. And mine, with my heart in't: and now farewell
Till half an hour hence.

Fer. A thousand thousand!

[*Exeunt Fer. and Mir. severally.*

Pros. So glad of this as they I cannot be,
Who are surpris'd withal; but my rejoicing
At nothing can be more. I'll to my book;
For yet, ere supper-time, must I perform
Much business appertaining. [*Exit.*

Scene II. *Another part of the island.*

Enter CALIBAN, STEPHANO, *and* TRINCULO, *with a bottle.*

Ste. Tell not me; — when the butt is out, we will drink
water; not a drop before: therefore bear up, and board 'em.
— Servant-monster, drink to me.

Trin. Servant-monster! the folly of this island! They
say there's but five upon this isle: we are three of them; if
th' other two be brained like us, the state totters.

Ste. Drink, servant-monster, when I bid thee: thy eyes
are almost set in thy head. [*Caliban drinks.*

Trin. Where should they be set else? he were a brave
monster indeed, if they were set in his tail.

Ste. My man-monster hath drowned his tongue in sack:
for my part, the sea cannot drown me; I swam, ere I could
recover the shore, five-and-thirty leagues off and on, by this
light.—Thou shalt be my lieutenant, monster, or my standard.

Trin. Your lieutenant, if you list; he's no standard.

Ste. We'll not run, Monsieur Monster.

Trin. Nor go neither: but you'll lie, like dogs; and yet say nothing neither.

Ste. Moon-calf, speak once in thy life, if thou beest a good moon-calf.

Cal. How does thy honour? Let me lick thy shoe. I'll not serve him, he is not valiant.

Trin. Thou liest, most ignorant monster: I am in case to justle a constable. Why, thou debauched fish, thou, was there ever man a coward that hath drunk so much sack as I to-day? Wilt thou tell a monstrous lie, being but half a fish and half a monster?

Cal. Lo, how he mocks me! wilt thou let him, my lord?

Trin. "Lord," quoth he! — that a monster should be such a natural!

Cal. Lo, lo, again! bite him to death, I prithee.

Ste. Trinculo, keep a good tongue in your head: if you prove a mutineer, — the next tree! The poor monster's my subject, and he shall not suffer indignity.

Cal. I thank my noble lord. Wilt thou be pleas'd
To hearken once again to the suit I made to thee?

Ste. Marry, will I: kneel and repeat it; I will stand, and so shall Trinculo.

Enter ARIEL, *invisible.*

Cal. As I told thee before, I am subject to a tyrant, — a sorcerer, that by his cunning hath cheated me of the island.

Ari. Thou liest.

Cal.   Thou liest, thou jesting monkey, thou:
I would my valiant master would destroy thee!
I do not lie.

Ste. Trinculo, if you trouble him any more in 's tale, by this hand, I will supplant some of your teeth.

Trin. Why, I said nothing.

Ste. Mum, then, and no more. — [*To Caliban*] Proceed.

Cal. I say, by sorcery he got this isle;
From me he got it. If thy greatness will

Revenge it on him, — for I know thou dar'st,
But this thing dare not, —

Ste. That's most certain.

Cal. Thou shalt be lord of it, and I'll serve thee.

Ste. How now shall this be compassed? Canst thou bring
me to the party?

Cal. Yea, yea, my lord: I'll yield him thee asleep,
Where thou mayst knock a nail into his head.

Ari. Thou liest; thou canst not.

Cal. What a pied ninny's this! — Thou scurvy patch!—
I do beseech thy greatness, give him blows,
And take his bottle from him: when that's gone,
He shall drink naught but brine; for I'll not show him
Where the quick freshes are.

Ste. Trinculo, run into no further danger: interrupt the
monster one word further, and, by this hand, I'll turn my
mercy out o' doors, and make a stock-fish of thee.

Trin. Why, what did I? I did nothing. I'll go further
off.

Ste. Didst thou not say he lied?

Ari. Thou liest.

Ste. Do I so? take thou that [*Strikes Trin.*]. As you like
this, give me the lie another time.

Trin. I did not give thee the lie. — Out o' your wits, and
hearing too?—A pox o' your bottle! this can sack and drinking do.—A murrain on your monster, and the devil take your
fingers!

Cal. Ha, ha, ha!

Ste. Now, forward with your tale.—Prithee, stand further
off.

Cal. Beat him enough: after a little time,
I'll beat him too.

Ste.　　　　　Stand further. — Come, proceed.

Cal. Why, as I told thee, 'tis a custom with him
I' th' afternoon to sleep: then thou mayst brain him,
Having first seiz'd his books; or with a log
Batter his skull, or paunch him with a stake,

8*

Or cut his wesand with thy knife: remember,
First to possess his books; for without them
He's but a sot, as I am, nor hath not
One spirit to command: they all do hate him
As rootedly as I:— burn but his books.
He has brave utensils, — for so he calls them, —
Which, when he has a house, he'll deck't withal:
And that most deeply to consider is
The beauty of his daughter; he himself
Calls her a nonpareil: I ne'er saw woman,
But only Sycorax my dam and she;
But she as far surpasseth Sycorax
As great'st does least.

  Ste.   Is it so brave a lass?

  Cal. Ay, lord; she will become thy bed, I warrant,
And bring thee forth brave brood.

  Ste. Monster, I will kill this man: his daughter and I will
be king and queen, — save our graces! — and Trinculo and
thyself shall be viceroys. — Dost thou like the plot, Trinculo?

  Trin. Excellent.

  Ste. Give me thy hand: I am sorry I beat thee; but,
while thou livest, keep a good tongue in thy head.

  Cal. Within this half hour will he be asleep:
Wilt thou destroy him then?

  Ste.   Ay, on mine honour.

  Ari. This will I tell my master.

  Cal. Thou mak'st me merry; I am full of pleasure:
Let us be jocund: will you troll the catch
You taught me but while-ere?

  Ste. At thy request, monster, I will do reason, any reason.
— Come on, Trinculo, let us sing.   [*Sings.*

  Flout 'em and scout 'em, and scout 'em and flout 'em;
   Thought is free.

  Cal. That's not the tune.

      [*Ariel plays the tune on a tabor and pipe.*

  Ste. What is this same?

Trin. This is the tune of our catch, played by the picture
of Nobody.

Ste. If thou beest a man, show thyself in thy likeness: if
thou beest a devil, take't as thou list.

Trin. O, forgive me my sins!

Ste. He that dies pays all debts: I defy thee. — Mercy
upon us!

Cal. Art thou afeard?

Ste. No, monster, not I.

Cal. Be not afeard; the isle is full of noises,
Sounds, and sweet airs, that give delight, and hurt not.
Sometime a thousand twangling instruments
Will hum about mine ears; and sometime voices,
That, if I then had wak'd after long sleep,
Will make me sleep again: and then, in dreaming,
The clouds methought would open, and show riches
Ready to drop upon me; that, when I wak'd,
I cried to dream again.

Ste. This will prove a brave kingdom to me, where I shall
have my music for nothing.

Cal. When Prospero is destroyed.

Ste. That shall be by and by: I remember the story.

Trin. The sound is going away; let's follow it, and after
do our work.

Ste. Lead, monster; we'll follow. — I would I could see
this taborer! he lays it on. — Wilt come?

Trin. I'll follow, Stephano.   [*Exeunt.*

SCENE III. *Another part of the island.*

Enter ALONSO, SEBASTIAN, ANTONIO, GONZALO, ADRIAN, FRAN-
CISCO, *and others.*

Gon. By'r lakin, I can go no further, sir;
My old bones ache: here's a maze trod, indeed,
Through forth-rights and meanders! by your patience,
I needs must rest me.

Alon.   Old lord, I cannot blame thee,

Who am myself attach'd with weariness,
To the dulling of my spirits: sit down, and rest.
Even here I will put off my hope, and keep it
No longer for my flatterer: he is drown'd
Whom thus we stray to find; and the sea mocks
Our frustrate search on land.   Well, let him go.

    Ant. [*aside to Seb.*] I am right glad that he's so out of hope.
Do not, for one repulse, forgo the purpose
That you resolv'd t' effect.

    Seb. [*aside to Ant.*]   The next advantage
Will we take throughly.

    Ant. [*aside to Seb.*] Let it be to-night;
For, now they are oppress'd with travel, they
Will not, nor cannot, use such vigilance
As when they're fresh.

    Seb. [*aside to Ant.*] I say, to-night: no more.
                          [*Solemn and strange music.*
    Alon. What harmony is this? — My good friends, hark!
    Gon. Marvellous sweet music!

Enter PROSPERO *above, invisible.   Enter, below, several strange
Shapes, bringing in a banquet: they dance about it with gentle
actions of salutation; and, inviting the King, &c. to eat, they
depart.*

    Alon. Give us kind keepers, heavens! — What were these?
    Seb. A living drollery.   Now I will believe
That there are unicorns; that in Arabia
There is one tree, the phœnix' throne; one phœnix
At this hour reigning there.

    Ant.   I'll believe both;
And what does else want credit, come to me,
And I'll be sworn 'tis true: travellers ne'er did lie,
Though fools at home condemn 'em.

    Gon.   If in Naples
I should report this now, would they believe me?
If I should say, I saw such islanders, —
For, certes, these are people of the island, —

Who, though they are of monstrous shape, yet, note,
Their manners are more gentle-kind than of
Our human generation you shall find
Many, nay, almost any.
  Pros. [*aside*]   Honest lord,
Thou hast said well; for some of you there present
Are worse than devils.
  Alon.   I cannot too much muse
Such shapes, such gesture, and such sound, expressing —
Although they want the use of tongue — a kind
Of excellent dumb discourse.
  Pros. [*aside*]   Praise in departing.
  Fran. They vanish'd strangely.
  Seb.   No matter, since
They've left their viands behind; for we have stomachs. —
Will't please you taste of what is here?
  Alon.   Not I.
  Gon. Faith, sir, you need not fear. When we were boys,
Who would believe that there were mountaineers
Dew-lapp'd like bulls, whose throats had hanging at 'em
Wallets of flesh? or that there were such men
Whose heads stood in their breasts? which now we find
Each putter-out of one for five will bring us
Good warrant of.
  Alon.   I will stand to, and feed,
Although my last: no matter, since I feel
The best is past. — Brother, my lord the duke,
Stand to, and do as we.

  Thunder and lightning. Enter ARIEL, *like a harpy; claps his
  wings upon the table; and, with a quaint device, the banquet
          vanishes.*

  Ari. You are three men of sin, whom Destiny, —
That hath to instrument this lower world
And what is in't, — the never-surfeited sea
Hath caus'd to belch up you; and on this island,
Where man doth not inhabit, — you 'mongst men

Being most unfit to live. I've made you mad;
And even with such-like valour men hang and drown
Their proper selves.   [*Alon., Seb., &c. draw their swords.*
                    You fools! I and my fellows
Are ministers of Fate: the elements,
Of whom your swords are temper'd, may as well
Wound the loud winds, or with bemock'd-at stabs
Kill the still-closing waters, as diminish
One dowle that's in my plume: my fellow-ministers
Are like invulnerable. If you could hurt,
Your swords are now too massy for your strengths,
And will not be uplifted. But remember, —
For that's my business to you, — that you three
From Milan did supplant good Prospero;
Expos'd unto the sea, which hath requit it,
Him and his innocent child: for which foul deed
The powers, delaying, not forgetting, have
Incens'd the seas and shores, yea, all the creatures,
Against your peace. Thee of thy son, Alonso,
They have bereft; and do pronounce, by me,
Lingering perdition — worse than any death
Can be at once — shall step by step attend
You and your ways; whose wrath to guard you from, —
Which here, in this most desolate isle, else falls
Upon your heads, — is nothing but heart's-sorrow
And a clear life ensuing.

*He vanishes in thunder; then, to soft music, enter the Shapes
again, and dance with mocks and mows, and carry out the
table.*

Pros. [*aside*] Bravely the figure of this harpy hast thou
Perform'd, my Ariel; a grace it had, devouring:
Of my instruction hast thou nothing bated
In what thou hadst to say: so, with good life,
And observation strange, my meaner ministers
Their several kinds have done. My high charms work,
And these, mine enemies, are all knit up

In their distractions: they now are in my power;
And in these fits I leave them, while I visit
Young Ferdinand, — whom they suppose is drown'd, —
And his and mine lov'd darling.   [*Exit above.*

   Gon. I' the name of something holy, sir, why stand you
In this strange stare?

   Alon.   O, it is monstrous, monstrous!
Methought the billows spoke, and told me of it;
The winds did sing it to me; and the thunder,
That deep and dreadful organ-pipe, pronounc'd
The name of Prosper: it did bass my trespass.
Therefore my son i' th' ooze is bedded; and
I'll seek him deeper than e'er plummet sounded,
And with him there lie mudded.   [*Exit.*

   Seb.   But one fiend at a time,
I'll fight their legions o'er.

   Ant.   I'll be thy second.
[*Exeunt Seb. and Ant.*

   Gon. All three of them are desperate: their great guilt,
Like poison given to work a great time after,
Now gins to bite the spirits. — I do beseech you,
That are of suppler joints, follow them swiftly,
And hinder them from what this ecstasy
May now provoke them to.

   Adr.   Follow, I pray you.   [*Exeunt.*

ACT IV.

SCENE I. *Before* PROSPERO's *cell.*

Enter PROSPERO, FERDINAND, *and* MIRANDA.

   Pros. If I have too austerely punish'd you,
Your compensation makes amends; for I
Have given you here a thread of mine own life,
Or that for which I live: who once again
I tender to thy hand: all thy vexations
Were but my trials of thy love, and thou

Hast strangely stood the test: here, afore Heaven,
I ratify this my rich gift. O Ferdinand,
Do not smile at me that I boast her off,
For thou shalt find she will outstrip all praise,
And make it halt behind her.

    Fer.   I do believe it
Against an oracle.

    Pros. Then, as my gift, and thine own acquisition
Worthily purchas'd, take my daughter: but
If thou dost break her virgin-knot before
All sanctimonious ceremonies may
With full and holy rite be minister'd,
No sweet aspersion shall the heavens let fall
To make this contract grow; but barren hate,
Sour-ey'd disdain, and discord, shall bestrew
The union of your bed with weeds so loathly
That you shall hate it both: therefore take heed,
As Hymen's lamps shall light you.

    Fer.   As I hope
For quiet days, fair issue, and long life,
With such love as 'tis now, — the murkiest den,
The most opportune place, the strong'st suggestion
Our worser Genius can, shall never melt
Mine honour into lust; to take away
The edge of that day's celebration,
When I shall think, or Phœbus' steeds are founder'd,
Or Night kept chain'd below.

    Pros.   Fairly spoke.
Sit, then, and talk with her; she is thine own. —
What, Ariel! my industrious servant, Ariel!

Enter ARIEL.

    Ari. What would my potent master? here I am.

    Pros. Thou and thy meaner fellows your last service
Did worthily perform; and I must use you
In such another trick. Go bring the rabble,
O'er whom I give thee power, here, to this place:

Incite them to quick motion; for I must
Bestow upon the eyes of this young couple
Some vanity of mine art: it is my promise,
And they expect it from me.

  Ari.   Presently?

  Pros. Ay, with a twink.

  Ari. Before you can say, "Come," and "Go,"
And breathe twice, and cry, "So, so,"
Each one, tripping on his toe,
Will be here with mop and mow.
Do you love me, master? no?

  Pros. Dearly, my delicate Ariel.   Do not approach
Till thou dost hear me call.

  Ari.   Well, I conceive.   [*Exit.*

  Pros. Look thou be true; do not give dalliance
Too much the rein; the strongest oaths are straw
To the fire i' the blood: be more abstemious,
Or else good night your vow!

  Fer.   I warrant you, sir;
The white-cold virgin snow upon my heart
Abates the ardour of my liver.

  Pros.   Well. —
Now come, my Ariel! bring a corollary,
Rather than want a spirit: appear, and pertly! —
No tongue; all eyes; be silent.   [*Soft music.*

     Enter IRIS.

  Iris. Ceres, most bounteous lady, thy rich leas
Of wheat, rye, barley, vetches, oats, and pease;
Thy turfy mountains, where live nibbling sheep,
And flat meads thatch'd with stover, them to keep;
Thy banks with peonèd and lilied brims,
Which spongy April at thy hest betrims,
To make cold nymphs chaste crowns; and thy broom-groves,
Whose shadow the dismissèd bachelor loves,
Being lass-lorn; thy pole-clipt vineyard;
And thy sea-marge, sterile and rocky-hard,

Where thou thyself dost air; — the queen o' the sky,
Whose watery arch and messenger am I,
Bids thee leave these; and with her sovereign grace,
Here on this grass-plot, in this very place,
To come and sport: — her peacocks fly amain:
Approach, rich Ceres, her to entertain.

Enter CERES.

Cer. Hail, many-colour'd messenger, that ne'er
Dost disobey the wife of Jupiter;
Who, with thy saffron wings, upon my flowers
Diffusest honey-drops, refreshing showers;
And with each end of thy blue bow dost crown
My bosky acres and my unshrubb'd down,
Rich scarf to my proud earth; — why hath thy queen
Summon'd me hither, to this short-grass'd green?

Iris. A contract of true love to celebrate;
And some donation freely to estate
On the bless'd lovers.

Cer.   Tell me, heavenly bow,
If Venus or her son, as thou dost know,
Do now attend the queen? Since they did plot
The means that dusky Dis my daughter got,
Her and her blind boy's scandal'd company
I have forsworn.

Iris.   Of her society
Be not afraid: I met her deity
Cutting the clouds towards Paphos, and her son
Dove-drawn with her. Here thought they to have done
Some wanton charm upon this man and maid,
Whose vows are, that no bed-rite shall be paid
Till Hymen's torch be lighted: but in vain;
Mars's hot minion is return'd again;
Her waspish-headed son has broke his arrows,
Swears he will shoot no more, but play with sparrows,
And be a boy right out.

Cer.　　　　　　　　　High'st queen of state,
Great Juno, comes; I know her by her gait.

Enter Juno.

Juno.　How does my bounteous sister?　Go with me
To bless this twain, that they may prosperous be,
And honour'd in their issue.

Song.

Juno.　*Honour, riches, marriage-blessing,*
　　　　Long continuance, and increasing,
　　　　Hourly joys be still upon you!
　　　　Juno sings her blessings on you.

Cer.　*Earth's increase, and foison plenty,*
　　　　Barns and garners never empty;
　　　　Vines with clustering bunches growing;
　　　　Plants with goodly burden bowing;
　　　　Spring come to you at the farthest
　　　　In the very end of harvest!
　　　　Scarcity and want shall shun you;
　　　　Ceres' blessing so is on you.

Fer.　This is a most majestic vision, and
Harmonious charmingly.　May I be bold
To think these spirits?
Pros.　　　　　　　　　Spirits, which by mine art
I have from their confines call'd to enact
My present fancies.
Fer.　　　　　　　Let me live here ever;
So rare a wonder'd father and a wife
Make this place Paradise.
　　　　　　　[*Juno and Ceres whisper, and send Iris on employment.*
Pros.　　　　　　　　Sweet, now, silence!
Juno and Ceres whisper seriously;
There's something else to do; hush, and be mute,
Or else our spell is marr'd.
　Iris. You nymphs, call'd Naiades, of the wandering brooks,

With your sedg'd crowns and ever-harmless looks,
Leave your crisp channels, and on this green land
Answer your summons; Juno does command:
Come, temperate nymphs, and help to celebrate
A contract of true love; be not too late.

Enter certain Nymphs.

You sunburn'd sicklemen, of August weary,
Come hither from the furrow, and be merry:
Make holiday; your rye-straw hats put on,
And these fresh nymphs encounter every one
In country footing.

*Enter certain Reapers, properly habited: they join with the Nymphs
in a graceful dance; towards the end whereof PROSPERO starts
suddenly, and speaks; after which, to a strange, hollow, and confused noise, they heavily vanish.*

    Pros. [*aside*] I had forgot that foul conspiracy
Of the beast Caliban and his confederates
Against my life: the minute of their plot
Is almost come. — [*To the Spirits*] Well done; — avoid, — no
        more.
    Fer. This is most strange: your father 's in some passion
That works him strongly.
    Mir.   Never till this day
Saw I him touch'd with anger so distemper'd.
    Pros. Sure, you do look, my son, in a mov'd sort,
As if you were dismay'd: be cheerful, sir.
Our revels now are ended. These our actors,
As I foretold you, were all spirits, and
Are melted into air, into thin air:
And, like the baseless fabric of this vision,
The cloud-capp'd towers, the gorgeous palaces,
The solemn temples, the great globe itself,
Yea, all which it inherit, shall dissolve,
And, like this insubstantial pageant faded,
Leave not a wreck behind. We are such stuff

As dreams are made on; and our little life
Is rounded with a sleep. — Sir, I am vex'd;
Bear with my weakness; my old brain is troubled:
Be not disturb'd with my infirmity:
If you be pleas'd, retire into my cell,
And there repose: a turn or two I'll walk,
To still my beating mind.
    Fer. Mir.   We wish your peace.
    Pros. [*to Ariel*] Come with a thought! — I thank ye [*Exeunt*
        Fer. and Mir.]. — Ariel, come!

Re-enter ARIEL.

    Ari. Thy thoughts I cleave to. What's thy pleasure?
    Pros.   Spirit,
We must prepare to meet with Caliban.
    Ari. Ay, my commander: when I presented Ceres,
I thought t' have told thee of it; but I fear'd
Lest I might anger thee.
    Pros. Say again, where didst thou leave these varlets?
    Ari. I told you, sir, they were red-hot with drinking;
So full of valour that they smote the air
For breathing in their faces; beat the ground
For kissing of their feet; yet always bending
Towards their project. Then I beat my tabor;
At which, like unback'd colts, they prick'd their ears,
Advanc'd their eyelids, lifted up their noses
As they smelt music: so I charm'd their ears,
That, calf-like, they my lowing follow'd through
Tooth'd briers, sharp furzes, pricking goss, and thorns,
Which enter'd their frail shins: at last I left them
I' the filthy-mantled pool beyond your cell,
There dancing up to the chins, that the foul lake
O'erstunk their feet.
    Pros.   This was well done, my bird.
Thy shape invisible retain thou still:
The trumpery in my house, go bring it hither,
For stale to catch these thieves.

Ari.   I go, I go.   [*Exit.*
Pros. A devil, a born devil, on whose nature
Nurture can never stick; on whom my pains,
Humanely taken, are all lost, quite lost;
And as with age his body uglier grows,
So his mind cankers. I will plague them all,

    Re-enter ARIEL, *loaden with glistering apparel, &c.*
Even to roaring. — Come, hang them on this line.

   PROSPERO *and* ARIEL *remain, invisible.   Enter* CALIBAN,
        STEPHANO, *and* TRINCULO, *all wet.*

Cal. Pray you, tread softly, that the blind mole may not
Hear a foot fall: we now are near his cell.
Ste. Monster, your fairy, which you say is a harmless
fairy, has done little better than played the Jack with us.
Trin. Monster, I do smell all horse-piss; at which my
nose is in great indignation.
Ste. So is mine. — Do you hear, monster? If I should
take a displeasure against you, look you, —
. *Trin.* Thou wert but a lost monster.
Cal. Good my lord, give me thy favour still.
Be patient, for the prize I'll bring thee to
Shall hoodwink this mischance: therefore speak softly; —
All's hush'd as midnight yet.
Trin. Ay, but to lose our bottles in the pool, —
Ste. There is not only disgrace and dishonour in that,
monster, but an infinite loss.
Trin. That's more to me than my wetting: yet this is
your harmless fairy, monster.
Ste. I will fetch off my bottle, though I be o'er ears for
my labour.
Cal. Prithee, my king, be quiet. See'st thou here,
This is the mouth o' the cell: no noise, and enter.
Do that good mischief which may make this island
Thine own for ever, and I, thy Caliban,
For aye thy foot-licker.

Ste. Give me thy hand. I do begin to have bloody thoughts.

Trin. O King Stephano! O peer! O worthy Stephano! look what a wardrobe here is for thee!

Cal. Let it alone, thou fool; it is but trash.

Trin. O, ho, monster! we know what belongs to a frippery. — O King Stephano!

Ste. Put off that gown, Trinculo: by this hand, I'll have that gown.

Trin. Thy grace shall have it.

Cal. The dropsy drown this fool! what do you mean
To dote thus on such luggage? Let's along,
And do the murder first: if he awake,
From toe to crown he'll fill our skins with pinches,
Make us strange stuff.

Ste. Be you quiet, monster.—Mistress line, is not this my jerkin? Now is the jerkin under the line: now, jerkin, you are like to lose your hair, and prove a bald jerkin.

Trin. Do, do: we steal by line and level, an 't like your grace.

Ste. I thank thee for that jest; here's a garment for't: wit shall not go unrewarded while I am king of this country. "Steal by line and level" is an excellent pass of pate; there's another garment for't.

— *Trin.* Monster, come, put some lime upon your fingers, and away with the rest.

Cal. I will have none on't: we shall lose our time,
And all be turn'd to barnacles, or apes
With foreheads villanous low.

Ste. Monster, lay-to your fingers: help to bear this away where my hogshead of wine is, or I'll turn you out of my kingdom: go to, carry this.

Trin. And this.

Ste. Ay, and this.

A noise of hunters heard. Enter divers Spirits, in shape of dogs and hounds, and hunt them about, PROSPERO *and* ARIEL *setting them on.*

Pros. Hey, Mountain, hey!

Ari.   Silver! there it goes, Silver!
Pros.   Fury, Fury! there, Tyrant, there! hark, hark!

> [*Cal., Ste.,* and *Trin. are driven out.*

Go charge my goblins that they grind their joints
With dry convulsions; shorten up their sinews
With agèd cramps; and more pinch-spotted make them
Than pard or cat-o'-mountain.
    Ari.   Hark, they roar!
    Pros.   Let them be hunted soundly.   At this hour
Lie at my mercy all mine enemies:
Shortly shall all my labours end, and thou
Shalt have the air at freedom: for a little
Follow, and do me service.   [*Exeunt.*

ACT V.

Scene I.   *Before the cell of* Prospero.

Enter Prospero *in his magic robes,* and Ariel.

    Pros.   Now does my project gather to a head:
My charms crack not; my spirits obey; and Time
Goes upright with his carriage.   How's the day?
    Ari.   On the sixth hour; at which time, my lord,
You said our work should cease.
    Pros.   I did say so,
When first I rais'd the tempest.   Say, my spirit,
How fares the king and 's followers?
    Ari.   Confin'd together
In the same fashion as you gave in charge,
Just as you left them; all are prisoners, sir,
In the line-grove which weather-fends your cell;
They cannot budge till your release.   The king,
His brother, and yours, abide all three distracted;
And the remainder mourning over them,
Brimful of sorrow and dismay; but chiefly
Him that you term'd, sir, "The good old lord, Gonzalo;"
His tears run down his beard, like winter-drops

From eaves of reeds. Your charm so strongly works 'em,
That if you now beheld them, your affections
Would become tender.

    Pros.   Dost thou think so, spirit?

    Ari. Mine would, sir, were I human.

    Pros.   And mine shall.
Hast thou, which art but air, a touch, a feeling
Of their afflictions, and shall not myself,
One of their kind, that relish all as sharply
Passion as they, be kindlier mov'd than thou art?
Though with their high wrongs I am struck to the quick,
Yet, with my nobler reason, 'gainst my fury
Do I take part: the rarer action is
In virtue than in vengeance: they being penitent,
The sole drift of my purpose doth extend
Not a frown further. Go release them, Ariel:
My charms I'll break, their senses I'll restore,
And they shall be themselves.

    Ari.   I'll fetch them, sir. ·   [*Exit.*

    Pros. Ye elves of hills, brooks, standing lakes, and groves;
And ye that on the sands with printless foot
Do chase the ebbing Neptune, and do fly him
When he comes back; you demi-puppets that
By moonshine do the green-sour ringlets make,
Whereof the ewe not bites; and you whose pastime
Is to make midnight mushrooms, that rejoice
To hear the solemn curfew; by whose aid —
Weak masters though ye be — I have bedimm'd
The noontide sun, call'd forth the mutinous winds,
And 'twixt the green sea and the azur'd vault
Set roaring war: to the dread-rattling thunder
Have I given fire, and rifted Jove's stout oak
With his own bolt: the strong-bas'd promontory
Have I made shake; and by the spurs pluck'd up
The pine and cedar: graves at my command
Have wak'd their sleepers, op'd, and let 'em forth
By my so potent art. But this rough magic

I here abjure; and, when I have requir'd
Some heavenly music, — which even now I do, —
To work mine end upon their senses that
This airy charm is for, I'll break my staff,
Bury it certain fathoms in the earth,
And deeper than did ever plummet sound
I'll drown my book.   [*Solemn music.*

Re-enter ARIEL: *after him,* ALONSO, *with a frantic gesture, attended by* GONZALO; SEBASTIAN *and* ANTONIO *in like manner, attended by* ADRIAN *and* FRANCISCO: *they all enter the circle which* PROSPERO *had made, and there stand charmed; which* PROSPERO *observing, speaks.*

A solemn air, and the best comforter
To an unsettled fancy, cure thy brains,
Now useless, boil'd within thy skull! There stand,
For you are spell-stopp'd. —
Holy Gonzalo, honourable man,
Mine eyes, even sociable to the shew of thine,
Fall fellowly drops. — The charm dissolves apace;
And as the morning steals upon the night,
Melting the darkness, so their rising senses
Begin to chase the ignorant fumes that mantle
Their clearer reason. — O thou good Gonzalo,
My true preserver, and a loyal sir
To him thou follow'st! I will pay thy graces
Home both in word and deed. — Most cruelly
Didst thou, Alonso, use me and my daughter:
Thy brother was a furtherer in the act, —
Thou'rt pinch'd for't now, Sebastian, flesh and blood. —
You, brother mine, that entertain'd ambition,
Expell'd remorse and nature; who, with Sebastian, —
Whose inward pinches therefore are most strong, —
Would here have kill'd your king; I do forgive thee,
Unnatural though thou art — Their understanding
Begins to swell; and the approaching tide
Will shortly fill the reasonable shore,

That now lies foul and muddy.   Not one of them
That yet looks on me, or would know me: — Ariel,
Fetch me the hat and rapier in my cell: —   [*Exit Ariel.*
I will discase me, and myself present
As I was sometime Milan: — quickly, spirit;
Thou shalt ere long be free.

> *Re-enter* ARIEL; *who sings while helping to attire* PROSPERO.

> *Where the bee sucks, there suck I:*
> *In a cowslip's bell I lie;*
> > *There I couch when owls do cry.*
> > *On the bat's back I do fly*
> > *After summer merrily.*
> *Merrily, merrily shall I live now*
> *Under the blossom that hangs on the bough.*

Pros.   Why, that's my dainty Ariel! I shall miss thee;
But yet thou shalt have freedom: — so, so, so. —
To the king's ship, invisible as thou art:
There shalt thou find the mariners asleep
Under the hatches; the master and the boatswain
Being awake, enforce them to this place,
And presently, I prithee.

Ari.   I drink the air before me, and return
Or e'er your pulse twice beat.   [*Exit.*

Gon.   All torment, trouble, wonder, and amazement,
Inhabit here: some heavenly power guide us
Out of this fearful country!

Pros.   Behold, sir king,
The wrongèd Duke of Milan, Prospero:
For more assurance that a living prince
Does now speak to thee, I embrace thy body;   .
And to thee and thy company I bid
A hearty welcome.

Alon.   Whêr thou be'st he or no,
Or some enchanted trifle to abuse me,
As late I have been, I not know: thy pulse
Beats, as of flesh and blood; and, since I saw thee,

Th' affliction of my mind amends, with which,
I fear, a madness held me: this must crave —
An if this be at all — a most strange story.
Thy dukedom I resign, and do entreat
Thou pardon me my wrongs. — But how should Prospero
Be living and be here?
    Pros.   First, noble friend,
Let me embrace thine age, whose honour cannot
Be measur'd or confin'd.
    Gon.   Whether this be
Or be not, I'll not swear.
    Pros.   You do yet taste
Some subtilties o' th' isle, that will not let you
Believe things certain. — Welcome, my friends all: —
[*Aside to Seb. and Ant.*] But you, my brace of lords, were I
            so minded,
I here could pluck his highness' frown upon you,
And justify you traitors: at this time
I'll tell no tales.
    Seb. [*aside*] The devil speaks in him.
    Pros.   No. —
For you, most wicked sir, whom to call brother
Would even infect my mouth, I do forgive
Thy rankest faults, — all of them; and require
My dukedom of thee, which perforce, I know,
Thou must restore.
    Alon.   If thou be'st Prospero,
Give us particulars of thy preservation;
How thou hast met us here, who three hours since
Were wreck'd upon this shore; where I have lost —
How sharp the point of this remembrance is! —
My dear son Ferdinand.
    Pros.   I'm woe for't, sir.
    Alon. Irreparable is the loss; and patience
Says it is past her cure.
    Pros.   I rather think
You have not sought her help; of whose soft grace,

For the like loss I have her sovereign aid,
And rest myself content.

Alon.   You the like loss!

Pros.   As great to me as late; and, súpportable
To make the dear loss, have I means much weaker
Than you may call to comfort you; for I,
Have lost my daughter.

· *Alon.*   A daughter!
O heavens, that they were living both in Naples,
The king and queen there! that they were, I wish
Myself were mudded in that oozy bed
Where my son lies. When did you lose your daughter?

Pros.   In this last tempest. I perceive, these lords
At this encounter do so much admire,
That they devour their reason, and scarce think
Their eyes do offices of truth, their words
Are natural breath: but, howso'er you have
Been justled from your senses, know for certain
That I am Prospero, and that very duke
Which was thrust forth of Milan; who most strangely
Upon this shore, where you were wreck'd, was landed,
To be the lord on't. No more yet of this;
For 'tis a chronicle of day by day,
Not a relation for a breakfast, nor
Befitting this first meeting. Welcome, sir;
This cell's my court: here have I few attendants,
And subjects none abroad: pray you, look in.
My dukedom since you've given me again,
I will requite you with as good a thing;
At least bring forth a wonder, to content ye
As much as me my dukedom.

The cell opens, and discovers FERDINAND *and* MIRANDA *playing
at chess.*

Mir.   Sweet lord, you play me false.

Fer.   No, my dear'st love,
I would not for the world.

Mir. **Yes**, for a score of kingdoms you should wrangle,
And I would call it fair play.

Alon.　　　　　　　　　If this prove
A vision of the island, one dear son
Shall I twice lose.

Seb.　　　　　A most high miracle!

Fer. Though the seas threaten, they are merciful:
I've curs'd them without cause.　　　　*[Kneels to Alon.*

Alon.　　　　　　　Now all the blessings
Of a glad father compass thee about!
Arise, and say how thou cam'st here.

Mir.　　　　　　　　　O, wonder!
How many goodly creatures are there here!
How beauteous mankind is!　O brave new world,
That has such people in't!

Pros.　　　　　　　'Tis new to thee.

Alon. What is this maid with whom thou wast at play?
Your eld'st acquaintance cannot be three hours:
Is she the goddess that hath sever'd us,
And brought us thus together?

Fer.　　　　　　　Sir, she's mortal;
But by immortal Providence she's mine:
I chose her when I could not ask my father
For his advice, nor thought I had one. She
Is daughter to this famous Duke of Milan,
Of whom so often I have heard renown,
But never saw before; of whom I have
Receiv'd a second life; and second father
This lady makes him to me.

Alon.　　　　　　　I am hers:
But, O, how oddly will it sound that I
Must ask my child forgiveness!

Pros.　　　　　　　There, sir, stop:
Let us not burden our remembrance with
A heaviness that's gone.

Gon.　　　　　　I've inly wept,
Or should have spoke ere this. — Look down, you gods,

And on this couple drop a blessèd crown!
For it is you that have chalk'd forth the way
Which brought us hither.
    Alon.   I say, Amen, Gonzalo!
    Gon. Was Milan thrust from Milan, that his issue
Should become kings of Naples? O, rejoice
Beyond a common joy! and set it down
With gold on lasting pillars, — In one voyage
Did Claribel her husband find at Tunis;
And Ferdinand, her brother, found a wife
Where he himself was lost; Prospero, his dukedom
In a poor isle; and all of us, ourselves
When no man was his own.
    Alon. [*to Fer. and Mir.*] Give me your hands:
Let grief and sorrow still embrace his heart
That doth not wish you joy!
    Gon.   Be't so! Amen!

Re-enter ARIEL, *with the* Master *and* Boatswain *amazedly
following.*

O, look, sir, look, sir! here is more of us:
I prophesied, if a gallows were on land,
This fellow could not drown. — Now, blasphemy,
That swear'st grace o'erboard, not an oath on shore?
Hast thou no mouth by land? What is the news?
    Boats. The best news is, that we have safely found
Our king and company; the next, our ship —
Which, but three glasses since, we gave out split —
Is tight, and yare, and bravely rigg'd, as when
We first put out to sea.
    Ari. [*aside to Pros.*] Sir, all this service
Have I done since I went.
    Pros. [*aside to Ari.*] My tricksy spirit!
    Alon. These are not natural events; they strengthen
From strange to stranger. — Say, how came you hither?
    Boats. If I did think, sir, I were well awake,
I'd strive to tell you. We were dead of sleep,

And — how we know not — all clapp'd under hatches;
Where, but even now, with strange and several noises
Of roaring, shrieking, howling, jingling chains,
And more diversity of sounds, all horrible,
We were awak'd; straightway, at liberty:
When we, in all her trim, freshly beheld
Our royal, good, and gallant ship; our master
Capering to eye her: on a trice, so please you,
Even in a dream, were we divided from them,
And were brought moping hither.

  Ari. [*aside to Pros.*]   Was't well done?

  Pros. [*aside to Ari.*] Bravely, my diligence. Thou shalt
  be free.

  Alon. This is as strange a maze as e'er men trod;
And there is in this business more than nature
Was ever conduct of: some oracle
Must rectify our knowledge.

  Pros.   Sir, my liege,
Do not infest your mind with beating on
The strangeness of this business; at pick'd leisure,
Which shall be shortly, single I'll resolve you —
Which to you shall seem probable — of every
These happen'd accidents: till when, be cheerful,
And think of each thing well. — [*Aside to Ari.*] Come hither,
    spirit:
Set Caliban and his companions free;
Untie the spell. [*Exit Ariel.*] — How fares my gracious sir?
There are yet missing of your company
Some few odd lads that you remember not.

Re-enter ARIEL, *driving in* CALIBAN, STEPHANO, *and* TRINCULO,
    in their stolen apparel.

  Ste. Every man shift for all the rest, and let no man take
care for himself; for all is but fortune. — Coragio, bully-
monster, coragio!

  Trin. If these be true spies which I wear in my head,
here's a goodly sight.

Cal.   O Setebos, these be brave spirits indeed!
How fine my master is! I am afraid
He will chastise me.
    Seb.   Ha, ha!
What things are these, my lord Antonio?
Will money buy 'em?
    Ant.   Very like; one of them
Is a plain fish, and, no doubt, marketable.
    Pros.   Mark but the badges of these men, my lords,
Then say if they be true. — This mis-shapen knave, —
His mother was a witch; and one so strong
That could control the moon, make flows and ebbs,
And deal in her command, without her power.
These three have robb'd me; and this demi-devil —
For he's a bastard one — had plotted with them
To take my life: two of these fellows you
Must know and own; this thing of darkness I
Acknowledge mine.
    Cal.   I shall be pinch'd to death.
    Alon.   Is not this Stephano, my drunken butler?
    Seb.   He is drunk now: where had he wine?
    Alon.   And Trinculo is reeling ripe: where should they
Find this grand liquor that hath gilded 'em? —
How cam'st thou in this pickle?
    Trin.   I have been in such a pickle, since I saw you last,
that, I fear me, will never out of my bones: I shall not fear
fly-blowing.
    Seb.   Why, how now, Stephano!
    Ste.   O, touch me not; — I am not Stephano, but a cramp.
    Pros.   You'd be king o' the isle, sirrah?
    Ste.   I should have been a sore one, then.
    Alon.   This is as strange a thing as e'er I look'd on.
                              [Pointing to Caliban.
    Pros.   He is as disproportion'd in his manners
As in his shape. — Go, sirrah, to my cell;
Take with you your companions; as you look
To have my pardon, trim it handsomely.

 Cal. Ay, that I will; and I'll be wise hereafter,
And seek for grace. What a thrice-double ass
Was I, to take this drunkard for a god,
And worship this dull fool!
 Pros.   Go to; away!
 Alon. Hence, and bestow your luggage where you found it.
 Seb. Or stole it, rather. [*Exeunt Cal., Ste., and Trin.*
 Pros. Sir, I invite your highness and your train
To my poor cell, where you shall take your rest
For this one night; which — part of it — I'll waste
With such discourse as, I not doubt, shall make it
Go quick away, — the story of my life,
And the particular accidents gone by
Since I came to this isle: and in the morn
I'll bring you to your ship, and so to Naples,
Where I have hope to see the nuptial
Of these our dear-belov'd solémnizèd;
And thence retire me to my Milan, where
Every third thought shall be my grave.
 Alon.   I long
To hear the story of your life, which must
Take the ear strangely.
 Pros.   I'll deliver all;
And promise you calm seas, auspicious gales,
And sail so expeditious, that shall catch
Your royal fleet far off. — [*Aside to Ari.*] My Ariel, — chick, —
That is thy charge: then to the elements
Be free, and fare thou well! — Please you, draw near.
                [*Exeunt.*

EPILOGUE.

SPOKEN BY PROSPERO.

Now my charms are all o'erthrown,
And what strength I have's mine own,—
Which is most faint: now, 'tis true,
I must be here confin'd by you,
Or sent to Naples. Let me not,
Since I have my dukedom got,
And pardon'd the deceiver, dwell
In this bare island by your spell;
But release me from my bands
With the help of your good hands:
Gentle breath of yours my sails
Must fill, or else my project fails,
Which was to please: now I want
Spirits to enforce, art to enchant;
And my ending is despair,
Unless I be reliev'd by prayer,
Which pierces so, that it assaults
Mercy itself, and frees all faults.
As you from crimes would pardon'd be,
Let your indulgence set me free.

TWO GENTLEMEN OF VERONA.

DRAMATIS PERSONÆ.

Duke of Milan.	PANTHINO, servant to Antonio.
ANTONIO.	Host.
PROTEUS, his son.	Outlaws.
VALENTINE.	
THURIO.	SILVIA, daughter to the Duke.
EGLAMOUR.	JULIA.
SPEED, servant to Valentine.	LUCETTA, her waiting-woman.
LAUNCE, servant to Proteus.	

Servants, Musicians.

SCENE — *In Verona; in Milan; and in a forest near Milan.*

ACT I.

SCENE I. *Verona. An open place in the city.*

Enter VALENTINE *and* PROTEUS.

Val. Cease to persuade, my loving Proteus:
Home-keeping youth have ever homely wits.
Were't not affection chains thy tender days
To the sweet glances of thy honour'd love,
I rather would entreat thy company
To see the wonders of the world abroad,
Than, living dully sluggardiz'd at home,
Wear out thy youth with shapeless idleness.
But since thou lov'st, love still, and thrive therein,
Even as I would, when I to love begin.
Pro. Wilt thou be gone? Sweet Valentine, adieu!

Think on thy Proteus, when thou haply see'st
Some rare note-worthy object in thy travel:
Wish me partaker in thy happiness,
When thou dost meet good hap; and in thy danger,
If ever danger do environ thee,
Commend thy grievance to my holy prayers,
For I will be thy beadsman, Valentine.

Val. And on a love-book pray for my success?

Pro. Upon some book I love I'll pray for thee.

Val. That's on some shallow story of deep love;
How young Leander cross'd the Hellespont.

Pro. That's a deep story of a deeper love;
For he was more than over shoes in love.

Val. 'Tis true; for you are over boots in love,
And yet you never swam the Hellespont.

Pro. Over the boots! nay, give me not the boots.

Val. No, I will not, for it boots thee not.

Pro.   What?

Val. To be in love, where scorn is bought with groans;
Coy looks with heart-sore sighs; one fading moment's mirth
With twenty watchful, weary, tedious nights:
If haply won, perhaps a hapless gain;
If lost, why then a grievous labour won;
However, but a folly bought with wit,
Or else a wit by folly vanquishèd.

Pro. So, by your circumstance, you call me fool.

Val. So, by your circumstance, I fear you'll prove.

Pro. 'Tis love you cavil at: I am not Love.

Val. Love is your master, for he masters you:
And he that is so yokèd by a fool,
Methinks, should not be chronicled for wise.

Pro. Yet writers say, as in the sweetest bud
The eating canker dwells, so eating love
Inhabits in the finest wits of all.

Val. And writers say, as the most forward bud
Is eaten by the canker ere it blow,
Even so by love the young and tender wit

Is turn'd to folly; blasting in the bud,
Losing his verdure even in the prime,
And all the fair effects of future hopes.
But wherefore waste I time to counsel thee,
That art a votary to fond desire?
Once more adieu! my father at the road
Expects my coming, there to see me shipp'd.

Pro. And thither will I bring thee, Valentine.

Val. Sweet Proteus, no; now let us take our leave.
To Milan let me hear from thee by letters
Of thy success in love, and what news else
Betideth here in absence of thy friend;
And I likewise will visit thee with mine.

Pro. All happiness bechance to thee in Milan!

Val. As much to you at home! and so, farewell.   [*Exit.*

Pro. He after honour hunts, I after love:
He leaves his friends to dignify them more;
I leave myself, my friends, and all, for love.
Thou, Julia, thou hast metamorphos'd me, —
Made me neglect my studies, lose my time,
War with good counsel, set the world at naught;
Made wit with musing weak, heart sick with thought.

Enter SPEED.

Speed. Sir Proteus, save you! Saw you my master?

Pro. But now he parted hence, t' embark for Milan.

Speed. Twenty to one, then, he is shipp'd already,
And I have play'd the sheep in losing him.

Pro. Indeed, a sheep doth very often stray,
An if the shepherd be awhile away.

Speed. You conclude that my master is a shepherd, then,
          and I a sheep?

Pro. I do.

Speed. Why, then, my horns are his horns, whether I
          wake or sleep.

Pro. A silly answer, and fitting well a sheep.

Speed. This proves me still a sheep.

Pro.   True; and thy master a shepherd.

Speed.   Nay, that I can deny by a circumstance.

Pro.   It shall go hard but I'll prove it by another.

Speed.   The shepherd seeks the sheep, and not the sheep the shepherd; but I seek my master, and my master seeks not me: therefore I am no sheep.

Pro.   The sheep for fodder follow the shepherd, the shepherd for food follows not the sheep; thou for wages followest thy master, thy master for wages follows not thee: therefore thou art a sheep.

Speed.   Such another proof will make me cry "baa."

Pro.   But, dost thou hear? gavest thou my letter to Julia?

Speed.   Ay, sir: I, a lost mutton, gave your letter to her, a laced mutton; and she, a laced mutton, gave me, a lost mutton, nothing for my labour.

Pro.   Here's too small a pasture for such store of muttons.

Speed.   If the ground be overcharged, you were best stick her.

Pro.   Nay, in that you are a stray, 'twere best pound you.

Speed.   Nay, sir, less than a pound shall serve me for carrying your letter.

Pro.   You mistake; I mean the pound, — a pinfold.

Speed.   From a pound to a pin? fold it over and over, 'Tis threefold too little for carrying a letter to your lover.

Pro.   But what said she?

Speed. [*nodding*] Ay.

Pro.   Nod, Ay? — why, that's noddy.

Speed.   You mistook, sir; I say, she did nod: and you ask me if she did nod; and I say, Ay.

Pro.   And that set together is — noddy.

Speed.   Now you have taken the pains to set it together, take it for your pains.

Pro.   No, no; you shall have it for bearing the letter.

Speed.   Well, I perceive I must be fain to bear with you.

Pro.   Why, sir, how do you bear with me?

Speed.   Marry, sir, the letter very orderly; having nothing but the word "noddy" for my pains.

Pro. Beshrew me, but you have a quick wit.

Speed. And yet it cannot overtake your slow purse.

Pro. Come, come, open the matter in brief; what said she?

Speed. Open your purse, that the money and the matter may be both at once delivered.

Pro. Well, sir, here is for your pains [*Giving him money*]. What said she?

Speed. Truly, sir, I think you'll hardly win her.

Pro. Why, couldst thou perceive so much from her?

Speed. Sir, I could perceive nothing at all from her; no, not so much as a ducat for delivering your letter: and being so hard to me that brought your mind, I fear she'll prove as hard to you in telling your mind. Give her no token but stones; for she's as hard as steel.

Pro. What, said she nothing?

Speed. No, not so much as "Take this for thy pains." To testify your bounty, I thank you, you have testerned me; in requital whereof, henceforth carry your letters yourself: and so, sir, I'll commend you to my master.

Pro. Go, go, be gone, to save your ship from wreck,
Which cannot perish having thee aboard,
Being destin'd to a drier death on shore.   [*Exit Speed.*
I must go send some better messenger:
I fear my Julia would not deign my lines,
Receiving them from such a worthless post.   · [*Exit.*

SCENE II. *The same. The garden of* JULIA'S *house.*

Enter JULIA *and* LUCETTA.

Jul. But say, Lucetta, now we are alone,
Wouldst thou, then, counsel me to fall in love?

Luc. Ay, madam; so you stumble not unheedfully.

Jul. Of all the fair resort of gentlemen
That every day with parle encounter me,
In thy opinion which is worthiest love?

Luc. Please you repeat their names, I'll show my mind
According to my shallow-simple skill.

10*

Jul. What think'st thou of the fair Sir Eglamour?
Luc. As of a knight well-spoken, neat, and fine;
But, were I you, he never should be mine.
Jul. What think'st thou of the rich Mercatio?
Luc. Well of his wealth; but of himself, so-so.
Jul. What think'st thou of the gentle Proteus?
Luc. Lord, Lord! to see what folly reigns in us!
Jul. How now! what means this passion at his name?
Luc. Pardon, dear madam: 'tis a passing shame
That I, unworthy body as I am,
Should censure thus on lovely gentlemen.
Jul. Why not on Proteus, as of all the rest?
Luc. Then thus, — of many good I think him best.
Jul. Your reason?
Luc. I have no other but a woman's reason;
I think him so, because I think him so.
Jul. And wouldst thou have me cast my love on him?
Luc. Ay, if you thought your love not cast away.
Jul. Why, he, of all the rest, hath never mov'd me.
Luc. Yet he, of all the rest, I think, best loves ye.
Jul. His little speaking shows his love but small.
Luc. Fire that's closest kept burns most of all.
Jul. They do not love that do not show their love.
Luc. O, they love least that let men know their love.
Jul. I would I knew his mind.
Luc. Peruse this paper, madam.   [*Gives a letter.*
Jul. [*reads*] "*To Julia.*" — Say, from whom?
Luc. That the contents will show.
Jul. Say, say, who gave it thee?
Luc. Sir Valentine's page; and sent, I think, from Proteus.
He would have given it you; but I, being in the way,
Did in your name receive it: pardon the fault, I pray.
Jul. Now, by my modesty, a goodly broker!
Dare you presume to harbour wanton lines?
To whisper and conspire against my youth?
Now, trust me, 'tis an office of great worth,
And you an officer fit for the place.

There, take the paper: see it be return'd;
Or else return no more into my sight.

    Luc.   To plead for love deserves more fee than hate.
    Jul.   Will ye be gone?
    Luc.   That you may ruminate.   [*Exit.*
    Jul.   And yet I would I had o'erlook'd the letter:
It were a shame to call her back again,
And pray her to a fault for which I chid her.
What fool is she, that knows I am a maid,
And would not force the letter to my view, —
Since maids, in modesty, say "No" to that
Which they would have the profferer construe "Ay"!
Fie, fie, how wayward is this foolish love,
That, like a testy babe, will scratch the nurse,
And presently, all humbled, kiss the rod!
How churlishly I chid Lucetta hence,
When willingly I would have had her here!
How angerly I taught my brow to frown,
When inward joy enforc'd my heart to smile!
My penance is, to call Lucetta back,
And ask remission for my folly past. —
What, ho! Lucetta!

              Re-enter LUCETTA.

    Luc.   What would your ladyship?
    Jul.   Is it near dinner-time?
    Luc.   I would it were,
That you might kill your stomach on your meat,
And not upon your maid.
    Jul.   What is't that you took up so gingerly?
    Luc.   Nothing.
    Jul.   Why didst thou stoop, then?
    Luc.   To take a paper up that I let fall.
    Jul.   And is that paper nothing?
    Luc.   Nothing concerning me.
    Jul.   Then let it lie for those that it concerns.

Luc. Madam, it will not lie where it concerns,
Unless it have a false interpreter.

Jul. Some love of yours hath writ to you in rhyme.

Luc. That I might sing it, madam, to a tune.
Give me a note: your ladyship can set.

Jul. As little by such toys as may be possible.
Best sing it to the tune of *Light o' love.*

Luc. It is too heavy for so light a tune.

Jul. Heavy! belike it hath some burden, then?

Luc. Ay; and melodious were it, would you sing it.

Jul. And why not you?

Luc. I cannot reach so high.

Jul. Let's see your song [*Taking the letter*]. How now,
minion!

Luc. Keep tune there still, so you will sing it out:
And yet methinks I do not like this tune.

Jul. You do not?

Luc. No, madam; it is too sharp.

Jul. You, minion, are too saucy.

Luc. Nay, now you are too flat,
And mar the concord with too harsh a descant:
There wanteth but a mean to fill your song.

Jul. The mean is drown'd with your unruly base.

Luc. Indeed, I bid the base for Proteus.

Jul. This babble shall not henceforth trouble me: —
Here is a coil with protestation! — [*Tears the letter.*
Go get you gone, and let the papers lie:
You would be fingering them, to anger me.

Luc. She makes it strange; but she would be best pleas'd
To be so anger'd with another letter. [*Exit.*

Jul. Nay, would I were so anger'd with the same!
O hateful hands, to tear such loving words!
Injurious wasps, to feed on such sweet honey,
And kill the bees, that yield it, with your stings!
I'll kiss each several paper for amends.
Look, here is writ — "kind Julia:" — unkind Julia!
As in revenge of thy ingratitude,

I throw thy name against the bruising stones,
Trampling contemptuously on thy disdain.·
And here is writ — "love-wounded Proteus:" —
Poor wounded name! my bosom, as a bed,
Shall lodge thee, till thy wound be throughly heal'd;
And thus I search it with a sovereign kiss.
But twice or thrice was "Proteus" written down: —
Be calm, good wind, blow not a word away,
Till I have found each letter in the letter,
Except mine own name: that some whirlwind bear
Unto a raggèd, fearful-hanging rock,
And throw it thence into the raging sea! —
Lo, here in one line is his name twice writ, —
"Poor forlorn Proteus, passionate Proteus,
To the sweet Julia:" — that I'll tear away; —
And yet I will not, sith so prettily
He couples it to his complaining names.
Thus will I fold them one upon another:
Now kiss, embrace, contend, do what you will.

Re-enter LUCETTA.

Luc. Madam,
Dinner is ready, and your father stays.
Jul. Well, let us go.
Luc. What, shall these papers lie like tell-tales here?
Jul. If you respect them, best to take them up.
Luc. Nay, I was taken up for laying them down:
Yet here they shall not lie, for catching cold.
Jul. I see you have a month's mind to them.
Luc. Ay, madam, you may say what sights you see;
I see things too, although you judge I wink.
Jul. Come, come; will't please you go?   [*Exeunt.*

SCENE III. *The same.   A room in* ANTONIO'S *house.*

Enter ANTONIO *and* PANTHINO.

Ant. Tell me, Panthino, what sad talk was that
Wherewith my brother held you in the cloister?

Pan.   'Twas of his nephew Proteus, your son.

Ant.   Why, what of him?

Pan.   He wonder'd that your lordship
Would suffer him to spend his youth at home,
While other men, of slender reputation,
Put forth their sons to seek preferment out:
Some to the wars, to try their fortune there;
Some to discover islands far away;
Some to the studious universities.
For any, or for all these exercises,
He said that Proteus your son was meet;
And did request me to impórtune you
To let him spend his time no more at home,
Which would be great impeachment to his age,
In having known no travel in his youth.

Ant.   Nor need'st thou much impórtune me to that
Whereon this month I have been hammering.
I have consider'd well his loss of time,
And how he cannot be a perfect man,
Not being tried and tutor'd in the world:
Experience is by industry achiev'd,
And perfected by the swift course of time.
Then, tell me, whither were I best to send him?

Pan.   I think your lordship is not ignorant
How his companion, youthful Valentine,
Attends the emperor in his royal court.

Ant.   I know it well.

Pan.   'Twere good, I think, your lordship sent him thither:
There shall he practise tilts and tournaments,
Hear sweet discourse, converse with noblemen,
And be in eye of every exercise
Worthy his youth and nobleness of birth.

Ant.   I like thy counsel; well hast thou advis'd:
And that thou mayst perceive how well I like it,
The execution of it shall make known.
Even with the speediest expedition
I will dispatch him to the emperor's court.

Pan. To-morrow, may it please you, Don Alphonso,
With other gentlemen of good esteem,
Are journeying to salute the emperor,
And to commend their service to his will.

Ant. Good company; with them shall Proteus go:
And, — in good time: — now will we break with him.

Enter PROTEUS.

Pro. Sweet love! sweet lines! sweet life!
Here is her hand, the agent of her heart;
Here is her oath for love, her honour's pawn.
O, that our fathers would applaud our loves,
To seal our happiness with their consents!
O heavenly Julia!

Ant. How now! what letter are you reading there?

Pro. May't please your lordship, 'tis a word or two
Of commendations sent from Valentine,
Deliver'd by a friend that came from him.

Ant. Lend me the letter; let me see what news.

Pro. There is no news, my lord; but that he writes
How happily he lives, how well belov'd,
And daily gracèd by the emperor;
Wishing me with him, partner of his fortune.

Ant. And how stand you affected to his wish?

Pro. As one relying on your lordship's will,
And not depending on his friendly wish.

Ant. My will is something sorted with his wish.
Muse not that I thus suddenly proceed;
For what I will, I will, and there an end.
I am resolv'd that thou shalt spend some time
With Valentinus in the emperor's court:
What maintenance he from his friends receives,
Like exhibition thou shalt have from me.
To-morrow be in readiness to go:
Excuse it not, for I am peremptory.

Pro. My lord, I cannot be so soon provided:
Please you, deliberate a day or two.

Ant. Look, what thou want'st shall be sent after thee:
No more of stay; to-morrow thou must go. —
Come on, Panthino: you shall be employ'd
To hasten on his expedition.   [*Exeunt Ant. and Pan.*
    Pro. Thus have I shunn'd the fire for fear of burning,
And drench'd me in the sea, where I am drown'd.
I fear'd to show my father Julia's letter,
Lest he should take exceptions to my love
And with the vantage of mine own excuse
Hath he excepted most against my love.
O, how this spring of love resembleth
    Th' uncertain glory of an April day,
Which now shows all the beauty of the sun,
    And by and by a cloud takes all away!

Re-enter PANTHINO.

Pan. Sir Proteus, your father calls for you:
    He is in haste; therefore, I pray you, go.
    Pro. Why, this it is, — my heart accords thereto,
    And yet a thousand times it answers, No.   [*Exeunt.*

ACT II.

SCENE I. *Milan.* *A room in the* Duke's *palace.*

Enter VALENTINE *and* SPEED.

Speed. [*picking up a glove*] Sir, your glove.
Val.   Not mine; my gloves are on.
Speed. Why, then, this may be yours, for this is but one.
    Val. . Ha, let me see: ay, give it me, it's mine: —
Sweet ornament that decks a thing divine!
Ah, Silvia, Silvia!
    Speed. [*calling*] Madam Silvia, Madam Silvia!
    Val. How now, sirrah!
    Speed. She is not within hearing, sir.
    Val. Why, sir, who bade you call her?
    Speed. Your worship, sir; or else I mistook.

Val. Well, you'll still be too forward.

Speed. And yet I was last chidden for being too slow.

Val. Go to, sir: tell me, do you know Madam Silvia?

Speed. She that your worship loves?

Val. Why, how know you that I am in love?

Speed. Marry, by these special marks: first, you have learned, like Sir Proteus, to wreathe your arms, like a malcontent; to relish a love-song, like a robin-redbreast; to walk alone, like one that had the pestilence; to sigh, like a schoolboy that had lost his A B C; to weep, like a young wench that had buried her grandam; to fast, like one that takes diet; to watch, like one that fears robbing; to speak puling, like a beggar at Hallowmas. You were wont, when you laughed, to crow like a cock; when you walked, to walk like one of the lions; when you fasted, it was presently after dinner; when you looked sadly, it was for want of money: and now you are metamorphosed with a mistress, that, when I look on you, I can hardly think you my master.

Val. Are all these things perceived in me?

Speed. They are all perceived without ye.

Val. Without me! they cannot.

Speed. Without you! nay, that's certain, for, without you were so simple, none else would: but you are so without these follies, that these follies are within you, and shine through you like the water in an urinal, that not an eye that sees you but is a physician to comment on your malady.

Val. But tell me, dost thou know my lady Silvia?

Speed. She that you gaze on so as she sits at supper?

Val. Hast thou observed that? even she I mean.

Speed. Why, sir, I know her not.

Val. Dost thou know her by my gazing on her, and yet knowest her not?

Speed. Is she not hard-favoured, sir?

Val. Not so fair, boy, as well-favoured.

Speed. Sir, I know that well enough.

Val. What dost thou know?

Speed. That she is not so fair as, of you, well favoured.

Val. I mean, that her beauty is exquisite, but her favour infinite.

Speed. That's because the one is painted, and the other out of all count.

Val. How painted? and how out of count?

Speed. Marry, sir, so painted, to make her fair, that no man counts of her beauty.

Val. How esteemest thou me? I account of her beauty.

Speed. You never saw her since she was deformed.

Val. How long hath she been deformed?

Speed. Ever since you loved her.

Val. I have loved her ever since I saw her; and still I see her beautiful.

Speed. If you love her, you cannot see her.

Val. Why?

Speed. Because Love is blind. O, that you had mine eyes; or your own eyes had the lights they were wont to have when you chid at Sir Proteus for going ungartered!

Val. What should I see then?

Speed. Your own present folly, and her passing deformity: for he, being in love, could not see to garter his hose; and you, being in love, cannot see to put on your hose.

Val. Belike, boy, then, you are in love; for last morning you could not see to wipe my shoes.

Speed. True, sir; I was in love with my bed: I thank you, you swinged me for my love, which makes me the bolder to chide you for yours.

Val. In conclusion, I stand affected to her.

Speed. I would you were set; so your affection would cease.

Val. Last night she enjoined me to write some lines to one she loves.

Speed. And have you?

Val. I have.

Speed. Are they not lamely writ?

Val. No, boy, but as well as I can do them. — Peace here she comes.

Speed. [*aside*] O excellent motion! O exceeding puppet!
Now will he interpret to her.

Enter SILVIA.

Val. Madam and mistress, a thousand good-morrows!

Speed. [*aside*] O, give ye good even! here's a million of
manners.

Sil. Sir Valentine and servant, to you two thousand.

Speed. [*aside*] He should give her interest, and she gives
it him.

Val. As you enjoin'd me, I have writ your letter
Unto the secret nameless friend of yours;
Which I was much unwilling to proceed in,
But for my duty to your ladyship.   [*Gives a letter.*

Sil. I thank you, gentle servant: 'tis very clerkly done.

Val. Now trust me, madam, it came hardly off;
For, being ignorant to whom it goes,
I writ at random, very doubtfully.

Sil. Perchance you think too much of so much pains?

Val. No, madam; so it stead you, I will write,
Please you command, a thousand times as much:
And yet, —

Sil. A pretty period! Well, I guess the sequel;
And yet I will not name 't; — and yet I care not; —
And yet take this again; — and yet I thank you;
Meaning henceforth to trouble you no more.

Speed. [*aside*] And yet you will; and yet another "yet."

Val. What means your ladyship? do you not like it?

Sil. Yes, yes; the lines are very quaintly writ:
But since unwillingly, take them again;
Nay, take them.   [*Gives back the letter.*

Val. Madam, they are for you.

Sil. Ay, ay, you writ them, sir, at my request;
But I will none of them; they are for you:
I would have had them writ more movingly.

Val. Please you, I'll write your ladyship another

Sil. And when it's writ, for my sake read it over:
And if it please you, so; if not, why, so.

Val. If it please me, madam! what then?

Sil. Why, if it please you, take it for your labour:
And so, good morrow, servant.   [*Exit.*

Speed. O jest unseen, inscrutable, invisible,
As a nose on a man's face, or a weathercock on a steeple!
My master sues to her; and she hath taught her suitor,
He being her pupil, to become her tutor.
O excellent device! was there ever heard a better,
That my master, being scribe, to himself should write the
            letter?

Val. How now, sir! what are you reasoning with yourself?
Speed. Nay, I was rhyming: 'tis you that have the reason.
Val. To do what?
Speed. To be a spokesman from Madam Silvia.
Val. To whom?
Speed. To yourself: why, she wooes you by a figure.
Val. What figure?
Speed. By a letter, I should say.
Val. Why, she hath not writ to me?
Speed. What need she, when she hath made you write to
yourself? Why, do you not perceive the jest?
Val. No, believe me.
Speed. No believing you, indeed, sir. But did you per-
ceive her earnest?
Val. She gave me none, except an angry word.
Speed. Why, she hath given you a letter.
Val. That's the letter I writ to her friend.
Speed. And that letter hath she delivered, and there an end.
Val. I would it were no worse.
Speed. I'll warrant you, 'tis as well:

For often have you writ to her; and she, in modesty,
Or else for want of idle time, could not again reply;
Or fearing else some messenger that might her mind discover,
Herself hath taught her love himself to write unto her lover.

All this I speak in print, for in print I found it. — Why muse
you, sir? 'tis dinner-time.

Val. I have dined.

Speed. Ay, but hearken, sir; though the chameleon Love can feed on the air, I am one that am nourished by my victuals, and would fain have meat. O, be not like your mistress; be moved, be moved.　　　　　　　　　*[Exeunt.*

SCENE II.　*Verona. The garden of* JULIA'S *house.*

Enter PROTEUS *and* JULIA.

Pro. Have patience, gentle Julia.

Jul. I must, where is no remedy.

Pro. When possibly I can, I will return.

Jul. If you turn not, you will return the sooner.
Keep this remembrance for thy Julia's sake.
　　　　　　　　　　　　　[Gives him a ring.

Pro. Why, then, we'll make exchange; here, take you
　　　　this.　　　　　　　　*[Gives her another.*

Jul. And seal the bargain with a holy kiss.

Pro. Here is my hand for my true constancy;
And when that hour o'erslips me in the day
Wherein I sigh not, Julia, for thy sake,
The next ensuing hour some foul mischance
Torment me for my love's forgetfulness!
My father stays my coming; answer not;
The tide is now: — nay, not thy tide of tears;
That tide will stay me longer than I should:
Julia, farewell!　　　　　　　　　*[Exit Julia.*
　　　　　　What, gone without a word?
Ay, so true love should do: it cannot speak;
For truth hath better deeds than words to grace it.

Enter PANTHINO.

Pan. Sir Proteus, you are stay'd for.

Pro. Go; I come, I come: —
Alas, this parting strikes poor lovers dumb!

　　　　　　　　　　　　　　　　[Exeunt.

SCENE III. *The same. A street.*

Enter LAUNCE, *leading a dog.*

Launce. Nay, 'twill be this hour ere I have done weeping; all the kind of the Launces have this very fault. I have received my proportion, like the prodigious son, and am going with Sir Proteus to the imperial's court. I think Crab my dog be the sourest-natured dog that lives: my mother weeping, my father wailing, my sister crying, our maid howling, our cat wringing her hands, and all our house in a great perplexity, yet did not this cruel-hearted cur shed one tear: he is a stone, a very pebble-stone, and has no more pity in him than a dog: a Jew would have wept to have seen our parting; why, my grandam, having no eyes, look you, wept herself blind at my parting. Nay, I'll show you the manner of it. This shoe is my father;— no, this left shoe is my father; — no, no, this left shoe is my mother; — nay, that cannot be so neither; — yes, it is so, it is so, — it hath the worser sole. This shoe, with the hole in it, is my mother, and this my father; a vengeance on't! there 'tis: now, sir, this staff is my sister; for, look you, she is as white as a lily, and as small as a wand: this hat is Nan, our maid: I am the dog; — no, the dog is himself, and I am the dog, — O, the dog is me, and I am myself; ay, so, so. Now come I to my father; "Father, your blessing!" now should not the shoe speak a word for weeping: now should I kiss my father; well, he weeps on. Now come I to my mother; — O, that the shoe could speak now like a wood woman! — well, I kiss her; — why, there 'tis; here's my mother's breath up and down. Now come I to my sister: mark the moan she makes. Now the dog all this while sheds not a tear, nor speaks a word: but see how I lay the dust with my tears.

Enter PANTHINO.

Pan. Launce, away, away, aboard! thy master is shipped, and thou art to post after with oars. What's the matter? why weepest thou, man? Away, ass! you'll lose the tide, if you tarry any longer.

Launce. It is no matter if the tied were lost; for it is the unkindest tied that ever any man tied.

Pan. What's the unkindest tide?

Launce. Why, he that's tied here, — Crab, my dog.

Pan. Tut, man, I mean thou'lt lose the flood: and, in losing the flood, lose thy voyage; and, in losing thy voyage, lose thy master; and, in losing thy master, lose thy service; and, in losing thy service, — Why dost thou stop my mouth?

Launce. For fear thou shouldst lose thy tongue.

Pan. Where should I lose my tongue?

Launce. In thy tale.

Pan. In my tail!

Launce. Lose the tide, and the voyage, and the master, and the service, and the tied! Why, man, if the river were dry, I am able to fill it with my tears; if the wind were down, I could drive the boat with my sighs.

Pan. Come, come away, man; I was sent to call thee.

Launce. Sir, call me what thou darest.

Pan. Wilt thou go?

Launce. Well, I will go.　　　　　　　　　　　　*[Exeunt.*

SCENE IV. *Milan. A room in the* Duke's *palace.*

Enter SILVIA, VALENTINE, THURIO, *and* SPEED.

Sil. Servant, —

Val. Mistress?

Speed. Master, Sir Thurio frowns on you.

Val. Ay, boy, it's for love.

Speed. Not of you.

Val. Of my mistress, then.

Speed. 'Twere good you knocked him.

Sil. Servant, you are sad.

Val. Indeed, madam, I seem so.

Thu. Seem you that you are not?

Val. Haply I do.

Thu. So do counterfeits.

Val. So do you.

Thu. What seem I that I am not?

Val. Wise.

Thu. What instance of the contrary?

Val. Your folly.

Thu. And how quote you my folly?

Val. I quote it in your jerkin.

Thu. My jerkin is a doublet.

Val. Well, then, I'll double your folly.

Thu. How!

Sil. What, angry, Sir Thurio! do you change colour?

Val. Give him leave, madam; he is a kind of chameleon.

Thu. That hath more mind to feed on your blood than live in your air.

Val. You have said, sir.

Thu. Ay, sir, and done too, for this time.

Val. I know it well, sir; you always end ere you begin.

Sil. A fine volley of words, gentlemen, and quickly shot off.

Val. 'Tis indeed, madam; we thank the giver.

Sil. Who is that, servant?

Val. Yourself, sweet lady; for you gave the fire. Sir Thurio borrows his wit from your ladyship's looks, and spends what he borrows kindly in your company.

Thu. Sir, if you spend word for word with me, I shall make your wit bankrupt.

Val. I know it well, sir; you have an exchequer of words, and, I think, no other treasure to give your followers, — for it appears, by their bare liveries, that they live by your bare words.

Sil. No more, gentlemen, no more: — here comes my father.

Enter Duke.

Duke. Now, daughter Silvia, you are hard beset. —
Sir Valentine, your father's in good health:
What say you to a letter from your friends
Of much good news?

Val.   My lord, I will be thankful
To any happy messenger from thence.

Duke. Know ye Don Antonio, your countryman?

Val. Ay, my good lord, I know the gentleman
To be of worth and worthy estimation,
And not without desert so well reputed.

Duke. Hath he not a son?

Val. Ay, my good lord; a son that well deserves
The honour and regard of such a father.

Duke. You know him well?

Val. I know him as myself; for from our infancy.
We have convers'd and spent our hours together:
And though myself have been an idle truant,
Omitting the sweet benefit of time
To clothe mine age with angel-like perfection,
Yet hath Sir Proteus, for that's his name,
Made use and fair advantage of his days;
His years but young, but his experience old;
His head unmellow'd, but his judgment ripe;
And, in a word, — for far behind his worth
Come all the praises that I now bestow, —
He is complete in feature and in mind,
With all good grace to grace a gentleman.

Duke. Beshrew me, sir, but if he make this good,
He is as worthy for an empress' love
As meet to be an emperor's counsellor.
Well, sir; this gentleman is come to me,
With commendation from great potentates;
And here he means to spend his time awhile:
I think 'tis no unwelcome news to you.

Val. Should I have wish'd a thing, it had been he.

Duke. Welcome him, then, according to his worth;
Silvia, I speak to you; and you, Sir Thurio: —
For Valentine, I need not cite him to it:
I'll send him hither to you presently.   [*Exit.*

Val. This is the gentleman I told your ladyship
Had come along with me, but that his mistress
Did hold his eyes lock'd in her crystal looks.

                              11*

Sil. Belike that now she hath enfranchis'd them,
Upon some other pawn for fealty.
 Val. Nay, sure, I think she holds them prisoners still.
 Sil. Nay, then, he should be blind; and, being blind,
How could he see his way to seek out you?
 Val. Why, lady, Love hath twenty pair of eyes.
 Thu. They say that Love hath not an eye at all.
 Val. To see such lovers, Thurio, as yourself:
Upon a homely object Love can wink.
 Sil. Have done, have done; here comes the gentleman.

Enter PROTEUS.

 Val. Welcome, dear Proteus! — Mistress, I beseech you,
Confirm his welcome with some special favour.
 Sil. His worth is warrant for his welcome hither,
If this be he you oft have wish'd to hear from.
 Val. Mistress, it is: sweet lady, entertain him
To be my fellow-servant to your ladyship.
 Sil. Too low a mistress for so high a servant.
 Pro. Not so, sweet lady; but too mean a servant
To have a look of such a worthy mistress.
 Val. Leave off discourse of disability: —
Sweet lady, entertain him for your servant.
 Pro. My duty will I boast of, nothing else.
 Sil. And duty never yet did want his meed:
Servant, you're welcome to a worthless mistress.
 Pro. I'll die on him that says so, but yourself.
 Sil. That you are welcome?
 Pro.   That you are worthless.

Enter a Servant.

 Serv. Madam, my lord your father would speak with you.
 Sil. I wait upon his pleasure.   [*Exit Servant.*
                    Come, Sir Thurio,
Go you with me. — Once more, new servant, welcome:
I'll leave you to confer of home affairs;
When you have done, we look to hear from yow.

Pro. We'll both attend upon your ladyship.

         [Exeunt Silvia and Thurio.

Val. Now, tell me, how do all from whence you came?

Pro. Your friends are well, and have them much commended.

Val. And how do yours?

Pro.   I left them all in health.

Val. How does your lady? and how thrives your love?

Pro. My tales of love were wont to weary you;
I know you joy not in a love-discourse.

Val. Ay, Proteus, but that life is alter'd now.
I have done penance for contemning Love:
Those high-imperious thoughts have punish'd me
With bitter fasts, with penitential groans,
With nightly tears, and daily heart-sore sighs;
For, in revenge of my contempt of love,
Love hath chas'd sleep from my enthrallèd eyes,
And made them watchers of mine own heart's sorrow.
O gentle Proteus, Love's a mighty lord,
And hath so humbled me, as, I confess,
There is no woe to his correction,
Nor to his service no such joy on earth!
Now, no discourse, except it be of love;
Now can I break my fast, dine, sup, and sleep,
Upon the very naked name of love.

Pro. Enough; I read your fortune in your eye.
Was this the idol that you worship so?

Val. Even she; and is she not a heavenly saint?

Pro. No; but she is an earthly paragon

Val. Call her divine.

Pro.   I will not flatter her.

Val. O, flatter me; for love delights in praise.

Pro. When I was sick, you gave me bitter pills;
And I must minister the like to you.

Val. Then speak the truth by her: if not **divine**,
Yet let her be a principality,
Sovereign to all the creatures on the earth.

Pro.   Except my mistress.

Val.   Sweet, except not any;
Except thou wilt except against my love.

Pro.   Have I not reason to prefer mine own?

Val.   And I will help thee to prefer her too:
She shall be dignified with this high honour, —
To bear my lady's train, lest the base earth
Should from her vesture chance to steal a kiss,
And, of so great a favour growing proud,
Disdain to root the summer-swelling flower,
And make rough winter everlastingly.

Pro.   Why, Valentine, what braggardism is this?

Val.   Pardon me, Proteus: all I can is nothing
To her, whose worth makes other worthies nothing;
She is alone.

Pro.   Then let her alone.

Val.   Not for the world: why, man, she is mine own;
And I as rich in having such a jewel
As twenty seas, if all their sand were pearl,
The water nectar, and the rocks pure gold.
Forgive me, that I do not dream on thee,
Because thou see'st me dote upon my love.
My foolish rival, that her father likes
Only for his possessions are so huge,
Is gone with her along; and I must after,
For love, thou know'st, is full of jealousy.

Pro.   But she loves you?

Val.   Ay,
And we're betroth'd: nay, more, our marriage-hour
With all the cunning manner of our flight,
Determin'd of; how I must climb her window,
The ladder made of cords; and all the means
Plotted and greed on for my happiness.
Good Proteus, go with me to my chamber,
In these affairs to aid me with thy counsel.

Pro.   Go on before; I shall inquire you forth:
I must unto the road, to disembark

Some necessaries that I needs must use;
And then I'll presently attend on you.
    Val. Will you make haste?
    Pro. I will.   *[Exeunt Valentine and Speed.*
Even as one heat another heat expels,
Or as one nail by strength drives out another,
So the remembrance of my former love
Is by a newer object quite forgotten.
Is it mine eye, or Valentinus' praise,
Her true perfection, or my false transgression,
That makes me, reasonless, to reason thus?
She's fair; and so is Julia, that I love, —
That I did love, for now my love is thaw'd;
Which, like a waxen image 'gainst a fire,
Bears no impression of the thing it was.
Methinks my zeal to Valentine is cold,
And that I love him not as I was wont:
O, but I love his lady too-too much;
And that's the reason I love him so little.
How shall I dote on her with more advice,
That thus without advice begin to love her!
'Tis but her picture I have yet beheld,
And that hath dazzled my reason's light;
But when I look on her perfections,
There is no reason but I shall be blind.
If I can check my erring love, I will;
If not, to compass her I'll use my skill.   *[Exit.*

SCENE V. *The same. A street.*

Enter SPEED *and* LAUNCE *severally.*

    Speed. Launce! by mine honesty, welcome to Milan!
    Launce. Forswear not thyself, sweet youth; for I am not welcome. I reckon this always — that a man is never undone till he be hanged; nor never welcome to a place till some certain shot be paid, and the hostess say, "Welcome."
    Speed. Come on, you madcap, I'll to the alehouse with

you presently; where, for one shot of five pence, thou shalt have five thousand welcomes. But, sirrah, how did thy master part with Madam Julia?

Launce. Marry, after they closed in earnest, they parted very fairly in jest.

Speed. But shall she marry him?

Launce. No.

Speed. How, then? shall he marry her?

Launce. No, neither.

Speed. What, are they broken?

Launce. No, they are both as whole as a fish.

Speed. Why, then, how stands the matter with them?

Launce. Marry, thus; when it stands well with him, it stands well with her.

Speed. What an ass art thou! I understand thee not.

Launce. What a block art thou, that thou canst not! My staff understands me.

Speed. What thou sayest?

Launce. Ay, and what I do too: look thee, I'll but lean, and my staff understands me.

Speed. It stands under thee, indeed.

Launce. Why, stand-under and under-stand is all one.

Speed. But tell me true, will't be a match?

Launce. Ask my dog: if he say ay, it will; if he say no, it will; if he shake his tail and say nothing, it will.

Speed. The conclusion is, then, that it will.

Launce. Thou shalt never get such a secret from me but by a parable.

Speed. 'Tis well that I get it so. But, Launce, how sayest thou, that my master is become a notable lover?

Launce. I never knew him otherwise.

Speed. Than how?

Launce. A notable lubber, as thou reportest him to be.

Speed. Why, thou whoreson ass, thou mistakest me.

Launce. Why, fool, I meant not thee; I meant thy master.

Speed. I tell thee, my master is become a hot lover.

Launce. Why, I tell thee, I care not though he burn himself in love. If thou wilt go with me to the alehouse, so; if not, thou art an Hebrew, a Jew, and not worth the name of a Christian.

Speed. Why?

Launce. Because thou hast not so much charity in thee as to go to the ale with a Christian. Wilt thou go?

Speed. At thy service. [*Exeunt.*

SCENE VI. *The same. A room in the* Duke's *palace.*

Enter PROTEUS.

Pro. To leave my Julia, shall I be forsworn;
To love fair Silvia, shall I be forsworn;
To wrong my friend, I shall be much forsworn;
And even that power, which gave me first my oath,
Provokes me to this threefold perjury:
Love bade me swear, and Love bids me forswear:
O sweet-suggesting Love, if thou hast sinn'd,
Teach me, thy tempted subject, to excuse it!
At first I did adore a twinkling star,
But now I worship a celestial sun:
Unheedful vows may heedfully be broken;
And he wants wit that wants resolvèd will
To learn his wit t' exchange the bad for better.
Fie, fie, unreverend tongue! to call her bad,
Whose sovereignty so oft thou hast preferr'd
With twenty thousand soul-confirming oaths.
I cannot leave to love, and yet I do;
But there I leave to love where I should love.
Julia I lose, and Valentine I lose:
If I keep them, I needs must lose myself;
If I lose them, this find I by their loss, —
For Valentine, myself; for Julia, Silvia.
I to myself am dearer than a friend,
For love is still most precious in itself;
And Silvia — witness Heaven, that made her fair! —
Shows Julia but a swarthy Ethiop.

I will forget that Julia is alive,
Remembering that my love to her is dead;
And Valentine I'll hold an enemy,
Aiming at Silvia as a sweeter friend.
I cannot now prove constant to myself,
Without some treachery us'd to Valentine.
This night he meaneth with a corded ladder
To climb celestial Silvia's chamber-window;
Myself in counsel his competitor:
Now presently I'll give her father notice
Of their disguising and pretended flight;
Who, all enrag'd, will banish Valentine,
For Thurio he intends shall wed his daughter:
But, Valentine being gone, I'll quickly cross,
By some sly trick, blunt Thurio's dull proceeding.
Love, lend me wings to make my purpose swift,
As thou hast lent me wit to plot this drift! [*Exit*

SCENE VII. *Verona. A room in* JULIA'*s house.*

Enter JULIA *and* LUCETTA.

Jul.　Counsel, Lucetta; gentle girl, assist me;
And, even in kind love, I do cónjure thee, —
Who art the table wherein all my thoughts
Are visibly charácter'd and engrav'd, —
To lesson me; and tell me some good mean,
How, with my honour, I may undertake
A journey to my loving Proteus.

Luc.　Alas, the way is wearisome and long!

Jul.　A true-devoted pilgrim is not weary
To measure kingdoms with his feeble steps;
Much less shall she that hath Love's wings to fly,
And when the flight is made to one so dear,
Of such divine perfection, as Sir Proteus.

Luc.　Better forbear till Proteus make return.

Jul.　O, know'st thou not, his looks are my soul's food?
Pity the dearth that I have pinèd in,

By longing for that food so long a time.
Didst thou but know the inly touch of love,
Thou wouldst as soon go kindle fire with snow
As seek to quench the fire of love with words.

Luc. I do not seek to quench your love's hot fire,
But qualify the fire's extreme rage,
Lest it should burn above the bounds of reason.

Jul. The more thou damm'st it up, the more it burns:
The current that with gentle murmur glides,
Thou know'st, being stopp'd, impatiently doth rage;
But when his fair course is not hindered,
He makes sweet music with th' enamell'd stones,
Giving a gentle kiss to every sedge
He overtaketh in his pilgrimage;
And so by many winding nooks he strays,
With willing sport, to the wide ocean.
Then let me go, and hinder not my course:
I'll be as patient as a gentle stream,
And make a pastime of each weary step,
Till the last step have brought me to my love;
And there I'll rest, as, after much turmoil,
A blessèd soul doth in Elysium.

Luc. But in what habit will you go along?

Jul. Not like a woman; for I would prevent
The loose encounters of lascivious men:
Gentle Lucetta, fit me with such weeds
As may beseem some well-reputed page.

Luc. Why, then, your ladyship must cut your hair.

Jul. No, girl; I'll knit it up in silken strings
With twenty odd-conceited true-love knots:
To be fantastic may become a youth
Of greater time than I shall show to be.

Luc. What fashion, madam, shall I make your breeches?

Jul. That fits as well as — "Tell me, good my lord,
What compass will you wear your farthingale?"
Why, even what fashion thou best lik'st, Lucetta.

Luc. You must needs have them with a codpiece, madam.

Jul. Out, out, Lucetta! that will be ill-favour'd.

Luc. A round hose, madam, now's not worth a pin,
Unless you have a codpiece to stick pins on.

Jul. Lucetta, as thou lov'st me, let me have
What thou think'st meet, and is most mannerly.
But tell me, wench, how will the world repute me
For undertaking so unstaid a journey?
I fear me, it will make me scandaliz'd.

Luc. If you think so, then stay at home, and go not.

Jul. Nay, that I will not.

Luc. Then never dream on infamy, but go.
If Proteus like your journey when you come,
No matter who's displeas'd when you are gone:
I fear me, he will scarce be pleas'd withal.

Jul. That is the least, Lucetta, of my fear:
A thousand oaths, an ocean of his tears,
And instances of infinite of love,
Warrant me welcome to my Proteus.

Luc. All these are servants to deceitful men.

Jul. Base men, that use them to so base effect!
But truer stars did govern Proteus' birth:
His words are bonds, his oaths are oracles;
His love sincere, his thoughts immaculate;
His tears pure messengers sent from his heart;
His heart as far from fraud as heaven from earth.

Luc. Pray heaven he prove so, when you come to him!

Jul. Now, as thou lov'st me, do him not that wrong,
To bear a hard opinion of his truth:
Only deserve my love by loving him;
And presently go with me to my chamber,
To take a note of what I stand in need of,
To furnish me upon my longing journey.
All that is mine I leave at thy dispose,
My goods, my lands, my reputation;
Only, in lieu thereof, dispatch me hence.
Come, answer not, but to it presently;
I am impatient of my tarriance.   [*Exeunt.*

ACT III.

SCENE I. *Milan.   An ante-room in the* Duke's *palace.*

Enter DUKE, THURIO, *and* PROTEUS.

Duke. Sir Thurio, give us leave, I pray, awhile;
We have some secrets to confer about.   [*Exit Thurio.*
Now, tell me, Proteus, what's your will with me?

Pro. My gracious lord, that which I would discover
The law of friendship bids me to conceal;
But when I call to mind your gracious favours
Done to me, undeserving as I am,
My duty pricks me on to utter that
Which else no worldly good should draw from me.
Know, worthy prince, Sir Valentine, my friend,
This night intends to steal away your daughter;
Myself am one made privy to the plot.
I know you have determin'd to bestow her
On Thurio, whom your gentle daughter hates;
And should she thus be stol'n away from you,
It would be much vexation to your age.
Thus, for my duty's sake, I rather chose
To cross my friend in his intended drift
Than, by concealing it, heap on your head
A pack of sorrows, which would press you down,
Being unprevented, to your timeless grave.

Duke. Proteus, I thank thee for thine honest care;
Which to requite, command me while I live.
This love of theirs myself have often seen,
Haply when they have judg'd me fast asleep;
And oftentimes have purpos'd to forbid
Sir Valentine her company and my court:
But, fearing lest my jealous aim might err,
And so, unworthily, disgrace the man, —
A rashness that I ever yet have shunn'd, —
I gave him gentle looks; thereby to find
That which thyself hast now disclos'd to me.
And, that thou mayst perceive my fear of this,

Knowing that tender youth is soon suggested,
I nightly lodge her in an upper tower,
The key whereof myself have ever kept;
And thence she cannot be convey'd away.

Pro.   Know, noble lord, they have devis'd a mean
How he her chamber-window will ascend,
And with a corded ladder fetch her down;
For which the youthful lover now is gone,
And this way comes he with it presently;
Where, if it please you, you may intercept him.
But, good my lord, do it so cunningly
That my discovery be not aim'd at;
For love of you, not hate unto my friend,
Hath made me publisher of this pretence.

Duke.   Upon mine honour, he shall never know
That I had any light from thee of this.

Pro.   Adieu, my lord; Sir Valentine is coming.   [*Exit.*

Enter VALENTINE.

Duke.   Sir Valentine, whither away so fast?

Val.   Please it your grace, there is a messenger
That stays to bear my letters to my friends,
And I am going to deliver them.

Duke.   Be they of much import?

Val.   The tenour of them doth but signify
My health, and happy being at your court.

Duke.   Nay, then, no matter; stay with me awhile;
I am to break with thee of some affairs
That touch me near, wherein thou must be secret.
'Tis not unknown to thee that I have sought
To match my friend Sir Thurio to my daughter.

Val.   I know it well, my lord; and, sure, the match
Were rich and honourable; besides, the gentleman
Is full of virtue, bounty, worth, and qualities
Beseeming such a wife as your fair daughter:
Cannot your grace win her to fancy him?

Duke.   No, trust me; she is peevish, sullen, froward,

Proud, disobedient, stubborn, lacking duty;
Neither regarding that she is my child,
Nor fearing me as if I were her father:
And, may I say to thee, this pride of hers,
Upon advice, hath drawn my love from her;
And, where I thought the remnant of mine age
Should have been cherish'd by her child-like duty,
I now am full resolv'd to take a wife,
And turn her out to who will take her in:
Then let her beauty be her wedding-dower;
For me and my possessions she esteems not.

    Val.   What would your grace have me to do in this?

    Duke.   There is a lady in Milano here
Whom I affect; but she is nice and coy,
And naught esteems my agèd eloquence:
Now, therefore, would I have thee to my tutor —
For long agone I have forgot to court;
Besides, the fashion of the time is chang'd, —
How, and which way, I may bestow myself,
To be regarded in her sun-bright eye.

    Val.   Win her with gifts, if she respect not words:
Dumb jewels often, in their silent kind,
More than quick words, do move a woman's mind.

    Duke.   But she did scorn a present that I sent her.

    Val.   A woman sometime scorns what best contents her:
Send her another; never give her o'er;
For scorn at first makes after-love the more.
If she do frown, 'tis not in hate of you,
But rather to beget more love in you:
If she do chide, 'tis not to have you gone;
For why the fools are mad, if left alone.
Take no repulse, whatever she doth say;
For "get you gone," she doth not mean "away!"
Flatter and praise, commend, extol their graces;
Though ne'er so black, say they have angels' faces.
That man that hath a tongue, I say, is no man,
If with his tongue he cannot win a woman.

Duke. But she I mean is promis'd by her friends
Unto a youthful gentleman of worth;
And kept severely from resort of men,
That no man hath access by day to her.

Val. Why, then, I would resort to her by night.

Duke. Ay, but the doors be lock'd, and keys kept safe,
That no man hath recourse to her by night.

Val. What lets but one may enter at her window?

Duke. Her chamber is aloft, far from the ground,
And built so shelving, that one cannot climb it
Without apparent hazard of his life.

Val. Why, then, a ladder, quaintly made of cords,
To cast up, with a pair of anchoring hooks,
Would serve to scale another Hero's tower,
So bold Leander would adventure it.

Duke. Now, as thou art a gentleman of blood,
Advise me where I may have such a ladder.

Val. When would you use it? pray, sir, tell me that.

Duke. This very night; for Love is like a child,
That longs for every thing that he can come by.

Val. By seven o'clock I'll get you such a ladder.

Duke. But, hark thee; I will go to her alone:
How shall I best convey the ladder thither?

Val. It will be light, my lord, that you may bear it
Under a cloak that is of any length.

Duke. A cloak as long as thine will serve the turn?

Val. Ay, my good lord.

Duke.   Then let me see thy cloak:
I'll get me one of such another length.

Val. Why, any cloak will serve the turn, my lord.

Duke. How shall I fashion me to wear a cloak? —
I pray thee, let me feel thy cloak upon me. —
What letter is this same? What's here? — *"To Silvia"!*
And here an engine fit for my proceeding!
I'll be so bold to break the seal for once.   [*Reads.*

"My thoughts do harbour with my Silvia nightly;
    And slaves they are to me, that send them flying:

O, could their master come and go as lightly,
 Himself would lodge where senseless they are lying!
My herald thoughts in thy pure bosom rest them;
 While I, their king, that thither them impórtune,
Do curse the grace that with such grace hath bless'd them,
 Because myself do want my servants' fortune:
I curse myself, for they are sent by me,
That they should harbour where their lord would be."
What's here?
"*Silvia, this night I will enfranchise thee:*"
'Tis so; and here's the ladder for the purpose.
Why, Phaëthon, — for thou art Merops' son, —
Wilt thou aspire to guide the heavenly car,
And with thy daring folly burn the world?
Wilt thou reach stars, because they shine on thee?
Go, base intruder! overweening slave!
Bestow thy fawning smiles on equal mates;
And think my patience, more than thy desert,
Is privilege for thy departure hence:
Thank me for this, more than for all the favours
Which, all too much, I have bestow'd on thee.
But if thou linger in my territories
Longer than swiftest expedition
Will give thee time to leave our royal court,
By heaven, my wrath shall far exceed the love
I ever bore my daughter or thyself.
Be gone! I will not hear thy vain excuse;
But, as thou lov'st thy life, make speed from hence.   [*Exit.*
    Val. And why not death, rather than living torment?
To die, is to be banish'd from myself;
And Silvia is myself: banish'd from her,
Is self from self, — a deadly banishment!
What light is light, if Silvia be not seen?
What joy is joy, if Silvia be not by?
Unless it be to think that she is by,
And feed upon the shadow of perfection,
Except I be by Silvia in the night,

There is no music in the nightingale;
Unless I look on Silvia in the day,
There is no day for me to look upon:
She is my essence; and I leave to be,
If I be not by her fair influence
Foster'd, illumin'd, cherish'd, kept alive.
I fly not death, to fly this deadly doom:
Tarry I here, I but attend on death;
But, fly I hence, I fly away from life.

Enter PROTEUS *and* LAUNCE.

Pro. Run, boy, run, run, and seek him out.
Launce. So-ho, so-ho!
Pro. What see'st thou?
Launce. Him we go to find: there 's not a hair on 's head
but 'tis a Valentine.
Pro. Valentine!
Val. No.
Pro. Who then? his spirit?
Val. Neither.
Pro. What then?
Val. Nothing.
Launce. Can nothing speak? Master, shall I strike?
Pro. Who wouldst thou strike?
Launce. Nothing.
Pro. Villain, forbear.
Launce. Why, sir, I'll strike nothing: I pray you, —
Pro. Sirrah, I say, forbear. — Friend Valentine, a word.
Val. My ears are stopp'd, and cannot hear good news,
So much of bad already hath possess'd them.
Pro. Then in dumb silence will I bury mine,
For they are harsh, untuneable, and bad.
Val. Is Silvia dead?
Pro. No, Valentine.
Val. No Valentine, indeed, for sacred Silvia! —
Hath she forsworn me?
Pro. No, Valentine.

Val.   No Valentine, if Silvia have forsworn me! —
What is your news?

    Launce.   Sir, there is a proclamation that you are vanished.

    Pro.   That thou art banishèd — O, that's the news! —
From hence, from Silvia, and from me thy friend.

    Val.   O, I have fed upon this woe already,
And now excess of it will make me surfeit.
Doth Silvia know that I am banishèd?

    Pro.   Ay, ay; and she hath offer'd to the doom —
Which, unrevers'd, stands in effectual force —
A sea of melting pearl, which some call tears:
Those at her father's churlish feet she tender'd;
With them, upon her knees, her humble self;
Wringring her hands, whose whiteness so became them
As if but now they waxèd pale for woe:
But neither bended knees, pure hands held up,
Sad sighs, deep groans, nor silver-shedding tears,
Could penetrate her uncompassionate sire;
But Valentine, if he be ta'en, must die.
Besides, her intercession chaf'd him so,
When she for thy repeal was suppliant,
That to close prison he commanded her,
With many bitter threats of biding there.

    Val.   No more; unless the next word that thou speak'st
Have some malignant power upon my life:
If so, I pray thee, breathe it in mine ear,
As ending anthem of my endless dolour.

    Pro.   Cease to lament for that thou canst not help,
And study help for that which thou lament'st.
Time is the nurse and breeder of all good.
Here if thou stay, thou canst not see thy love;
Besides, thy staying will abridge thy life.
Hope is a lover's staff; walk hence with that,
And manage it against despairing thoughts.
Thy letters may be here, though thou art hence;
Which, being writ to me, shall be deliver'd
Even in the milk-white bosom of thy love.

                                                  12•

The time now serves not to expostulate: .
Come, I'll convey thee through the city-gate;
And, ere I part with thee, confer at large
Of all that may concern thy love-affairs.
As thou lov'st Silvia, though not for thyself,
Regard thy danger, and along with me.

Val. I pray thee, Launce, an if thou see'st my boy,
Bid him make huste, and meet me at the nórth-gate.

Pro. Go, sirrah, find him out. — Come, Valentine.

Val. O my dear Silvia! — Hapless Valentine!

[*Exeunt Valentine and Proteus.*

Launce. I am but a fool, look you; and yet I have the
wit to think my master is a kind of a knave: but that's all
one, if he be but one knave. He lives not now that knows
me to be in love; yet I am in love; but a team of horse' shall
not pluck that from me; nor who 'tis I love; and yet 'tis a
woman; but what woman, I will not tell myself; and yet 'tis
a milkmaid; yet 'tis not a maid, for she hath had gossips;
yet 'tis a maid, for she is her master's maid, and serves for
wages. She hath more qualities than a water-spaniel, —
which is much in a bare Christian. [*Pulling out a paper.*]
Here is the cate-log of her conditions. [*Reads*] "Imprimis,
She can fetch and carry." Why, a horse can do no more: nay,
a horse cannot fetch, but only carry; therefore is she better
than a jade. "Item, She can milk;" look you, a sweet virtue .
in a maid with clean hands.

Enter SPEED.

Speed. How now, Signior Launce! what news with your
mastership?

Launce. With my master's ship? why, it is at sea.

Speed. Well, your old vice still; mistake the word. What
news, then, in your paper?

Launce. The blackest news that ever thou heardest.

Speed. Why, man, how black?

Launce. Why, as black as ink.

Speed. Let me read them.

Launce. Fie on thee, jolt-head! thou canst not read.

Speed. Thou liest; I can.

Launce. I will try thee. Tell me this: who begot thee?

Speed. Marry, the son of my grandfather.

Launce. O illiterate loiterer! it was the son of thy grandmother: this proves that thou canst not read.

Speed. Come, fool, come; try me in thy paper.

Launce. There; and Saint Nicholas be thy speed!

Speed. [*reads*] "Imprimis, She can milk."

Launce. Ay, that she can.

Speed. "Item, She brews good ale."

Launce. And thereof comes the proverb, — Blessing of your heart, you brew good ale.

Speed. "Item, She can sew."

Launce. That's as much as to say, Can she so?

Speed. "Item, She can knit."

Launce. What need a man care for a stock with a wench, when she can knit him a stock?

Speed. "Item, She can wash and scour."

Launce. A special virtue; for then she need not be washed and scoured.

Speed. "Item, She can spin."

Launce. Then may I set the world on wheels, when she can spin for her living.

Speed. "Item, She hath many nameless virtues."

Launce. That's as much as to say, bastard virtues; that, indeed, know not their fathers, and therefore have no names.

Speed. "Here follow her vices."

Launce. Close at the heels of her virtues.

Speed. "Item, She is not to be kissed fasting, in respect of her breath."

Launce. Well, that fault may be mended with a breakfast. Read on.

Speed. "Item, She hath a sweet mouth."

Launce. That makes amends for her sour breath.

Speed. "Item, She doth talk in her sleep."

Launce. It's no matter for that, so she sleep not in her talk.

Speed. "Item, She is slow in words."

Launce. O villain, that set this down among her vices! To be slow in words is a woman's only virtue: I pray thee, out with't, and place it for her chief virtue.

Speed. "Item, She is proud."

Launce. Out with that too; it was Eve's legacy, and cannot be ta'en from her.

Speed. "Item, She hath no teeth."

Launce. I care not for that neither, because I love crusts.

Speed. "Item, She is curst."

Launce. Well, the best is, she hath no teeth to bite.

Speed. "Item, She will often praise her liquor."

Launce. If her liquor be good, she shall: if she will not, I will; for good things should be praised.

Speed. "Item, She is too liberal."

Launce. Of her tongue she cannot, for that's writ down she is slow of; of her purse she shall not, for that I'll keep shut: now, of another thing she may, and that cannot I help. Well, proceed.

Speed. "Item, She hath more hair than wit, and more faults than hairs, and more wealth than faults."

Launce. Stop there; I'll have her: she was mine, and not mine, twice or thrice in that last article. Rehearse that once more.

Speed. "Item, She hath more hair than wit," —

Launce. More hair than wit, — it may be: I'll prove it. The cover of the salt hides the salt, and therefore it is more than the salt; the hair that covers the wit is more than the wit, for the greater hides the less. What's next?

Speed. "And more faults than hairs," —

Launce. That's monstrous: O, that that were out!

Speed. "And more wealth than faults."

Launce. Why, that word makes the faults gracious. Well, I'll have her: and if it be a match, as nothing is impossible, —

Speed. What then?

Launce. Why, then will I tell thee—that thy master stays for thee at the north-gate.

Speed. For me!

Launce. For thee! ay; who art thou? he hath stayed for a better man than thee.

Speed. And must I go to him?

Launce. Thou must run to him, for thou hast stayed so long, that going will scarce serve the turn.

Speed. Why didst not tell me sooner? pox of your love-letters!   [*Exit.*

Launce. Now will he be swinged for reading my letter, — an unmannerly slave, that will thrust himself into secrets! I'll after, to rejoice in the boy's correction.   [*Exit.*

SCENE II. *The same. A room in the* Duke's *palace.*

Enter Duke *and* THURIO.

Duke. Sir Thurio, fear not but that she will love you, Now Valentine is banish'd from her sight.

Thu. Since his exile she hath despis'd me most, Forsworn my company, and rail'd at me, That I am desperate of obtaining her.

Duke. This weak impress of love is as a figure Trenchèd in ice, which with an hour's heat Dissolves to water, and doth lose his form. A little time will melt her frozen thoughts, And worthless Valentine shall be forgot.

Enter PROTEUS.

How now, Sir Proteus! Is your countryman, According to our proclamation, gone?

Pro. Gone, my good lord.

Duke. My daughter takes his going grievously.

Pro. A little time, my lord, will kill that grief.

Duke. So I believe; but Thurio thinks not so. Proteus, the good conceit I hold of thee — For thou hast shown some sign of good desert — Makes me the better to confer with thee.

Pro. Longer than I prove loyal to your grace Let me not live to look upon your grace.

Duke.   Thou know'st how willingly I would effect
The match between Sir Thurio and my daughter.
Pro.   I do, my lord.
Duke.   And also, I think, thou art not ignorant
How she opposes her against my will.
Pro.   She did, my lord, when Valentine was here.
Duke.   Ay, and perversely she persévers so.
What might we do to make the girl forget
The love of Valentine, and love Sir Thurio?
Pro.   The best way is to slander Valentine
With falsehood, cowardice, and poor descent, —
Three things that women highly hold in hate.
Duke.   Ay, but she'll think that it is spoke in hate.
Pro.   Ay, if his enemy deliver it:
Therefore it must with circumstance be spoken
By one whom she esteemeth as his friend.
Duke.   Then you must undertake to slander him.
Pro.   And that, my lord, I shall be loth to do:
'Tis an ill office for a gentleman,
Especially against his very friend.
Duke.   Where your good word cannot advantage him,
Your slander never can endamage him;
Therefore the office is indifferent,
Being entreated to it by your friend.
Pro.   You have prevail'd, my lord: if I can do it
By aught that I can speak in his dispraise,
She shall not long continue love to him.
But say, this weed her love from Valentine,
It follows not that she will love Sir Thurio.
Thu.   Therefore, as you unwind her love from him,
Lest it should ravel and be good to none,
You must provide to bottom it on me;
Which must be done by praising me as much
As you in worth dispraise Sir Valentine.
Duke.   And, Proteus, we dare trust you in this kind,
Because we know, on Valentine's report,
You are already Love's firm votary,

And cannot soon revolt and change your mind.
Upon this warrant shall you have access
Where you with Silvia may confer at large;
For she is lumpish, heavy, melancholy,
And, for your friend's sake, will be glad of you;
When you may temper her, by your persuasion,
To hate young Valentine, and love my friend.

Pro. As much as I can do, I will effect: —
But you, Sir Thurio, are not sharp enough;
You must lay lime to tangle her desires
By wailful sonnets, whose composèd rhymes
Should be full-fraught with serviceable vows.

Duke. Ay,
Much is the force of heaven-bred poesy.

Pro. Say, that upon the altar of her beauty
You sacrifice your tears, your sighs, your heart:
Write till your ink be dry, and with your tears
Moist it again; and frame some feeling line
That may discover such integrity:
For Orpheus' lute was strung with poets' sinews;
Whose golden touch could soften steel and stones,
Make tigers tame, and huge leviathans
Forsake unsounded deeps to dance on sands.
After your dire-lamenting elegies,
Visit by night your lady's chamber-window
With some sweet consort; to their instruments
Tune a deploring dump: the night's dead silence
Will well become such sweet-complaining grievance.
This, or else nothing, will inherit her.

Duke. This discipline shows thou hast been in love.

Thu. And thy advice this night I'll put in practice.
Therefore, sweet Proteus, my direction-giver,
Let us into the city presently
To sort some gentlemen well skill'd in music:
I have a sonnet that will serve the turn
To give the onset to thy good advice.

Duke. About it, gentlemen.

Prc. We'll wait upon your grace till after supper,
And afterward determine our proceedings.

Duke. Even now about it; I will pardon you.   [*Exeunt.*

ACT IV.

Scene I. *A forest near Milan.*

Enter certain Outlaws.

First Out. Fellows, stand fast; I see a passenger.

Sec. Out. If there be ten, shrink not, but down with 'em.

Enter Valentine *and* Speed.

Third Out. Stand, sir, and throw us that you have about ye:
If not, we'll make you sit, and rifle you.

Speed.   O, sir, we are undone! these are the villains
That all the travellers do fear so much.

Val. My friends, —

First Out. That's not so, sir, — we are your enemies.

Sec. Out. Peace! we'll hear him.

Third Out. Ay, by my beard, will we;
For he's a proper man.

Val. Then know that I have little wealth to lose;
A man I am cross'd with adversity:
My riches are these poor habiliments,
Of which if you should here disfurnish me,
You take the sum and substance that I have.

Sec. Out. Whither travel you?

Val. To Verona.

First Out. Whence came you?

Val. From Milan.

Third Out. Have you long sojourn'd there?

Val. Some sixteen months; and longer might have stay'd,
If crookèd fortune had not thwarted me.

First Out. What, were you banish'd thence?

Val. I was.

Sec. Out. For what offence?   .

Val. For that which now torments me to rehearse:
I kill'd a man, whose death I much repent;
But yet I slew him manfully in fight,
Without false vantage or base treachery.

First Out. Why, ne'er repent it, if it were done so.
But were you banish'd for so small a fault?

Val. I was, and held me glad of such a doom.

Sec. Out. Have you the tongues?

Val. My youthful travel therein made me happy,
Or else I often had been miserable.

Third Out. By the bare scalp of Robin Hood's fat friar,
This fellow were a king for our wild faction!

First Out. We'll have him: — sirs, a word.

Speed. Master, be one of them;
It is an honourable kind of thievery.

Val. Peace, villain!

Sec. Out. Tell us this: have you any thing to take to?

Val. Nothing but my fortune.

Third Out. Know, then, that some of us are gentlemen,
Such as the fury of ungovern'd youth
Thrust from the company of awful men:
Myself was from Verona banishèd
For practising to steal away a lady,
An heir, and near allied unto the duke.

Sec. Out. And I from Mantua, for a gentleman,
Who, in my mood, I stabb'd unto the heart.

First Out. And I for such-like petty crimes as these
But to the purpose, — for we cite our faults,
That they may hold excus'd our lawless lives;
And partly, seeing you are beautified
With goodly shape, and by your own report
A linguist, and a man of such perfection
As we do in our quality much want, —

Sec. Out. Indeed, because you are a banish'd man,
Therefore, above the rest, we parley to you:
Are you content to be our general?

To make a virtue of necessity,
And live, as we do, in this wilderness?

   Third Out. What say'st thou? wilt thou be of our consórt?
Say ay, and be the captain of us all:
We'll do thee homage and be rul'd by thee,
Love thee as our commander and our king.

   First Out. But if thou scorn our courtesy, thou diest.

   Sec. Out. Thou shalt not live to brag what we have offer'd.

   Val. I take your offer, and will live with you,
Provided that you do no outrages
On silly women or poor passengers.

   Third Out. No, we detest such vile base practices.
Come, go with us, we'll bring thee to our cave,
And show thee all the treasure we have got;
Which, with ourselves, shall rest at thy dispose.   [*Exeunt.*

    Scene II. *Milan. The court of the* Duke's *palace.*

        Enter Proteus.

   Pro. Already have I been false to Valentine,
And now I must be as unjust to Thurio.
Under the colour of commending him,
I have access my own love to prefer:
But Silvia is too fair, too true, too holy,
To be corrupted with my worthless gifts.
When I protest true loyalty to her,
She twits me with my falsehood to my friend;
When to her beauty I commend my vows,
She bids me think how I have been forsworn
In breaking faith with Julia whom I lov'd:
And notwithstanding all her sudden quips,   :
The least whereof would quell a lover's hope,
Yet, spaniel-like, the more she spurns my love,
The more it grows, and fawneth on her still.
But here comes Thurio: now must we to her window,
And give some evening music to her ear.

Enter THURIO *and* Musicians.

Thu. How now, Sir Proteus! are you crept before us?
Pro. Ay, gentle Thurio; for you know that love
Will creep in service where it cannot go.
Thu. Ay, but I hope, sir, that you love not here.
Pro. Sir, but I do; or else I would be hence.
Thu. Who? Silvia?
Pro.   Ay, Silvia, — for your sake.
Thu. I thank you for your own. — Now, gentlemen,
Let's tune, and to it lustily awhile.

Enter, at a distance, Host, *and* JULIA *in boy's clothes.*

Host. Now, my young guest, — methinks you're allicholy:
I pray you, why is it?
Jul. Marry, mine host, because I cannot be merry.
Host. Come, we'll have you merry: I'll bring you where
you shall hear music, and see the gentleman that you
asked for.
Jul. But shall I hear him speak?
Host. Ay, that you shall.
Jul. That will be music.   [*Music plays.*
Host. Hark, hark!
Jul. Is he among these?
Host. Ay: but, peace! let's hear 'em.

Song.

Who is Silvia? what is she,
That all our swains commend her?
Holy, fair, and wise is she;
The heaven such grace did lend her,
That she might admirèd be.

Is she kind as she is fair, —
For beauty lives with kindness?
Love doth to her eyes repair,
To help him of his blindness;
And, being help'd, inhabits there.

Then to Silvia let us sing,
  That Silvia is excelling;
She excels each mortal thing
  Upon the dull earth dwelling:
To her let us garlands bring.

Host. How now! you are sadder than you were before:
How do you, man? the music likes you not.

Jul. You mistake; the musician likes me not.

Host. Why, my pretty youth?

Jul. He plays false, father.

Host. How? out of tune on the strings?

Jul. Not so; but yet so false that he grieves my very
heart-strings.

Host. You have a quick ear.

Jul. Ay, I would I were deaf; it makes me have a slow
heart.

Host. I perceive you delight not in music.

Jul. Not a whit, — when it jars so.

Host. Hark, what fine change is in the music!

Jul. Ay, that change is the spite.

Host. You would have them always play but one thing?

Jul. I would always have one play but one thing.
But, host, doth this Sir Proteus that we talk on
Often resort unto this gentlewoman?

Host. I tell you what Launce, his man, told me, — he
loved her out of all nick.

Jul. Where is Launce?

Host. Gone to seek his dog; which to-morrow, by his
master's command, he must carry for a present to his lady.

Jul. Peace! stand aside: the company parts.

Pro. Sir Thurio, fear not you: I will so plead,
That you shall say my cunning drift excels.

Thu. Where meet we?

Pro.   At Saint Gregory's well.

Thu.   Farewell.
                    [*Exeunt Thurio and Musicians.*

SILVIA *appears above, at her window.*

Pro.   Madam, good even to your ladyship.

Sil.   I thank you for your music, gentlemen.
Who is that that spake?

Pro.   One, lady, if you knew his pure heart's truth,
You'd quickly learn to know him by his voice.

Sil.   Sir Proteus, as I take it.

Pro.   Sir Proteus, gentle lady, and your servant.

Sil.   What is your will?

Pro.   That I may compass yours.

Sil.   You have your wish; my will is even this,—
That presently you hie you home to bed.
Thou subtle, perjur'd, false, disloyal man!
Think'st thou I am so shallow, so conceitless,
To be reducèd by thy flattery,
That hast deceiv'd so many with thy vows?
Return, return, and make thy love amends.
For me, — by this pale queen of night I swear,
I am so far from granting thy request,
That I despise thee for thy wrongful suit;
And by and by intend to chide myself
Even for this time I spend in talking to thee.

Pro.   I grant, sweet love, that I did love a lady;
But she is dead.

Jul. [*aside*] 'Twere false, if I should speak it;
For I am sure she is not burièd.

Sil.   Say that she be; yet Valentine thy friend
Survives; to whom, thyself art witness,
I am betroth'd: and art thou not asham'd
To wrong him with thy importúnacy?

Pro.   I likewise hear that Valentine is dead.

Sil.   And so suppose am I; for in his grave
Assure thyself my love is burièd.

Pro.   Sweet lady, let me rake it from the earth.

Sil.   Go to thy lady's grave, and call hers thence;
Or, at the least, in hers sepulchre thine.

Jul. [*aside*] He heard not that.

Pro. Madam, if your heart be so obdurate,
Vouchsafe me yet your picture for my love,
The picture that is hanging in your chamber;
To that I'll speak, to that I'll sigh and weep:
For since the substance of your perfect self
Is else devoted, I am but a shadow;
And to your shadow will I make true love.
    Jul. [*aside*] If 'twere a substance, you would, sure, de-
          ceive it,
And make it but a shadow, as I am.
    Sil. I'm very loth to be your idol, sir;
But since your falsehood shall become you well
To worship shadows and adore false shapes,
Send to me in the morning, and I'll send it:
And so, good rest.
    Pro.   As wretches have o'ernight
That wait for execution in the morn.

                   [*Exeunt Proteus, and Silvia above.*

    Jul. Host, will you go?
    Host. By my halidom, I was fast asleep.
    Jul. Pray you, where lies Sir Proteus?
    Host. Marry, at my house. Trust me, I think 'tis al-
most day.
    Jul. Not so; but it hath been the longest night
That e'er I watch'd, and the most heaviest.   [*Exeunt.*

Enter EGLAMOUR.

    Egl. This is the hour that Madam Silvia
Entreated me to call and know her mind:
There's some great matter she'd employ me in. —
Madam, madam!

        SILVIA *re-appears above, at her window.*
    Sil.   Who calls?
    Egl.   Your servant and your friend;
One that attends your ladyship's command.
    Sil. Sir Eglamour, a thousand times good morrow.

Egl. As many, worthy lady, to yourself.
According to your ladyship's impose,
I am thus early come to know what service
It is your pleasure to command me in.
   Sil. O Eglamour, thou art a gentleman, —
Think not I flatter, for I swear I do not, —
Valiant, wise, remorseful, well accomplish'd:
Thou art not ignorant what dear good will
I bear unto the banish'd Valentine;
Nor how my father would enforce me marry
Vain Thurio, whom my very soul abhors.
Thyself hast lov'd; and I have heard thee say
No grief did ever come so near thy heart
As when thy lady and thy true love died,
Upon whose grave thou vow'dst pure chastity.
Sir Eglamour, I would to Valentine,
To Mantua, where I hear he makes abode;
And, for the ways are dangerous to pass,
I do desire thy worthy company,
Upon whose faith and honour I repose.
Urge not my father's anger, Eglamour,
But think upon my grief, — a lady's grief, —
And on the justice of my flying hence,
To keep me from a most unholy match,
Which heaven and fortune still reward with plagues.
I do desire thee, even from a heart
As full of sorrows as the sea of sands,
To bear me company, and go with me:
If not, to hide what I have said to thee,
That I may venture to depart alone.
   Egl. Madam, I pity much your grievances;
Which since I know they virtuously are plac'd,
I give consent to go along with you;
Recking as little what betideth me
As much I wish all good befortune you.
When will you go?
   Sil.   This evening coming.

Egl. Where shall I meet you?

Sil.   At Friar Patrick's cell,
Where I intend holy confession.

Egl. I will not fail your ladyship. Good morrow,
Gentle lady.

Sil.   Good morrow, kind Sir Eglamour.

[*Exeunt Eglamour, and Silvia above.*

Enter LAUNCE, *with his Dog.*

Launce. When a man's servant shall play the cur with him,
look you, it goes hard: one that I brought up of a puppy;
one that I saved from drowning, when three or four of his
blind brothers and sisters went to it! I have taught him —
even as one would say precisely, Thus I would teach a dog.
I was sent to deliver him as a present to Mistress Silvia from
my master; and I came no sooner into the dining-chamber,
but he steps me to her trencher, and steals her capon's leg:
O, 'tis a foul thing when a cur cannot keep himself in all
companies! I would have, as one should say, one that takes
upon him to be a dog indeed, to be, as it were, a dog at all
things. If I had not had more wit than he, to take a fault
upon me that he did, I think verily he had been hanged for't;
sure as I live, he had suffered for't: you shall judge. He
thrusts me himself into the company of three or four gentle-
manlike dogs, under the duke's table: he had not been there
(bless the mark!) a pissing while, but all the chamber smelt
him. "Out with the dog," says one; "What cur is that?"
says another; "Whip him out," says the third; "Hang him
up," says the duke. I, having been acquainted with the smell
before, knew it was Crab; and goes me to the fellow that whips
the dogs: "Friend," quoth I, "you mean to whip the dog?"
"Ay, marry, do I," quoth he. "You do him the more wrong,"
quoth I; "'twas I did the thing you wot of." He makes me
no more ado, but whips me out of the chamber. How many
masters would do this for his servant? Nay, I'll be sworn,
I have sat in the stocks for puddings he hath stolen, otherwise
he had been executed; I have stood on the pillory for geese

he hath killed, otherwise he had suffered for't. — Thou
thinkest not of this now! Nay, I remember the trick you
served me when I took my leave of Madam Silvia; did not I
bid thee still mark me, and do as I do? when didst thou see
me heave up my leg, and make water against a gentlewoman's
farthingale? didst thou ever see me do such a trick?

Re-enter PROTEUS, *and* JULIA *in boy's clothes.*

Pro. Sebastian is thy name? I like thee well,
And will employ thee in some service presently.

Jul. In what you please: I will do what I can.

Pro. I hope thou wilt. — [*To Launce*] How now, you
　　　　whoreson peasant!
Where have you been these two days loitering?

Launce. Marry, sir, I carried Mistress Silvia the dog you
bade me.

Pro. And what says she to my little jewel?

Launce. Marry, she says your dog was a cur, and tells you
currish thanks is good enough for such a present.

Pro. But she received my dog?

Launce. No, indeed, did she not: here have I brought
him back again.

Pro. What, didst thou offer her this from me?

Launce. Ay, sir; the other squirrel was stolen from me
by the hangman boys in the market-place: and then I offered
her mine own, — who is a dog as big as ten of yours, and
therefore the gift the greater.

Pro. Go get thee hence, and find my dog again,
Or ne'er return again into my sight.
Away, I say! stay'st thou to vex me here?
A slave, that still an end turns me to shame!　　[*Exit Launce.*
Sebastian, I have entertainèd thee,
Partly that I have need of such a youth,
That can with some discretion do my business,
For 'tis no trusting to yond foolish lout;
But chiefly for thy face and thy behaviour,
Which — if my augury deceive me not —

13*

Witness good bringing up, fortune, and truth:
Therefore know thou, for this I entertain thee.
Go presently, and take this ring with thee,
Deliver it to Madam Silvia:
She lov'd me well deliver'd it to me.

  Jul. It seems you lov'd not her, to leave her token.
She's dead, belike?

    Pro.   Not so; I think she lives.

    Jul. Alas!

    Pro. Why dost thou cry, "Alas"?

    Jul.   I cannot choose
But pity her.

    Pro. Wherefore shouldst thou pity her?

    Jul. Because methinks that she lov'd you as well
As you do love your lady Silvia:
She dreams on him that has forgot her love;
You dote on her that cares not for your love.
'Tis pity love should be so contrary;
And thinking on it makes me cry, "Alas!"

    Pro. Well, well, give her that ring, and therewithal
This letter: — that's her chamber: — tell my lady
I claim the promise for her heavenly picture.
Your message done, hie home unto my chamber,
Where thou shalt find me, sad and solitary.   *[Exit*

  Jul. How many women would do such a message?
Alas, poor Proteus! thou hast entertain'd
A fox to be the shepherd of thy lambs: —
Alas, poor fool! why do I pity him,
That with his very heart despiseth me?
Because he loves her, he despiseth me;
Because I love him, I must pity him.
This ring I gave him when he parted from me,
To bind him to remember my good will:
And now am I — unhappy messenger —
To plead for that which I would not obtain;
To carry that which I would have refus'd;
To praise his faith which I would have disprais'd.

I am my master's true-confirmèd love;
But cannot be true servant to my master,
Unless I prove false traitor to myself.
Yet will I woo for him; but yet so coldly
As, heaven it knows, I would not have him speed.

Enter SILVIA *below, attended.*

Gentlewoman, good day! I pray you, be my mean
To bring me where to speak with Madam Silvia.
　　Sil. What would you with her, if that I be she?
　　Jul. If you be she, I do entreat your patience
To hear me speak the message I am sent on.
　　Sil. From whom?
　　Jul. From my master, Sir Proteus, madam.
　　Sil. O, — he sends you for a picture?
　　Jul. Ay, madam.
　　Sil. Ursula, bring my picture there. —
　　　　　　　　　　　　　　[*The picture is brought.*
Go give your master this: tell him, from me,
One Julia, that his changing thoughts forget,
Would better fit his chamber than this shadow.
　　Jul. Madam, please you peruse this letter: —
　　　　　　　　　　　　　　[*Gives a letter.*
Pardon me, madam; I have unadvis'd
Deliver'd you a paper that I should not:
This is the letter to your ladyship.　　　　[*Gives another.*
　　Sil. I pray thee, let me look on that again.
　　Jul. It may not be; good madam, pardon me.
　　Sil. There, hold: —　　　　[*Gives back the first letter.*
I will not look upon your master's lines:
I know they're stuff'd with protestations,
And full of new-found oaths; which he will break
As easily as I do tear his paper. ·　　[*Tears the second letter.*
　　Jul. Madam, he sends your ladyship this ring.
　　Sil. The more shame for him that he sends it me;
For I have heard him say a thousand times
His Julia gave it him at his departure.

Though his false finger have profan'd the ring,
Mine shall not do his Julia so much wrong.

Jul. She thanks you.

Sil. What say'st thou?

Jul. I thank you, madam, that you tender her.
Poor gentlewoman! my master wrongs her much.

Sil. Dost thou know her?

Jul. Almost as well as I do know myself:
To think upon her woes I do protest
That I have wept a hundred several times.

Sil. Belike she thinks that Proteus hath forsook her.

Jul. I think she doth; and that's her cause of sorrow.

Sil. Is she not passing fair?

Jul. She hath been fairer, madam, than she is:
When she did think my master lov'd her well,
She, in my judgment, was as fair as you;
But since she did neglect her looking-glass,
And threw her sun-expelling mask away,
The air hath starv'd the roses in her cheeks,
And pinch'd the lily-tincture of her face,
That now she is become as black as I.

Sil. How tall was she?

Jul. About my stature: for, at Pentecost,
When all our pageants of delight were play'd,
Our youth got me to play the woman's part,
And I was trimm'd in Madam Julia's gown;
Which servèd me as fit, by all men's judgments,
As if the garment had been made for me:
Therefore I know she is about my height.
And at that time I made her weep a-good,
For I did play a lamentable part;
Madam, 'twas Ariadne, passioning
For Theseus' perjury and unjust flight;
Which I so lively acted with my tears,
That my poor mistress, movèd therewithal,
Wept bitterly; and, would I might be dead,
If I in thought felt not her very sorrow!

Sil. She is beholding to thee, gentle youth:—
Alas, poor lady, desolate and left!—
I weep myself to think upon thy words.
Here, youth, there is my purse: I give thee this
For thy sweet mistress' sake, because thou lov'st her.
Farewell.
  Jul. And she shall thank you for't, if e'er you know her.
         [*Exit Silvia with Attendants.*
A virtuous gentlewoman, mild and beautiful!
I hope my master's suit will be but cold,
Since she respects my mistress' love so much.
Alas, how love can trifle with itself!
Here is her picture: let me see; I think,
If I had such a tire, this face of mine
Were full as lovely as is this of hers:
And yet the painter flatter'd her a little,
Unless I flatter with myself too much.
Her hair is auburn, mine is perfect yellow:
If that be all the difference in his love,
I'll get me such a colour'd periwig.
Her eyes are grey as glass; and so are mine:
Ay, but her forehead's low, and mine's as high.
What should it be that he respects in her,
But I can make respective in myself,
If this fond Love were not a blinded god?
Come, shadow, come, and take this shadow up,
For 'tis thy rival. O thou senseless form,
Thou shalt be worshipp'd, kiss'd, lov'd, and ador'd!
And, were there sense in his idolatry,
My substance should be statue in thy stead.
I'll use thee kindly for thy mistress' sake,
That us'd me so; or else, by Jove I vow,
I should have scratch'd out your unseeing eyes,
To make my master out of love with thee!

             [*Exit.*

ACT V.

Scene I. *Milan. An abbey.*

Enter Eglamour.

Egl. The sun begins to gild the western sky;
And now it is about the very hour
That Silvia, at Friar Patrick's cell, should meet me.
She will not fail; for lovers break not hours,
Unless it be to come before their time;
So much they spur their expedition.
See where she comes.

Enter Silvia.

Lady, a happy evening!
Sil. Amen, amen! Go on, good Eglamour,
Out at the postern by the abbey-wall:
I fear I am attended by some spies.
Egl. Fear not: the forest is not three leagues off;
If we recover that, we're sure enough.   [*Exeunt.*

Scene II. *The same. A room in the Duke's palace.*

Enter Thurio, Proteus, and Julia in boy's clothes.

Thu. Sir Proteus, what says Silvia to my suit?
Pro. O, sir, I find her milder than she was;
And yet she takes exceptions at your person.
Thu. What, that my leg is too long?
Pro. No; that it is too little.
Thu. I'll wear a boot, to make it somewhat rounder.
Jul. [*aside*] But love will not be spurr'd to what it loathes.
Thu. What says she to my face?
Pro. She says it is a fair one.
Thu. Nay, then, the wanton lies; my face is black.
Pro. But pearls are fair; and the old saying is,
Black men are pearls in beauteous ladies' eyes.
Jul. [*aside*] 'Tis true, such pearls as put out ladies' eyes;
For I had rather wink than look on them.

Thu. How likes she my discourse?

Pro. Ill, when you talk of war.

Thu. But well, when I discourse of love and peace?

Jul. [*aside*] But, indeed, better when you hold your peace.

Thu. What says she to my valour?

Pro.   O, sir, she makes
No doubt of that.

Jul. [*aside*] She needs not, when she knows it cowardice.

Thu. What says she to my birth?

Pro. That you are well deriv'd.

Jul. [*aside*] True; from a gentleman to a fool.

Thu. Considers she my possessions?

Pro. O, ay; and pities them.

Thu. Wherefore?

Jul. [*aside*] That such an ass should owe them.

Pro. That they are out by lease.

Jul. Here comes the duke.

Enter Duke.

Duke. How now, Sir Proteus! how now, Thurio!
Which of you saw Sir Eglamour of late?

Thu. Not I.

Pro.   Nor I.

Duke.   Saw you my daughter?

Pro.   Neither.

Duke. Why, then, she's fled unto that peasant Valentine;
And Eglamour is in her company.
"Tis true; for Friar Laurence met them both,
As he in penance wander'd through the forest:
Him he knew well; and guess'd that it was she,
But, being mask'd, he was not sure of it:
Besides, she did intend confession
At Patrick's cell this even; and there she was not:
These likelihoods confirm her flight from hence.
Therefore, I pray you, stand not to discourse,
But mount you presently; and meet with me
Upon the rising of the mountain-foot

That leads toward Mantua, whither they are fled:
Dispatch, sweet gentlemen, and follow me.   [*Exit.*

 Thu. Why, this it is to be a peevish girl,
That flies her fortune when it follows her.
I'll after, more to be reveng'd on Eglamour
Than for the love of reckless Silvia.   [*Exit.*

 Pro. And I will follow, more for Silvia's love
Than hate of Eglamour, that goes with her. [*Exit.*

 Jul. And I will follow, more to cross that love
Than hate for Silvia, that is gone for love. [*Exit.*

Scene III. *The forest.*

Enter Outlaws *with* Silvia.

 First Out. Come, come;
Be patient; we must bring you to our captain.

 Sil. A thousand more mischances than this one
Have learn'd me how to brook this patiently.

 Sec. Out. Come, bring her away.

 First Out. Where is the gentleman that was with her?

 Third Out. Being nimble-footed, he hath outrun us,
But Moses and Valerius follow him.
Go thou with her to the west end of the wood;
There is our captain: we'll follow him that's fled;
The thicket is beset, he cannot scape.
     [*Exeunt all except the First Outlaw and Silvia.*

 First Out. Come, I must bring you to our captain's cave:
Fear not; he bears an honourable mind,
And will not use a woman lawlessly.

 Sil. O Valentine, this I endure for thee!   [*Exeunt.*

Scene IV. *Another part of the forest.*   •

Enter Valentine.

 Val. How use doth breed a habit in a man!
These shadowy, desert, unfrequented woods
I better brook than flourishing peopled towns:

Here can I sit alone, unseen of any,
And to the nightingale's complaining notes
Tune my distresses and record my woes.
O thou that dost inhabit in my breast,
Leave not the mansion so long tenantless,
Lest, growing ruinous, the building fall,
And leave no memory of what it was!
Repair me with thy presence, Silvia;
Thou gentle nymph, cherish thy fórlorn swain! [*Noise within.*
What halloing and what stir is this to-day?
These are my mates, that make their wills their law,
Have some unhappy passenger in chase:
They love me well; yet I have much to do
To keep them from uncivil outrages. —
Withdraw thee, Valentine: who's this comes here? [*Retires.*

　　　Enter PROTEUS, SILVIA, *and* JULIA *in boy's clothes.*

　Pro. Madam, this service I have done for you, —
Though you respect not aught your servant doth, —
To hazard life, and rescue you from him
That would have forc'd your honour and your love:
Vouchsafe me, for my meed, but one fair look;
A smaller boon than this I cannot beg,
And less than this, I'm sure, you cannot give.
　Val. [*aside*] How like a dream is this I see and hear!
Love, lend me patience to forbear awhile.
　Sil. O miserable, unhappy that I am!
　Pro. Unhappy were you, madam, ere I came;
But by my coming I have made you happy.
　Sil. By thy approach thou mak'st me most unhappy.
　Jul. [*aside*] And me, when he approacheth to your pre-
　　　sence.
　Sil. Had I been seizèd by a hungry lion,
I would have been a breakfast to the beast,
Rather than have false Proteus rescue me.
O, Heaven be judge how I love Valentine,
Whose life's as tender to me as my soul;

And full as much — for more there cannot be —
I do detest false perjur'd Proteus!
Therefore be gone, solicit me no more.

Pro. What dangerous action, stood it next to death,
Would I not undergo for one calm look?
O, 'tis the curse in love, and still approv'd,
When women cannot love where they're belov'd!

Sil. When Proteus cannot love where he's belov'd.
Read over Julia's heart, thy first best love,
For whose dear sake thou didst then rend thy faith
Into a thousand oaths; and all those oaths
Descended into perjury, to love me.
Thou hast no faith left now, unless thou'dst two,
And that's far worse than none; better have none
Than plural faith, which is too much by one:
Thou counterfeit to thy true friend!

Pro.   In love
Who respects friend?

Sil.   All men but Proteus.

Pro. Nay, if the gentle spirit of moving words
Can no way change you to a milder form,
I'll woo you like a soldier, at arms' end,
And love you 'gainst the nature of love, — force ye.

Sil. O heaven!

Pro.   I'll force thee yield to my desire.

Val. [*coming forward*] Ruffian, let go that rude uncivil
              touch, —
Thou friend of an ill fashion!

Pro.   Valentine!

Val. Thou common friend, that's without faith or love, —
For such is a friend now; — thou treacherous man!
Thou hast beguil'd my hopes; naught but mine eye*
Could have persuaded me: now I dare not say
I have one friend alive; thou wouldst disprove me.
Who should be trusted, when one's own right hand
Is perjur'd to the bosom? Proteus,
I'm sorry I must never trust thee more,

But count the world a stranger for thy sake.
The private wound is deep'st: O time most curst,
'Mongst all foes that a friend should be the worst!

Pro.　My shame and guilt confound me. —
Forgive me, Valentine: if hearty sorrow
Be a sufficient ransom for offence,
I tender't here; I do as truly suffer
As e'er I did commit.

Val.　　　　Then I am paid;
And once again I do receive thee honest: —
Who by repentance is not satisfied
Is nor of heaven nor earth; for these are pleas'd;
By penitence th' Eternal's wrath's appeas'd: —
And, that my love may appear plain and free,
All that was mine in Silvia I give thee.

Jul.　O me unhappy!　　　　　　　　　[*Faints.*

Pro.　Look to the boy.

Val. Why, boy! why, wag! how now! what is the matter?
Look up; speak.

Jul.　　　　O good sir, my master charg'd me
To deliver a ring to Madam Silvia;
Which, out of my neglect, was never done.

Pro.　Where is that ring, boy?

Jul.　　　　　　Here 'tis; this is it. [*Gives a ring.*

Pro.　How! let me see: —
Why, this is the ring I gave to Julia.

Jul.　O, cry you mercy, sir, I have mistook:
This is the ring you sent to Silvia.　　[*Shows another ring.*

Pro.　But how cam'st thou by this ring?
At my depart I gave this unto Julia.

Jul.　And Julia herself did give it me;
And Julia herself hath brought it hither.

Pro.　How! Julia!

Jul.　Behold her that gave aim to all thy oaths,
And entertain'd 'em deeply in her heart:
How oft hast thou with perjury cleft the root!
O Proteus, let this habit make thee blush!

Be thou asham'd that I have took upon me
Such an immodest raiment, — if shame live
In a disguise of love:
It is the lesser blot, modesty finds,
Women to change their shapes than men their minds.

   Pro. Than men their minds! 'tis true. O heaven, were man
But constant, he were perfect! that one error
Fills him with faults; makes him run through all sins:
Inconstancy falls off ere it begins.
What is in Silvia's face, but I may spy
More fresh in Julia's with a constant eye?

   Val. Come, come, a hand from either:
Let me be bless'd to make this happy close;
'Twere pity two such friends should be long foes.

   Pro. Bear witness, Heaven, I have my wish for ever.

   Jul. And I mine.

           Enter Outlaws, *with* Duke *and* THURIO.

   Outlaws.   A prize, a prize, a prize!

   Val.   Forbear, —
Forbear, I say! it is my lord the duke. —
Your grace is welcome to a man disgrac'd,
Banishèd Valentine.

   Duke.   Sir Valentine!

   Thu. Yonder is Silvia; and Silvia's mine.

   Val. Thurio, give back, or else embrace thy death;
Come not within the measure of my wrath:
Do not name Silvia thine; if once again,
Milano shall not hold thee. Here she stands:
Take but possession of her with a touch; —
I dare thee but to breathe upon my love.

   Thu. Sir Valentine, I care not for her, I;
I hold him but a fool that will endanger
His body for a girl that loves him not:
I claim her not, and therefore she is thine.

   Duke. The more degenerate and base art thou,
To make such means for her as thou hast done,

And leave her on such slight conditions. —
Now, by the honour of my ancestry,
I do applaud thy spirit, Valentine,
And think thee worthy of an empress' love:
Know, then, I here forget all former griefs,
Cancel all grudge, repeal thee home again.
Plead a new state in thy unrivall'd merit,
To which I thus subscribe, — Sir Valentine,
Thou art a gentleman, and well deriv'd;
Take thou thy Silvia, for thou hast deserv'd her.

    Val. I thank your grace; the gift hath made me happy.
I now beseech you, for your daughter's sake,
To grant one boon that I shall ask of you.

    Duke. I grant it, for thine own, whate'er it be.

    Val. These banish'd men, that I have kept withal,
Are men endu'd with worthy qualities:
Forgive them what they have committed here,
And let them be recall'd from their exile:
They are reformèd, civil, full of good,
And fit for great employment, worthy lord.

    Duke. Thou hast prevail'd; I pardon them and thee:
Dispose of them as thou know'st their deserts. —
Come, let us go: we will include all jars
With triumphs, mirth, and rare solemnity.

    Val. And, as we walk along, I dare be bold
With our discourse to make your grace to smile.
What think you of this page, my lord?

    Duke. I think the boy hath grace in him; he blushes.

    Val. I warrant you, my lord, more grace than boy.

    Duke. What mean you by that saying?

    Val. Please you, I'll tell you as we pass along,
That you will wonder what hath fortunèd. —
Come, Proteus; 'tis your penance, but to hear
The story of your loves discoverèd:
That done, our day of marriage shall be yours;
One feast, one house, one mutual happiness.

                                                 [Exeunt.

MERRY WIVES OF WINDSOR.

—

DRAMATIS PERSONÆ.

SIR JOHN FALSTAFF.
FENTON, a young gentleman.
SHALLOW, a country justice.
SLENDER, cousin to Shallow.
FORD, } two gentlemen dwelling
PAGE, } at Windsor.
WILLIAM PAGE, a boy, son to Page.
SIR HUGH EVANS, a Welsh parson.
DOCTOR CAIUS, a French physician.
Host of the Garter Inn.

BARDOLPH,
PISTOL, } followers of Falstaff.
NYM,
ROBIN, page to Falstaff.
SIMPLE, servant to Slender.
RUGBY, servant to Doctor Caius.

MISTRESS FORD.
MISTRESS PAGE.
ANNE PAGE, her daughter.
MISTRESS QUICKLY, servant to Doctor Caius.

Servants to Page, Ford, &c.

SCENE — *Windsor, and the neighbourhood.*

———

ACT I.

SCENE I. *Windsor. Before* PAGE'S *house.*

Enter JUSTICE SHALLOW, SLENDER, *and* SIR HUGH EVANS.

Shal. Sir Hugh, persuade me not; I will make a Star-Chamber matter of it: if he were twenty Sir John Falstaffs, he shall not abuse Robert Shallow, esquire.

Slen. In the county of Gloster, justice of peace and *coram.*

Shal. Ay, cousin Slender, and *cust-alorum.*

Slen. Ay, and *rato-lorum* too; and a gentleman born,

master parson; who writes himself *armigero*, — in any bill, warrant, quittance, or obligation, *armigero*.

Shal. Ay, that I do; and have done any time these three hundred years.

Slen. All his successors gone before him have done't; and all his ancestors that come after him may: they may give the dozen white luces in their coat.

Shal. It is an old coat.

Evans. The dozen white louses do become an old coat well; it agrees well, passant; it is a familiar beast to man, and signifies — love.

Shal. The luce is the fresh fish; the salt fish is an old coat.

Slen. I may quarter, coz?

Shal. You may, by marrying.

Evans. It is marring indeed, if he quarter it.

Shal. Not a whit.

Evans. Yes, py'r lady; if he has a quarter of your coat, there is but three skirts for yourself, in my simple conjectures: but that is all one. If Sir John Falstaff have committed disparagements unto you, I am of the church, and will be glad to do my benevolence to make atonements and compremises between you.

Shal. The Council shall hear it; it is a riot.

Evans. It is not meet the Council hear a riot; there is no fear of Got in a riot: the Council, look you, shall desire to hear the fear of Got, and not to hear a riot; take your vizaments in that.

Shal. Ha! o' my life, if I were young again, the sword should end it.

Evans. It is petter that friends is the sword, and end it: and there is also another device in my prain, which peradventure prings goot discretions with it: — there is Anne Page, which is daughter to Master George Page, which is pretty virginity.

Slen. Mistress Anne Page! She has brown hair, and speaks small like a woman.

Evans. It is that fery person for all the orld, as just as you will desire; and seven hundred pounds of moneys, and gold, and silver, is her grandsire upon his death's-bed (Got deliver to a joyful resurrections!) give, when she is able to overtake seventeen years old: it were a goot motion if we leave our pribbles and prabbles, and desire a marriage between Master Abraham and Mistress Anne Page.

Shal. Did her grandsire leave her seven hundred pound?

Evans. Ay, and her father is make her a petter penny.

Shal. I know the young gentlewoman; she has good gifts.

Evans. Seven hundred pounds and possibilities is goot gifts.

Shal. Well, let us see honest Master Page. Is Falstaff there?

Evans. Shall I tell you a lie? I do despise a liar as I do despise one that is false, or as I despise one that is not true. The knight, Sir John, is there; and, I beseech you, be ruled by your well-willers. I will peat the door for Master Page. [*Knocks*] What, ho! Got pless your house here!

Page. [*appearing above*] Who's there?

Evans. Here is Got's plessing, and your friend, and Justice Shallow; and here young Master Slender, that peradventures shall tell you another tale, if matters grow to your likings.

Enter PAGE.

Page. I am glad to see your worships well. I thank you for my venison, Master Shallow.

Shal. Master Page, I am glad to see you: much good do it your good heart! I wished your venison better; it was ill killed. — How doth good Mistress Page? — and I thank you always with my heart, la; with my heart.

Page. Sir, I thank you.

Shal. Sir, I thank you; by yea and no, I do.

Page. I am glad to see you, good Master Slender.

Slen. How does your fallow greyhound, sir? I heard say he was outrun on Cotsol'.

Page. It could not be judged, sir.

14*

Slen. You'll not confess, you'll not confess.

Shal. That he will not. — 'Tis your fault, 'tis your fault: — 'tis a good dog.

Page. A cur, sir.

Shal. Sir, he's a good dog, and a fair dog: can there be more said? he is good and fair. — Is Sir John Falstaff here?

Page. Sir, he is within; and I would I could do a good office between you.

Evans. It is spoke as a Christians ought to speak.

Shal. He hath wronged me, Master Page.

Page. Sir, he doth in some sort confess it.

Shal. If it be confessed, it is not redressed: is not that so, Master Page? He hath wronged me; indeed he hath; — at a word, he hath; — believe me; Robert Shallow, esquire, saith he is wronged.

Page. Here comes Sir John.

Enter SIR JOHN FALSTAFF, BARDOLPH, NYM, *and* PISTOL.

Fal. Now, Master Shallow, — you'll complain of me to the king?

Shal. Knight, you have beaten my men, killed my deer, and broke open my lodge.

Fal. But not kissed your keeper's daughter?

Shal. Tut, a pin! this shall be answered.

Fal. I will answer it straight; I have done all this: — that is now answered.

Shal. The Council shall know this.

Fal. 'Twere better for you if it were known in counsel: you'll be laughed at.

Evans. *Pauca verba*, Sir John, goot worts.

Fal. Good worts! good cabbage. — Slender, I broke your head: what matter have you against me?

Slen. Marry, sir, I have matter in my head against you: and against your cony-catching rascals, Bardolph, Nym, and Pistol; they carried me to the tavern and made me drunk, and afterward picked my pocket.

Bard. You Banbury cheese!

Slen. Ay, it is no matter.

Pist. How now, Mephostophilus!

Slen. Ay, it is no matter.

Nym. Slice, I say! *pauca, pauca;* slice! that's my humour.

Slen. Where's Simple, my man?— can you tell, cousin?

Evans. Peace, I pray you. — Now let us understand. There is three umpires in this matter, as I understand; that is, Master Page, *fidelicet* Master Page; and there is myself, *fidelicet* myself; and the three party is, lastly and finally, mine host of the Garter.

Page. We three, to hear it and end it between them.

Evans. Fery goot: I will make a prief of it in my note-book; and we will afterwards ork upon the cause with as great discreetly as we can.

Fal. Pistol, —

Pist. He hears with ears.

Evans. The tevil and his tam! what phrase is this, "He hears with ear"? why, it is affectations.

Fal. Pistol, did you pick Master Slender's purse?

Slen. Ay, by these gloves, did he — or I would I might never come in mine own great chamber again else— of seven groats in mill-sixpences, and two Edward shovel-boards, that cost me two shilling and two pence a-piece of Yead Miller, by these gloves.

Fal. Is this true, Pistol?

Evans. No; it is false, if it is a pick-purse.

Pist. Ha, thou mountain-foreigner! — Sir John and mas-
　　　　ter mine,
I combat challenge of this latten bilbo. —
Word of denial in thy labras here;
Word of denial: — froth and scum, thou liest!

Slen. By these gloves, then, 'twas he.

Nym. Be avised, sir, and pass good humours: I will say "marry trap" with you, if you run the nuthook's humour on me; that is the very note of it.

Slen. By this hat, then, he in the red face ·had it; for

though I cannot remember what I did when you made me drunk, yet I am not altogether an ass.

Fal. What say you, Scarlet and John?

Bard. Why, sir, for my part, I say the gentleman had drunk himself out of his five sentences, —

Evans. It is his five senses: fie, what the ignorance is!

Bard. And being fap, sir, was, as they say, cashiered; and so conclusions passed the careers.

Slen. Ay, you spake in Latin then too; but 'tis no matter: I'll ne'er be drunk whilst I live again, but in honest, civil, godly company, for this trick: if I be drunk, I'll be drunk with those that have the fear of God, and not with drunken knaves.

Evans. So Got udge me, that is a virtuous mind.

Fal. You hear all these matters denied, gentlemen; you hear it.

    Enter ANNE PAGE, *with wine;* MISTRESS FORD *and*
                MISTRESS PAGE

Page. Nay, daughter, carry the wine in; we'll drink within.   *[Exit Anne Page.*

Slen. O heaven! this is Mistress Anne Page.

Page. How now, Mistress Ford!

Fal. Mistress Ford, by my troth, you are very well met: by your leave, good mistress.   *[Kisses her.*

Page. Wife, bid these gentlemen welcome. — Come, we have a hot venison-pasty to dinner: come, gentlemen, I hope we shall drink down all unkindness.

                [Exeunt all except Shal., Slen., and Evans.

Slen. I had rather than forty shillings I had my Book of Songs and Sonnets here.

              Enter SIMPLE.

How now, Simple! where have you been? I must wait on myself, must I? You have not the Book of Riddles about you, have you?

Sim. Book of Riddles! why, did you not lend it to Alice

Shortcake upon All-hallowmas last, a fortnight afore Michaelmas?

Shal. Come, coz; come, coz; we stay for you. A word with you, coz; marry, this, coz; — there is, as 'twere, a tender, a kind of tender, made afar off by Sir Hugh here. Do you understand me?

Slen. Ay, sir, you shall find me reasonable; if it be so, I shall do that that is reason.

Shal. Nay, but understand me.

Slen. So I do, sir.

Evans. Give ear to his motions, Master Slender: I will description the matter to you, if you be capacity of it.

Slen. Nay, I will do as my cousin Shallow says: I pray you, pardon me; he's a justice of peace in his country, simple though I stand here.

Evans. But that is not the question: the question is concerning your marriage.

Shal. Ay, there's the point, sir.

Evans. Marry, is it; the very point of it; to Mistress Anne Page.

Slen. Why, if it be so, I will marry her upon any reasonable demands.

Evans. But can you affection the oman? Let us command to know that of your mouth or of your lips; for divers philosophers hold that the lips is parcel of the mouth. Therefore, precisely, can you carry your good will to the maid?

Shal. Cousin Abraham Slender, can you love her?

Slen. I hope, sir, I will do as it shall become one that would do reason.

Evans. Nay, Got's lords and his ladies, you must speak positable, if you can carry her your desires towards her.

Shal. That you must. Will you, upon good dowry, marry her?

Slen. I will do a greater thing than that, upon your request, cousin, in any reason.

Shal. Nay, conceive me, conceive me, sweet coz: what I do is to pleasure you, coz. Can you love the maid?

Slen. I will marry her, sir, at your request: but if there be no great love in the beginning, yet heaven may decrease it upon better acquaintance, when we are married and have more occasion to know one another; I hope, upon familiarity will grow more contempt: but if you say, "marry her," I will marry her; that I am freely dissolved, and dissolutely.

Evans. It is a fery discretion answer; save the faul is in the ort "dissolutely:" the ort is, according to our meaning, "resolutely:" — his meaning is goot.

Shal. Ay, I think my cousin meant well.

Slen. Ay, or else I would I might be hanged, la.

Shal. Here comes fair Mistress Anne.

Re-enter ANNE PAGE.

Would I were young for your sake, Mistress Anne!

Anne. The dinner is on the table; my father desires your worships' company.

Shal. I will wait on him, fair Mistress Anne.

Evans. Od's plessed will! I will not be absence at the grace.   [*Exeunt Shallow and Sir H. Evans.*

Anne. Will't please your worship to come in, sir?

Slen. No, I thank you, forsooth, heartily; I am very well.

Anne. The dinner attends you, sir.

Slen. I am not a-hungry, I thank you, forsooth. — Go, sirrah, for all you are my man, go wait upon my cousin Shallow. [*Exit Simple.*] A justice of peace sometime may be beholding to his friend for a man. — I keep but three men and a boy yet, till my mother be dead: but what though? yet I live like a poor gentleman born.

Anne. I may not go in without your worship: they will not sit till you come.

Slen. I' faith, I'll eat nothing; I thank you as much as though I did.

Anne. I pray you, sir, walk in.

Slen. I had rather walk here, I thank you. I bruised my shin th' other day with playing at sword and dagger with a master of fence, — three veneys for a dish of stewed prunes;

and, by my troth, I cannot abide the smell of hot meat since.
— Why do your dogs bark so? be there bears i' the town?

Anne. I think there are, sir; I heard them talked of.

Slen. I love the sport well; but I shall as soon quarrel
at it as any man in Eugland. — You are afraid, if you see the
bear loose, are you not?

Anne. Ay, indeed, sir.

Slen. That's meat and drink to me, now. I have seen
Sackerson loose twenty times, and have taken him by the
chain; but, I warrant you, the women have so cried and
shricked at it, that it passed: — but women, indeed, cannot
abide 'em; they are very ill-favoured rough things.

Re-enter PAGE.

Page. Come, gentle Master Slender, come; we stay for
you.

Slen. I'll eat nothing, I thank you, sir.

Page. By cock and pie, you shall not choose, sir: come,
come.

Slen. Nay, pray you, lead the way.

Page. Come on, sir.

Slen. Mistress Anne, yourself shall go first

Anne. Not I, sir; pray you, keep on.

Slen. Truly, I will not go first; truly, la; I will not do
you that wrong.

Anne. I pray you, sir.

Slen. I'll rather be unmannerly than troublesome. You
do yourself wrong, indeed, la.   [*Exeunt.*

SCENE II. *An outer room in* PAGE's *house.*

Enter SIR HUGH EVANS *and* SIMPLE.

Evans. Go your ways, and ask of Doctor Caius' house
which is the way: and there dwells one Mistress Quickly,
which is in the manner of his nurse, or his try nurse, or his
cook, or his laundry, his washer, and his wringer.

Sim. Well, sir.

Evans. Nay, it is petter yet. — Give her this letter; for it is a oman that altogether's acquaintance with Mistress Anne Page: and the letter is, to desire and require her to solicit your master's desires to Mistress Anne Page. I pray you, be gone: I will make an end of my dinner; there's pippins and seese to come.   [*Exeunt.*

SCENE III. *A room in the Garter Inn.*

Enter FALSTAFF, Host, BARDOLPH, NYM, PISTOL, *and* ROBIN.

Fal. Mine host of the Garter, —

Host. What says my bully-rook? speak scholarly and wisely.

Fal. Truly, mine host, I must turn away some of my followers.

Host. Discard, bully Hercules; cashier: let them wag; trot, trot.

Fal. I sit at ten pounds a-week.

Host. Thou'rt an emperor, Cæsar, Keisar, and Pheezar. I will entertain Bardolph; he shall draw, he shall tap: said I well, bully Hector?

Fal. Do so, good mine host.

Host. I have spoke; let him follow. — Let me see thee froth and lime: I am at a word; follow.   [*Exit.*

Fal. Bardolph, follow him. A tapster is a good trade: an old cloak makes a new jerkin; a withered serving-man a fresh tapster. Go; adieu.

Bard. It is a life that I have desired: I will thrive.

Pist. O base Hungarian wight! wilt thou the spigot wield?
                    [*Exit Bardolph.*

Nym. He was gotten in drink: is not the humour conceited?

Fal. I am glad I am so acquit of this tinder-box: his thefts were too open; his filching was like an unskilful singer, — he kept not time.

Nym. The good humour is to steal at a minim's rest.

Pist. "Convey" the wise it call. "Steal"! foh! a fico for the phrase!

Fal. Well, sirs, I am almost out at heels.

Pist. Why, then, let kibes ensue.

Fal. There is no remedy; I must cony-catch; I must shift.

Pist. Young ravens must have food.

Fal. Which of you know Ford of this town?

Pist. I ken the wight: he is of substance good.

Fal. My honest lads, I will tell you what I am about.

Pist. Two yards, and more.

Fal. No quips now, Pistol:—indeed, I am in the waist two yards about; but I am now about no waste; I am about thrift. Briefly, I do mean to make love to Ford's wife: I spy entertainment in her; she discourses, she carves, she gives the leer of invitation: I can construe the action of her familiar style; and the hardest voice of her behaviour, to be Englished rightly, is, "I am Sir John Falstaff's."

Pist. He hath studied her well, and translated her well, — out of honesty into English.

Nym. The anchor is deep: will that humour pass?

Fal. Now, the report goes she has all the rule of her husband's purse: — he hath a legion of angels.

Pist. As many devils entertain; and, "To her, boy," say I.

Nym. The humour rises; it is good: humour me the angels.

Fal. I have writ me here a letter to her: and here another to Page's wife, who even now gave me good eyes too, examined my parts with most judicious œilliads; sometimes the beam of her view gilded my foot, sometimes my portly belly.

Pist. Then did the sun on dunghill shine.

Nym. I thank thee for that humour.

Fal. O, she did so course o'er my exteriors with such a greedy intention, that the appetite of her eye did seem to scorch me up like a burning-glass! Here's another letter to her: she bears the purse too; she is a region in Guiana, all gold and bounty. I will be cheater to them both, and they shall be exchequers to me; they shall be my East and West

Indies, and I will trade to them both. Go bear thou this
letter to Mistress Page ; and thou this to Mistress Ford: we
will thrive, lads, we will thrive.

Pist.   Shall I Sir Pandarus of Troy become,
And by my side wear steel? then, Lucifer take all!

Nym.   I will run no base humour: here, take the humour-
letter: I will keep the haviour of reputation.

Fal. [*to Robin*] Hold, sirrah, bear you these letters tightly;
Sail like my pinnace to the golden shores. —   [*Exit Robin*
Rogues, hence, avaunt! vanish like hailstones, go;
Trudge, plod away o' th' hoof; seek shelter, pack!
Falstaff will learn the humour of the age,
French thrift, you rogues; myself and skirted page.   [*Exit.*

Pist.   Let vultures gripe thy guts! for gourd and fullam
            hold,
And high and low beguile the rich and poor:
Tester I'll have in pouch when thou shalt lack,
Base Phrygian Turk!

Nym.   I have operations in my head, which be humours
of revenge.

Pist.   Wilt thou revenge? ·

Nym.   By welkin and her stars!

Pist.   With wit or steel?

Nym.   With both the humours, I:
I will discuss the humour of this love to Page.

Pist.   And I to Ford shall eke unfold
            How Falstaff, varlet vile,
            His dove will prove, his gold will hold,
            And his soft couch defile.

Nym.   My humour shall not cool: I will incense Page
to deal with poison; I will possess him with yellowness, for
this revolt of mine is dangerous: that is my true humour.

Pist.   Thou art the Mars of malcontents: I second thee;
troop on.   [*Exeunt.*

SCENE IV. *A room in* DOCTOR CAIUS'S *house.*

Enter MISTRESS QUICKLY *and* SIMPLE.

Quick. What, John Rugby!

Enter RUGBY.

I pray thee, go to the casement, and see if you can see my master, Master Doctor Caius, coming. If he do, i' faith, and find any body in the house, here will be an old abusing of God's patience and the king's English.

Rug. I'll go watch.

Quick. Go; and we'll have a posset for't soon at night, in faith, at the latter end of a sea-coal fire. [*Exit Rugby.*] An honest, willing, kind fellow, as ever servant shall come in house withal; and, I warrant you, no tell-tale nor no breed-bate: his worst fault is, that he is given to prayer; he is something peevish that way: but nobody but has his fault; — but let that pass. — Peter Simple you say your name is?

Sim. Ay, for fault of a better.

Quick. And Master Slender's your master?

Sim. Ay, forsooth.

Quick. Does he not wear a great round beard, like a glover's paring-knife?

Sim. No, forsooth: he hath but a little wee face, with a little yellow beard, — a Cain-coloured beard.

Quick. A softly-sprighted man, is he not?

Sim. Ay, forsooth: but he is as tall a man of his hands as any is between this and his head; he hath fought with a warrener.

Quick. How say you? — O, I should remember him: does he not hold up his head, as it were, and strut in his gait?

Sim. Yes, indeed, does he.

Quick. Well, heaven send Anne Page no worse fortune! Tell Master Parson Evans I will do what I can for your master: Anne is a good girl, and I wish —

Re-enter RUGBY.

Rug. Out, alas! here comes my master.

Quick. We shall all be shent. [*Exit Rugby.*] — Run in here, good young man; go into this closet:—he will not stay long. [*Shuts Simple in the closet.*] — What, John Rugby! John! what, John, I say! Go, John, go inquire for my master; I doubt he be not well, that he comes not home. [*Sings.*

   And down, down, adown-a, &c.

Enter Doctor Caius.

Caius. Vat is you sing? I do not like dese toys. Pray you, go and vetch me in my closet *un boîtier vert,* — a box, a green-a box: do intend vat I speak? a green-a box.

Quick. Ay, forsooth; I'll fetch it you. — [*Aside*] I am glad he went not in himself: if he had found the young man, he would have been horn-mad.

Caius. Fe, fe, fe, fe! ma foi, il fait fort chaud. Je m'en vais à la cour, — la grande affaire.

Quick. Is it this, sir?

Caius. Oui; mette le au mon pocket: dépêche, quickly. — Vere is dat knave Rugby?

Quick. What, John Rugby! John!

Re-enter Rugby.

Rug. Here, sir.

Caius. You are John Rugby, and you are Jack Rugby. Come, take-a your rapier, and come after my heel to de court.

Rug. 'Tis ready, sir, here in the porch.

Caius. By my trot, I tarry too long. — Od's me! Qu'ai-j'oublié! dere is some simples in my closet, dat I vill not for de varld I shall leave behind.

Quick. Ay me, he'll find the young man there, and be mad!

Caius. O diable, diable! vat is in my closet? Villain! larron! [*Pulling Simple out.*] — Rugby, my rapier!

Quick. Good master, be content.

Caius. Verefore shall I be content-a?

Quick. The young man is an honest man.

Caius. Vat shall de honest man do in my closet? dere is no honest man dat shall come in my closet.

Quick. I beseech you, be not so phlegmatic. Hear the truth of it: he came of an errand to me from Parson Hugh.

Caius. Vell.

Sim. Ay, forsooth; to desire her to —

Quick. Peace, I pray you.

Caius. Peace-a your tongue. — Speak-a your tale.

Sim. To desire this honest gentlewoman, your maid, to speak a good word to Mistress Anne Page for my master in the way of marriage.

Quick. This is all, indeed, la; but I'll ne'er put my finger in the fire, and need not.

Caius. Sir Hugh send-a you? — Rugby, *baillez* me some paper. — Tarry you a little-a while. [*Writes.*

Quick. I am glad he is so quiet: if he had been throughly moved, you should have heard him so loud and so melancholy. — But notwithstanding, man, I'll do for your master what good I can: and the very yea and the no is, the French doctor, my master, — I may call him my master, look you, for I keep his house; and I wash, wring, brew, bake, scour, dress meat and drink, make the beds, and do all myself, —

Sim. 'Tis a great charge to come under one body's hand.

Quick. Are you avised o' that? you shall find it a great charge: and to be up early and down late; — but notwithstanding, to tell you in your ear, — I would have no words of it, — my master himself is in love with Mistress Anne Page: but notwithstanding that, I know Anne's mind, — that's neither here nor there.

Caius. You jack'nape, — give-a dis letter to Sir Hugh; by gar, it is a shallenge: I vill cut his troat in de park; and I vill teach a scurvy jack-a-nape priest to meddle or make: — you may be gone; it is not good you tarry here: — by gar, I vill cut all his two stones; by gar, he shall not have a stone to trow at his dog. [*Exit Simple.*

Quick. Alas, he speaks but for his friend.

Caius. It is no matter-a for dat: — do not you tell-a me dat I shall have Anne Page for myself? — by gar, I vill kill de Jack priest; and I have appointed mine host of de

Jartecr to measure our weapon: — by gar, I vill myself have
Anne Page.

Quick. Sir, the maid loves you, and all shall be well. We
must give folks leave to prate: what, the good-jer!

Caius. Rugby, come to de court vit me. — By gar, if I
have not Anne Page, I shall turn your head out of my door.
— Follow my heels, Rugby.   [*Exeunt Caius and Rugby.*

Quick. You shall have An fool's-head of your own. No,
I know Anne's mind for that: never a woman in Windsor
knows more of Anne's mind than I do; nor can do more than
I do with her, I thank heaven.

Fent. [*within*] Who's within there? ho!

Quick. Who's there, I trow? Come near the house, I
pray you.

Enter Fenton

Fent. How now, good woman! how dost thou?

Quick. The better that it pleases your good worship to ask.

Fent. What news? how does pretty Mistress Anne?

Quick. In truth, sir, and she is pretty, and honest, and
gentle; and one that is your friend, I can tell you that by
the way; I praise heaven for it.

Fent. Shall I do any good, thinkest thou? shall I not lose
my suit?

Quick. Troth, sir, all is in his hands above: but notwithstanding, Master Fenton, I'll be sworn on a book, she loves
you. — Have not your worship a wart above your eye?

Fent. Yes, marry, have I; what of that?

Quick. Well, thereby hangs a tale: — good faith, it is such
another Nan; — but, I detest, an honest maid as ever broke
bread: — we had an hour's talk of that wart: — I shall never
laugh but in that maid's company! — But, indeed, she is given
too much to allicholy and musing: but for you — well, go to.

Fent. Well, I shall see her to-day. Hold, there's money
for thee; let me have thy voice in my behalf: if thou see'st
her before me, commend me.

Quick. Will I? i' faith, that we will; and I will tell your

worship more of the wart the next time we have confidence;
and of other wooers.

Fent. Well, farewell; I am in great haste now.

Quick. Farewell to your worship. [*Exit Fenton.*] Truly,
an honest gentleman: but Anne loves him not; for I know
Anne's mind as well as another does. — Out upon't! what have
I forgot?   [*Exit.*

ACT II.

Scene I. *Before Page's house.*

Enter Mistress Page, *with a letter.*

Mrs. Page. What, have I scaped love-letters in the holi-
day-time of my beauty, and am I now a subject for them? Let
me see.   [*Reads.*

"Ask me no reason why I love you; for though Love use
Reason for his physician, he admits him not for his counsellor.
You are not young, no more am I; go to, then, there's sympathy: you are merry, so am I; ha, ha! then there's more
sympathy: you love sack, and so do I; would you desire better
sympathy? Let it suffice thee, Mistress Page, — at the least,
if the love of a soldier can suffice, — that I love thee. I will
not say, pity me, — 'tis not a soldier-like phrase; but I say,
love me. By me,

> Thine own true knight,
> By day or night,
> Or any kind of light,
> With all his might
> For thee to fight,   *John Falstaff.*"

What a Herod of Jewry is this! — O wicked, wicked world! —
one that is well-nigh worn to pieces with age to show himself
a young gallant! What unweighed behaviour hath this
Flemish drunkard picked — with the devil's name — out of
my conversation, that he dares in this manner assay me?
Why, he hath not been thrice in my company! — What should
I say to him? — I was then frugal of my mirth: — Heaven

forgive me! — Why, I'll exhibit a bill in the parliament for the putting-down of fat men. How shall I be revenged on him? for revenged I will be, as sure as his guts are made of puddings.

Enter MISTRESS FORD.

Mrs. Ford. Mistress Page! trust me, I was going to your house.

Mrs. Page. And, trust me, I was coming to you. You look very ill.

Mrs. Ford. Nay, I'll ne'er believe that; I have to show to the contrary.

Mrs. Page. Faith, but you do, in my mind.

Mrs. Ford. Well, I do, then; yet, I say, I could show you to the contrary. O Mistress Page, give me some counsel!

Mrs. Page. What's the matter, woman?

Mrs. Ford. O woman, if it were not for one trifling respect, I could come to such honour!

Mrs. Page. Hang the trifle, woman! take the honour. What is it? — dispense with trifles; — what is it?

Mrs. Ford. If I would but go to hell for an eternal moment or so, I could be knighted.

Mrs. Page. What? thou liest! — Sir Alice Ford! These knights will hack; and so thou shouldst not alter the article of thy gentry.

Mrs. Ford. We burn daylight: — here, read, read; perceive how I might be knighted. — I shall think the worse of fat men, as long as I have an eye to make difference of men's liking: and yet he would not swear; praised women's modesty; and gave such orderly and well-behaved reproof to all uncomeliness, that I would have sworn his disposition would have gone to the truth of his words; but they do no more adhere and keep pace together than the Hundredth Psalm to the tune of *Green sleeves*. What tempest, I trow, threw this whale, with so many tuns of oil in his belly, ashore at Windsor? How shall I be revenged on him? I think the best way were to entertain him with hope, till the wicked fire of lust have melted him in his own grease. — Did you ever hear the like?

Mrs. Page. Letter for letter, but that the name of Page and Ford differs! — To thy great comfort in this mystery of ill opinions, here's the twin-brother of thy letter: but let thine inherit first; for, I protest, mine never shall. I warrant he hath a thousand of these letters, writ with blank space for different names, — sure, more, — and these are of the second edition: he will print them, out of doubt; for he cares not what he puts into the press, when he would put us two. I had rather be a giantess, and lie under Mount Pelion. Well, I will find you twenty lascivious turtles, ere one chaste man.

Mrs. Ford. Why, this is the very same; the very hand, the very words. What doth he think of us?

Mrs. Page. Nay, I know not: it makes me almost ready to wrangle with mine own honesty. I'll entertain myself like one that I am not acquainted withal; for, sure, unless he know some strain in me, that I know not myself, he would never have boarded me in this fury.

Mrs. Ford. Boarding, call you it? I'll be sure to keep him above deck.

Mrs. Page. So will I: if he come under my hatches, I'll never to sea again. Let's be revenged on him: let's appoint him a meeting; give him a show of comfort in his suit; and lead him on with a fine-baited delay, till he hath pawned his horses to mine host of the Garter.

Mrs. Ford. Nay, I will consent to act any villany against him, that may not sully the chariness of our honesty. O, that my husband saw this letter! it would give eternal food to his jealousy.

Mrs. Page. Why, look where he comes; — and my good man too: he's as far from jealousy as I am from giving him cause; and that, I hope, is an unmeasurable distance.

Mrs. Ford. You are the happier woman.

Mrs. Page. Let's consult together against this greasy knight. Come hither   [*They retire.*

Enter FORD, PISTOL, PAGE, *and* NYM.

Ford. Well, I hope it be not so.

15*

Pist. Hope is a curtal dog in some affairs:
Sir John affects thy wife.

Ford. Why, sir, my wife is not young.

Pist. He wooes both high and low, both rich and poor,
Both young and old, one with another, Ford;
He loves the gallimaufry: Ford, perpend.

Ford. Love my wife!

Pist. With liver burning hot. Prevent, or go thou,
Like Sir Actæon he, with Ringwood at thy heels: —
O, odious is the name!

Ford. What name, sir?

Pist. The horn, I say. Farewell.
Take heed; have open eye; for thieves do foot by night:
Take heed, ere summer comes, or cuckoo-birds do sing. —
Away, Sir Corporal Nym! —
Believe it, Page; he speaks sense.   [*Exit.*

Ford. [*aside*] I will be patient; I will find out this.

Nym. [*to Page*] And this is true; I like not the humour of
lying. He hath wronged me in some humours: I should have
borne the humoured letter to her; but I have a sword, and it
shall bite upon my necessity. He loves your wife; there's
the short and the long. My name is Corporal Nym; I speak,
and I avouch 'tis true: my name is Nym, and Falstaff loves
your wife. — Adieu. I love not the humour of bread and
cheese; and there's the humour of it. Adieu.   [*Exit.*

Page. [*aside*] "The humour of it," quoth 'a! here's a fellow
frights humour out of his wits.

Ford. [*aside*] I will seek out Falstaff.

Page. [*aside*] I never heard such a drawling, affecting rogue.

Ford. [*aside*] If I do find it: — well.

Page. [*aside*] I will not believe such a Cataian, though the
priest o' the town commended him for a true man.

Ford. [*aside*] 'Twas a good sensible fellow: — well.

       [*Mistress Page and Mistress Ford come forward.*

Page. How now, Meg!

Mrs. Page. Whither go you, George? — Hark you.

Mrs. Ford. How now, sweet Frank! why art thou melancholy?

Ford. I melancholy! I am not melancholy. — Get you home, go.

Mrs. Ford. Faith, thou hast some crotchet in thy head now. — Will you go, Mistress Page?

Mrs. Page. Have with you. — You'll come to dinner, George? — [*Aside to Mrs. Ford*] Look who comes yonder: she shall be our messenger to this paltry knight.

Mrs. Ford. [*aside to Mrs. Page*] Trust me, I thought on her: she'll fit it.

Enter MISTRESS QUICKLY.

Mrs. Page. You are come to see my daughter Anne?

Quick. Ay, forsooth; and, I pray, how does good Mistress Anne?

Mrs. Page. Go in with us and see: we have an hour's talk with you.

[*Exeunt Mistress Page, Mistress Ford, and Mistress Quickly.*

Page. How now, Master Ford!

Ford. You heard what this knave told me, did you not?

Page. Yes: and you heard what the other told me?

Ford. Do you think there is truth in them?

Page. Hang 'em, slaves! I do not think the knight would offer it: but these that accuse him in his intent towards our wives are a yoke of his discarded men; very rogues, now they be out of service.

Ford. Were they his men?

Page. Marry, were they.

Ford. I like it never the better for that. — Does he lie at the Garter?

Page. Ay, marry, does he. If he should intend this voyage toward my wife, I would turn her loose to him; and what he gets more of her than sharp words, let it lie on my head.

Ford. I do not misdoubt my wife; but I would be loth to turn them together. A man may be too confident: I would have nothing lie on my head: I cannot be thus satisfied.

Page. Look where my ranting host of the Garter comes:

there is either liquor in his pate, or money in his purse, when he looks so merrily.

Enter Host.

How now, mine host!

Host. How now, bully-rook! thou'rt a gentleman. — Cavalero-justice, I say!

Enter SHALLOW.

Shal. I follow, mine host, I follow. — Good even and twenty, good Master Page! Master Page, will you go with us? we have sport in hand.

Host. Tell him, cavalero-justice; tell him, bully-rook.

Shal. Sir, there is a fray to be fought between Sir Hugh the Welsh priest and Caius the French doctor.

Ford. Good mine host o' the Garter, a word with you.

Host. What sayest thou, my bully-rook? [*They go aside.*

Shal. [*to Page.*] Will you go with us to behold it? My merry host hath had the measuring of their weapons; and, I think, hath appointed them contrary places; for, believe me, I hear the parson is no jester. Hark, I will tell you what our sport shall be.   [*They go aside.*

Host. Hast thou no suit against my knight, my guest-cavalier?

Ford. None, I protest: but I'll give you a pottle of burnt sack to give me recourse to him, and tell him my name is Brook; only for a jest.

Host. My hand, bully; thou shalt have egress and regress; — said I well? — and thy name shall be Brook. It is a merry knight. — Will you go, mynheers?

Shal. Have with you, mine host.

Page. I have heard the Frenchman hath good skill in his rapier.

Shal. Tut, sir, I could have told you more. In these times you stand on distance, your passes, stoccadoes, and I know not what: 'tis the heart, Master Page; 'tis here, 'tis here. I have seen the time, with my long sword I would have made you four tall fellows skip like rats.

Host. Here, boys, here, here! shall we wag?

Page. Have with you. — I had rather hear them scold than see them fight.　　　　　　　[*Exeunt Host, Shal., and Page.*

Ford. Though Page be a secure fool, and stands so firmly on his wife's frailty, yet I cannot put off my opinion so easily: she was in his company at Page's house; and what they made there, I know not. Well, I will look further into't: and I have a disguise to sound Falstaff. If I find her honest, I lose not my labour; if she be otherwise, 'tis labour well bestowed.　　　　　　　　　　　[*Exit.*

SCENE II. *A room in the Garter Inn.*

Enter FALSTAFF *and* PISTOL.

Fal. I will not lend thee a penny.

Pist. Why, then the world's mine oyster,
Which I with sword will open.

Fal. Not a penny. I have been content, sir, you should lay my countenance to pawn: I have grated upon my good friends for three reprieves for you and your coach-fellow Nym; or else you had looked through the grate, like a geminy of baboons. I am damned in hell for swearing to gentlemen my friends, you were good soldiers and tall fellows; and when Mistress Bridget lost the handle of her fan, I took't upon mine honour thou hadst it not.

Pist. Didst not thou share? hadst thou not fifteen pence?

Fal. Reason, you rogue, reason: thinkest thou I'll endanger my soul gratis? At a word, hang no more about me, I am no gibbet for you: — go: — a short knife and a throng; — to your manor of Pickt-hatch, go. — You'll not bear a letter for me, you rogue! — you stand upon your honour! — Why, thou unconfinable baseness, it is as much as I can do to keep the terms of my honour precise: I, I, I myself sometimes, leaving the fear of God on the left hand, and hiding mine honour in my necessity, am fain to shuffle, to hedge, and to lurch; and yet you, rogue, will ensconce your rags, your cat-a-mountain looks, your red-lattice phrases, and your bull-

baiting oaths, under the shelter of your honour! You will
not do it, you!

Pist. I do relent: — what would thou more of man?

Enter ROBIN.

Rob. Sir, here's a woman would speak with you.

Fal. Let her approach.

Enter MISTRESS QUICKLY.

Quick. Give your worship good morrow.

Fal. Good morrow, good wife.

Quick. Not so, an't please your worship.

Fal. Good maid, then.

Quick. I'll be sworn;
As my mother was, the first hour I was born.

Fal. I do believe the swearer. What with me?

Quick. Shall I vouchsafe your worship a word or two?

Fal. Two thousand, fair woman: and l'll vouchsafe thee
the hearing.

Quick. There is one Mistress Ford, sir: — I pray, come a
little nearer this ways: — I myself dwell with Master Doctor
Caius, —

Fal. Well, one Mistress Ford, you say, —

Quick. Your worship says very true: — I pray your worship, come a little nearer this ways.

Fal. I warrant thee, nobody hears; — mine own people,
mine own people.

Quick. Are they so? God bless them, and make them his
servants!

Fal. Well, Mistress Ford; — what of her?

Quick. Why, sir, she's a good creature. — Lord, Lord!
your worship's a wanton! Well, heaven forgive you, and all
of us, I pray! —

Fal. Mistress Ford; — come, Mistress Ford, —

Quick. Marry, this is the short and the long of it; you
have brought her into such a canaries as 'tis wonderful. The
best courtier of them all, when the court lay at Windsor,
could never have brought her to such a canary. Yet there

has been knights, and lords, and gentlemen, with their
coaches; I warrant you, coach after coach, letter after letter,
gift after gift; smelling so sweetly—all musk—and so rush-
ling, I warrant you, in silk and gold; and in such alligant
terms; and such wine and sugar of the best and the fairest,
that would have won any woman's heart; and, I warrant you,
they could never get an eye-wink of her: — I had myself
twenty angels given me this morning; but I defy all angels
— in any such sort, as they say—but in the way of honesty:
— and, I warrant you, they could never get her so much as
sip on a cup with the proudest of them all: and yet there has
been earls, nay, which is more, pensioners; but, I warrant
you, all is one with her.

Fal. But what says she to me? be brief, my good she-
Mercury.

Quick. Marry, she hath received your letter; for the which
she thanks you a thousand times; and she gives you to notify,
that her husband will be absence from his house between ten
and eleven.

Fal. Ten and eleven?

Quick. Ay, forsooth; and then you may come and see the
picture, she says, that you wot of; — Master Ford, her husband,
will be from home. Alas, the sweet woman leads an ill life
with him! he's a very jealousy man: she leads a very frampold
life with him, good heart.

Fal. Ten and eleven: — woman, commend me to her; I
will not fail her.

Quick. Why, you say well. But I have another messenger
to your worship. Mistress Page hath her hearty commendations to you, too: — and let me tell you in your ear, she's as
fartuous a civil modest wife, and one, I tell you, that will not
miss you morning nor evening prayer, as any is in Windsor,
whoe'er be the other: — and she bade me tell your worship
that her husband is seldom from home; but, she hopes, there
will come a time. I never knew a woman so dote upon a
man: surely, I think you have charms, la; yes, in truth.

Fal.   Not I, I assure thee: setting the attraction of my good parts aside, I have no other charms.

Quick.   Blessing on your heart for't!

Fal.   But, I pray thee, tell me this, — has Ford's wife and Page's wife acquainted each other how they love me?

Quick.   That were a jest indeed! — they have not so little grace, I hope:—that were a trick indeed!—But Mistress Page would desire you to send her your little page, of all loves: her husband has a marvellous infection to the little page; and, truly, Master Page is an honest man.   Never a wife in Windsor leads a better life than she does: do what she will, say what she will, take all, pay all, go to bed when she list, rise when she list, all is as she will: and, truly, she deserves it; for if there be a kind woman in Windsor, she is one.   You must send her your page; no remedy.

Fal.   Why, I will.

Quick.   Nay, but do so, then: and, look you, he may come and go between you both; and, in any case, have a nay-word, that you may know one another's mind, and the boy never need to understand any thing; for 'tis not good that children should know any wickedness: old folks, you know, have dis-crètion, as they say, and know the world.

Fal.   Fare thee well: commend me to them both: there's my purse; I am yet thy debtor. — Boy, go along with this woman.   [*Exeunt Mistress Quickly and Robin.*] — This news distracts me!

Pist.   This punk is one of Cupid's carriers: —
Clap on more sails; pursue; up with your fights;
Give fire; she is my prize, or ocean whelm them all!   [*Exit.*

Fal.   Sayest thou so, old Jack? go thy ways; I'll make more of thy old body than I have done.   Will they yet look after thee?   Wilt thou, after the expense of so much money, be now a gainer?   Good body, I thank thee.   Let them say 'tis grossly done; so it be fairly done, no matter.

Enter BARDOLPH, *with a cup of sack.*

Bard.   Sir John, there's one Master Brook below would

fain speak with you, and be acquainted with you; and hath
sent your worship a morning's draught of sack.

Fal. Brook is his name?

Bard. Ay, sir.

Fal. Call him in. [*Exit Bardolph.*] Such Brooks are welcome to me, that o'erflow such liquor. — Ah, ha! Mistress
Ford and Mistress Page, have I encompassed you? go to; *via!*

Re-enter Bardolph, *with* Ford *disguised.*

Ford. Bless you, sir!

Fal. And you, sir! Would you speak with me?

Ford. I make bold to press with so little preparation upon
you.

Fal. You're welcome. What's your will? — Give us leave,
drawer.   [*Exit Bardolph.*

Ford. Sir, I am a gentleman that have spent much; my
name is Brook.

Fal. Good Master Brook, I desire more acquaintance of you.

Ford. Good Sir John, I sue for yours: not to charge you;
for I must let you understand I think myself in better plight
for a lender than you are: the which hath something embold-
ened me to this unseasoned intrusion; for they say, if money
go before, all ways do lie open.

Fal. Money is a good soldier, sir, and will on.

Ford. Troth, and I have a bag of money here troubles me:
if you will help to bear it, Sir John, take all, or half, for
easing me of the carriage.

Fal. Sir, I know not how I may deserve to be your porter.

Ford. I will tell you, sir, if you will give me the hearing.

Fal. Speak, good Master Brook: I shall be glad to be your
servant.

Ford. Sir, I hear you are a scholar, — I will be brief with
you; — and you have been a man long known to me, though
I had never so good means, as desire, to make myself ac-
quainted with you. I shall discover a thing to you, wherein
I must very much lay open mine own imperfection: but, good
Sir John, as you have one eye upon my follies, as you hear

them unfolded, turn another into the register of your own; that I may pass with a reproof the easier, sith you yourself know how easy it is to be such an offender.

Fal. Very well, sir; proceed.

Ford. There is a gentlewoman in this town, her husband's name is Ford.

Fal. Well, sir.

Ford. I have long loved her, and, I protest to you, bestowed much on her; followed her with a doting observance; engrossed opportunities to meet her; fee'd every slight occasion that could but niggardly give me sight of her; not only bought many presents to give her, but have given largely to many to know what she would have given; briefly, I have pursued her as love hath pursued me; which hath been on the wing of all occasions. But whatsoever I have merited, either in my mind or in my means, meed, I am sure, I have received none; unless experience be a jewel: that I have purchased at an infinite rate; and that hath taught me to say this;

Love like a shadow flies when substance love pursues;
Pursuing that that flies, and flying what pursues.

Fal. Have you received no promise of satisfaction at her hands?

Ford. Never.

Fal. Have you importuned her to such a purpose?

Ford. Never.

Fal. Of what quality was your love, then?

Ford. Like a fair house built on another man's ground; so that I have lost my edifice by mistaking the place where I erected it.

Fal. To what purpose have you unfolded this to me?

Ford. When I have told you that, I have told you all. Some say, that though she appear honest to me, yet in other places she enlargeth her mirth so far that there is shrewd construction made of her. Now, Sir John, here is the heart of my purpose: you are a gentleman of excellent breeding, admirable discourse, of great admittance, authentic in your

place and person, generally allowed for your many war-like,
court-like, and learned preparations, —

Fal. O, sir!

Ford. Believe it, for you know it. — There is money; spend
it, spend it; spend more; spend all I have; only give me so
much of your time in exchange of it, as to lay an amiable
siege to the honesty of this Ford's wife: use your art of wooing; win her to consent to you: if any man may, you may as
soon as any.

Fal. Would it apply well to the vehemency of your affection, that I should win what you would enjoy? Methinks you
prescribe to yourself very preposterously.

Ford. O, understand my drift. She dwells so securely
on the excellency of her honour, that the folly of my soul
dares not present itself: she is too bright to be looked against.
Now, could I come to her with any detection in my hand, my
desires had instance and argument to commend themselves: I
could drive her then from the ward of her purity, her reputation, her marriage-vow, and a thousand other her defences,
which now are too-too strongly embattled against me. What
say you to't, Sir John?

Fal. Master Brook, I will first make bold with your money;
next, give me your hand; and last, as I am a gentleman, you
shall, if you will, enjoy Ford's wife.

Ford. O good sir!

Fal. I say you shall.

Ford. Want no money, Sir John; you shall want none.

Fal. Want no Mistress Ford, Master Brook; you shall
want none. I shall be with her — I may tell you — by her
own appointment; even as you came in to me, her assistant,
or go-between, parted from me: I say I shall be with her
between ten and eleven; for at that time the jealous rascally
knave her husband will be forth. Come you to me at night;
you shall know how I speed.

Ford. I am blest in your acquaintance. Do you know
Ford, sir?

Fal. Hang him, poor cuckoldly knave! I know him not:

— yet I wrong him to call him poor; they say the jealous
wittolly knave hath masses of money; for the which his wife
seems to me well-favoured.   I will use her as the key of the
cuckoldly rogue's coffer; and there's my harvest-home.

Ford.   I would you knew Ford, sir, that you might avoid
him, if you saw him.

Fal. Hang him, mechanical salt-butter rogue!   I will
stare him out of his wits; I will awe him with my cudgel, —
it shall hang like a meteor o'er the cuckold's horns.   Master
Brook, thou shalt know I will predominate over the peasant,
and thou shalt lie with his wife.—Come to me soon at night:
—Ford's a knave, and I will aggravate his style; thou, Master
Brook, shalt know him for knave and cuckold:— come to me
soon at night.   [*Exit.*

Ford. What a damned Epicurean rascal is this!—My heart
is ready to crack with impatience.— Who says this is improvi-
dent jealousy? my wife hath sent to him, the hour is fixed, the
match is made. Would any man have thought this?—See the
hell of having a false woman!   My bed shall be abused, my
coffers ransacked, my reputation gnawn at; and I shall not
only receive this villanous wrong, but stand under the adop-
tion of abominable terms, and by him that does me this wrong.
Terms! names!—Amaimon sounds well; Lucifer, well; Barbason, well; yet they are devils' additions, the names of fiends:
but cuckold! wittol-cuckold! the devil himself hath not such
a name.   Page is an ass, a secure ass: he will trust his wife;
he will not be jealous. I will rather trust a Fleming with my
butter, Parson Hugh the Welshman with my cheese, an Irish-
man with my aqua-vitæ bottle, or a thief to walk my ambling
gelding, than my wife with herself: then she plots, then she
ruminates, then she devises; and what they think in their
hearts they may effect, they will break their hearts but they
will effect.   Heaven be praised for my jealousy! — Eleven
o'clock the hour: — I will prevent this, detect my wife, be
revenged on Falstaff, and laugh at Page. I will about it;
better three hours too soon than a minute too late. Fie, fie,
fie! cuckold! cuckold! cuckold!   [*Exit.*

SCENE III. *A field near Windsor.*

Enter CAIUS *and* RUGBY.

Caius. Jack Rugby, —

Rug. Sir?

Caius. Vat is de clock, Jack?

Rug. 'Tis past the hour, sir, that Sir Hugh promised to meet.

Caius. By gar, he has save his soul, dat he is no come; he has pray his Pible vell, dat he is no come: by gar, Jack Rugby, he is dead already, if he be come.

Rug. He is wise, sir; he knew your worship would kill him, if he came.

Caius. By gar, de herring is no dead so as I vill kill him. Take your rapier, Jack; I vill tell you how I vill kill him.

Rug. Alas, sir, I cannot fence.

Caius. Villain, take your rapier.

Rug. Forbear; here's company.

Enter HOST, SHALLOW, SLENDER, *and* PAGE.

Host. Bless thee, bully doctor!

Shal. Save you, Master Doctor Caius!

Page. Now, good master doctor!

Slen. Give you good morrow, sir.

Caius. Vat be all you, one, two, tree, four, come for?

Host. To see thee fight, to see thee foin, to see thee traverse; to see thee here, to see thee there; to see thee pass thy punto, thy stock, thy reserve, thy distance, thy montánt. Is he dead, my Ethiopian? is he dead, my Francisco? ha, bully! What says my Æsculapius? my Galen? my heart of elder? ha! is he dead, bully Stale? is he dead?

Caius. By gar, he is de coward Jack priest of de varld; he is not show his face.

Host. Thou art a Castilian, King Urinal! Hector of Greece, my boy!

Caius. I pray you, bear vitness that me have stay six or seven, two, tree hours for him, and he is no come

Shal. He is the wiser man, master doctor: he is a curer of souls, and you a curer of bodies; if you should fight, you go against the hair of your professions. — Is it not true, Master Page?

Page. Master Shallow, you have yourself been a great fighter, though now a man of peace.

Shal. Bodikins, Master Page, though I now be old, and of the peace, if I see a sword out, my finger itches to make one. Though we are justices, and doctors, and churchmen, Master Page, we have some salt of our youth in us; we are the sons of women, Master Page.

Page. 'Tis true, Master Shallow.

Shal. It will be found so, Master Page. — Master Doctor Caius, I am come to fetch you home. I am sworn of the peace: you have showed yourself a wise physician, and Sir Hugh hath shown himself a wise and patient churchman. You must go with me, master doctor.

Host. Pardon, guest-justice. — A word, Monsieur Mock-water.

Caius. Mock-vater! vat is dat?

Host. Mock-water, in our English tongue, is valour, bully.

Caius. By gar, den, I have as mush mock-vater as de Englishman. — Scurvy jack-dog priest! by gar, me vill cut his ears.

Host. He will clapper-claw thee tightly, bully.

Caius. Clapper-de-claw! vat is dat?

Host. That is, he will make thee amends.

Caius. By gar, me do look he shall clapper-de-claw me; for, by gar, me vill have it.

Host. And I will provoke him to't, or let him wag.

Caius. Me dank you for dat.

Host. And, moreover, bully, — But first, master guest, and Master Page, and eke Cavalero Slender, go you through the town to Frogmore.   [*Aside to them.*

Page. Sir Hugh is there, is he?

Host. He is there: see what humour he is in; and I will bring the doctor about by the fields. Will it do well?

Shal. We will do it.

Page, Shal., and Slen. Adieu, good master doctor.

[*Exeunt Page, Shal., and Slen.*

Caius. By gar, me vill kill de priest; for he speak for a jack-an-ape to Anne Page.

Host. Let him die: sheathe thy impatience, throw cold water on thy choler: go about the fields with me through Frogmore: I will bring thee where Mistress Anne Page is, at a farm-house a-feasting; and thou shalt woo her. Cried I aim? said I well?

Caius. By gar, me dank you for dat: by gar, I love you; and I shall procure-a you de good guest, de earl, de knight, de lords, de gentlemen, my patients.

Host. For the which I will be thy adversary toward Anne Page. Said I well?

Caius. By gar, 'tis good; vell said.

Host. Let us wag, then.

Caius. Come at my heels, Jack Rugby.   [*Exeunt.*

ACT III.

Scene I. *A field near Frogmore.*

Enter Sir Hugh Evans *and* Simple.

Evans. I pray you now, good Master Slender's serving-man, and friend Simple by your name, which way have you looked for Master Caius, that calls himself doctor of physic?

Sim. Marry, sir, the Pitty-ward, the Park-ward, every way; old Windsor way, and every way but the town way.

Evans. I most fehemently desire you you will also look that way.

Sim. I will, sir.   [*Retires.*

Evans. Pless my soul, how full of cholers I am, and trempling of mind! — I shall be glad if he have deceived me: — how melancholies I am! — I will knog his urinals about his knave's costard when I have goot opportunities for the ork: — Pless my soul! —   [*Sings.*

> *To shallow rivers, to whose falls*
> *Melodious birds sing madrigals;*
> *There will we make our peds of roses,*
> *And a thousand fragrant posies.*
>   *To shallow —*

Mercy on me! I have a great dispositions to cry. —   [*Sings.*

> *Melodious birds sing madrigals; —*
> *Whenas I sat in Pabylon, —*
> *And a thousand vagram posies.*
>   *To shallow, &c.*

Sim. [*coming forward*] Yonder he is, coming this way, Sir Hugh.

Evans. He's welcome. —   [*Sings.*

> *To shallow rivers, to whose falls —*

Heaven prosper the right! — What weapons is he?

Sim. No weapons, sir. There comes my master, Master Shallow, and another gentleman, from Frogmore, over the stile, this way.

Evans. Pray you, give me my gown; or else keep it in your arms.   [*Reads in a book.*

Enter PAGE, SHALLOW, *and* SLENDER.

Shal. How now, master parson! Good morrow, good Sir Hugh. Keep a gamester from the dice, and a good student from his book, and it is wonderful.

Slen. [*aside*] Ah, sweet Anne Page!

Page. Save you, good Sir Hugh!

Evans. Pless you from his mercy sake, all of you!

Shal. What, the sword and the word! do you study them both, master parson?

Page. And youthful still, in your doublet and hose this raw rheumatic day?

Evans. There is reasons and causes for it.

Page. We are come to you to do a good office, master parson.

Evans. Fery well: what is it?

Page. Yonder is a most reverend gentleman, who, belike having received wrong by some person, is at most odds with his own gravity and patience that ever you saw.

Shal. I have lived fourscore years and upward; I never heard a man of his place, gravity, and learning, so wide of his own respect.

Evans. What is he?

Page. I think you know him; Master Doctor Caius, the renowned French physician.

Evans. Got's will, and his passion of my heart! I had as lief you would tell me of a mess of porridge.

Page. Why?

Evans. He has no more knowledge in Hibbocrates and Galen, — and he is a knave besides; a cowardly knave as you would desires to be acquainted withal.

Page. I warrant you, he's the man should fight with him.

Slen. [*aside*] O sweet Anne Page!

Shal. It appears so, by his weapons. — Keep them asunder: — here comes Doctor Caius.

Enter Host, CAIUS, *and* RUGBY.

Page. Nay, good master parson, keep in your weapon.

Shal. So do you, good master doctor.

Host. Disarm them, and let them question: let them keep their limbs whole, and hack our English.

Caius. I pray you, let-a me speak a word vit your ear. Verefore vill you not meet-a me?

Evans. [*aside to Caius*] Pray you, use your patience: in goot time.

Caius. By gar, you are de coward, de Jack dog, John ape.

Evans. [*aside to Caius*] Pray you, let us not be laughing-stogs to other men's humours; I desire you in friendship, and I will one way or other make you amends. — [*Aloud*] I will knog your urinals about your knave's cogscomb for missing your meetings and appointments.

Caius. *Diable!* — Jack Rugby, — mine host de Jarteer, —

16*

have I not stay for him to kill him? have I not, at de place
I did appoint?

Evans. As I am a Christians soul, now, look you, this is
the place appointed: I'll be judgment by mine host of the
Garter.

Host. Peace, I say, Gallia and Guallia, French and
Welsh, soul-curer and body-curer!

Caius. Ay, dat is very good; excellent.

Host. Peace, I say! hear mine host of the Garter. Am
I politic? am I subtle? am I a Machiavel? Shall I lose my
doctor? no; he gives me the potions and the motions. Shall
I lose my parson, my priest, my Sir Hugh? no; he gives me
the proverbs and the no-verbs. — Give me thy hand, terres-
trial; so. — Give me thy hand, celestial; so. — Boys of art,
I have deceived you both; I have directed you to wrong
places: your hearts are mighty, your skins are whole, and
let burnt sack be the issue. — Come, lay their swords to
pawn. — Follow me, lads of peace; follow, follow, follow.

Shal. Trust me, a mad host. — Follow, gentlemen, follow.

Slen. [*aside*] O sweet Anne Page!

> [*Exeunt Shal., Slen., Page, and Host.*

Caius. Ha, do I perceive dat? have you make-a de sot
of us, ha, ha?

Evans. This is well; he has made us his vlouting-stog.—
I desire you that we may be friends; and let us knog our
prains together to be revenge on this same scall, scurvy, cog-
ging companion, the host of the Garter.

Caius. By gar, vit all my heart. He promise to bring
me vere is Anne Page; by gar, he deceive me too.

Evans. Well, I will smite his noddles. Pray you, follow.

> [*Exeunt.*

Scene II.   *The street, in Windsor*

Enter Mistress Page *and* Robin.

Mrs. Page. Nay, keep your way, little gallant; you were
wont to be a follower, but now you are a leader. Whether
had you rather lead mine eyes, or eye your master's heels?

Rob. I had rather, forsooth, go before you like a man than follow him like a dwarf.

Mrs. Page. O, you are a flattering boy: now I see you'll be a courtier.

Enter FORD.

Ford. Well met, Mistress Page. Whither go you?

Mrs. Page. Truly, sir, to see your wife. Is she at home?

Ford. Ay, and as idle as she may hang together, for want of company. I think, if your husbands were dead, you two would marry.

Mrs. Page. Be sure of that, — two other husbands.

Ford. Where had you this pretty weathercock?

Mrs. Page. I cannot tell what the dickens his name is my husband had him of. — What do you call your knight's name, sirrah?

Rob. Sir John Falstaff.

Ford. Sir John Falstaff!

Mrs. Page. He, he; I can never hit on's name. — There is such a league between my good man and he! — Is your wife at home indeed?

Ford. Indeed she is.

Mrs. Page. By your leave, sir: I am sick till I see her.
　　　　　　　　　　　[*Exeunt Mrs. Page and Robin.*

Ford. Has Page any brains? hath he any eyes? hath he any thinking? Sure, they sleep; he hath no use of them. Why, this boy will carry a letter twenty mile, as easy as a cannon will shoot point-blank twelve score. He pieces out his wife's inclination; he gives her folly motion and advantage: and now she's going to my wife, and Falstaff's boy with her: — a man may hear this shower sing in the wind: — and Falstaff's boy with her! — Good plots! — they are laid; and our revolted wives share damnation together. Well; I will take him, then torture my wife, pluck the borrowed veil of modesty from the so seeming Mistress Page, divulge Page himself for a secure and wilful Actæon; and to these violent proceedings all my neighbours shall cry aim. [*Clock strikes.*] The clock gives me my cue, and my assurance bids me search where I shall find Falstaff: I shall be rather praised for this than mocked; for it is as positive as the earth is firm that Falstaff is there: I will go.

Enter PAGE, SHALLOW, SLENDER, Host, SIR HUGH EVANS, CAIUS, *and* RUGBY.

Shal., *Page*, &c. Well met, Master Ford.

Ford. Trust me, a good knot: I have good cheer at home; and I pray you all, go with me.

Shal. I must excuse myself, Master Ford.

Slen. And so must I, sir: we have appointed to dine with Mistress Anne, and I would not break with her for more money than I'll speak of.

Shal. We have lingered about a match between Anne Page and my cousin Slender, and this day we shall have our answer.

Slen. I hope I have your good will, father Page.

Page. You have, Master Slender; I stand wholly for you: — but my wife, master doctor, is for you altogether.

Caius. Ay, by gar; and de maid is love-a me; my nursh-a Quickly tell me so mush.

Host. What say you to young Master Fenton? he capers, he dances, he has eyes of youth, he writes verses, he speaks holiday, he smells April and May: he will carry't, he will carry't; 'tis in his buttons; he will carry't.

Page. Not by my consent, I promise you. The gentleman is of no having: he kept company with the wild prince and Pointz; he is of too high a region; he knows too much. No, he shall not knit a knot in his fortunes with the finger of my substance: if he take her, let him take her simply; the wealth I have waits on my consent, and my consent goes not that way.

Ford. I beseech you heartily, some of you go home with me to dinner: besides your cheer, you shall have sport; I will show you a monster. — Master doctor, you shall go — so shall you, Master Page; — and you, Sir Hugh.

Shal. Well, fare you well: — we shall have the freer wooing at Master Page's. 　　　　　　　　[*Exeunt Shal. and Slen.*

Caius. Go home, John Rugby; I come anon.
　　　　　　　　　　　　　　　　　　　[*Exit Rugby.*

Host. Farewell, my hearts: I will to my honest knight
Falstaff, and drink canary with him. 　　　　　[*Exit.*

Ford. [*aside*] I think I shall drink in pipe-wine first with
him; I'll make him dance. — Will you go, gentles?

All. Have with you to see this monster. 　　　[*Exeunt.*

SCENE III.　*A room in* FORD'S *house.*

Enter MISTRESS FORD *and* MISTRESS PAGE.

Mrs. Ford. What, John! What, Robert!

Mrs. Page. Quickly, quickly: — is the buck-basket —

Mrs. Ford. I warrant. — What, Robin, I say!

Enter Servants *with a basket.*

Mrs. Page. Come, come, come.

Mrs. Ford. Here, set it down.

Mrs. Page. Give your men the charge; we must be brief.

Mrs. Ford. Marry, as I told you before, John and Robert,
be ready here hard by in the brew-house; and when I suddenly call you, come forth, and, without any pause or stag-
gering, take this basket on your shoulders: that done, trudge
with it in all haste, and carry it among the whitsters in
Datchet-mead, and there empty it in the muddy ditch close
by the Thames side.

Mrs. Page. You will do it?

Mrs. Ford. I ha' told them over and over; they lack no
direction. — Be gone, and come when you are called.
　　　　　　　　　　　　　　　　　　　[*Exeunt Servants.*

Mrs. Page. Here comes little Robin.

Enter ROBIN.

Mrs. Ford. How now, my eyas-musket! what news with you?

Rob. My master, Sir John, is come in at your back-door,
Mistress Ford, and requests your company.

Mrs. Page. You little Jack-a-Lent, have you been true to us?

Rob. Ay, I'll be sworn. My master knows not of your being here, and hath threatened to put me into everlasting liberty, if I tell you of it; for he swears he'll turn me away. .

Mrs. Page. Thou'rt a good boy: this secrecy of thine shall be a tailor to thee, and shall make thee a new doublet and hose. — I'll go hide me.

Mrs. Ford. Do so. — Go tell thy master I am alone. — Mistress Page, remember you your cue.   [*Exit Robin.*

Mrs. Page. I warrant thee; if I do not act it, hiss me.

[*Exit.*

Mrs. Ford. Go to, then: we'll use this unwholesome humidity, this gross watery pumpion; we'll teach him to know turtles from jays.

Enter FALSTAFF.

Fal. "Have I caught my heavenly jewel?" Why, now let me die, for I have lived long enough; this is the period of my ambition: O this blessed hour!

Mrs. Ford. O sweet Sir John!

Fal. Mistress Ford, I cannot cog, I cannot prate, Mistress Ford. Now shall I sin in my wish, — I would thy husband were dead: I'll speak it before the best lord, — I would make thee my lady.

Mrs. Ford. I your lady, Sir John! alas, I should be a pitiful lady!

Fal. Let the court of France show me such another. I see how thine eye would emulate the diamond: thou hast the right arched beauty of the brow that becomes the ship-tire, the tire-valiant, or any tire of Venetian admittance.

Mrs. Ford. A plain kerchief, Sir John: my brows become nothing else; nor that well neither.

Fal. By the Lord, thou art a traitor to say so: thou wouldst make an absolute courtier; and the firm fixture of thy foot would give an excellent motion to thy gait in a semicircled farthingale. I see what thou wert, if Fortune thy foe were not, Nature thy friend. Come, thou canst not hide it

Mrs. Ford　Believe me, there's no such thing in me.

Fal.　What made me love thee? let that persuade thee there's something extraordinary in thee.　Come, I cannot cog, and say thou art this and that, like a many of these lisping hawthorn-buds, that come like women in men's apparel, and smell like Bucklersbury in simple-time; I cannot: but I love thee; none but thee; and thou deservest it.

Mrs. Ford.　Do not betray me, sir.　I fear you love Mistress Page.

Fal.　Thou mightst as well say I love to walk by the Counter-gate, which is as hateful to me as the reek of a lime-kiln.

Mrs. Ford.　Well, heaven knows how I love you; and you shall one day find it.

Fal.　Keep in that mind; I'll deserve it.

Mrs. Ford.　Nay, I must tell you, so you do; or else I could not be in that mind.

Rob. [*within*]　Mistress Ford, Mistress, Ford! here's Mistress Page at the door, sweating, and blowing, and looking wildly, and would needs speak with you presently.

Fal.　She shall not see me: I will ensconce me behind the arras.

Mrs. Ford.　Pray you, do so: she's a very tattling woman.
　　　　　　　[*Falstaff hides himself behind the arras.*

Re-enter MISTRESS PAGE *and* ROBIN.

What's the matter? how now!

Mrs. Page.　O Mistress Ford, what have you done? You're shamed, you're overthrown, you're undone for ever!

Mrs. Ford.　What's the matter, good Mistress Page?

Mrs. Page.　O well-a-day, Mistress Ford! having an honest man to your husband, to give him such cause of suspicion!

Mrs. Ford.　What cause of suspicion?

Mrs. Page.　What cause of suspicion! Out upon you! how am I mistook in you!

Mrs. Ford.　Why, alas, what's the matter?

Mrs. Page.　Your husband's coming hither, woman, with

all the officers in Windsor, to search for a gentleman that he
says is here now in the house, by your consent, to take an ill
advantage of his absence: you are undone.

Mrs. Ford.   'Tis not so, I hope.

Mrs. Page.   Pray heaven it be not so, that you have such
a man here! but 'tis most certain your husband's coming, with
half Windsor at his heels, to search for such a one.   I come
before to tell you.   If you know yourself clear, why, I am
glad of it; but if you have a friend here, convey, convey him
out.   Be not amazed; call all your senses to you; defend your
reputation, or bid farewell to your good life for ever.

Mrs. Ford.   What shall I do? — There is a gentleman my
dear friend; and I fear not mine own shame so much as his
peril: I had rather than a thousand pound he were out of the
house.

Mrs. Page.   For shame! never stand "you had rather" and
"you had rather:" your husband's here at hand; bethink you
of some conveyance: in the house you cannot hide him. — O,
how have you deceived me! — Look, here is a basket: if he be
of any reasonable stature, he may creep in here; and throw
foul linen upon him, as if it were going to bucking: or, — it is
whiting-time, — send him by your two men to Datchet-mead.

Mrs. Ford.   He's too big to go in there.   What shall I do?

Re-enter FALSTAFF.

Fal.   Let me see't, let me see't, O, let me see't! — I'll in,
I'll in: — follow your friend's counsel: — I'll in.

Mrs. Page.   What, Sir John Falstaff!   Are these your
letters, knight?

Fal.   I love thee, and none but thee; help me away: let
me creep in here.   I'll never —
        [*Goes into the basket; they cover him with foul linen.*

Mrs. Page.   Help to cover your master, boy. — Call your
men, Mistress Ford. — You dissembling knight! [*Exit Robin.*

Mrs. Ford.   What, John! Robert! John!

Re-enter Servants.

Go take up these clothes here quickly: — where's the cowl-

staff? look, how you drumble! — carry them to the laundress
in Datchet-mead; quickly, come.

Enter FORD, PAGE, CAIUS, *and* SIR HUGH EVANS.

Ford. Pray you, come near: if I suspect without cause,
why then make sport at me; then let me be your jest; I deserve it. — How now! whither bear you this?

Serv. To the laundress, forsooth.

Mrs. Ford. Why, what have you to do whither they bear
it? You were best meddle with buck-washing.

Ford. Buck! — I would I could wash myself of the buck!
— Buck, buck, buck! Ay, buck; I warrant you, buck; and
of the season too, it shall appear. [*Exeunt Servants with the
basket.*] — Gentlemen, I have dreamed to-night; I'll tell you
my dream. Here, here, here be my keys: ascend my chambers; search, seek, find out: I'll warrant we'll unkennel the
fox. — Let me stop this way first [*Locks the door*]. — So, now
uncape.

Page. Good Master Ford, be contented: you wrong yourself too much.

Ford. True, Master Page. — Up, gentlemen; you shall
see sport anon: follow me, gentlemen. [*Exit.*

Evans. This is fery fantastical humours and jealousies.

Caius. By gar, 'tis no de fashion of France; it is not jealous
in France.

Page. Nay, follow him, gentlemen; see the issue of his
search. [*Exeunt Page, Caius, and Evans.*

Mrs. Page. Is there not a double excellency in this?

Mrs. Ford. I know not which pleases me better, that my
husband is deceived, or Sir John.

Mrs. Page. What a taking was he in when your husband
asked what was in the basket!

Mrs. Ford. I am half afraid he will have need of washing;
so throwing him into the water will do him a benefit.

Mrs. Page. Hang him, dishonest rascal! I would all of the
same strain were in the same distress.

Mrs. Ford. I think my husband hath some special suspicion

of Falstaff's being here; for I never saw him so gross in his jealousy till now.

Mrs. Page. I will lay a plot to try that; and we will yet have more tricks with Falstaff: his dissolute disease will scarce obey this medicine.

Mrs. Ford. Shall we send that foolish carrion Mistress Quickly to him, and excuse his throwing into the water; and give him another hope, to betray him to another punishment?

Mrs. Page. We will do it: let him be sent for to-morrow eight o'clock, to have amends.

Re-enter FORD, PAGE, CAIUS, *and* SIR HUGH EVANS.

Ford. I cannot find him: may be the knave bragged of that he could not compass.

Mrs. Page. [aside to Mrs. Ford] Heard you that?

Mrs. Ford. [aside to Mrs. Page] Ay, ay, peace. — You use me well, Master Ford, do you?

Ford. Ay, I do so.

Mrs. Ford. . Heaven make you better than your thoughts!

Ford. Amen!

Mrs. Page. You do yourself mighty wrong, Master Ford.

Ford. Ay, ay; I must bear it.

Evans. If there be any pody in the house, and in the chambers, and in the coffers, and in the presses, heaven forgive my sins at the day of judgment!

Caius. By gar, nor I too: dere is no bodies.

Page. Fie, fie, Master Ford! are you not ashamed? What spirit, what devil suggests this imagination? I would not ha' your distemper in this kind for the wealth of Windsor Castle.

Ford. 'Tis my fault, Master Page: I suffer for it.

Evans. You suffer for a pad conscience: your wife is as honest a omans as I will desires among five thousand, and five hundred too.

Caius. By gar, I see 'tis an honest woman.

Ford. Well; — I promised you a dinner: — come, come,

walk in the Park: I pray you, pardon me; I will hereafter
make known to you why I have done this. — Come, wife; —
come, Mistress Page. — I pray you, pardon me; pray heartily,
pardon me.

Page. Let's go in, gentlemen; but, trust me, we'll mock
him. I do invite you to-morrow morning to my house to
breakfast: after, we'll a-birding together; I have a fine hawk
for the bush. Shall it be so?

Ford. Any thing.

Evans. If there is one, I shall make two in the company.

Caius. If dere be one or two, I shall make-a de turd.

Ford. Pray you, go, Master Page.

Evans. I pray you now, remembrance to-morrow on the
lousy knave, mine host.

Caius. Dat is good; by gar, vit all my heart.

Evans. A lousy knave, to have his gibes and his mockeries!

                                                  [Exeunt.

SCENE IV. *A room in* PAGE'S *house.*

Enter FENTON *and* ANNE PAGE.

Fent. I see I cannot get thy father's love;
Therefore no more turn me to him, sweet Nan.

Anne. Alas, how then?

Fent.   Why, thou must be thyself.
He doth object I am too great of birth;
And that, my state being gall'd with my expense,
I seek to heal it only by his wealth:
Besides, these other bars he lays before me, —
My riots past, my wild societies;
And tells me 'tis a thing impossible
I should love thee but as a property.

Anne. May be he tells you true.

Fent. No, heaven so speed me in my time to come!
Albeit I will confess thy father's wealth
Was the first motive that I woo'd thee, Anne:
Yet, wooing thee, I found thee of more value

Than stamps in gold or sums in sealèd bags;
And 'tis the very riches of thyself
That now I aim at.

  Anne.   Gentle Master Fenton,
Yet seek my father's love; still seek it, sir:
If opportunity and humblest suit
Cannot attain it, why, then — Hark you hither.
            [*They converse apart.*

  Enter SHALLOW, SLENDER, *and* MISTRESS QUICKLY.

  Shal. Break their talk, Mistress Quickly: my kinsman shall speak for himself.

  Slen. I'll make a shaft or a bolt on't: slid, 'tis but venturing.

  Shal. Be not dismayed.

  Slen. No, she shall not dismay me: I care not for that, — but that I am afeard.

  Quick. Hark ye; Master Slender would speak a word with you.

  Anne. I come to him.—[*Aside*] This is my father's choice. O, what a world of vile ill-favour'd faults
Looks handsome in three hundred pounds a-year!

  Quick. And how does good Master Fenton? Pray you, a word with you.

  Shal. She's coming; to her, coz. O boy, thou hadst a father!

  Slen. I had a father, Mistress Anne; — my uncle can tell you good jests of him. — Pray you, uncle, tell Mistress Anne the jest, how my father stole two geese out of a pen, good uncle.

  Shal. Mistress Anne, my cousin loves you.

  Slen. Ay, that I do; as well as I love any woman in Glostershire.

  Shal. He will maintain you like a gentlewoman.

  Slen. Ay, that I will, come cut and long-tail, under the degree of a squire.

  Shal. He will make you a hundred and fifty pounds jointure.

Anne. Good Master Shallow, let him woo for himself.

Shal. Marry, I thank you for it; I thank you for that good comfort — She calls you, coz: I'll leave you.

Anne. Now, Master Slender, —

Slen. Now, good Mistress Anne, —

Anne. What is your will?

Slen. My will! od's heartlings, that's a pretty jest indeed! I ne'er made my will yet, I thank heaven; I am not such a sickly creature, I give heaven praise.

Anne. I mean, Master Slender, what would you with me?

Slen. Truly, for mine own part, I would little or nothing with you. Your father and my uncle have made motions: if it be my luck, so; if not, happy man be his dole! They can tell you how things go better than I can: you may ask your father; here he comes.

Enter PAGE *and* MISTRESS PAGE.

Page. Now, Master Slender: — love him, daughter Anne. — Why, how now! what does Master Fenton here?
You wrong me, sir, thus still to haunt my house:
I told you, sir, my daughter is dispos'd of.

Fent. Nay, Master Page, be not impatient.

Mrs. Page. Good Master Fenton, come not to my child.

Page. She is no match for you.

Fent. Sir, will you hear me?

Page.   No, good Master Fenton. —
Come, Master Shallow; come, son Slender; in. —
Knowing my mind, you wrong me, Master Fenton.
                                        [*Exeunt Page, Shal., and Slen.*

Quick. Speak to Mistress Page.

Fent. Good Mistress Page, for that I love your daughter
In such a righteous fashion as I do,
Perforce, against all checks, rebukes, and manners,
I must advance the colours of my love,
And not retire: let me have your good will.

Anne. Good mother, do not marry me to yond fool.

Mrs. Page. I mean it not; I seek you a better husband.

Quick. That's my master, master doctor.

Anne. Alas, I had rather be set quick i' th' earth,
And bowl'd to death with turnips!

Mrs. Page. Come, trouble not yourself. — Good Master
         Fenton,
I will not be your friend nor enemy:
My daughter will I question how she loves you,
And as I find her, so am I affected.
Till then farewell, sir: she must needs go in;
Her father will be angry.

Fent. Farewell, gentle mistress. — Farewell, Nan.

                [*Exeunt Mrs. Page and Anne.*

Quick. This is my doing now: — "Nay," said I, "will you
cast away your child on a fool and a physician? Look on
Master Fenton:" — this is my doing.

Fent. I thank thee; and I pray thee, once to-night
Give my sweet Nan this ring: there's for thy pains.

Quick. Now heaven send thee good fortune! [*Exit Fenton.*]
A kind heart he hath: a woman would run through fire and
water for such a kind heart. But yet I would my master had
Mistress Anne; or I would Master Slender had her; or, in
sooth, I would Master Fenton had her: I will do what I can
for them all three; for so I have promised, and I'll be as good
as my word; but speciously for Master Fenton. Well, I must
of another errand to Sir John Falstaff from my two mistresses:
what a beast am I to slack it!   [*Exit.*

SCENE V.   *A room in the Garter Inn.*

Enter FALSTAFF *and* BARDOLPH.

Fal. Bardolph, I say, —

Bard. Here, sir.

Fal. Go fetch me a quart of sack; put a toast in't. [*Exit
Bard.*] Have I lived to be carried in a basket, like a barrow
of butcher's offal, and to be thrown in the Thames? Well,
if I be served such another trick, I'll have my brains ta'en
out, and buttered, and give them to a dog for a new-year's

gift. The rogues slighted me into the river with as little remorse as they would have drowned a bitch's blind puppies, fifteen i' the litter: and you may know by my size that I have a kind of alacrity in sinking; if the bottom were as deep as hell, I should down. I had been drowned, but that the shore was shelvy and shallow,—a death that I abhor; for the water swells a man; and what a thing should I have been when I had been swelled! I should have been a mountain of mummy.

Re-enter BARDOLPH *with sack.*

Bard. Here's Mistress Quickly, sir, to speak with you.

Fal. Come, let me pour in some sack to the Thames water; for my belly's as cold as if I had swallowed snowballs for pills to cool the reins. Call her in.

Bard. Come in, woman!

Enter MISTRESS QUICKLY.

Quick. By your leave; I cry you mercy: — give your worship good morrow.

Fal. Take away these chalices. Go brew me a pottle of sack finely.

Bard. With eggs, sir?

Fal. Simple of itself; I'll no pullet-sperm in my brewage. [*Exit Bardolph.*] How now!

Quick. Marry, sir, I come to your worship from Mistress Ford.

Fal. Mistress Ford! I have had ford enough; I was thrown into the ford; I have my belly full of ford.

Quick. Alas the day! good heart, that was not her fault: she does so take on with her men; they mistook their erection.

Fal. So did I mine, to build upon a foolish woman's promise.

Quick. Well, she laments, sir, for it, that it would yearn your heart to see it. Her husband goes this morning a-birding; she desires you once more to come to her between eight and nine: I must carry her word quickly: she'll make you amends, I warrant you.

Fal. Well, I will visit her: tell her so; and bid her think

what a man is: let her consider his frailty, and then judge of
my merit.

Quick. I will tell her.

Fal. Do so. Between nine and ten, sayest thou?

Quick. Eight and nine, sir.

Fal. Well, be gone: I will not miss her.

Quick. Peace be with you, sir.   [*Exit.*

Fal. I marvel I hear not of Master Brook; he sent me
word to stay within: I like his money well. — O, here he
comes.

Enter FORD *disguised.*

Ford. Bless you, sir!

Fal. Now, Master Brook, — you come to know what hath
passed between me and Ford's wife?

Ford. That, indeed, Sir John, is my business.

Fal. Master Brook, I will not lie to you: I was at her
house the hour she appointed me.

Ford. And how sped you, sir?

Fal. Very ill-favouredly, Master Brook.

Ford. How so, sir? Did she change her determination?

Fal. No, Master Brook; but the peaking cornuto her husband, Master Brook, dwelling in a continual 'larum of jealousy,
comes me in the instant of our encounter, after we had em-
braced, kissed, protested, and, as it were, spoke the prologue
of our comedy; and at his heels a rabble of his companions,
thither provoked and instigated by his distemper, and, forsooth, to search his house for his wife's love.

Ford. What, while you were there?

Fal. While I was there?

Ford. And did he search for you, and could not find you?

Fal. You shall hear. As good luck would have it, comes
in one Mistress Page; gives intelligence of Ford's approach;
and, by her invention and Ford's wife's direction, they con-
veyed me into a buck-basket.

Ford. A buck-basket!

Fal. By the Lord, a buck-basket! — rammed me in with
foul shirts and smocks, socks, foul stockings, greasy napkins;

that, Master Brook, there was the rankest compound of villanous smell that ever offended nostril.

Ford. And how long lay you there?

Fal. Nay, you shall hear, Master Brook, what I have
suffered to bring this woman to evil for your good. Being
thus crammed in the basket, a couple of Ford's knaves, his
hinds, were called forth by their mistress to carry me in the
name of foul clothes to Datchet-lane: they took me on their
shoulders; met the jealous knave their master in the door,
who asked them once or twice what they had in their basket: I quaked for fear, lest the lunatic knave would have
searched it; but fate, ordaining he should be a cuckold, held
his hand. Well: on went he for a search, and away went I
for foul clothes. But mark the sequel, Master Brook: I suffered the pangs of three several deaths; first, an intolerable
fright, to be detected with a jealous rotten bell-wether;
next, to be compassed, like a good bilbo, in the circumference
of a peck, hilt to point, heel to head; and then, to be stopped
in, like a strong distillation, with stinking clothes that fretted
in their own grease: think of that,— a man of my kidney,—
think of that, — that am as subject to heat as butter; a man
of continual dissolution and thaw;— it was a miracle to scape
suffocation. And in the height of this bath, when I was more
than half stewed in grease, like a Dutch dish, to be thrown
into the Thames, and cooled, glowing hot, in that surge, like
a horse-shoe; think of that, — hissing hot, — think of that,
Master Brook.

Ford. In good sadness, sir, I am sorry that for my sake
you have suffered all this. My suit, then, is desperate; you'll
undertake her no more?

Fal. Master Brook, I will be thrown into Etna, as I have
been into Thames, ere I will leave her thus. Her husband
is this morning gone a-birding: I have received from her
another embassy of meeting; 'twixt eight and nine is the
hour, Master Brook.

Ford. 'Tis past eight already, sir.

Fal Is it? I will then address me to my appointment.

17*

Come to me at your convenient leisure, and you shall know how I speed; and the conclusion shall be crowned with your enjoying her. Adieu. You shall have her, Master Brook; Master Brook, you shall cuckold Ford.   [*Exit.*

Ford. Hum, — ha! is this a vision? is this a dream? do I sleep?´ Master Ford, awake! awake, Master Ford! there's a hole made in your best coat, Master Ford. This 'tis to be married! this 'tis to have linen and buck-baskets! — Well, I will proclaim myself what I am: I will now take the lecher; he is at my house; he cannot scape me; 'tis impossible he should; he cannot creep into a halfpenny purse, nor into a pepper-box: but, lest the devil that guides him should aid him, I will search impossible places. Though what I am I cannot avoid, yet to be what I would not shall not make me tame: if I have horns to make me mad, let the proverb go with me, — I'll be horn-mad.   [*Exit.*

ACT IV.

Scene I. *The street.*

Enter Mistress Page, Mistress Quickly, *and* William.

Mrs. Page. Is he at Master Ford's already, thinkest thou?

Quick. Sure he is by this, or will be presently: but, truly, he is very courageous mad about his throwing into the water. Mistress Ford desires you to come suddenly.

Mrs. Page. I'll be with her by and by; I'll but bring my young man here to school. Look, where his master comes: 'tis a playing-day, I see.

Enter Sir Hugh Evans.

How now, Sir Hugh! no school to-day?

Evans. No; Master Slender is let the boys leave to play.

Quick. Blessing of his heart!

Mrs. Page. Sir Hugh, my husband says my son profits nothing in the world at his book. I pray you, ask him some questions in his accidence.

Evans. Come hither, William; hold up your head; come.

Mrs. Page. Come on, sirrah; hold up your head; answer your master, be not afraid.

Evans. William, how many numbers is in nouns?

Will. Two.

Quick. Truly, I thought there had been one number more, because they say, Od's-nouns.

Evans. Peace your tattlings. — What is *fair*, William?

Will. *Pulcher*.

Quick. Polecats! there are fairer things than polecats, sure.

Evans. You are a very simplicity oman: I pray you, peace. — What is *lapis*, William?

Will. A stone.

Evans. And what is a stone, William?

Will. A pebble.

Evans. No, it is *lapis*: I pray you, remember in your prain.

Will. *Lapis*.

Evans. That is a good William. What is he, William, that does lend articles?

Will. Articles are borrowed of the pronoun, and be thus declined, *Singulariter*, *nominativo*, *hic*, *hæc*, *hoc*.

Evans. *Nominativo*, *hig*, *hag*, *hog;* — pray you, mark: *genitivo*, *hujus*. Well, what is your accusative case?

Will. *Accusativo*, *hunc*.

Evans. I pray you, have your remembrance, child; *accusativo*, *hung*, *hang*, *hog*.

Quick. Hang-hog is Latin for bacon, I warrant you.

Evans. Leave your prabbles, oman. — What is the focative case, William?

Will. *O*, — *vocativo*, *O*.

Evans. Remember, William; focative is *caret*.

Quick. And that's a good root.

Evans. Oman, forbear.

Mrs. Page. Peace!

Evans. What is your genitive case plural, William?

Will.   Genitive case!

Evans.   Ay.

Will.   Genitivo, — *horum, harum, horum.*

Quick.   Vengeance of Jenny's case! fie on her! — never name her, child, if she be a whore.

Evans.   For shame, oman.

Quick.   You do ill to teach the child such words: — he teaches him to hick and to hack, which they'll do fast enough of themselves, and to call whorum: — fie upon you!

Evans.   Oman, art thou lunatics? hast thou no understandings for thy cases, and the numbers and the genders? Thou art as foolish Christian creatures as I would desires.

Mrs. Page.   Prithee, hold thy peace.

Evans.   Show me now, William, some declensions of your pronouns.

Will.   Forsooth, I have forgot.

Evans.   It is *qui, quæ, quod:* if you forget your *quies,* your *quæs,* and your *quods,* you must be preeches. Go your ways, and play; go.

Mrs. Page.   He is a better scholar than I thought he was.

Evans.   He is a good sprag memory. Farewell, Mistress Page.

Mrs. Page.   Adieu, good Sir Hugh. [*Exit Sir Hugh.*] — Get you home, boy. — Come, we stay too long.   [*Exeunt.*

SCENE II.   *A room in* FORD'S *house.*

Enter FALSTAFF *and* MISTRESS FORD.

Fal.   Mistress Ford, your sorrow hath eaten up my sufferance. I see you are obsequious in your love, and I profess requital to a hair's breadth; not only, Mistress Ford, in the simple office of love, but in all the accoutrement, complement, and ceremony of it. But are you sure of your husband now?

Mrs. Ford.   He's a-birding, sweet Sir John.

Mrs. Page. [*within*] What, ho, gossip Ford! what, ho!

Mrs. Ford.   Step into the chamber, Sir John.

[*Exit Falstaff.*

Enter MISTRESS PAGE.

Mrs. Page. How now, sweetheart! who's at home besides yourself?

Mrs. Ford. Why, none but mine own people.

Mrs. Page. Indeed!

Mrs. Ford. No, certainly. — [*Aside to her*] Speak louder.

Mrs. Page. Truly, I am so glad you have nobody here.

Mrs. Ford. Why?

Mrs. Page. Why, woman, your husband is in his old lunes again: he so takes on yonder with my husband; so rails against all married mankind; so curses all Eve's daughters, of what complexion soever; and so buffets himself on the forehead, crying, "Peer out, peer out!" that any madness I ever yet beheld seemed but tameness, civility, and patience, to this his distemper he is in now: I am glad the fat knight is not here.

Mrs. Ford. Why, does he talk of him?

Mrs. Page. Of none but him; and swears he was carried out, the last time he searched for him, in a basket; protests to my husband he is now here; and hath drawn him and the rest of their company from their sport, to make another experiment of his suspicion: but I am glad the knight is not here; now he shall see his own foolery.

Mrs. Ford. How near is he, Mistress Page?

Mrs. Page. Hard by; at street end; he will be here anon.

Mrs. Ford. I am undone! — the knight is here.

Mrs. Page. Why, then, you are utterly shamed, and he's but a dead man. What a woman are you! — Away with him, away with him! better shame than murder.

Mrs. Ford. Which way should he go? how should I bestow him? Shall I put him into the basket again?

Re-enter FALSTAFF.

Fal. No, I'll come no more i' the basket. May I not go out ere he come?

Mrs. Page. Alas, three of Master Ford's brothers watch

the door with pistols, that none shall issue out; otherwise you might slip away ere he came. But what make you here?

Fal. What shall I do? — I'll creep up into the chimney.

Mrs. Ford. There they always use to discharge their birding-pieces.

Mrs. Page. Creep into the kiln-hole.

Fal. Where is it?

Mrs. Ford. He will seek there, on my word. Neither press, coffer, chest, trunk, well, vault, but he hath an abstract for the remembrance of such places, and goes to them by his note: there is no hiding you in the house.

Fal. I'll go out, then.

Mrs. Page. If you go out in your own semblance, you die, Sir John. Unless you go out disguised, —

Mrs. Ford. How might we disguise him?

Mrs. Page. Alas the day, I know not! There is no woman's gown big enough for him; otherwise he might put on a hat, a muffler, and a kerchief, and so escape.

Fal. Good hearts, devise something: any extremity rather than a mischief.

Mrs. Ford. My maid's aunt, the fat woman of Brentford, has a gown above.

Mrs. Page. On my word, it will serve him; she's as big as he is: and there's her thrummed hat, and her muffler too. — Run up, Sir John.

Mrs. Ford. Go, go, sweet Sir John: Mistress Page and I will look some linen for your head.

Mrs. Page. Quick, quick! we'll come dress you straight: put on the gown the while. 			[*Exit Falstaff.*

Mrs. Ford. I would my husband would meet him in this shape: he cannot abide the old woman of Brentford; he swears she's a witch; forbade her my house, and hath threatened to beat her.

Mrs. Page. Heaven guide him to thy husband's cudgel, and the devil guide his cudgel afterwards!

Mrs. Ford. But is my husband coming?

Mrs. Page. Ay, in good sadness, is he; and talks of the basket too, howsoever he hath had intelligence.

Mrs. Ford. We'll try that; for I'll appoint my men to carry the basket again, to meet him at the door with it, as they did last time.

Mrs. Page. Nay, but he'll be here presently: let's go dress him like the witch of Brentford.

Mrs. Ford. I'll first direct my men what they shall do with the basket. Go up; I'll bring linen for him straight. [*Exit.*

Mrs. Page. Hang him, dishonest varlet! we cannot misuse him enough.

　　　We'll leave a proof, by that which we will do,
　　　Wives may be merry, and yet honest too:
　　　We do not act that often jest and laugh;
　　　'Tis old, but true, — Still swine eat all the draff. [*Exit.*

Re-enter MISTRESS FORD *with two* Servants.

Mrs. Ford. Go, sirs, take the basket again on your shoulders: your master is hard at door; if he bid you set it down, obey him: quickly, dispatch. 　　　　　　　[*Exit.*

First Serv. Come, come, take it up.

Sec. Serv. Pray heaven it be not full of knight again.

First Serv. I hope not; I had as lief bear so much lead.

Enter FORD, PAGE, SHALLOW, CAIUS, *and* SIR HUGH EVANS.

Ford. Ay, but if it prove true, Master Page, have you any way then to unfool me again? — Set down the basket, villains! — Somebody call my wife. — Youth in a basket! — O you panderly rascals! there's a knot, a ging, a pack, a conspiracy against me: now shall the devil be shamed. — What, wife, I say! come, come forth! behold what honest clothes you send forth to bleaching!

Page. Why, this passes! Master Ford, you are not to go loose any longer; you must be pinioned.

Evans. Why, this is lunatics! this is mad as a mad dog!

Shal. Indeed, Master Ford, this is not well; indeed.

Ford. So say I too, sir.

Re-enter MISTRESS FORD.

Come hither, Mistress Ford; Mistress Ford, the honest
woman, the modest wife, the virtuous creature, that hath the
jealous fool to her husband! — I suspect without cause, mistress, do I?

Mrs. Ford. Heaven be my witness you do, if you suspect
me in any dishonesty.

Ford. Well said, brazen-face! hold it out. — Come forth,
sirrah!   [*Pulling the clothes out of the basket.*

Page. This passes!

Mrs. Ford. Are you not ashamed? let the clothes alone.

Ford. I shall find you anon.

Evans. 'Tis unreasonable! Will you take up your wife's
clothes? Come away.

Ford. Empty the basket, I say!

Mrs. Ford. Why, man, why, —

Ford. Master Page, as I am a man, there was one con-
veyed out of my house yesterday in this basket: why may
not he be there again? In my house I am sure he is: my
intelligence is true; my jealousy is reasonable. — Pluck me
out all the linen.

Mrs. Ford. If you find a man there, he shall die a flea's
death.

Page. Here's no man.

Shal. By my fidelity, this is not well, Master Ford; this
wrongs you.

Evans. Master Ford, you must pray, and not follow the
imaginations of your own heart: this is jealousies.

Ford. Well, he's not here I seek for.

Page. No, nor nowhere else but in your brain.

Ford. Help to search my house this one time. If I find
not what I seek, show no colour for my extremity; let me
for ever be your table-sport; let them say of me, "As jealous
as Ford, that searched a hollow walnut for his wife's leman."
Satisfy me once more; once more search with me.

Mrs. Ford. What, ho, Mistress Page! come you and the
old woman down; my husband will come into the chamber.

Ford. Old woman! what old woman's that?

Mrs. Ford. Why, it is my maid's aunt of Brentford.

Ford. A witch, a quean, an old cozening quean! Have I not forbid her my house? She comes of errands, does she? We arc simple men; we do not know what's brought to pass under the profession of fortune-telling. She works by charms, by spells, by the figure; and such daubery as this is beyond our element; we know nothing. — Come down, you witch, you hag, you; come down, I say!

Mrs. Ford. Nay, good, sweet husband, — Good gentlemen, let him not strike the old woman.

Re-enter FALSTAFF *in women's clothes, led by* MISTRESS PAGE.

Mrs. Page. Come, Mother Prat; come, give me your hand.

Ford. I'll prat her. — [*Beating him*] Out of my door, you witch, you hag, you baggage, you polecat, you ronyon! out, out! I'll conjure you, I'll fortune-tell you.   [*Exit Falstaff.*

Mrs. Page. Are you not ashamed? I think you have killed the poor woman.

Mrs. Ford. Nay, he will do it. — 'Tis a goodly credit for you

Ford. Hang her, witch!

Evans. By yea and no, I think the oman is a witch indeed: I like not when a oman has a great peard: I spy a great peard under her muffler.

Ford. Will you follow, gentlemen? I beseech you, follow; see but the issue of my jealousy: if I cry out thus upon no trail, never trust me when I open again.

Page. Let's obey his humour a little further: come, gentlemen.   [*Exeunt Ford, Page, Shal., Caius, and Evans.*

Mrs. Page. Trust me, he beat him most pitifully.

Mrs. Ford. Nay, by the mass, that he did not; he beat him most unpitifully methought.

Mrs. Page. I'll have the cudgel hallowed, and hung o'er the altar; it hath done meritorious service.

Mrs. Ford. What think you? may we, with the warrant of womanhood and the witness of a good conscience, pursue him with any further revenge?

Mrs. Page. The spirit of wantonness is, sure, scared out of him: if the devil have him not in fee-simple, with fine and recovery, he will never, I think, in the way of waste, attempt us again.

Mrs. Ford. Shall we tell our husbands how we have served him?

Mrs. Page. Yes, by all means; if it be but to scrape the figures out of your husband's brains. If they can find in their hearts the poor unvirtuous fat knight shall be any further afflicted, we two will still be the ministers.

Mrs. Ford. I'll warrant they'll have him publicly shamed: and methinks there would be no period to the jest, should he not be publicly shamed.

Mrs. Page. Come, to the forge with it, then; shape it: I would not have things cool.   [*Exeunt.*

Scene III. *A room in the Garter Inn.*

Enter Host *and* Bardolph.

Bard. Sir, the Germans desire to have three of your horses: the duke himself will be to-morrow at court, and they are going to meet him.

Host. What duke should that be comes so secretly? I hear not of him in the court. Let me speak with the gentlemen: they speak English?

Bard. Ay, sir; I'll call them to you.

Host. They shall have my horses; but I'll make them pay; I'll sauce them: they have had my house a week at command; I have turned away my other guests: they must come off; I'll sauce them. Come   [*Exeunt.*

Scene IV. *A room in* Ford's *house.*

Enter Page, Ford, Mistress Page, Mistress Ford, *and* Sir Hugh Evans.

Evans. 'Tis one of the best discretions of a oman as ever I did look upon.

Page. And did he send you both these letters at an instant?

Mrs. Page. Within a quarter of an hour.

Ford. Pardon me, wife. Henceforth do what thou wilt;
I rather will suspect the sun with cold
Than thee with wantonness: now doth thy honour stand,
In him that was of late an heretic,
As firm as faith.

Page.   'Tis well, 'tis well; no more:
Be not as éxtreme in submission
As in offence.
But let our plot go forward: let our wives
Yet once again, to make us public sport,
Appoint a meeting with this old fat fellow,
Where we may take him, and disgrace him for it.

Ford. There is no better way than that they spoke of.

Page. How! to send him word they'll meet him in the
Park at midnight? Fie, fie! he'll never come.

Evans. You say he has been thrown in the rivers; and
has been grievously peaten, as au old oman: methinks there
should be terrors in him that he should not come; methinks
his flesh is punished, he shall have no desires.

Page. So think I too.

Mrs. Ford. Devise but how you'll use him when he comes,
And let us two devise to bring him thither.

Mrs. Page. There is an old tale goes, that Herne the hunter,
Sometime a keeper here in Windsor forest,
Doth all the winter-time, at still midnight,
Walk round about an oak, with great rugg'd horns;
And there he blasts the trees, and takes the cattle,
And makes milch-kine yield blood, and shakes a chain
In a most hideous and dreadful manner:
You've heard of such a spirit; and well you know
The superstitious idle-headed eld
Receiv'd, and did deliver to our age,
This tale of Herne the hunter for a truth.

Page. Why, yet there want not many that do fear

In deep of night to walk by this Herne's oak:
But what of this?

    Mrs. Ford.   Marry, this is our device;
That Falstaff at that oak shall meet with us,
Disguis'd like Herne, with huge horns on his head.

    Page. Well, let it not be doubted but he'll come:
And in this shape when you have brought him thither,
What shall be done with him? what is your plot?

    Mrs. Page. That likewise have we thought upon, and thus.
Nan Page my daughter, and my little son,
And three or four more of their growth, we'll dress
Like urchins, ouphs, and fairies, green and white,
With rounds of waxen tapers on their heads,
And rattles in their hands: upon a sudden,
As Falstaff, she, and I, are newly met,
Let them from forth a sawpit rush at once
With some diffusèd song: upon their sight,
We two in great amazedness will fly:
Then let them all encircle him about,
And, fairy-like, to-pinch the unclean knight;
And ask him why, that hour of fairy revel,
In their so sacred paths he dares to tread
In shape profane.

    Mrs. Ford.   And till he tell the truth,
Let the supposèd fairies pinch him sound,
And burn him with their tapers.

    Mrs. Page.   The truth being known,
We'll all present ourselves, dis-horn the spirit,
And mock him home to Windsor.

    Ford.   The children must
Be practis'd well to this, or they'll ne'er do't.

    Evans. I will teach the children their behaviours; and I
will be like a jack-an-apes also, to burn the knight with my
taber.

    Ford. That will be excellent. I'll go buy them visards.

    Mrs. Page. My Nan shall be the queen of all the fairies,
Finely attirèd in a robe of white.

Page. That silk will I go buy:—[*aside*] and in that tire
Shall Master Slender steal my Nan away,
And marry her at Eton. — Go send to Falstaff straight.

Ford. Nay, I'll to him again in name of Brook:
He'll tell me all his purpose: sure, he'll come.

Mrs. Page. Fear not you that. Go get us properties,
And tricking for our fairies.

Evans. Let us about it: it is admirable pleasures and fery
honest knaveries.　　　　　　　　[*Exeunt Page, Ford, and Evans.*

Mrs. Page. Go, Mistress Ford,
Send quickly to Sir John, to know his mind.
　　　　　　　　　　　　　　　　　　[*Exit Mrs. Ford.*
I'll to the doctor: he hath my good will,
And none but he, to marry with Nan Page.
That Slender, though well landed, is an idiot;
And he my husband best of all affects.
The doctor is well money'd, and his friends
Potent at court: he, none but he, shall have her,
Though twenty thousand worthier come to crave her.　[*Exit.*

　　　　　SCENE V. *A room in the Garter Inn.*

　　　　　　　　Enter Host *and* SIMPLE.

Host. What wouldst thou have, boor? what, thick-skin?
speak, breathe, discuss; brief, short, quick, snap.

Sim. Marry, sir, I come to speak with Sir John Falstaff
from Master Slender.

Host. There's his chamber, his house, his castle, his stand-
ing-bed, and truckle-bed; 'tis painted about with the story of
the Prodigal, fresh and new. Go knock and call; he'll speak
like an Anthropophaginian unto thee: knock, I say.

Sim. There's an old woman, a fat woman, gone up into
his chamber: I'll be so bold as stay, sir, till she come down;
I come to speak with her, indeed.

Host. Ha! a fat woman! the knight may be robbed: I'll
call. — Bully knight! bully Sir John! speak from thy lungs
military: art thou there? it is thine host, thine Ephesian, calls.

Fal. [*above*] How now, mine host!

Host. Here's a Bohemian-Tartar tarries the coming down of thy fat woman. Let her descend, bully, let her descend; my chambers are honourable: fie! privacy? fie!

Enter FALSTAFF.

Fal. There was, mine host, an old fat woman even now with me; but she's gone.

Sim. Pray you, sir, was't not the wise woman of Brentford?

Fal. Ay, marry, was it, muscle-shell: what would you with her?

Sim. My master, sir, Master Slender, sent to her, seeing her go thorough the streets, to know, sir, whether one Nym, sir, that beguiled him of a chain, had the chain or no.

Fal. I spake with the old woman about it.

Sim. And what says she, I pray, sir?

Fal. Marry, she says that the very same man that beguiled Master Slender of his chain cozened him of it.

Sim. I would I could have spoken with the woman herself; I had other things to have spoken with her too from him.

Fal. What are they? let us know.

Host. Ay, come; quick.

Sim. I may not conceal them, sir.

Host. Conceal them, or thou diest.

Sim. Why, sir, they were nothing but about Mistress Anne Page; to know if it were my master's fortune to have her or no.

Fal. 'Tis, 'tis his fortune.

Sim. What, sir?

Fal. To have her, — or no. Go; say the woman told me so.

Sim. May I be bold to say so, sir?

Fal. Ay, sir; like who more bold.

Sim. I thank your worship: I shall make my master glad with these tidings.   [*Exit.*

Host. Thou art clerkly, thou art clerkly, Sir John. Was there a wise woman with thee?

Fal. Ay, that there was, mine host; one that hath taught me more wit than ever I learned before in my life; and I paid nothing for it neither, but was paid for my learning.

Enter BARDOLPH.

Bard. Out, alas, sir! cozenage, mere cozenage!

Host. Where be my horses? speak well of them, varletto.

Bard. Run away with by the cozeners: for so soon as I came beyond Eton, they threw me off, from behind one of them, in a slough of mire; and set spurs and away, like three German devils, three Doctor Faustuses.

Host. They are gone but to meet the duke, villain: do not say they be fled; Germans are honest men.

Enter SIR HUGH EVANS.

Evans. Where is mine host?

Host. What is the matter, sir?

Evans. Have a care of your entertainments: there is a friend of mine come to town, tells me there is three cozen-germans that has cozened all the hosts of Readings, of Maidenhead, of Colebrook, of horses and money. I tell you for good will, look you: you are wise, and full of gibes and vlouting-stogs, and 'tis not convenient you should be cozened. Fare you well.   [*Exit.*

Enter DOCTOR CAIUS.

Caius. Vere is mine host de Jarteer?

Host. Here, master doctor, in perplexity and doubtful dilemma.

Caius. I cannot tell vat is dat: but it is tell-a me dat you make grand preparation for a duke de Jarmany: by my trot, dere is no duke dat de court is know to come. I tell you for good vill: adieu.   [*Exit.*

Host. Hue and cry, villain, go!—Assist me, knight.—I am undone!—Fly, run, hue and cry, villain!—I am undone!

[*Exeunt Host and Bard.*

Fal. I would all the world might be cozened; for I have been cozened and beaten too. If it should come to the ear

of the court, how I have been transformed, and how my trans-
formation hath been washed and cudgelled, they would melt
me out of my fat drop by drop, and liquor fishermen's boots
with me: I warrant they would whip me with their fine wits
till I were as crest-fallen as a dried pear. I never prospered
since I forswore myself at primero. Well, if my wind were
but long enough to say my prayers, I would repent.

Enter MISTRESS QUICKLY.

Now, whence come you?

Quick. From the two parties, forsooth.

Fal. The devil take one party, and his dam the other! and
so they shall be both bestowed. I have suffered more for their
sakes, more than the villanous inconstancy of man's disposition is able to bear.

Quick. And have not they suffered? Yes, I warrant; speciously one of them; Mistress Ford, good heart, is beaten
black and blue, that you cannot see a white spot about her.

Fal. What tellest thou me of black and blue? I was beaten
myself into all the colours of the rainbow; and I was like to be
apprehended for the witch of Brentford: but that my admirable dexterity of wit, my counterfeiting the action of an old
woman, delivered me, the knave constable had set me i' the
stocks, i' the common stocks, for a witch.

Quick. Sir, let me speak with you in your chamber: you
shall hear how things go; and, I warrant, to your content.
Here is a letter will say somewhat. Good hearts, what ado
here is to bring you together! Sure, one of you does not
serve heaven well, that you are so crossed.

Fal. Come up into my chamber.   [*Exeunt.*

SCENE VI. *Another room in the Garter Inn.*

Enter FENTON *and* HOST.

Host. Master Fenton, talk not to me; my mind is heavy:
I will give over all.

Fent. Yet hear me speak. Assist me in my purpose,

And, as I am a gentleman, I'll give thee
A hundred pound in gold more than your loss

　　Host. I will hear you, Master Fenton; and I will at the
least keep your counsel.

　　Fent. From time to time I have acquainted you
With the dear love I bear to fair Anne Page;
Who mutually hath answer'd my affection,
So far forth as herself might be her chooser,
Even to my wish: I have a letter from her
Of such contents as you will wonder at;
The mirth whereof so larded with my matter,
That neither singly can be manifested
Without the show of both; — wherein fat Falstaff
Hath a great share: the image of the jest
I'll show you here at large. Hark, good mine host.
To-night at Herne's oak, just 'twixt twelve and one,
Must my sweet Nan present the Fairy Queen;
The purpose why, is here: in which disguise,
While other jests are something rank on foot,
Her father hath commanded her to slip
Away with Slender, and with him at Eton
Immediately to marry: she hath consented:
Now, sir,
Her mother, ever strong against that match,
And firm for Doctor Caius, hath appointed
That he shall likewise shuffle her away,
While other sports are tasking of their minds,
And at the deanery, where a priest attends,
Straight marry her: to this her mother's plot
She seemingly obedient, likewise hath
Made promise to the doctor. — Now, thus it rests:
Her father means she shall be all in white;
And in that habit, when Slender sees his time
To take her by the hand, and bid her go,
She shall go with him: her mother hath intended,
The better to denote her to the doctor, —
For they must all be mask'd and visarded, —

18*

That quaint in green she shall be loose enrob'd,
With ribands pendent, flaring 'bout her head;
And when the doctor spies his vantage ripe,
To pinch her by the hand, and, on that token,
The maid hath given consent to go with him.

Host. Which means she to deceive, father or mother?

Fent. Both, my good host, to go along with me:
And here it rests, — that you'll procure the vicar
To stay for me at church 'twixt twelve and one,
And, in the lawful name of marrying,
To give our hearts united ceremony.

Host. Well, husband your device; I'll to the vicar:
Bring you the maid, you shall not lack a priest.

Fent. So shall I evermore be bound to thee;
Besides, I'll make a present recompense. [*Exeunt.*

ACT V.

Scene I. *A room in the Garter Inn.*

Enter Falstaff *and* Mistress Quickly.

Fal. Prithee, no more prattling; go: — I'll hold. This is
the third time; I hope good luck lies in odd numbers. Away,
go. They say there is divinity in odd numbers, either in
nativity, chance, or death. Away.

Quick. I'll provide you a chain; and I'll do what I can to
get you a pair of horns.

Fal. Away, I say; time wears: hold up your head, and
mince. [*Exit Mrs. Quickly.*

Enter Ford *disguised.*

How now, Master Brook! Master Brook, the matter will be
known to-night, or never. Be you in the Park about midnight, at Herne's oak, and you shall see wonders.

Ford. Went you not to her yesterday, sir, as you told me
you had appointed?

Fal. I went to her, Master Brook, as you see, like a poor

old man: but I came from her, Master Brook, like a poor
old woman. That same knave Ford, her husband, hath the
finest mad devil of jealousy in him, Master Brook, that ever
governed frenzy:— I will tell you: — he beat me grievously,
in the shape of a woman; for in the shape of man, Master
Brook, I fear not Goliath with a weaver's beam; because I
know also life is a shuttle. I am in haste; go along with
me: I'll tell you all, Master Brook. Since I plucked geese,
played truant, and whipped top, I knew not what 'twas to be
beaten till lately. Follow me: I'll tell you strange things
of this knave Ford; on whom to-night I will be revenged,
and I will deliver his wife into your hand. Follow:— strange
things in hand, Master Brook: — follow.   [*Exeunt.*

SCENE II. *Windsor Park.*

Enter PAGE, SHALLOW, *and* SLENDER.

Page. Come, come; we'll couch i' the castle-ditch till
we see the light of our fairies. — Remember, son Slender, my
daughter.

Slen. Ay, forsooth; I have spoke with her, and we have a
nay-word how to know one another: I come to her in white,
and cry "mum;" she cries "budget;" and by that we know
one another.

Shal. That's good too; but what needs either your "mum"
or her "budget"? the white will decipher her well enough.—
It hath struck ten o'clock.

Page. The night is dark; light and spirits will become it
well. Heaven prosper our sport! No man means evil but
the devil, and we shall know him by his horns. Let's away;
follow me.   [*Exeunt.*

SCENE III. *A street leading to the Park.*

Enter MISTRESS PAGE, MISTRESS FORD, *and* DOCTOR CAIUS.

Mrs. Page. Master doctor, my daughter is in green: when
you see your time, take her by the hand, away with her to

the deanery, and dispatch it quickly. Go before into the
Park: we two must go together.

Caius. I know vat I have to do. Adieu.

Mrs. Page. Fare you well, sir. [*Exit Caius.*] — My husband will not rejoice so much at the abuse of Falstaff as he
will chafe at the doctor's marrying my daughter: but 'tis
no matter; better a little chiding than a great deal of heart-
break.

Mrs. Ford. Where is Nan now and her troop of fairies?
and the Welsh devil Hugh?

Mrs. Page. They are all couched in a pit hard by Herne's
oak, with obscured lights; which, at the very instant of Falstaff's and our meeting, they will at once display to the night.

Mrs. Ford. That cannot choose but amaze him.

Mrs. Page. If he be not amazed, he will be mocked; if
he be amazed, he will every way be mocked.

Mrs. Ford. We'll betray him finely.

Mrs. Page. Against such lewdsters and their lechery
Those that betray them do no treachery.

Mrs. Ford. The hour draws on. To the oak, to the oak!
                                              [*Exeunt.*

Scene IV. *Windsor Park.*

Enter Sir Hugh Evans *disguised as a Satyr, with* Anne Page
and others as Fairies.

Evans. Trib, trib, fairies; come; and remember your
parts: be pold, I pray you; follow me into the pit; and when
I give the watch-ords, do as I pid you: come, come; trib,
trib.   [*Exeunt.*

Scene V. *Another part of the Park.*

Enter Falstaff *disguised as Herne, with a buck's head on.*

Fal. The Windsor bell hath struck twelve; the minute
draws on. Now, the hot-blooded gods assist me! — Remember, Jove, thou wast a bull for thy Europa; love set
on thy horns: — O powerful love! that, in some respects,
makes a beast a man; in some other, a man a beast. — You

were also, Jupiter, a swan for the love of Leda: — O omni-
potent love! how near the god drew to the complexion of a
goose! — A fault done first in the form of a beast; — O Jove,
a beastly fault! — and then another fault in the semblance
of a fowl; — think on't, Jove; a foul fault! When gods have
hot backs, what shall poor men do? For me, I am here a
Windsor stag; and the fattest, I think, i' the forest. — Send
me a cool rut-time, Jove, or who can blame me to piss my
tallow? — Who comes here? my doe?

Enter MISTRESS FORD *and* MISTRESS PAGE.

Mrs. Ford. Sir John! art thou there, my deer? my male
deer?

Fal. My doe with the black scut! — Let the sky rain
potatoes; let it thunder to the tune of *Green sleeves*, hail
kissing-comfits, and snow eryngoes; let there come a tempest
of provocation, I will shelter me here.   [*Embracing her.*

Mrs. Ford. Mistress Page is come with me, sweetheart.

Fal. Divide me like a bribed buck, each a haunch: I
will keep my sides to myself, my shoulders for the fellow of
this walk, and my horns I bequeath your husbands. Am I a
woodman, ha? Speak I like Herne the hunter? — Why, now
is Cupid a child of conscience; he makes restitution. As I
am a true spirit, welcome!   [*Noise within.*

Mrs. Page. Alas, what noise?

Mrs. Ford. Heaven forgive our sins!

Fal. What should this be?

Mrs. Ford. |
Mrs. Page. | Away, away!   [*They run off.*

Fal. I think the devil will not have me damned, lest the
oil that's in me should set hell on fire; he would never else
cross me thus.

Enter SIR HUGH EVANS, *as a Satyr; another person, as Hobgoblin;* ANNE PAGE, *as the Fairy Queen, attended by her Brother
and others, as Fairies, with waxen tapers on their heads.*

Anne. Fairies, black, gray, green, and white,
You moonshine revellers, and shades of night,

You orphan heirs of fixèd destiny,
Attend your office and your quality. —
Crier Hobgoblin, make the fairy oyes.

 Hobgob. Elves, list your names; silence, you airy toys.
Cricket, to Windsor chimneys shalt thou leap:
Where fires thou find'st unrak'd and hearths unswep,
There pinch the maids as blue as bilberry:
Our radiant queen hates sluts and sluttery.

 Fal. They're fairies; he that speaks to them shall die:
I'll wink and couch: no man their works must eye.

          [*Lies down upon his face.*

 Evans. Where's Pead? — Go you, and where you find
    a maid
That, ere she sleep, has thrice her prayers said,
Rein up the organs of her fantasy;
Sleep she as sound as careless infancy:
But those as sleep and think not on their sins,
Pinse them, arms, legs, backs, shoulders, sides, and shins.

 Anne. About, about;
Search Windsor Castle, elves, within and out:
Strew good luck, ouphs, on every sacred room;
That it may stand till the perpetual doom,
In state as wholesome as in state 'tis fit,
Worthy the owner, and the owner it.
The several chairs of order look you scour
With juice of balm and every precious flower:
Each fair instalment, coat, and several crest,
With loyal blazon, evermore be blest!
And nightly, meadow-fairies, look you sing,
Like to the Garter's compass, in a ring:
Th' expressure that it bears, green let it be,
More fertile-fresh than all the field to see;
And *Honi soit qui mal y pense* write
In emerald tufts, flowers purple, blue, and white;
Like sapphire, pearl, and rich embroidery,
Buckled below fair knighthood's bending knee: —
Fairies use flowers for their charàctery.

Away; disperse: but till 'tis one o'clock,
Our dance of custom round about the oak
Of Herne the hunter let us not forget.

    Evans. Pray you, lock hand in hand; yourselves in
              order set;
And twenty glow-worms shall our lanterns be,
To guide our measure round about the tree. —
But, stay; I smell a man of middle-earth.

    Fal. Heavens defend me from that Welsh fairy, lest he
transform me to a piece of cheese!

    Hobgob. Vile worm, thou wast o'erlook'd even in thy birth.

    Anne. With trial-fire touch me his finger-end:
If he be chaste, the flame will back descend,
And turn him to no pain; but if he start,
It is the flesh of a corrupted heart.

    Hobgob. A trial, come.

    Evans.   Come, will this wood take fire?
                          [They burn him with their tapers.

    Fal. O, O, O!

    Anne. Corrupt, corrupt, and tainted in desire! —
About him, fairies; sing a scornful rhyme;
And, as you trip, still pinch him to your time.

Song.

       Fie on sinful fantasy!
       Fie on lust and luxury!
       Lust is but a bloody fire,
       Kindled with unchaste desire,
       Fed in heart; whose flames aspire,
       As thoughts do blow them, higher and higher.
       Pinch him, fairies, mutually;
       Pinch him for his villany;
    Pinch him, and burn him, and turn him about,
    Till candles and starlight and moonshine be out.

During this song the Fairies pinch FALSTAFF. DOCTOR CAIUS
comes one way, and steals away a Fairy in green; SLENDER

another way, and takes off a Fairy in white; and FENTON *comes,
and steals away* ANNE PAGE. *A noise of hunting is heard within.
The Fairies run away.* FALSTAFF *pulls off his buck's head, and
rises.*

Enter PAGE, FORD, MISTRESS PAGE, *and* MISTRESS FORD.
They lay hold on FALSTAFF.

Page. Nay, do not fly; I think we've watch'd you now:
Will none but Herne the hunter serve your turn?

Mrs. Page. I pray you, come, hold up the jest no higher.—
Now, good Sir John, how like you Windsor wives? —
See you these, husband? do not these fair oaks
Become the forest better than the town?

Ford. Now, sir, who's a cuckold now? — Master Brook,
Falstaff's a knave, a cuckoldly knave; here are his horns,
Master Brook: and, Master Brook, he hath enjoyed nothing
of Ford's but his buck-basket, his cudgel, and twenty pounds
of money, which must be paid to Master Brook; his horses
are arrested for it, Master Brook.

Mrs. Ford. Sir John, we have had ill luck; we could
never meet. I will never take you for my love again; but
I will always count you my deer.

Fal. I do begin to perceive that I am made an ass.

Ford. Ay, and an ox too: both the proofs are extant.

Fal. And these are not fairies? I was three or four times
in the thought they were not fairies: and yet the guiltiness
of my mind, the sudden surprise of my powers, drove the
grossness of the foppery into a received belief, in despite of
the teeth of all rhyme and reason, that they were fairies.
See now how wit may be made a Jack-a-Lent, when 'tis upon
ill employment!

Evans. Sir John Falstaff, serve Got, and leave your desires, and fairies will not pinse you.

Ford. Well said, fairy Hugh.

Evans. And leave you your jealousies too, I pray you.

Ford. I will never mistrust my wife again, till thou art
able to woo her in good English.

Fal. Have I laid my brain in the sun, and dried it, that it wants matter to prevent so gross o'er-reaching as this? Am I ridden with a Welsh goat too? shall I have a coxcomb of frize? 'Tis time I were choked with a piece of toasted cheese.

Evans. Scese is not goot to give putter; your pelly is all putter.

Fal. "Seese" and "putter"! have I lived to stand at the taunt of one that makes fritters of English? This is enough to be the decay of lust and late-walking through the realm.

Mrs. Page. Why, Sir John, do you think, though we would have thrust virtue out of our hearts by the head and shoulders, and have given ourselves without scruple to hell, that ever the devil could have made you our delight?

Ford. What, a hodge-pudding? a bag of flax?

Mrs. Page. A puffed man?

Page. Old, cold, withered, and of intolerable entrails?

Ford. And one that is as slanderous as Satan?

Page. And as poor as Job?

Ford. And as wicked as his wife?

Evans. And given to fornications, and to taverns, and sack, and wine, and metheglins, and to drinkings, and swearings and starings, pribbles and prabbles?

Fal. Well, I am your theme: you have the start of me; I am dejected; I am not able to answer the Welsh flannel; ignorance itself is a plummet o'er me: use me as you will.

Ford. Marry, sir, we'll bring you to Windsor, to one Master Brook, that you have cozened of money, to whom you should have been a pander: over and above that you have suffered, I think to repay that money will be a biting affliction.*

Page. Yet be cheerful, knight: thou shalt eat a posset to-night at my house; where I will desire thee to laugh at

---

* Here Theobald inserted from the quartos 1602, 1619;

"*Mrs. Ford.* Nay, husband, let that go to make amends;
Forgive that sum, and so we'll all be friends.
Ford. Well, here's my hand: all is forgiven at last.""

my wife, that now laughs at thee: tell her Master Slender
hath married her daughter.

Mrs. Page. [*aside*] Doctors doubt that: if Anne Page be
my daughter, she is, by this, Doctor Caius' wife.

Enter SLENDER.

Slen. Whoa, ho! ho, father Page!

Page. Son, how now! how now, son! have you dispatched?

Slen. Dispatched! — I'll make the best in Glostershire
know on't; would I were hanged, la, else!

Page. Of what, son?

Slen. I came yonder at Eton to marry Mistress Anne
Page, and she's a great lubberly boy. If it had not been i'
the church, I would have swinged him, or he should have
swinged me. If I did not think it had been Anne Page,
would I might never stir! — and 'tis a postmaster's boy.

Page. Upon my life, then, you took the wrong.

Slen. What need you tell me that? I think so, when I
took a boy for a girl. If I had been married to him, for all
he was in woman's apparel, I would not have had him.

Page. Why, this is your own folly. Did not I tell you
how you should know my daughter by her garments?

Slen. I went to her in white, and cried "mum," and she
cried "budget," as Anne and I had appointed; and yet it was
not Anne, but a postmaster's boy.

Mrs. Page. Good George, be not angry: I knew of your
purpose; turned my daughter into green; and, indeed, she is
now with the doctor at the deanery, and there married.

Enter CAIUS.

Caius. Vere is Mistress Page? By gar, I am cozened: I
ha' married *un garçon*, a boy; *un paysan*, by gar, a boy; it is
not Anne Page: by gar, I am cozened.

Mrs. Page. Why, did you take her in green?

Caius. Ay, by gar, and 'tis a boy: by gar, I'll raise all
Windsor.·   [*Exit.*

Ford. This is strange. Who hath got the right Anne?

Page. My heart misgives me: — here comes Master Fenton.

Enter FENTON *and* ANNE PAGE.

How now, Master Fenton!

　Anne. Pardon, good father! — good my mother, pardon!

　Page. Now, mistress, — how chance you went not with
Master Slender?

　Mrs. Page. Why went you not with master doctor, maid?

　Fent. You do amaze her: hear the truth of it.
You would have married her most shamefully,
Where there was no proportion held in love.
The truth is, she and I, long since contracted,
Are now so sure that nothing can dissolve us.
Th' offence is holy that she hath committed;
And this deceit loses the name of craft,
Of disobedience, or unduteous wile;
Since therein she doth evitate and shun
A thousand irreligious cursèd hours,
Which forcèd marriage would have brought upon her.

　Ford. Stand not amaz'd; here is no remedy:
In love the heavens themselves do guide the state;
Money buys lands, and wives are sold by fate.

　Fal. I am glad, though you have ta'en a special stand to
strike at me, that your arrow hath glanced.

　Page. Well, what remedy? — Fenton, heaven give thee
　　　　　joy! —
What cannot be eschew'd must be embrac'd.

　Fal. When night-dogs run, all sorts of deer are chas'd.

　Mrs. Page. Well, I will muse no further. — Master Fenton,
Heaven give you many, many merry days! —
Good husband, let us every one go home,
And laugh this sport o'er by a country fire;
Sir John and all.

　Ford.　　　　　Let it be so. — Sir John,
To Master Brook you yet shall hold your word;
For he to-night shall lie with Mistress Ford.

　　　　　　　　　　　　　　　　　　[*Exeunt.*

THE POEMS
OF
WILLIAM SHAKESPEARE.

VENUS AND ADONIS.

TO THE
RIGHT HONOURABLE
HENRY WRIOTHESLY,
EARL OF SOUTHAMPTON, AND BARON OF TICHFIELD.

RIGHT HONOURABLE,

I KNOW not how I shall offend in dedicating my unpolished lines to your lordship, nor how the world will censure me for choosing so strong a prop to support so weak a burden: only, if your honour seem but pleased, I account myself highly praised, and vow to take advantage of all idle hours, till I have honoured you with some graver labour. But if the first heir of my invention prove deformed, I shall be sorry it had so noble a godfather, and never after ear so barren a land, for fear it yield me still so bad a harvest. I leave it to your honourable survey, and your honour to your heart's content; which I wish may always answer your own wish, and the world's hopeful expectation.

Your honour's in all duty,
WILLIAM SHAKESPEARE.

VENUS AND ADONIS.

Vilia miretur vulgus; mihi flavus Apollo
Pocula Castalia plena ministret aqua.

[OVID, I. *Am.* xv. 35.]

EVEN as the sun with purple-colour'd face
Had ta'en his last leave of the weeping morn,
Rose-cheek'd Adonis hied him to the chase;
Hunting he lov'd, but love he laugh'd to scorn:
    Sick-thoughted Venus makes amain unto him,
    And like a bold-fac'd suitor gins to woo him.

"Thrice-fairer than myself," thus she began,
"The field's chief flower, sweet above compare,
Stain to all nymphs, more lovely than a man,
More white and red than doves or roses are;
    Nature that made thee, with herself at strife,
    Saith that the world hath ending with thy life.

"Vouchsafe, thou wonder, to alight thy steed,
And rein his proud head to the saddle-bow;
If thou wilt deign this favour, for thy meed
A thousand honey secrets shalt thou know:
    Here come and sit, where never serpent hisses,
    And being set, I'll smother thee with kisses;

"And yet not cloy thy lips with loath'd satiety,
But rather famish them amid their plenty,
Making them red and pale with fresh variety, —
Ten kisses short as one, one long as twenty:
    A summer's day will seem an hour but short,
    Being wasted in such time-beguiling sport."

With this she seizeth on his sweating palm,
The precedent of pith and livelihood,
And, trembling in her passion, calls it balm,
Earth's sovereign salve to do a goddess good:
    Being so enrag'd, desire doth lend her force
    Courageously to pluck him from his horse.

Over one arm the lusty courser's rein,
Under her other was the tender boy,
Who blush'd and pouted in a dull disdain,
With leaden appetite, unapt to toy;
    She red and hot as coals of glowing fire,
    He red for shame, but frosty in desire.

The studded bridle on a raggèd bough
Nimbly she fastens: — O, how quick is love! —
The steed is stallèd up, and even now
To tie the rider she begins to prove:
    Backward she push'd him, as she would be thrust,
    And govern'd him in strength, though not in lust.

So soon was she along as he was down,
Each leaning on their elbows and their hips:
Now doth she stroke his cheek, now doth he frown,
And gins to chide, but soon she stops his lips;
    And kissing speaks, with lustful language broken,
    "If thou wilt chide, thy lips shall never open."

He burns with bashful shame; she with her tears
Doth quench the maiden burning of his cheeks;
Then with her windy sighs and golden hairs
To fan and blow them dry again she seeks:
    He saith she is immodest, blames her miss;
    What follows more she murders with a kiss.

Even as an empty eagle, sharp by fast,
Tires with her beak on feathers, flesh, and bone,
Shaking her wings, devouring all in haste,
Till either gorge be stuff'd, or prey be gone;

Even so she kiss'd his brow, his cheek, his chin,
And where she ends she doth anew begin.

Forc'd to content, but never to obey,
Panting he lies, and breatheth in her face;
She feedeth on the steam as on a prey,
And calls it heavenly moisture, air of grace;
   Wishing her cheeks were gardens full of flowers,
   So they were dew'd with such-distilling showers.

Look how a bird lies tangled in a net,
So fasten'd in her arms Adonis lies;
Pure shame and aw'd resistance made him fret,
Which bred more beauty in his angry eyes:
   Rain added to a river that is rank
   Perforce will force it overflow the bank.

Still she entreats, and prettily entreats,
And to a pretty ear she tunes her tale;
Still is he sullen, still he lours and frets,
"Twixt crimson shame and anger ashy-pale;
   Being red, she loves him best; and being white,
   Her best is better'd with a more delight.

Look how he can, she cannot choose but love;
And by her fair immortal hand she swears,
From his soft bosom never to remove,
Till he take truce with her contending tears,
   Which long have rain'd, making her cheeks all wet;
   And one sweet kiss shall pay this countless debt.

Upon this promise did he raise his chin,
Like a dive-dapper peering through a wave,
Who, being look'd on, ducks as quickly in;
So offers he to give what she did crave;
   But when her lips were ready for his pay,
   He winks, and turns his lips another way.

Never did passenger in summer's heat
More thirst for drink than she for this good turn.

Her help she sees, but help she cannot get;
She bathes in water, yet her fire must burn:
  "O, pity," gan she cry, "flint-hearted boy!
  'Tis but a kiss I beg; why art thou coy?

"I have been woo'd, as I entreat thee now,
Even by the stern and direful god of war,
Whose sinewy neck in battle ne'er did bow,
Who conquers where he comes in every jar;
  Yet hath he been my captive and my slave,
  And begg'd for that which thou unask'd shalt have.

"Over my altars hath he hung his lance,
His batter'd shield, his uncontrollèd crest,
And for my sake hath learn'd to sport and dance,
To toy, to wanton, dally, smile, and jest;
  Scorning his churlish drum and ensign red,
  Making my arms his field, his tent my bed.

"Thus he that overrul'd I oversway'd,
Leading him prisoner in a red-rose chain:
Strong-temper'd steel his stronger strength obey'd,
Yet was he servile to my coy disdain.
  O, be not proud, nor brag not of thy might,
  For mastering her that foil'd the god of fight!

"Touch but my lips with those fair lips of thine, —
Though mine be not so fair, yet are they red, —
The kiss shall be thine own as well as mine: —
What see'st thou in the ground? hold up thy head:
  Look in mine eyeballs, there thy beauty lies;
  Then why not lips on lips, since eyes in eyes?

"Art thou asham'd to kiss? then wink again,
And I will wink; so shall the day seem night;
Love keeps his revels where there are but twain;
Be bold to play, our sport is not in sight:
  These blue-vein'd violets whereon we lean
  Never can blab, nor know not what we mean.

"The tender spring upon thy tempting lip
Shows thee unripe; yet mayst thou well be tasted:
Make use of time, let not advantage slip;
Beauty within itself should not be wasted:
   Fair flowers that are not gather'd in their prime
   Rot and consume themselves in little time.

"Were I hard-favour'd, foul, or wrinkled-old,
Ill-nurtur'd, crookèd, churlish, harsh in voice,
O'erworn, despisèd, rheumatic, and cold,
Thick-sighted, barren, lean, and lacking juice,
   Then mightst thou pause, for then I were not for thee;
   But having no defects, why dost abhor me?

"Thou canst not see one wrinkle in my brow;
Mine eyes are gray, and bright, and quick in turning;
My beauty as the spring doth yearly grow,
My flesh is soft and plump, my marrow burning;
   My smooth moist hand, were it with thy hand felt,
   Would in thy palm dissolve, or seem to melt.

"Bid me discourse, I will enchant thine ear,
Or, like a fairy, trip upon the green,
Or, like a nymph, with long dishevell'd hair,
Dance on the sands, and yet no footing seen:
   Love is a spirit all compact of fire,
   Not gross to sink, but light, and will aspire.

"Witness this primrose bank whereon I lie;
These forceless flowers like sturdy trees support me;
Two strengthless doves will draw me through the sky,
From morn till night, even where I list to sport me:
   Is love so light, sweet boy, and may it be
   That thou shouldst think it heavy unto thee?

"Is thine own heart to thine own face affected?
Can thy right hand seize love upon thy left?
Then woo thyself, be of thyself rejected,
Steal thine own freedom, and complain on theft.

Narcissus so himself himself forsook,
And died to kiss his shadow in the brook.

"Torches are made to light, jewels to wear,
Dainties to taste, fresh beauty for the use,
Herbs for their smell, and sappy plants to bear;
Things growing to themselves are growth's abuse:
　Seeds spring from seeds, and beauty breedeth beauty;
　Thou wast begot, — to get it is thy duty.

"Upon the earth's increase why shouldst thou feed,
Unless the earth with thy increase be fed?
By law of nature thou art bound to breed,
That thine may live when thou thyself art dead;
　And so, in spite of death, thou dost survive,
　In that thy likeness still is left alive."

By this, the love-sick queen began to sweat,
For, where they lay, the shadow had forsook them,
And Titan, tirèd in the mid-day heat,
With burning eye did hotly overlook them;
　Wishing Adonis had his team to guide,
　So he were like him, and by Venus' side.

And now Adonis, with a lazy spright,
And with a heavy, dark, disliking eye,
His louring brows o'erwhelming his fair sight,
Like misty vapours when they blot the sky, —
　Souring his cheeks, cries, "Fie, no more of love!
　The sun doth burn my face; I must remove."

"Ay me," quoth Venus, "young, and so unkind?
What bare excuses mak'st thou to be gone!
I'll sigh celestial breath, whose gentle wind
Shall cool the heat of this descending sun:
　I'll make a shadow for thee of my hairs;
　If they burn too, I'll quench them with my tears.

"The sun that shines from heaven shines but warm,
And, lo, I lie between that sun and thee:

The heat I have from thence doth little harm,
Thine eye darts forth the fire that burneth me;
 And were I not immortal, life were done
 Between this heavenly and earthly sun.

"Art thou obdurate, flinty, hard as steel,
Nay, more than flint, for stone at rain relenteth?
Art thou a woman's son, and canst not feel
What 'tis to love? how want of love tormenteth?
 O, had thy mother borne so hard a mind,
 She had not brought forth thee, but died unkind.

"What am I, that thou shouldst contemn me this?
Or what great danger dwells upon my suit?
What were thy lips the worse for one poor kiss?
Speak, fair; but speak fair words, or else be mute:
 Give me one kiss, I'll give it thee again,
 And one for interest, if thou wilt have twain.

"Fie, lifeless picture, cold and senseless stone,
Well-painted idol, image dull and dead,
Statue contenting but the eye alone,
Thing like a man, but of no woman bred!
 Thou art no man, though of a man's complexion,
 For men will kiss even by their own direction."

This said, impatience chokes her pleading tongue,
And swelling passion doth provoke a pause;
Red cheeks and fiery eyes blaze forth her wrong;
Being judge in love, she cannot right her cause:
 And now she weeps, and now she fain would speak,
 And now her sobs do her intendments break

Sometimes she shakes her head, and then his hand,
Now gazeth she on him, now on the ground;
Sometimes her arms infold him like a band:
She would, he will not in her arms be bound;
 And when from thence he struggles to be gone,
 She locks her lily fingers one in one.

"Fondling," she saith, "since I have hemm'd thee here
Within the circuit of this ivory pale,
I'll be a park, and thou shalt be my deer;
Feed where thou wilt, on mountain or in dale:
　Graze on my lips; and if those hills be dry,
　Stray lower, where the pleasant fountains lie.

"Within this limit is relief enough,
Sweet bottom-grass, and high delightful plain,
Round rising hillocks, brakes obscure and rough,
To shelter thee from tempest and from rain:
　Then be my deer, since I am such a park;
　No dog shall rouse thee, though a thousand bark."

At this Adonis smiles as in disdain,
That in each cheek appears a pretty dimple:
Love made those hollows, if himself were slain,
He might be buried in a tomb so simple;
　Foreknowing well, if there he came to lie,
　Why, there Love liv'd, and there he could not die.

These lovely caves, these round enchanting pits,
Open'd their mouths to swallow Venus' liking.
Being mad before, how doth she now for wits?
Struck dead at first, what needs a second striking?
　Poor queen of love, in thine own law forlorn,
　To love a cheek that smiles at thee in scorn!

Now which way shall she turn? what shall she say?
Her words are done, her woes the more increasing;
The time is spent, her object will away,
And from her twining arms doth urge releasing.
　"Pity," she cries, "some favour, some remorse!"
　Away he springs, and hasteth to his horse.

But, lo, from forth a copse that neighbours by,
A breeding jennet, lusty, young, and proud,
Adonis' trampling courser doth espy,
And forth she rushes, snorts, and neighs aloud:

The strong-neck'd steed, being tied unto a tree,
Breaketh his rein, and to her straight goes he.

Imperiously he leaps, he neighs, he bounds,
And now his woven girths he breaks asunder;
The bearing earth with his hard hoof he wounds,
Whose hollow womb resounds like heaven's thunder;
   The iron bit he crusheth 'tween his teeth,
   Controlling what he was controllèd with.

His ears up-prick'd; his braided hanging mane
Upon his compass'd crest now stand on end;
His nostrils drink the air, and forth again,
As from a furnace, vapours doth he send;
   His eye, which scornfully glisters like fire,
   Shows his hot courage and his high desire.

Sometime he trots, as if he told the steps,
With gentle majesty and modest pride;
Anon he rears upright, curvets and leaps,
As who should say, "Lo, thus my strength is tried;
   And this I do to captivate the eye
   Of the fair breeder that is standing by."

What recketh he his rider's angry stir,
His flattering "Holla" or his "Stand, I say"?
What cares he now for curb or pricking spur?
For rich caparisons or trapping gay?
   He sees his love, and nothing else he sees,
   For nothing else with his proud sight agrees.

Look, when a painter would surpass the life
In limning out a well-proportion'd steed,
His art with nature's workmanship at strife,
As if the dead the living should exceed;
   So did this horse excel a common one
   In shape, in courage, colour, pace, and bone.

Round-hoof'd, short-jointed, fetlocks shag and long,
Broad breast, full eye, small head, and nostril wide,

High crest, short ears, straight legs and passing strong,
Thin mane, thick tail, broad buttock, tender hide:
  Look, what a horse should have he did not lack,
  Save a proud rider on so proud a back.

Sometime he scuds far off, and there he stares;
Anon he starts at stirring of a feather;
To bid the wind a base he now prepares,
And whêr he run or fly they know not whether;
  For through his mane and tail the high wind sings,
  Fanning the hairs, who wave like feather'd wings.

He looks upon his love, and neighs unto her;
She answers him, as if she knew his mind:
Being proud, as females are, to see him woo her,
She puts on outward strangeness, seems unkind;
  Spurns at his love, and scorns the heat he feels,
  Beating his kind embracements with her heels.

Then, like a melancholy malcontent,
He vails his tail, that, like a falling plume,
Cool shadow to his melting buttock lent:
He stamps, and bites the poor flies in his fume.
  His love, perceiving how he is enrag'd,
  Grew kinder, and his fury was assuag'd.

His testy master goeth about to take him;
When, lo, the unback'd breeder, full of fear,
Jealous of catching, swiftly doth forsake him,
With her the horse, and left Adonis there:
  As they were mad, unto the wood they hie them,
  Out-stripping crows that strive to over-fly them.

All swoln with chafing, down Adonis sits,
Banning his boisterous and unruly beast:
And now the happy season once more fits,
That love-sick Love by pleading may be blest;
  For lovers say, the heart hath treble wrong
  When it is barr'd the aidance of the tongue.

An oven that is stopp'd, or river stay'd,
Burneth more hotly, swelleth with more rage:
So of concealèd sorrow may be said;
Free vent of words love's fire doth assuage;
　　But when the heart's attorney once is mute,
　　The client breaks, as desperate in his suit.

He sees her coming, and begins to glow,
Even as a dying coal revives with wind,
And with his bonnet hides his angry brow;
Looks on the dull earth with disturbèd mind;
　　Taking no notice that she is so nigh,
　　For all askance he holds her in his eye.

O, what a sight it was, wistly to view
How she came stealing to the wayward .boy!
To note the fighting conflict of her hue,
How white and red each other did destroy!
　　But now her cheek was pale, and by and by
　　It flash'd forth fire, as lightning from the sky.

Now was she just before him as he sat,
And like a lowly lover down she kneels;
With one fair hand she heaveth up his hat,
Her other tender hand his fair cheek feels:
　　His tenderer cheek receives her soft hand's print,
　　As apt as new-fall'n snow takes any dint.

O, what a war of looks was then between them!
Her eyes petitioners to his eyes suing;
His eyes saw her eyes as they had not seen them;
Her eyes woo'd still, his eyes disdain'd the wooing:
　　And all this dumb-play had his acts made plain
　　With tears, which, chorus-like, her eyes did rain.

Full gently now she takes him by the hand,
A lily prison'd in a gaol of snow,
Or ivory in an alabaster band;
So white a friend engirts so white a foe:

This beauteous combat, wilful and unwilling,
Show'd like two silver doves that sit a-billing.

Once more the engine of her thoughts began:
"O fairest mover on this mortal round,
Would thou wert as I am, and I a man,
My heart all whole as thine, thy heart my wound;
  For one sweet look thy help I would assure thee,
  Though nothing but my body's bane would cure thee."

"Give me my hand," saith he; "why dost thou feel it?"
"Give me my heart," saith she, "and thou shalt have it;
O, give it me, lest thy hard heart do steel it,
And being steel'd, soft sighs can never grave it:
  Then love's deep groans I never shall regard,
  Because Adonis' heart hath made mine hard."

"For shame," he cries, "let go, and let me go;
My day's delight is past, my horse is gone,
And 'tis your fault I am bereft him so:
I pray you hence, and leave me here alone;
  For all my mind, my thought, my busy care
  Is how to get my palfrey from the mare."

Thus she replies: "Thy palfrey, as he should,
Welcomes the warm approach of sweet desire:
Affection is a coal that must be cool'd;
Else, suffer'd, it will set the heart on fire:
  The sea hath bounds, but deep desire hath none;
  Therefore no marvel though thy horse be gone.

"How like a jade he stood, tied to the tree,
Servilely master'd with a leathern rein!
But when he saw his love, his youth's fair fee,
He held such petty bondage in disdain;
  Throwing the base thong from his bending crest,
  Enfranchising his mouth, his back, his breast.

"Who sees his true-love in her naked bed,
Teaching the sheets a whiter hue than white,

But, when his glutton eye so full hath fed,
His other agents aim at like delight?
  Who is so faint, that dare not be so bold
  To touch the fire, the weather being cold?

"Let me excuse thy courser, gentle boy;
And learn of him, I heartily beseech thee,
To take advantage on presented joy;
Though I were dumb, yet his proceedings teach thee:
  O, learn to love; the lesson is but plain,
  And once made perfect, never lost again."

"I know not love," quoth he, "nor will not know it,
Unless it be a boar, and then I chase it;
'Tis much to borrow, and I will not owe it;
My love to love is love but to disgrace it;
  For I have heard it is a life in death,
  That laughs, and weeps, and all but with a breath.

"Who wears a garment shapeless and unfinish'd?
Who plucks the bud before one leaf put forth?
If springing things be any jot diminish'd,
They wither in their prime, prove nothing worth:
  The colt that's back'd and burden'd being young
  Loseth his pride, and never waxeth strong.

"You hurt my hand with wringing; let us part,
And leave this idle theme, this bootless chat:
Remove your siege from my unyielding heart;
To love's alarms it will not ope the gate:
  Dismiss your vows, your feignèd tears, your flattery;
  For where a heart is hard they make no battery."

"What! canst thou talk?" quoth she, "hast thou a tongue?
O, would thou hadst not, or I had no hearing!
Thy mermaid's voice hath done me double wrong;
I had my load before, now press'd with bearing:
  Melodious discord, heavenly tune harsh-sounding,
  Ear's deep-sweet music, and heart's deep-sore wounding.

"Had I no eyes but ears, my ears would love
That inward beauty and invisible;
Or were I deaf, thy outward parts would move
Each part in me that were but sensible:
  Though neither eyes nor ears, to hear nor see,
  Yet should I be in love by touching thee.

"Say, that the sense of feeling were bereft me,
And that I could not see, nor hear, nor touch,
And nothing but the very smell were left me,
Yet would my love to thee be still as much;
  For from the still'tory of thy face excelling
  Comes breath perfum'd, that breedeth love by smelling.

"But, O, what banquet wert thou to the taste,
Being nurse and feeder of the other four!
Would they not wish the feast might ever last,
And bid Suspicion double-lock the door,
  Lest Jealousy, that sour unwelcome guest,
  Should, by his stealing in, disturb the feast?"

Once more the ruby-colour'd portal open'd,
Which to his speech did honey passage yield;
Like a red morn, that ever yet betoken'd
Wreck to the seaman, tempest to the field,
  Sorrow to shepherds, woe unto the birds,
  Gusts and foul flaws to herdmen and to herds.

This ill presage advisedly she marketh:
Even as the wind is hush'd before it raineth,
Or as the wolf doth grin before he barketh,
Or as the berry breaks before it staineth,
  Or like the deadly bullet of a gun,
  His meaning struck her ere his words begun.

And at his look she flatly falleth down,
For looks kill love, and love by looks reviveth:
A smile recures the wounding of a frown;
But blessèd bankrupt, that by love so thriveth!

The silly boy, believing she is dead,
Claps her pale cheek, till clapping makes it red;

And all-amaz'd brake off his late intent,
For sharply he did think to reprehend her,
Which cunning love did wittily prevent:
Fair fall the wit that can so well defend her!
    For on the grass she lies as she were slain,
    Till his breath breatheth life in her again.

He wrings her nose, he strikes her on the cheeks,
He bends her fingers, holds her pulses hard,
He chafes her lips; a thousand ways he seeks
To mend the hurt that his unkindness marr'd:
    He kisses her; and she, by her good will,
    Will never rise, so he will kiss her still.

The night of sorrow now is turn'd to day:
Her two blue windows faintly she up-heaveth,
Like the fair sun, when in his fresh array
He cheers the morn, and all the earth relieveth:
    And as the bright sun glorifies the sky,
    So is her face illumin'd with her eye;

Whose beams upon his hairless face are fix'd,
As if from thence they borrow'd all their shine.
Were never four such lamps together mix'd,
Had not his clouded with his brow's repine;
    But hers, which through the crystal tears gave light,
    Shone like the moon in water seen by night.

"O, where am I?" quoth she; "in earth or heaven,
Or in the ocean drench'd, or in the fire?
What hour is this? or morn or weary even?
Do I delight to die, or life desire?
    But now I liv'd, and life was death's annoy;
    But now I died, and death was lively joy.

"O, thou didst kill me; — kill me once again:
Thy eyes' shrewd tutor, that hard heart of thine,

Hath taught them scornful tricks, and such disdain,
That they have murder'd this poor heart of mine;
 And these mine eyes, true leaders to their queen,
 But for thy piteous lips no more had seen.

"Long may they kiss each other, for this cure!
O, never let their crimson liveries wear!
And as they last, their verdure still endure,
To drive infection from the dangerous year!
 That the star-gazers, having writ on death,
 May say, the plague is banish'd by thy breath.

"Pure lips, sweet seals in my soft lips imprinted,
What bargains may I make, still to be sealing?
To sell myself I can be well contented,
So thou wilt buy, and pay, and use good dealing;
 Which purchase if thou make, for fear of slips
 Set thy seal-manual on my wax-red lips.

"A thousand kisses buys my heart from me;
And pay them at thy leisure, one by one.
What is ten hundred touches unto thee?
Are they not quickly told and quickly gone?
 Say, for non-payment that the debt should double,
 Is twenty hundred kisses such a trouble?"

"Fair queen," quoth he, "if any love you owe me,
Measure my strangeness with my unripe years:
Before I know myself, seek not to know me;
No fisher but the ungrown fry forbears:
 The mellow plum doth fall, the green sticks fast,
 Or being early pluck'd is sour to taste.

"Look, the world's comforter, with weary gait,
His day's hot task hath ended in the west;
The owl, night's herald, shrieks, 'tis very late;
The sheep are gone to fold, birds to their nest;
 And coal-black clouds that shadow heaven's light
 Do summon us to part, and bid good night.

"Now let me say 'Good night,' and so say you;
If you will say so, you shall have a kiss."
"Good night," quoth she; and, ere he says "Adieu,"
The honey-fee of parting tender'd is:
   Her arms do lend his neck a sweet embrace;
   Incorporate then they seem; face grows to face:

Till, breathless, he disjoin'd, and backward drew
The heavenly moisture, that sweet coral mouth,
Whose precious taste her thirsty lips well knew,
Whereon they surfeit, yet complain on drouth:
   He with her plenty press'd, she faint with dearth,
   Their lips together glu'd, fall to the earth.

Now quick desire hath caught the yielding prey,
And glutton-like she feeds, yet never filleth;
Her lips are conquerors, his lips obey,
Paying what ransom the insulter willeth;
   Whose vulture thought doth pitch the price so high,
   That she will draw his lips' rich treasure dry:

And having felt the sweetness of the spoil,
With blindfold fury she begins to forage;
Her face doth reek and smoke, her blood doth boil,
And careless lust stirs up a desperate courage;
   Planting oblivion, beating reason back,
   Forgetting shame's pure blush and honour's wrack.

Hot, faint, and weary with her hard embracing,
Like a wild bird being tam'd with too much handling,
Or as the fleet-foot roe that's tir'd with chasing,
Or like the froward infant still'd with dandling,
   He now obeys, and now no more resisteth,
   While she takes all she can, not all she listeth.

What wax so frozen but dissolves with tempering,
And yields at last to every light impression?
Things out of hope are compass'd oft with venturing,
Chiefly in love, whose leave exceeds commission:

Affection faints not like a pale-fac'd coward,
But then woos best when most his choice is froward.

When he did frown, O, had she then gave over,
Such nectar from his lips she had not suck'd.
Foul words and frowns must not repel a lover;
What though the rose have prickles, yet 'tis pluck'd:
  Were beauty under twenty locks kept fast,
  Yet love, breaks through, and picks them all at last.

For pity now she can no more detain him;
The poor fool prays her that he may depart:
She is resolv'd no longer to restrain him;
Bids him farewell, and look well to her heart,
  The which, by Cupid's bow she doth protest,
  He carries thence incagèd in his breast.

"Sweet boy," she says, "this night I'll waste in sorrow,
For my sick heart commands mine eyes to watch.
Tell me, Love's master, shall we meet to-morrow?
Say, shall we? shall we? wilt thou make the match?"
  He tells her, no; to-morrow he intends
  To hunt the boar with certain of his friends.

"The boar!" quoth she; whereat a sudden pale,
Like lawn being spread upon the blushing rose,
Usurps her cheek; she trembles at his tale,
And on his neck her yoking arms she throws:
  She sinketh down, still hanging by his neck
  He on her belly falls, she on her back.

Now is she in the very lists of love,
Her champion mounted for the hot encounter:
All is imaginary she doth prove,
He will not manage her, although he mount her;
  That worse than Tantalus' is her annoy,
  To clip Elysium, and to lack her joy.

Even as poor birds, deceiv'd with painted grapes,
Do surfeit by the eye and pine the maw,

Even so she languisheth in her mishaps
As those poor birds that helpless berries saw.
　The warm effects which she in him finds missing
　She seeks to kindle with continual kissing.

But all in vain; good queen, it will not be:
She hath assay'd as much as may be prov'd;
Her pleading hath deserv'd a greater fee;
She's Love, she loves, and yet she is not lov'd.
　"Fie, fie," he says, "you crush me; let me go;
　You have no reason to withhold me so."

"Thou hadst been gone," quoth she, "sweet boy, ere this,
But that thou told'st me thou wouldst hunt the boar.
O, be advis'd! thou know'st not what it is
With javelin's point a churlish swine to gore,
　Whose tushes never-sheath'd he whetteth still,
　Like to a mortal butcher bent to kill.

"On his bow-back he hath a battle set
Of bristly pikes, that ever threat his foes;
His eyes, like glow-worms, shine when he doth fret;
His snout digs sepulchres where'er he goes;
　Being mov'd, he strikes whate'er is in his way,
　And whom he strikes his cruel tushes slay.

"His brawny sides, with hairy bristles arm'd,
Are better proof than thy spear's point can enter;
His short thick neck cannot be easily harm'd;
Being ireful, on the lion he will venture:
　The thorny brambles and embracing bushes,
　As fearful of him, part; through whom he rushes.

"Alas, he naught esteems that face of thine,
To which Love's eyes pay tributary gazes;
Nor thy soft hands, sweet lips, and crystal eyne,
Whose full perfection all the world amazes;
　But having thee at vantage, — wondrous dread! —
　Would root these beauties as he roots the mead.

"O, let him keep his loathsome cabin still;
Beauty hath naught to do with such foul fiends:
Come not within his danger by thy will;
They that thrive well take counsel of their friends.
　　When thou didst name the boar, not to dissemble,
　　I fear'd thy fortune, and my joints did tremble.

"Didst thou not mark my face? was it not white?
Saw'st thou not signs of fear lurk in mine eye?
Grew I not faint? and fell I not downright?
Within my bosom, whereon thou dost lie,
　　My boding heart pants, beats, and takes no rest,
　　But, like an earthquake, shakes thee on my breast.

"For where Love reigns, disturbing Jealousy
Doth call himself Affection's sentinel;
Gives false alarms, suggesteth mutiny,
And in a peaceful hour doth cry 'Kill, kill!'
　　Distempering gentle Love in his desire,
　　As air and water do abate the fire.

"This sour informer, this bate-breeding spy,
This canker that eats up Love's tender spring,
This carry-tale, dissentious Jealousy,
That sometime true news, sometime false doth bring,
　　Knocks at my heart, and whispers in mine ear,
　　That if I love thee, I thy death should fear:

"And more than so, presenteth to mine eye
The picture of an angry-chafing boar,
Under whose sharp fangs on his back doth lie
An image like thyself, all stain'd with gore;
　　Whose blood upon the fresh flowers being shed
　　Doth make them droop with grief and hang the head.

"What should I do, seeing thee so indeed,
That tremble at th' imagination?
The thought of it doth make my faint heart bleed,
And fear doth teach it divination:

20*

I prophesy thy death, my living sorrow,
If thou encounter with the boar to-morrow.

"But if thou needs wilt hunt, be rul'd by me;
Uncouple at the timorous flying hare,
Or at the fox which lives by subtlety,
Or at the roe which no encounter dare:
　　Pursue these fearful creatures o'er the downs,
　　And on thy well-breath'd horse keep with thy hounds.

"And when thou hast on foot the purblind hare,
Mark the poor wretch, to overshoot his troubles,
How he outruns the wind, and with what care
He cranks and crosses with a thousand doubles:
　　The many musets through the which he goes
　　Are like a labyrinth to amaze his foes.

"Sometime he runs among a flock of sheep,
To make the cunning hounds mistake their smell,
And sometime where earth-delving conies keep,
To stop the loud pursuers in their yell;
　　And sometime sorteth with a herd of deer:
　　Danger deviseth shifts; wit waits on fear:

"For there his smell with others being mingled,
The hot scent-snuffing hounds are driven to doubt,
Ceasing their clamorous cry till they have singled
With much ado the cold fault cleanly out;
　　Then do they spend their mouths: Echo replies,
　　As if another chase were in the skies.

"By this, poor Wat, far off upon a hill,
Stands on his hinder legs with listening ear,
To hearken if his foes pursue him still:
Anon their loud alarums he doth hear;
　　And now his grief may be comparèd well
　　To one sore sick that hears the passing-bell.

"Then shalt thou see the dew-bedabbled wretch
Turn, and return, indenting with the way;

Each envious brier his weary legs doth scratch,
Each shadow makes him stop, each murmur stay;
  For misery is trodden on by many,
  And being low never reliev'd by any.

"Lie quietly, and hear a little more;
Nay, do not struggle, for thou shalt not rise:
To make thee hate the hunting of the boar,
Unlike myself thou hear'st me moralize,
  Applying this to that, and so to so;
  For love can comment upon every woe.

"Where did I leave?" "No matter where," quoth he;
"Leave me, and then the story aptly ends:
The night is spent." "Why, what of that?" quoth she.
"I am," quoth he, "expected of my friends;
  And now 'tis dark, and going I shall fall."
  "In night," quoth she, "desire sees best of all.

"But if thou fall, O, then imagine this,
The earth, in love with thee, thy footing trips,
And all is but to rob thee of a kiss.
Rich preys make true men thieves; so do thy lips
  Make modest Dian cloudy and forlorn,
  Lest she should steal a kiss, and die forsworn.

"Now of this dark night I perceive the reason:
Cynthia for shame obscures her silver shine,
Till forging Nature be condemn'd of treason,
For stealing moulds from heaven that were divine;
  Wherein she fram'd thee, in high heaven's despite,
  To shame the sun by day, and her by night.

"And therefore hath she brib'd the Destinies
To cross the curious workmanship of Nature,
To mingle beauty with infirmities,
And pure perfection with impure defeature;
  Making it subject to the tyranny
  Of mad mischances and much misery;

"As burning fevers, agues pale and faint,
Life-poisoning pestilence, and frenzies wood,
The marrow-eating sickness, whose attaint
Disorder breeds by heating of the blood:
　　Surfeits, imposthumes, grief, and damn'd despair,
　　Swear Nature's death for framing thee so fair.

"And not the least of all these maladies
But in one minute's fight brings beauty under:
Both favour, savour, hue, and qualities,
Whereat th' impartial gazer late did wonder,
　　Are on the sudden wasted, thaw'd, and done,
　　As mountain snow melts with the midday sun.

"Therefore, despite of fruitless chastity,
Love-lacking vestals, and self-loving nuns,
That on the earth would breed a scarcity
And barren dearth of daughters and of sons,
　　Be prodigal: the lamp that burns by night
　　Dries up his oil to lend the world his light.

"What is thy body but a swallowing grave,
Seeming to bury that posterity
Which by the rights of time thou needs must have,
If thou destroy them not in dark obscurity?
　　If so, the world will hold thee in disdain,
　　Sith in thy pride so fair a hope is slain.

"So in thyself thyself art made away;
A mischief worse than civil home-bred strife,
Or theirs whose desperate hands themselves do slay,
Or butcher-sire that reaves his son of life.
　　Foul-cankering rust the hidden treasure frets,
　　But gold that's put to use more gold begets."

"Nay, then," quoth Adon, "you will fall again
Into your idle over-handled theme:
The kiss I gave you is bestow'd in vain,
And all in vain you strive against the stream;

For, by this black-fac'd night, desire's foul nurse,
Your treatise makes me like you worse and worse.

"If love have lent you twenty thousand tongues,
And every tongue more moving than your own,
Bewitching like the wanton mermaid's songs,
Yet from mine ear the tempting tune is blown;
    For know, my heart stands armèd in mine ear,
    And will not let a false sound enter there;

"Lest the deceiving harmony should run
Into the quiet closure of my breast;
And then my little heart were quite undone,
In his bedchamber to be barr'd of rest.
    No, lady, no; my heart longs not to groan,
    But soundly sleeps, while now it sleeps alone.

"What have you urg'd that I cannot reprove?
The path is smooth that leadeth on to danger:
I hate not love, but your device in love,
That lends embracements unto every stranger.
    You do it for increase: O strange excuse,
    When reason is the bawd to lust's abuse!

"Call it not love, for Love to heaven is fled,
Since sweating Lust on earth usurp'd his name;
Under whose simple semblance he hath fed
Upon fresh beauty, blotting it with blame;
    Which the hot tyrant stains and soon bereaves,
    As caterpillars do the tender leaves.

"Love comforteth like sunshine after rain,
But Lust's effect is tempest after sun;
Love's gentle spring doth always fresh remain,
Lust's winter comes ere summer half be done;
    Love surfeits not, Lust like a glutton dies;
    Love is all truth, Lust full of forgèd lies.

"More I could tell, but more I dare not say;
The text is old, the orator too green.

Therefore, in sadness, now I will away;
My face is full of shame, my heart of teen:
   Mine ears, that to your wanton talk attended,
   Do burn themselves for having so offended."

With this, he breaketh from the sweet embrace
Of those fair arms which bound him to her breast,
And homeward through the dark laund runs apace;
Leaves Love upon her back deeply distress'd.
   Look, how a bright star shooteth from the sky,
   So glides he in the night from Venus' eye;

Which after him she darts, as one on shore
Gazing upon a late-embarkèd friend,
Till the wild waves will have him seen no more,
Whose ridges with the meeting clouds contend:
   So did the merciless and pitchy night
   Fold-in the object that did feed her sight.

Whereat amaz'd, as one that unaware
Hath dropp'd a precious jewel in the flood,
Or stonish'd as night-wanderers often are,
Their light blown out in some mistrustful wood;
   Even so confounded in the dark she lay,
   Having lost the fair discovery of her way.

And now she beats her heart, whereat it groans,
That all the neighbour caves, as seeming troubled,
Make verbal repetition of her moans;
Passion on passion deeply is redoubled:
   "Ay me!" she cries, and twenty times, "Woe, woe!"
   And twenty echoes twenty times cry so.

She, marking them, begins a wailing note,
And sings extemp'rally a woful ditty;
How love makes young men thrall, and old men dote;
How love is wise in folly, foolish-witty:
   Her heavy anthem still concludes in woe,
   And still the choir of echoes answer so.

Her song was tedious, and outwore the night,
For lovers' hours are long, though seeming short:
If pleas'd themselves, others, they think, delight
In such-like circumstance, with such-like sport:
    Their copious stories, oftentimes begun,
    End without audience, and are never done.

For who hath she to spend the night withal,
But idle sounds resembling parasites;
Like shrill-tongu'd tapsters answering every call,
Soothing the humour of fantastic wits?
    She says "'Tis so:" they answer all, "'Tis so;"
    And would say after her, if she said "No."

Lo, here the gentle lark, weary of rest,
From his moist cabinet mounts up on high,
And wakes the morning, from whose silver breast
The sun ariseth in his majesty;
    Who doth the world so gloriously behold,
    That cedar-tops and hills seem burnish'd gold.

Venus salutes him with this fair good-morrow:
"O thou clear god, and patron of all light,
From whom each lamp and shining star doth borrow
The beauteous influence that makes him bright,
    There lives a son, that suck'd an earthly mother,
    May lend thee light, as thou dost lend to other."

This said, she hasteth to a myrtle grove,
Musing the morning is so much o'erworn,
And yet she hears no tidings of her love:
She hearkens for his hounds and for his horn:
    Anon she hears them chant it lustily,
    And all in haste she coasteth to the cry.

And as she runs, the bushes in the way
Some catch her by the neck, some kiss her face,
Some twine about her thigh to make her stay:
She wildly breaketh from their strict embrace,

Like a milch doe, whose swelling dugs do ache,
Hasting to feed her fawn hid in some brake.

By this, she hears the hounds are at a bay:
Whereat she starts, like one that spies an adder
Wreath'd up in fatal folds just in his way,
The fear whereof doth make him shake and shudder;
   Even so the timorous yelping of the hounds
   Appals her senses and her spirit confounds.

For now she knows it is no gentle chase,
But the blunt boar, rough bear, or lion proud,
Because the cry remaineth in one place,
Where fearfully the dogs exclaim aloud:
   Finding their enemy to be so curst,
   They all strain courtesy who shall cope him first.

This dismal cry rings sadly in her ear,
Through which it enters to surprise her heart;
Who, overcome by doubt and bloodless fear,
With cold-pale weakness numbs each feeling part:
   Like soldiers, when their captain once doth yield,
   They basely fly, and dare not stay the field.

Thus stands she in a trembling ecstasy;
Till, cheering up her senses all dismay'd,
She tells them 'tis a causeless fantasy,
And childish error, that they are afraid;
   Bids them leave quaking, bids them fear no more: —
   And with that word she spied the hunted boar;

Whose frothy mouth, bepainted all with red,
Like milk and blood being mingled both together,
A second fear through all her sinews spread,
Which madly hurries her she knows not whither:
   This way she runs, and now she will no further,
   But back retires to rate the boar for murther.

A thousand spleens bear her a thousand ways;
She treads the path that she untreads again;

Her more than haste is mated with delays,
Like the proceedings of a drunken brain,
  Full of respects, yet naught at all respecting;
  In hand with all things, naught at all effecting.

Here kennell'd in a brake she finds a hound,
And asks the weary caitiff for his master;
And there another licking of his wound,
'Gainst venom'd sores the only sovereign plaster;
  And here she meets another sadly scowling,
  To whom she speaks, and he replies with howling.

When he hath ceas'd his ill-resounding noise,
Another flap-mouth'd mourner, black and grim,
Against the welkin volleys out his voice;
Another and another answer him,
  Clapping their proud tails to the ground below,
  Shaking their scratch'd ears, bleeding as they go.

Look how the world's poor people are amaz'd
At apparitions, signs, and prodigies,
Whereon with fearful eyes they long have gaz'd,
Infusing them with dreadful prophecies;
  So she at these sad signs draws up her breath,
  And, sighing it again, exclaims on Death.

"Hard-favour'd tyrant, ugly, meagre, lean,
Hateful divorce of love," — thus chides she Death, —
"Grim-grinning ghost, earth's worm, what dost thou mean
To stifle beauty and to steal his breath,
  Who when he liv'd, his breath and beauty set
  Gloss on the rose, smell to the violet?

"If he be dead, — O no, it cannot be,
Seeing his beauty, thou shouldst strike at it; —
O yes, it may; thou hast no eyes to see,
But hatefully at random dost thou hit.
  Thy mark is feeble age; but thy false dart
  Mistakes that aim, and cleaves an infant's heart.

"Hadst thou but bid beware, then he had spoke,
And, hearing him, thy power had lost his power.
The Destinies will curse thee for this stroke;
They bid thee crop a weed, thou pluck'st a flower:
    Love's golden arrow at him should have fled,
    And not Death's ebon dart, to strike him dead.

"Dost thou drink tears, that thou provok'st such weeping?
What may a heavy groan advantage thee?
Why hast thou cast into eternal sleeping
Those eyes that taught all other eyes to see?
    Now Nature cares not for thy mortal vigour,
    Since her best work is ruin'd with thy rigour."

Here overcome, as one full of despair,
She vail'd her eyelids, who, like sluices, stopp'd
The crystal tide that from her two cheeks fair
In the sweet channel of her bosom dropp'd;
    But through the flood-gates breaks the silver rain,
    And with his strong course opens them again.

O, how her eyes and tears did lend and borrow!
Her eyes seen in the tears, tears in her eye;
Both crystals, where they view'd each other's sorrow, —
Sorrow that friendly sighs sought still to dry;
    But like a stormy day, now wind, now rain,
    Sighs dry her cheeks, tears make them wet again.

Variable passions throng her constant woe,
As striving who should best become her grief;
All entertain'd, each passion labours so,
That every present sorrow seemeth chief,
    But none is best: then join they all together,
    Like many clouds consulting for foul weather.

By this, far off she hears some huntsman hollo;
A nurse's song ne'er pleas'd her babe so well:
The dire imagination she did follow
This sound of hope doth labour to expel;

For now reviving joy bids her rejoice,
And flatters her it is Adonis' voice.

Whereat her tears began to turn their tide,
Being prison'd in her eye like pearls in glass;
Yet sometimes falls an orient drop beside,
Which her cheek melts, as scorning it should pass,
    To wash the foul face of the sluttish ground,
    Who is but drunken when she seemeth drown'd.

O hard-believing love, how strange it seems
Not to believe, and yet too credulous!
Thy weal and woe are both of them extremes;
Despair and hope make thee ridiculous:
    The one doth flatter thee in thoughts unlikely,
    In likely thoughts the other kills thee quickly.

Now she unweaves the web that she hath wrought;
Adonis lives, and Death is not to blame;
It was not she that call'd him all to-naught:
Now she adds honours to his hateful name;
    She clepes him king of graves, and grave for kings,
    Imperious supreme of all mortal things.

"No, no" quoth she, "sweet Death, I did but jest;
Yet pardon me I felt a kind of fear
Whenas I met the boar, that bloody beast
Which knows no pity, but is still severe:
    Then, gentle shadow, — truth I must confess, —
    I rail'd on thee, fearing my love's decease.

"'Tis not my fault: the boar provok'd my tongue;
Be wreak'd on him, invisible commander;
'Tis he, foul creature, that hath done thee wrong;
I did but act, he's author of thy slander:
    Grief hath two tongues; and never woman yet
    Could rule them both without ten women's wit."

Thus hoping that Adonis is alive,
Her rash suspect she doth extenuate;

And that his beauty may the better thrive,
With Death she humbly doth insinuate;
  Tells him of trophies, statues, tombs, and stories,
  His victories, his triumphs, and his glories.

"O Jove," quoth she, "how much a fool was I
To be of such a weak and silly mind
To wail his death who lives, and must not die
Till mutual overthrow of mortal kind!
  For he being dead, with him is beauty slain,
  And, beauty dead, black chaos comes again.

"Fie, fie, fond love, thou art so full of fear
As one with treasure laden hemm'd with thieves;
'Trifles, unwitnessèd with eye or ear,
Thy coward heart with false bethinking grieves."
  Even at this word she hears a merry horn,
  Whereat she leaps that was but late forlorn.

As falcon to the lure, away she flies;
The grass stoops not, she treads on it so light;
And in her haste unfortunately spies
The foul boar's conquest on her fair delight;
  Which seen, her eyes, as murder'd with the view,
  Like stars asham'd of day, themselves withdrew;

Or as the snail, whose tender horns being hit,
Shrinks backward in his shelly cave with pain,
And there, all smother'd up in shade, doth sit,
Long after fearing to creep forth again;
  So at his bloody view her eyes are fled
  Into the deep-dark cabins of her head:

Where they resign their office and their light
To the disposing of her troubled brain;
Who bids them still consort witn ugly night,
And never wound the heart with looks again;
  Who, like a king perplexèd in his throne,
  By their suggestion gives a deadly groan,

Whereat each tributary subject quakes;
As when the wind, imprison'd in the ground,
Struggling for passage, earth's foundation shakes,
Which with cold terror doth men's minds confound.
  This mutiny each part doth so surprise,
  That from their dark beds once more leap her eyes;

And, being open'd, threw unwilling light
Upon the wide wound that the boar had trench'd
In his soft flank; whose wonted lily white
With purple tears, that his wound wept, was drench'd:
  No flower was nigh, no grass, herb, leaf, or weed,
  But stole his blood, and seem'd with him to bleed.

This solemn sympathy poor Venus noteth;
Over one shoulder doth she hang her head:
Dumbly she passions, franticly she doteth;
She thinks he could not die, he is not dead:
  Her voice is stopp'd, her joints forget to bow;
  Her eyes are mad that they have wept till now.

Upon his hurt she looks so steadfastly,
That her sight dazzling makes the wound seem three;
And then she reprehends her mangling eye,
That makes more gashes where no breach should be:
  His face seems twain, each several limb is doubled;
  For oft the eye mistakes, the brain being troubled.

"My tongue cannot express my grief for one,
And yet," quoth she, "behold two Adons dead!
My sighs are blown away, my salt tears gone,
Mine eyes are turn'd to fire, my heart to lead:
  Heavy heart's lead, melt at mine eyes' red fire!
  So shall I die by drops of hot desire.

"Alas, poor world, what treasure hast thou lost!
What face remains alive that's worth the viewing?
Whose tongue is music now? what canst thou boast
Of things long since, or any thing ensuing?

The flowers are sweet, their colours fresh and trim;
But true-sweet beauty liv'd and died with him.

"Bonnet nor veil henceforth no creature wear!
Nor sun nor wind will ever strive to kiss you:
Having no fair to lose, you need not fear;
The sun doth scorn you, and the wind doth hiss you:
  But when Adonis liv'd, sun and sharp air
  Lurk'd like two thieves, to rob him of his fair:

"And therefore would he put his bonnet on,
Under whose brim the gaudy sun would peep;
The wind would blow it off, and, being gone,
Play with his locks: then would Adonis weep;
  And straight, in pity of his tender years,
  They both would strive who first should dry his tears.

"To see his face the lion walk'd along
Behind some hedge, because he would not fear him;
To recreate himself when he hath sung,
The tiger would be tame, and gently hear him;
  If he had spoke, the wolf would leave his prey,
  And never fright the silly lamb that day.

"When he beheld his shadow in the brook,
The fishes spread on it their golden gills;
When he was by, the birds such pleasure took,
That some would sing, some other in their bills
  Would bring him mulberries and ripe-red cherries;
  He fed them with his sight, they him with berries.

"But this foul, grim, and urchin-snouted boar,
Whose downward eye still looketh for a grave,
Ne'er saw the beauteous livery that he wore;
Witness the entertainment that he gave:
  If he did see his face, why then I know
  He thought to kiss him, and hath kill'd him so.

"'Tis true, 'tis true; thus was Adonis slain:
He ran upon the boar with his sharp spear,

Who did not whet his teeth at him again,
But by a kiss thought to persuade him there;
   And nuzzling in his flank, the loving swine
   Sheath'd, unaware, the tusk in his soft groin.

"Had I been tooth'd like him, I must confess,
With kissing him I should have kill'd him first;
But he is dead, and never did he bless
My youth with his, — the more am I accurst."
   With this, she falleth in the place she stood,
   And stains her face with his congealèd blood.

She looks upon his lips, and they are pale;
She takes him by the hand, and that is cold;
She whispers in his ears a heavy tale,
As if they heard the woful words she told;
   She lifts the coffer-lids that close his eyes,
   Where, lo, two lamps, burnt out, in darkness lies;

Two glasses, where herself herself beheld
A thousand times, and now no more reflect;
Their virtue lost, wherein they late excell'd,
And every beauty robb'd of his effect:
   "Wonder of time," quoth she, "this is my spite,
   That, thou being dead, the day should yet be light.

"Since thou art dead, lo, here I prophesy
Sorrow on love hereafter shall attend:
It shall be waited on with jealousy,
Find sweet beginning, but unsavoury end;
   Ne'er settled equally, but high or low;
   That all love's pleasure shall not match his woe.

"It shall be fickle, false, and full of fraud;
Bud and be blasted in a breathing-while;
The bottom poison, and the top o'erstraw'd
With sweets that shall the truest sight beguile:
   The strongest body shall it make most weak,
   Strike the wise dumb, and teach the fool to speak.

"It shall be sparing and too full of riot,
Teaching decrepit age to tread the measures;
The staring ruffian shall it keep in quiet,
Pluck down the rich, enrich the poor with treasures;
   It shall be raging-mad and silly-mild,
   Make the young old, the old become a child.

"It shall suspect where is no cause of fear;
It shall not fear where it should most mistrust;
It shall be merciful and too severe,
And most deceiving when it seems most just;
   Perverse it shall be where it shows most toward,
   Put fear to valour, courage to the coward.

"It shall be cause of war and dire events,
And set dissension 'twixt the son and sire;
Subject and servile to all discontents,
As dry combustious matter is to fire:
   Sith in his prime Death doth my love destroy,
   They that love best their loves shall not enjoy."

By this, the boy that by her side lay kill'd
Was melted like a vapour from her sight;
And in his blood, that on the ground lay spill'd,
A purple flower sprung up, chequer'd with white,
   Resembling well his pale cheeks, and the blood
   Which in round drops upon their whiteness stood.

She bows her head the new-sprung flower to smell,
Comparing it to her Adonis' breath;
And says within her bosom it shall dwell,
Since he himself is reft from her by Death:
   She crops the stalk, and in the breach appears
   Green dropping sap, which she compares to tears.

"Poor flower," quoth she, "this was thy father's guise, —
Sweet issue of a more sweet-smelling sire, —
For every little grief to wet his eyes:
To grow unto himself was his desire,

And so 'tis thine; but know, it is as good
To wither in my breast as in his blood.

"Here was thy father's bed, here in my breast;
Thou art the next of blood, and 'tis thy right:
Lo in this hollow cradle take thy rest,
My throbbing heart shall rock thee day and night:
　　There shall not be one minute in an hour
　　Wherein I will not kiss my sweet love's flower."

Thus weary of the world, away she hies,
And yokes her silver doves; by whose swift aid
Their mistress, mounted, through the empty skies
In her light chariot quickly is convey'd;
　　Holding their course to Paphos, where their queen
　　Means to immure herself and not be seen.

LUCRECE.

TO THE

RIGHT HONOURABLE

HENRY WRIOTHESLY,

EARL OF SOUTHAMPTON, AND BARON OF TICHFIELD.

THE love I dedicate to your lordship is without end; whereof this pamphlet, without beginning, is but a superfluous moiety. The warrant I have of your honourable disposition, not the worth of my untutored lines, makes it assured of acceptance. What I have done is yours; what I have to do is yours; being part in all I have, devoted yours. Were my worth greater, my duty would show greater; meantime, as it is, it is bound to your lordship, to whom I wish long life, still lengthened with all happiness.

Your lordship's in all duty,

WILLIAM SHAKESPEARE.

FROM the besieged Ardea all in post,
Borne by the trustless wings of false desire,
Lust-breathed Tarquin leaves the Roman host,
And to Collatiun bears the lightless fire
Which, in pale embers hid, lurks to aspire
  And girdle with embracing flames the waist
  Of Collatine's fair love, Lucrece the chaste.

Haply that name of "chaste" unhappily set
This bateless edge on his keen appetite;
When Collatine unwisely did not let

To praise the clear unmatchèd red and white
Which triumph'd in that sky of his delight,
  Where mortal stars, as bright as heaven's beauties,
  With pure aspécts did him peculiar duties.

For he the night before, in Tarquin's tent,
Unlock'd the treasure of his happy state;
What priceless wealth the heavens had him lent
In the possession of his beauteous mate;
Reckoning his fortune at such high-proud rate,
  That kings might be espousèd to more fame,
  But king nor peer to such a peerless dame.

O happiness enjoy'd but of a few!
And, if possess'd, as soon decay'd and done
As is the morning's silver-melting dew
Against the golden splendour of the sun!
An expir'd date, cancell'd ere well begun:
  Honour and beauty, in the owner's arms,
  Are weakly fortress'd from a world of harms.

Beauty itself doth of itself persuade
The eyes of men without an orator;
What needeth, then, apologies be made,
To set forth that which is so singular?
Or why is Collatine the publisher
  Of that rich jewel he should keep unknown
  From thievish ears, because it is his own?

Perchance his boast of Lucrece' sovereignty
Suggested this proud issue of a king;
For by our ears our hearts oft tainted be:
Perchance that envy of so rich a thing,
Braving compare, disdainfully did sting
  His high-pitch'd thoughts, that meaner men should vaunt
  That golden hap which their superiors want.

But some untimely thought did instigate
His all-too-timeless speed, if none of those:
His honour, his affairs, his friends, his state,

Neglected all, with swift intent he goes
To quench the coal which in his liver glows.
  O rash-false heat, wrapp'd in repentant cold,
  Thy hasty spring still blasts, and ne'er grows old!

When at Collatium this false lord arriv'd
Well was he welcom'd by the Roman dame,
Within whose face beauty and virtue striv'd
Which of them both should underprop her fame:
When virtue bragg'd, beauty would blush for shame;
  When beauty boasted blushes, in despite
  Virtue would stain that o'er with silver white.

But beauty, in that white intituled,
From Venus' doves doth challenge that fair field:
Then virtue claims from beauty beauty's red,
Which virtue gave the golden age to gild
Their silver cheeks, and call'd it then their shield;
  Teaching them thus to use it in the fight, —
  When shame assail'd, the red should fence the white.

This heraldry in Lucrece' face was seen,
Argu'd by beauty's red and virtue's white:
Of either's colour was the other queen,
Proving from world's minority their right:
Yet their ambition makes them still to fight;
  The sovereignty of either being so great,
  That oft they interchange each other's seat.

This silent war of lilies and of roses,
Which Tarquin view'd in her fair face's field,
In their pure ranks his traitor eye encloses;
Where, lest between them both it should be kill'd,
The coward captive vanquishèd doth yield
  To those two armies that would let him go,
  Rather than triumph in so false a foe.

Now thinks he that her husband's shallow tongue, —
The niggard prodigal that prais'd her so, —
In that high task hath done her beauty wrong,

Which far exceeds his barren skill to show:
Therefore that praise which Collatine doth owe
  Enchanted Tarquin answers with surmise,
  In silent wonder of still-gazing eyes.

This earthly saint, adorèd by this devil,
Little suspecteth the false worshipper;
For unstain'd thoughts do seldom dream on evil;
Birds never lim'd no secret bushes fear:
So guiltless she securely gives good cheer
  And reverent welcome to her princely guest,
  Whose inward ill no outward harm express'd:

For that he colour'd with his high estate,
Hiding base sin in plaits of majesty;
That nothing in him seem'd inordinate,
Save sometime too much wonder of his eye,
Which, having all, all could not satisfy;
  But, poorly rich, so wanteth in his store,
  That, cloy'd with much, he pineth still for more.

But she, that never cop'd with stranger eyes,
Could pick no meaning from their parling looks,
Nor read the subtle-shining secrecies
Writ in the glassy margents of such books:
She touch'd no unknown baits, nor fear'd no hooks;
  Nor could she moralize his wanton sight,
  More than his eyes were open'd to the light.

He stories to her ears her husband's fame,
Won in the fields of fruitful Italy;
And decks with praises Collatine's high name,
Made glorious by his manly chivalry
With bruisèd arms and wreaths of victory:
  Her joy with heav'd-up hand she doth express,
  And, wordless, so greets heaven for his success.

Far from the purpose of his coming hither,
He makes excuses for his being there:
No cloudy show of stormy blustering weather

Doth yet in his fair welkin once appear;
Till sable Night, mother of Dread and Fear,
  Upon the world dim darkness doth display,
  And in her vaulty prison stows the Day.

For then is Tarquin brought unto his bed,
Intending weariness with heavy sprite;
For, after supper, long he questionèd
With modest Lucrece, and wore out the night:
Now leaden slumber with life's strength doth fight;
  And every one to rest themselves betake,
  Save thieves, and cares, and troubled minds, that wake.

As one of which doth Tarquin lie revolving
The sundry dangers of his will's obtaining;
Yet ever to obtain his will resolving,
Though weak-built hopes persuade him to abstaining:
Despair to gain doth traffic oft for gaining;
  And when great treasure is the meed propos'd,
  Though death be adjunct, there's no death suppos'd.

Those that much covet are with gain so fond,
That what they have not, that which they possess,
They scatter and unloose it from their bond,
And so, by hoping more, they have but less;
Or, gaining more, the profit of excess
  Is but to surfeit, and such griefs sustain,
  That they prove bankrupt in this poor-rich gain.

The aim of all is but to nurse the life
With honour, wealth, and ease, in waning age;
And in this aim there is such thwarting strife,
That one for all, or all for one we gage;
As life for honour in fell battle's rage;
  Honour for wealth; and oft that wealth doth cost
  The death of all, and all together lost.

So that in venturing ill we leave to be
The things we are for that which we expect;
And this ambitious-foul infirmity,

In having much, torments us with defect
Of that we have: so then we do neglect
　　The thing we have; and, all for want of wit,
　　Make something nothing by augmenting it.

Such hazard now must doting Tarquin make,
Pawning his honour to obtain his lust;
And for himself himself he must forsake:
Then where is truth, if there be no self-trust?
When shall he think to find a stranger just,
　　When he himself himself confounds, betrays
　　To slanderous tongues and wretched hateful days?

Now stole upon the time the dead of night,
When heavy sleep had clos'd up mortal eyes:
No comfortable star did lend his light,
No noise but owls' and wolves' death-boding cries;
Now serves the season that they may surprise
　　The silly lambs: pure thoughts are dead and still,
　　While lust and murder wake to stain and kill.

And now this lustful lord leap'd from his bed,
Throwing his mantle rudely o'er his arm;
Is madly toss'd between desire and dread;
Th' one sweetly flatters, th' other feareth harm;
But honest fear, bewitch'd with lust's foul charm,
　　Doth too-too oft betake him to retire,
　　Beaten away by brain-sick rude desire.

His falchion on a flint he softly smiteth,
That from the cold stone sparks of fire do fly;
Whereat a waxen torch forthwith he lighteth,
Which must be lode-star to his lustful eye;
And to the flame thus speaks advisedly,
　　"As from this cold flint I enforc'd this fire,
　　So Lucrece must I force to my desire."

Here pale with fear he doth premeditate
The dangers of his loathsome enterprise,
And in his inward mind he doth debate

What following sorrow may on this arise:
Then looking scornfully, he doth despise
  His naked armour of still-slaughter'd lust,
  And justly thus controls his thoughts unjust:

"Fair torch, burn out thy light, and lend it not
To darken her whose light excelleth thine:
And die, unhallow'd thoughts, before you blot
With your uncleanness that which is divine;
Offer pure incense to so pure a shrine:
  Let fair humanity abhor the deed
  That spots and stains love's modest snow-white weed.

"O shame to knighthood and to shining arms!
O foul dishonour to my household's grave!
O impious act, including all foul harms!
A martial man to be soft fancy's slave!
True valour still a true respect should have;
  Then my digression is so vile, so base,
  That it will live engraven in my face.

"Yea, though I die, the scandal will survive,
And be an eye-sore in my golden coat;
Some loathsome dash the herald will contrive,
To cipher me how fondly I did dote;
That my posterity, sham'd with the note,
  Shall curse my bones, and hold it for no sin
  To wish that I their father had not bin.

"What win I, if I gain the thing I seek?
A dream, a breath, a froth of fleeting joy.
Who buys a minute's mirth to wail a week?
Or sells eternity to get a toy?
For one sweet grape who will the vine destroy?
  Or what fond beggar, but to touch the crown,
  Would with the sceptre straight be strucken down?

"If Collatinus dream of my intent,
Will he not wake, and in a desperate rage
Post hither, this vile purpose to prevent?

This siege that hath engirt his marriage,
This blur to youth, this sorrow to the sage,
  This dying virtue, this surviving shame,
  Whose crime will bear an ever-during blame?

"O, what excuse can my invention make,
. When thou shalt charge me with so black a deed?
Will not my tongue be mute, my frail joints shake,
Mine eyes forgo their light, my false heart bleed?
The guilt being great, the fear doth still exceed;
  And extreme fear can neither fight nor fly,
  But coward-like with trembling terror die.

"Had Collatinus kill'd my son or sire,
Or lain in ambush to betray my life,
Or were he not my dear friend, this desire
Might have excuse to work upon his wife,
As in revenge or quittal of such strife:
  But as he is my kinsman, my dear friend,
  The shame and fault finds no excuse nor end.

"Shameful it is; — ay, if the fact be known:
Hateful it is; — there is no hate in loving:
I'll beg her love; — but she is not her own:
The worst is but denial and reproving:
My will is strong, past reason's weak removing.
  Who fears a sentence or an old man's saw
  Shall by a painted cloth be kept in awe."

Thus, graceless, holds he disputation
'Tween frozen conscience and hot-burning will,
And with good thoughts makes dispensation,
Urging the worser sense for vantage still;
Which in a moment doth confound and kill
  All pure effects, and doth so far proceed,
  That what is vile shows like a virtuous deed.

Quoth he, "She took me kindly by the hand,
And gaz'd for tidings in my eager eyes,
Fearing some hard news from the warlike band,

Where her belovèd Collatinus lies.
O, how her fear did make her colour rise!
  First red as roses that on lawn we lay,
  Then white as lawn, the roses took away.

"And how her hand, in my hand being lock'd,
Forc'd it to tremble with her loyal fear!
Which struck her sad, and then it faster rock'd,
Until her husband's welfare she did hear;
Whereat she smilèd with so sweet a cheer,
  That had Narcissus seen her as she stood,
  Self-love had never drown'd him in the flood.

"Why hunt I, then, for colour or excuses?
All orators are dumb when beauty pleadeth;
Poor wretches have remorse in poor abuses;
Love thrives not in the heart that shadows dreadeth:
Affection is my captain, and he leadeth;
  And when his gaudy banner is display'd,
  The coward fights, and will not be dismay'd.

"Then, childish fear, avaunt! debating, die!
Respect and reason, wait on wrinkled age!
My heart shall never countermand mine eye:
Sad pause and deep regard beseem the sage;
My part is youth, and beats these from the stage:
  Desire my pilot is, beauty my prize;
  Then who fears sinking where such treasure lies?"

As corn o'ergrown by weeds, so heedful fear
Is almost chok'd by unresisted lust.
Alway he steals with open listening ear,
Full of foul hope and full of fond mistrust;
Both which, as servitors to the unjust,
  So cross him with their opposite persuasion,
  That now he vows a league, and now invasion.

Within his thought her heavenly image sits,
And in the self-same seat sits Collatine:
That eye which looks on her confounds his wits;

That eye which him beholds, as more divine,
Unto a view so false will not incline;
  But with a pure appeal seeks to the heart,
  Which once corrupted takes the worser part;

And therein heartens up his servile powers,
Who, flatter'd by their leader's jocund show,
Stuff up his lust, as minutes fill up hours;
And as their captain, so their pride doth grow,
Paying more slavish tribute than they owe.
  By reprobate desire thus madly led,
  The Roman lord marcheth to Lucrece' bed.

The locks between her chamber and his will,
Each one by him enforc'd, retires his ward;
But, as they open, they all rate his ill,
Which drives the creeping thief to some regard:
The threshold grates the door to have him heard;
  Night-wandering weasels shriek to see him there;
  They fright him, yet he still pursues his fear.

As each unwilling portal yields him way,
Through little vents and crannies of the place
The wind wars with his torch to make him stay,
And blows the smoke of it into his face,
Extinguishing his conduct in this case;
  But his hot heart, which fond desire doth scorch,
  Puffs forth another wind that fires the torch:

And being lighted, by the light he spies
Lucretia's glove, wherein her needle sticks:
He takes it from the rushes where it lies,
And griping it, the neeld his finger pricks;
As who should say, "This glove to wanton tricks
  Is not inur'd; return again in haste;
  Thou see'st our mistress' ornaments are chaste."

But all these poor forbiddings could not stay him;
He in the worst sense construes their denial:
The doors, the wind, the glove, that did delay him,

He takes for accidental things of trial;
Or as those bars which stop the hourly dial,
  Who with a lingering stay his course doth let,
  Till every minute pays the hour his debt.

"So, so," quoth he, "these lets attend the time,
Like little frosts that sometime threat the spring,
To add a more rejoicing to the prime,
And give the sneapèd birds more cause to sing.
Pain pays the income of each precious thing;
  Huge rocks, high winds, strong pirates, shelves and sands,
  The merchant fears, ere rich at home he lands."

Now is he come unto the chamber-door
That shuts him from the heaven of his thought,
Which with a yielding latch, and with no more,
Hath barr'd him from the blessèd thing he sought.
So from himself impiety hath wrought,
  That for his prey to pray he doth begin,
  As if the heavens should countenance his sin.

But in the midst of his unfruitful prayer,
Having solicited th' eternal power
That his foul thoughts might compass his fair fair,
And they would stand auspicious to the hour,
Even there he starts: — quoth he, "I must deflower:
  The powers to whom I pray abhor this fact,
  How can they, then, assist me in the act?

"Then Love and Fortune be my gods, my guide!
My will is back'd with resolution:
Thoughts are but dreams till their effects be tried;
The blackest sin is clear'd with absolution;
Against love's fire fear's frost hath dissolution.
  The eye of heaven is out, and misty night
  Covers the shame that follows sweet delight."

This said, his guilty hand pluck'd up the latch,
And with his knee the door he opens wide.
The dove sleeps fast that this night-owl will catch:

Thus treason works ere traitors be espied.
Who sees the lurking serpent steps aside;
　But she, sound sleeping, fearing no such thing,
　Lies at the mercy of his mortal sting.

Into the chamber wickedly he stalks,
And gazeth on her yet-unstainèd bed.
The curtains being close, about he walks,
Rolling his greedy eyeballs in his head:
By their high treason is his heart misled;
　Which gives the watch-word to his hand full soon
　To draw the cloud that hides the silver moon.

Look, as the fair and fiery-pointed sun,
Rushing from forth a cloud, bereaves our sight;
Even so, the curtain drawn, his eyes begun
To wink, being blinded with a greater light:
Whether it is that she reflects so bright,
　That dazzleth them, or else some shame suppos'd;
　But blind they are, and keep themselves enclos'd.

O, had they in that darksome prison died!
Then had they seen the period of their ill;
Then Collatine again, by Lucrece' side,
In his clear bed might have reposèd still:
But they must ope, this blessèd league to kill;
　And holy-thoughted Lucrece to their sight
　Must sell her joy, her life, her world's delight.

Her lily hand her rosy cheek lies under,
Cozening the pillow of a lawful kiss;
Who, therefore angry, seems to part in sunder,
Swelling on either side to want his bliss;
Between whose hills her head entombèd is:
　Where, like a virtuous monument, she lies,
　To be admir'd of lewd unhallow'd eyes.

Without the bed her other fair hand was,
On the green coverlet; whose perfect white
Show'd like an April daisy on the grass,

With pearly sweat, resembling dew of night.
Her eyes, like marigolds, had sheath'd their light,
  And canopied in darkness sweetly lay,
  · Till they might open to adorn the day.

Her hair, like golden threads, play'd with her breath;
O modest wantons! wanton modesty!
Showing life's triumph in the map of death,
And death's dim look in life's mortality:
Each in her sleep themselves so beautify,
  As if between them twain there were no strife,
  But that life liv'd in death, and death in life.

Her breasts, like ivory globes circled with blue,
A pair of maiden worlds unconquerèd,
Save of their lord no bearing yoke they knew,
And him by oath they truly honourèd.
These worlds in Tarquin new ambition bred;
  Who, like a foul usurper, went about
  From this fair throne to heave the owner out.

What could he see but mightily he noted?
What did he note but strongly he desir'd?
What he beheld, on that he firmly doted,
And in his will his wilful eye he tir'd.
With more than admiration he admir'd
  Her azure veins, her alabaster skin,
  Her coral lips, her snow-white dimpled chin.

As the grim lion fawneth o'er his prey,
Sharp hunger by the conquest satisfied,
So o'er this sleeping soul doth Tarquin stay,
His rage of lust by gazing qualified;
Slack'd, not suppress'd; for standing by her side,
  His eye, which late this mutiny restrains,
  Unto a greater uproar tempts his veins:

And they, like straggling slaves for pillage fighting,
Obdurate vassals fell exploits effecting,
In bloody death and ravishment delighting,

Nor children's tears nor mothers' groans respecting,
Swell in their pride, the onset still expecting:
　　Anon his beating heart, alarum striking,
　　Gives the hot charge, and bids them do their liking.

His drumming heart cheers up his burning eye,
His eye commends the leading to his hand;
His hand, as proud of such a dignity,
Smoking with pride, march'd on to make his stand
On her bare breast, the heart of all her land;
　　Whose ranks of blue veins, as his hand did scale,
　　Left their round turrets destitute and pale.　.

They, mustering to the quiet cabinet
Where their dear governess and lady lies,
Do tell her she is dreadfully beset,
And fright her with confusion of their cries:
She, much amaz'd, breaks ope her lock'd-up eyes,
　　Who, peeping forth this tumult to behold,
　　Are by his flaming torch dimm'd and controll'd.˙

Imagine her as one in dead of night
From forth dull sleep by dreadful fancy waking,
That thinks she hath beheld some ghastly sprite,
Whose grim aspéct sets every joint a-shaking;
What terror 'tis! but she, in worser taking,
　　From sleep disturbèd, heedfully doth view
　　The sight which makes supposèd terror true.

Wrapp'd and confounded in a thousand fears,
Like to a new-kill'd bird she trembling lies;
She dares not look; yet, winking, there appears
Quick-shifting antics, ugly in her eyes:
Such shadows are the weak brain's forgeries;
　　Who, angry that the eyes fly from their lights,
　　In darkness daunts them with more dreadful sights.

His hand, that yet remains upon her breast, —
Rude ram, to batter such an ivory wall! —
May feel her heart — poor citizen! — distress'd,

Wounding itself to death, rise up and fall,
Beating her bulk, that his hand shakes withal.
   This moves in him more rage, and lesser pity,
   To make the breach, and enter this sweet city.

First, like a trumpet, doth his tongue begin
To sound a parley to his heartless foe;
Who o'er the white sheet peers her whiter chin,
The reason of this rash alarm to know,
Which he by dumb demeanour seeks to show;
   But she with vehement prayers urgeth still
   Under what colour he commits this ill.

Thus he replies: "The colour in thy face —
That even for anger makes the lily pale,
And the red rose blush at her own disgrace —
Shall plead for me, and tell my loving tale;
Under that colour am I come to scale
   Thy never-conquer'd fort: the fault is thine
   For those thine eyes betray thee unto mine.

"Thus I forestall thee, if thou mean to chide:
Thy beauty hath ensnar'd thee to this night,
Where thou with patience must my will abide;
My will that marks thee for my earth's delight,
Which I to conquer sought with all my might;
   But as reproof and reason beat it dead,
   By thy bright beauty was it newly bred.

"I see what crosses my attempt will bring;
I know what thorns the growing rose defends;
I think the honey guarded with a sting;
All this beforehand counsel comprehends:
But will is deaf, and hears no heedful friends;
   Only he hath an eye to gaze on beauty,
   And dotes on what he looks, 'gainst law or duty.

"I have debated, even in my soul,
What wrong, what shame, what sorrow I shall breed;
But nothing can affection's course control,

Or stop the headlong fury of his speed.
I know repentant tears ensue the deed,
   Reproach, disdain, and deadly enmity;
   Yet strive I to embrace mine infamy."

This said, he shakes aloft his Roman blade,
Which, like a falcon towering in the skies,
Coucheth the fowl below with his wings' shade,
Whose crookèd beak threats if he mount he dies:
So under his insulting falchion lies
   Harmless Lucretia, marking what he tells
   With trembling fear, as fowl hear falcon's bells.

"Lucrece," quoth he, "this night I must enjoy thee:
If thou deny, then force must work my way,
For in thy bed I purpose to destroy thee:
That done, some worthless slave of thine I'll slay,
To kill thine honour with thy life's decay;
   And in thy dead arms do I mean to place him,
   Swearing I slew him, seeing thee embrace him.

"So thy surviving husband shall remain
The scornful mark of every open eye;
Thy kinsmen hang their heads at this disdain,
Thy issue blurr'd with nameless bastardy:
And thou, the author of their obloquy,
   Shalt have thy trespass cited up in rhymes,
   And sung by children in succeeding times.

"But if thou yield, I rest thy secret friend:
The fault unknown is as a thought unacted;
A little harm done to a great good end
For lawful policy remains enacted.
The poisonous simple sometimes is compacted
   In a pure compound; being so applied,
   His venom in effect is purified.

"Then, for thy husband and thy children's sake,
Tender my suit: bequeath not to their lot
The shame that from them no device can take,

The blemish that will never be forgot;
Worse than a slavish wipe or birth-hour's blot:
  For marks descried in men's nativity
  Are nature's faults, not their own infamy."

Here with a cockatrice' dead-killing eye
He rouseth up himself, and makes a pause;
While she, the picture of true piety,
Like a white hind under the gripe's sharp claws.
Pleads, in a wilderness where are no laws,
  To the rough beast that knows no gentle right,
  Nor aught obeys but his foul appetite.

But when a black-fac'd cloud the world doth threat,
In his dim mist th' aspiring mountains hiding,
From earth's dark womb some gentle gust doth get,
Which blows these pitchy vapours from their biding,
Hindering their present fall by this dividing;
  So his unhallow'd haste her words delays,
  And moody Pluto winks while Orpheus plays.

Yet, foul night-waking cat, he doth but dally,
While in his hold-fast foot the weak mouse panteth:
Her sad behaviour feeds his vulture folly,
A swallowing gulf that even in plenty wanteth:
His ear her prayers admits, but his heart granteth
  No penetrable entrance to her plaining:
  Tears harden lust, though marble wear with raining.

Her pity-pleading eyes are sadly fix'd
In the remorseless wrinkles of his face;
Her modest eloquence with sighs is mix'd,
Which to her oratory adds more grace.
She puts the period often from his place;
  And midst the sentence so her accent breaks,
  That twice she doth begin ere once she speaks.

She conjures him by high almighty Jove,
By knighthood, gentry, and sweet friendship's oath,
By her untimely tears, her husband's love,

By holy human law, and common troth,
By heaven and earth, and all the power of both,
　That to his borrow'd bed he make retire,
　And stoop to honour, not to foul desire.

Quoth she, "Reward not hospitality
With such black payment as thou hast pretended;
Mud not the fountain that gave drink to thee;
Mar not the thing that cannot be amended;
End thy ill aim before thy shoot be ended;
　He is no woodman that doth bend his bow
　To strike a poor unseasonable doe.

"My husband is thy friend, — for his sake spare me;
Thyself art mighty, — for thine own sake leave me;
Myself a weakling, — do not, then, ensnare me;
Thou look'st not like deceit, — do not deceive me.
My sighs, like whirlwinds, labour hence to heave thee
　If ever man were mov'd with woman's moans,
　Be movèd with my tears, my sighs, my groans:

"All which together, like a troubled ocean,
Beat at thy rocky and wreck-threatening heart,
To soften it with their continual motion;
For stones dissolv'd to water do convert.
O, if no harder than a stone thou art,
　Melt at my tears, and be compassionate!
　Soft pity enters at an iron gate.

"In Tarquin's likeness I did entertain thee:
Hast thou put on his shape to do him shame?
To all the host of heaven I complain me,
Thou wrong'st his honour, wound'st his princely name.
Thou art not what thou seem'st; and if the same,
　Thou seem'st not what thou art, a god, a king;
　For kings like gods should govern every thing.

"How will thy shame be seeded in thine age,
When thus thy vices bud before thy spring!
If in thy hope thou dar'st do such outráge,

What dar'st thou not when once thou art a king?
O, be remember'd, no outrageous thing
　　From vassal actors can be wip'd away;
　　Then kings' misdeeds cannot be hid in clay.

"This deed will make thee only lov'd for fear;
But happy monarchs still are fear'd for love:
With foul offenders thou perforce must bear,
When they in thee the like offences prove:
If but for fear of this, thy will remove;
　　For princes are the glass, the school, the book,
　·　Where subjects' eyes do learn, do read, do look.

"And wilt thou be the school where Lust shall learn?
Must he in thee read lectures of such shame?
Wilt thou be glass wherein it shall discern
Authority for sin, warrant for blame,
To privilege dishonour in thy name?
　　Thou back'st reproach against long-living laud,
　　And mak'st fair reputation but a bawd.

"Hast thou command? by him that gave it thee,
From a pure heart command thy rebel will:
Draw not thy sword to guard iniquity,
For it was lent thee all that brood to kill.
Thy princely office how canst thou fulfil,
　　When, pattern'd by thy fault, foul Sin may say,
　　He learn'd to sin, and thou didst teach the way?

"Think but how vile a spectacle it were,
To view thy present trespass in another.
Men's faults do seldom to themselves appear;
Their own transgressions partially they smother:
This guilt would seem death-worthy in thy brother.
　　O, how are they wrapp'd in with infamies
　　That from their own misdeeds askance their eyes!

"To thee, to thee, my heav'd-up hands appeal,
Not to seducing lust, thy rash relicr:
I sue for exil'd majesty's repeal;

Let him return, and flattering thoughts retire:
His true respect will prison false desire,
  And wipe the dim mist from thy doting eyne,
  That thou shalt see thy state, and pity mine."

"Have done," quoth he: "my uncontrollèd tide
Turns not, but swells the higher by this let.
Small lights are soon blown out, huge fires abide,
And with the wind in greater fury fret:
The petty streams that pay a daily debt
  To their salt sovereign, with their fresh falls' haste
  Add to his flow, but alter not his taste."

"Thou art," quoth she, "a sea, a sovereign king;
And, lo, there falls into thy boundless flood
Black lust, dishonour, shame, misgoverning,
Who seek to stain the ocean of thy blood.
If all these petty ills shall change thy good,
  Thy sea within a puddle's womb is hears'd,
  And not the puddle in thy sea dispers'd.

"So shall these slaves be king, and thou their slave;
Thou nobly base, they basely dignified;
Thou their fair life, and they thy fouler grave:
Thou loathèd in their shame, they in thy pride:
The lesser thing should not the greater hide;
  The cedar stoops not to the base shrub's foot,
  But low shrubs wither at the cedar's root.

"So let thy thoughts, low vassals to thy state" —
"No more," quoth he; "by heaven, I will not hear thee:
Yield to my love; if not, enforcèd hate,
Instead of love's coy touch, shall rudely tear thee;
That done, despitefully I mean to bear thee
  Unto the base bed of some rascal groom,
  To be thy partner in this shameful doom."

This said, he sets his foot upon the light,
For light and lust are deadly enemies:
Shame folded up in blind-concealing night,

When most unseen, then most doth tyrannize.
The wolf hath seiz'd his prey, the poor lamb cries;
 Till with her own white fleece her voice controll'd
 Entombs her outcry in her lips' sweet fold:

For with the nightly linen that she wears
He pens her piteous clamours in her head;
Cooling his hot face in the chastest tears
That ever modest eyes with sorrow shed.
O, that prone lust should stain so pure a bed!
 The spots whereof could weeping purify,
 Her tears should drop on them perpetually.

But she hath lost a dearer thing than life,
And he hath won what he would lose again:
This forcèd league doth force a further strife;
This momentary joy breeds months of pain;
This hot desire converts to cold disdain:
 Pure Chastity is rifled of her store,
 And Lust, the thief, far poorer than before.

Look, as the full-fed hound or gorgèd hawk,
Unapt for tender smell or speedy flight,
Make slow pursuit, or altogether balk
The prey wherein by nature they delight;
So surfeit-taking Tarquin fares this night:
 His taste delicious, in digestion souring,
 Devours his will, that liv'd by foul devouring.

O, deeper sin than bottomless conceit
Can comprehend in still imagination!
Drunken Desire must vomit his receipt,
Ere he can see his own abomination.
While Lust is in his pride, no exclamation
 Can curb his heat, or rein his rash desire,
 Till, like a jade, Self-will himself doth tire.

And then with lank and lean discolour'd cheek,
With heavy eye, knit brow, and strengthless pace,
Feeble Desire, all recreant, poor, and meek,

Like to a bankrupt beggar wails his case:
The flesh being proud, Desire doth fight with Grace,
  For there it revels; and when that decays,
  The guilty rebel for remission prays.

So fares it with this faultful lord of Rome,
Who this accomplishment so hotly chas'd;
For now against himself he sounds this doom, —
That through the length of times he stands disgrac'd:
Besides, his soul's fair temple is defac'd;
  To whose weak ruins muster troops of cares,
  To ask the spotted princess how she fares.

She says, her subjects with foul insurrection
Have batter'd down her consecrated wall,
And by their mortal fault brought in subjection
Her immortality, and made her thrall
To living death and pain perpetual:
  Which in her prescience she controllèd still,
  But her foresight could not forestall their will.

Even in this thought through the dark night he stealeth,
A captive victor that hath lost in gain;
Bearing away the wound that nothing healeth,
The scar that will, despite of cure, remain;
Leaving his spoil perplex'd in greater pain.
  She bears the load of lust he left behind,
  And he the burden of a guilty mind.

He like a thievish dog creeps sadly thence;
She like a wearied lamb lies panting there;
He scowls, and hates himself for his offence;
She, desperate, with her nails her flesh doth tear;
He faintly flies, sweating with guilty fear;
  She stays, exclaiming on the direful night;
  He runs, and chides his vanish'd, loath'd delight.

He thence departs a heavy convertite;
She there remains a hopeless castaway;
He in his speed looks for the morning light;

She prays she never may behold the day,
"For day," quoth she, "night's scapes doth open lay,
 And my true eyes have never practis'd how
 To cloak offences with a cunning brow.

"They think not but that every eye can see
The same disgrace which they themselves behold;
And therefore would they still in darkness be,
To have their unseen sin remain untold;
For they their guilt with weeping will unfold,
 And grave, like water that doth eat in steel,
 Upon my cheeks what helpless shame I feel."

Here she exclaims against repose and rest,
And bids her eyes hereafter still be blind.
She wakes her heart by beating on her breast,
And bids it leap from thence, where it may find
Some purer chest to close so pure a mind.
 Frantic with grief thus breathes she forth her spite
 Against the unseen secrecy of night:

"O comfort-killing Night, image of hell!
Dim register and notary of shame!
Black stage for tragedies and murders fell!
Vast sin-concealing chaos! nurse of blame!
Blind muffled bawd! dark harbour for defame!
 Grim cave of death! whispering conspirator
 With close-tongu'd treason and the ravisher!

"O hateful, vaporous, and foggy Night!
Since thou art guilty of my cureless crime,
Muster thy mists to meet the eastern light,
Make war against proportion'd course of time;
Or if thou wilt permit the sun to climb
 His wonted height, yet ere he go to bed,
 Knit poisonous clouds about his golden head.

"With rotten damps ravish the morning air;
Let their exhal'd unwholesome breaths make sick
The life of purity, the supreme fair,

Ere he arrive his weary noon-tide prick;
And let thy misty vapours march so thick,
 That in their smoky ranks his smother'd light
 May set at noon, and make perpetual night.

"Were Tarquin Night, as he is but Night's child,
The silver-shining queen he would distain;
Her twinkling handmaids too, by him defil'd,
Through Night's black bosom should not peep again:
So should I have co-partners in my pain;
 And fellowship in woe doth woe assuage,
 As palmers' chat makes short their pilgrimage.

"Where now I have no one to blush with me,
To cross their arms, and hang their heads with mine,
To mask their brows, and hide their infamy;
But I alone alone must sit and pine,
Seasoning the earth with showers of silver brine,
 Mingling my talk with tears, my grief with groans,
 Poor wasting monuments of lasting moans.

"O Night, thou furnace of foul-reeking smoke,
Let not the jealous Day behold that face
Which underneath thy black all-hiding cloak
Immodestly lies martyr'd with disgrace!
Keep still possession of thy gloomy place,
 That all the faults which in thy reign are made
 May likewise be sepulchred in thy shade!

"Make me not object to the tell-tale Day!
The light will show, charácter'd in my brow,
The story of sweet chastity's decay,
The impious breach of holy wedlock vow:
Yea, the illiterate, that know not how
 To cipher what is writ in learnèd books,
 Will quote my loathsome trespass in my looks.

"The nurse, to still her child, will tell my story,
And fright her crying babe with Tarquin's name;
The orator, to deck his oratory,

Will couple my reproach to Tarquin's shame;
Feast-finding minstrels, tuning my defame,
　　Will tie the hearers to attend each line,
　　How Tarquin wrongèd me, I Collatine.

"Let my good name, that senseless reputation,
For Collatine's dear love be kept unspotted:
If that be made a theme for disputation,
The branches of another root are rotted,
And undeserv'd reproach to him allotted
　　That is as clear from this attaint of mine
　　As I, ere this, was pure to Collatine.

"O unseen shame! invisible disgrace!
O unfelt sore! crest-wounding, private scar!
Reproach is stamp'd in Collatinus' face,
And Tarquin's eye may read the mot afar,
How he in peace is wounded, not in war.
　　Alas, how many bear such shameful blows,
　　Which not themselves, but he that gives them knows!

"If, Collatine, thine honour lay in me,
From me by strong assault it is bereft.
My honey lost, and I, a drone-like bee,
Have no perfection of my summer left,
But robb'd and ransack'd by injurious theft:
　　In thy weak hive a wandering wasp hath crept,
　　And suck'd the honey which thy chaste bee kept.

"Yet am I guilty of thy honour's wrack, —
Yet for thy honour did I entertain him;
Coming from thee, I could not put him back,
For it had been dishonour to disdain him:
Besides, of weariness he did complain him,
　　And talk'd of virtue: — O unlook'd-for evil,
　　When virtue is profan'd in such a devil!

Why should the worm intrude the maiden bud?
Or hateful cuckoos hatch in sparrows' nests?
Or toads infect fair founts with venom mud?

Or tyrant folly lurk in gentle breasts?
Or kings be breakers of their own behests?
  But no perfection is so absolute,
  That some impurity doth not pollute.

"The agèd man that coffers-up his gold
Is plagu'd with cramps and gouts and painful fits;
And scarce hath eyes his treasure to behold,
But like still-pining Tantalus he sits,
And useless barns the harvest of his wits;
  Having no other pleasure of his gain
  But torment that it cannot cure his pain.

"So then he hath it when he cannot use it,
And leaves it to be master'd by his young;
Who in their pride do presently abuse it:
Their father was too weak, and they too strong,
To hold their cursèd-blessèd fortune long.
  The sweets we wish for turn to loathèd sours
  Even in the moment that we call them ours.

"Unruly blasts wait on the tender spring;
Unwholesome weeds take root with precious flowers;
The adder hisses where the sweet birds sing;
What virtue breeds iniquity devours:
We have no good that we can say is ours,
  But ill-annexèd Opportunity
  Or kills his life or else his quality.

"O Opportunity, thy guilt is great!
'Tis thou that execut'st the traitor's treason;
Thou sett'st the wolf where he the lamb may get;
Whoever plots the sin, thou point'st the season;
'Tis thou that spurn'st at right, at law, at reason;
  And in thy shady cell, where none may spy him,
  Sits Sin, to seize the souls that wander by him.

"Thou mak'st the vestal violate her oath;
Thou blow'st the fire when temperance is thaw'd;
Thou smother'st honesty, thou murder'st troth;

Thou foul abettor! thou notorious bawd!
Thou plantest scandal, and displacest laud:
  Thou ravisher, thou traitor, thou false thief,
  Thy honey turns to gall, thy joy to grief!

"Thy secret pleasure turns to open shame,
Thy private feasting to a public fast,
Thy smoothing titles to a ragged name,
Thy sugar'd tongue to bitter wormwood taste:
Thy violent vanities can never last.
  How comes it, then, vile Opportunity,
  Being so bad, such numbers seek for thee?

"When wilt thou be the humble suppliant's friend,
And bring him where his suit may be obtain'd?
When wilt thou sort an hour great strifes to end?
Or free that soul which wretchedness hath chain'd?
Give physic to the sick, ease to the pain'd?
  The poor, lame, blind, halt, creep, cry out for thee;
  But they ne'er meet with Opportunity.

"The patient dies while the physician sleeps;
The orphan pines while the oppressor feeds;
Justice is feasting while the widow weeps;
Advice is sporting while infection breeds:
Thou grant'st no time for charitable deeds:
  Wrath, envy, treason, rape, and murder's rages,
  Thy heinous hours wait on them as their pages.

"When Truth and Virtue have to do with thee,
A thousand crosses keep them from thy aid:
They buy thy help; but Sin ne'er gives a fee,
He gratis comes; and thou art well appaid
As well to hear as grant what he hath said.
  My Collatine would else have come to me
  When Tarquin did, but he was stay'd by thee.

"Guilty thou art of murder and of theft,
Guilty of perjury and subornation,
Guilty of treason, forgery, and shift,

Guilty of incest, that abomination;
An accessary by thine inclination
  To all sins past, and all that are to come,
  From the creation to the general doom.

"Mis-shapen Time, copesmate of ugly Night,
Swift subtle post, carrier of grisly care,
Eater of youth, false slave to false delight,
Base watch of woes, sin's pack-horse, virtue's snare;
Thou nursest all, and murder'st all that are:
  O, hear me, then, injurious-shifting Time!
  Be guilty of my death, since of my crime.

"Why hath thy servant Opportunity
Betray'd the hours thou gav'st me to repose,
Cancell'd my fortunes, and enchainèd me
To endless date of never-ending woes?
Time's office is to fine the hate of foes;
  To eat up errors by opinion bred,
  Not spend the dowry of a lawful bed.

"Time's glory is to calm contending kings,
To unmask falsehood, and bring truth to light,
To stamp the seal of time in agèd things,
To wake the morn, and sentinel the night,
To wrong the wronger till he render right,
  To ruinate proud buildings with thy hours,
  And smear with dust their glittering golden towers;

"To fill with worm-holes stately monuments,
To feed oblivion with decay of things,
To blot old books and alter their contents,
To pluck the quills from ancient ravens' wings,
To dry the old oak's sap, and cherish springs,
  To spoil antiquities of hammer'd steel,
  And turn the giddy round of Fortune's wheel;

"To show the beldam daughters of her daughter,
To make the child a man, the man a child,
To slay the tiger that doth live by slaughter,

To tame the unicorn and lion wild,
To mock the subtle in themselves beguil'd,
   To cheer the ploughman with increaseful crops,
   And waste huge stones with little water-drops.

"Why work'st thou mischief in thy pilgrimage,
Unless thou couldst return to make amends?
One poor retiring minute in an age
Would purchase thee a thousand thousand friends,
Lending him wit that to bad debtors lends:
   O, this dread night, wouldst thou one hour come back,
   I could prevent this storm, and shun thy wrack!

"Thou ceaseless lackey to eternity,
With some mischance cross Tarquin in his flight:
Devise extremes beyond extremity,
To make him curse this cursèd crimeful night:
Let ghastly shadows his lewd eyes affright;
   And the dire thought of his committed evil
   Shape every bush a hideous shapeless devil.

"Disturb his hours of rest with restless trances,
Afflict him in his bed with bedrid groans;
Let there bechance him pitiful mischances,
To make him moan; but pity not his moans:
Stone him with harden'd hearts, harder than stones;
   And let mild women to him lose their mildness,
   Wilder to him than tigers in their wildness.

"Let him have time to tear his curlèd hair,
Let him have time against himself to rave,
Let him have time of Time's help to despair,
Let him have time to live a loathèd slave,
Let him have time a beggar's orts to crave,
   And time to see one that by alms doth live
   Disdain to him disdainèd scraps to give.

"Let him have time to see his friends his foes,
And merry fools to mock at him resort;
Let him have time to mark how slow time goes

In time of sorrow, and how swift and short
His time of folly and his time of sport;
   And ever let his unrecalling crime
   Have time to wail th' abusing of his time.

"O Time, thou tutor both to good and bad,
Teach me to curse him that thou taught'st this ill!
At his own shadow let the thief run mad,
Himself himself seek every hour to kill!
Such wretched hands such wretched blood should spill;
   For who so base would such an office have
   As slanderous death's-man to so base a slave?

"The baser is he, coming from a king,
To shame his hope with deeds degenerate:
The mightier man, the mightier is the thing
That makes him honour'd, or begets him hate;
For greatest scandal waits on greatest state.
   The moon being clouded presently is miss'd,
   But little stars may hide them when they list.

"The crow may bathe his coal-black wings in mire,
And unperceiv'd fly with the filth away;
But if the like the snow-white swan desire,
The stain upon his silver down will stay.
Poor grooms are sightless night, kings glorious day:
   Gnats are unnoted wheresoe'er they fly,
   But eagles gaz'd upon with every eye.

"Out, idle words, servants to shallow fools!
Unprofitable sounds, weak arbitrators!
Busy yourselves in skill-contending schools;
Debate where leisure serves with dull debaters;
To trembling clients be you mediators:
   For me, I force not argument a straw,
   Since that my case is past the help of law.

"In vain I rail at Opportunity,
At Time, at Tarquin, and uncheerful Night;
In vain I cavil with mine infamy,

Shakespeare. VII.   23

In vain I spurn at my confirm'd despite:
This helpless smoke of words doth me no right.
   The remedy indeed to do me good
   Is to let forth my foul-defilèd blood.

"Poor hand, why quiver'st thou at this decree?
Honour thyself to rid me of this shame;
For if I die, my honour lives in thee;
But if I live, thou liv'st in my defame:
Since thou couldst not defend thy loyal dame,
   And wast afeard to scratch her wicked foe,
   Kill both thyself and her for yielding so."

This said, from her betumbled couch she starteth,
To find some desperate instrument of death:
But this no slaughterhouse no tool imparteth
To make more vent for passage of her breath;
Which, thronging through her lips, so vanisheth
   As smoke from Ætna, that in air consumes,
   Or that which from dischargèd cannon fumes.

"In vain," quoth she, "I live, and seek in vain
Some happy mean to end a hapless life.
I fear'd by Tarquin's falchion to be slain,
Yet for the self-same purpose seek a knife:
But when I fear'd I was a loyal wife:
   So am I now: — O no, that cannot be;
   Of that true type hath Tarquin rifled me.

"O, that is gone for which I sought to live,
And therefore now I need not fear to die.
To clear this spot by death, at least I give
A badge of fame to slander's livery;
A dying life to living infamy:
   Poor helpless help, the treasure stol'n away,
   To burn the guiltless casket where it lay!

"Well, well, dear Collatine, thou shalt not know
The stainèd taste of violated troth;
I will not wrong thy true affection so,

To flatter thee with an infringèd oath;
This bastard graff shall never come to growth:
  He shall not boast who did thy stock pollute
  That thou art doting father of his fruit.

"Nor shall he smile at thee in secret thought,
Nor laugh with his companions at thy state;
But thou shalt know thy interest was not bought
Basely with gold, but stol'n from forth thy gate.
For me, I am the mistress of my fate,
  And with my trespass never will dispense,
  Till life to death acquit my forc'd offence.

"I will not poison thee with my attaint,
Nor fold my fault in cleanly-coin'd excuses;
My sable ground of sin I will not paint,
To hide the truth of this false night's abuses:
My tongue shall utter all; mine eyes, like sluices,
  As from a mountain-spring that feeds a dale,
  Shall gush pure streams to purge my impure tale."

By this, lamenting Philomel had ended
The well-tun'd warble of her nightly sorrow,
And solemn night with slow-sad gait descended
To ugly hell; when, lo, the blushing morrow
Lends light to all fair eyes that light will borrow;
  But cloudy Lucrece shames herself to see,
  And therefore still in night would cloister'd be.

Revealing day through every cranny spies,
And seems to point her out where she sits weeping;
To whom she sobbing speaks: "O eye of eyes,
Why pry'st thou through my window? leave thy peeping:
Mock with thy tickling beams eyes that are sleeping:
  Brand not my forehead with thy piercing light,
  For day hath naught to do what's done by night."

Thus cavils she with every thing she sees:
True grief is fond and testy as a child,
Who wayward once, his mood with naught agrees:

23*

Old woes, not infant sorrows, bear them mild;
Continuance tames the one; the other wild,
　　Like an unpractis'd swimmer plunging still,
　　With too much labour drowns for want of skill.

So she, deep-drenchèd in a sea of care,
Holds disputation with each thing she views,
And to herself all sorrow doth compare;
No object but her passion's strength renews;
And as one shifts, another straight ensues:
　　Sometime her grief is dumb, and hath no words;
　　Sometime 'tis mad, and too much talk affords.

The little birds that tune their morning's joy
Make her moans mad with their sweet melody:
For mirth doth search the bottom of annoy;
Sad souls are slain in merry company;
Grief best is pleas'd with grief's society:
　　True sorrow then is feelingly suffic'd
　　When with like semblance it is sympathiz'd.

'Tis double death to drown in ken of shore;
He ten times pines that pines beholding food;
To see the salve doth make the wound ache more;
Great grief grieves most at that would do it good;
Deep woes roll forward like a gentle flood,
　　Who, being stopp'd, the bounding banks o'erflows;
　　Grief dallied with nor law nor limit knows.

"You mocking birds," quoth she, "your tunes entomb
Within your hollow-swelling feather'd breasts,
And in my hearing be you mute and dumb:
My restless discord loves no stops nor rests;
A woful hostess brooks not merry guests:
　　Relish your nimble notes to pleasing ears;
　　Distress likes dumps when time is kept with tears.

"Come, Philomel, that sing'st of ravishment,
Make thy sad grove in my dishevell'd hair:
As the dank earth weeps at thy languishment,

So I at each sad strain will strain a tear,
And with deep groans the diapason bear;
    For burden-wise I'll hum on Tarquin still,
    While thou on Tereus descant'st better skill.

"And whiles against a thorn thou bear'st thy part,
To keep thy sharp woes waking, wretched I,
To imitate thee well, against my heart
Will fix a sharp knife, to affright mine eye;
Who, if it wink, shall thereon fall and die.
    These means, as frets upon an instrument,
    Shall tune our heart-strings to true languishment.

"And for, poor bird, thou sing'st not in the day,
As shaming any eye should thee behold,
Some dark-deep desert, seated from the way,
That knows not parching heat nor freezing cold,
Will we find out; and there we will unfold
    To creatures stern sad tunes, to change their kinds:
    Since men prove beasts, let beasts bear gentle minds."

As the poor frighted deer, that stands at gaze,
Wildly determining which way to fly,
Or one encompass'd with a winding maze,
That cannot tread the way out readily;
So with herself is she in mutiny,
    To live or die which of the twain were better,
    When life is sham'd, and death reproach's debtor.

"To kill myself," quoth she, "alack, what were it,
But with my body my poor soul's pollution?
They that lose half with greater patience bear it
Than they whose whole is swallow'd in confusion.
That mother tries a merciless conclusion
    Who, having two sweet babes, when death takes one,
    Will slay the other, and be nurse to none.

"My body or my soul, which was the dearer,
When the one pure, the other made divine?
Whose love of either to myself was nearer,

When both were kept for heaven and Collatine?
Ay me! the bark peel'd from the lofty pine,
  His leaves will wither, and his sap decay;
  So must my soul, her bark being peel'd away.

"Her house is sack'd, her quiet interrupted,
Her mansion batter'd by the enemy;
Her sacred temple spotted, spoil'd, corrupted,
Grossly engirt with daring infamy:
Then let it not be call'd impiety,
  If in this blemish'd fort I make some hole
  Through which I may convey this troubled soul.

"Yet die I will not till my Collatine
Have heard the cause of my untimely death;
That he may vow, in that sad hour of mine,
Revenge on him that made me stop my breath.
My stainèd blood to Tarquin I'll bequeath,
  Which by him tainted shall for him be spent,
  And as his due writ in my testament.

"My honour I'll bequeath unto the knife
That wounds my body so dishonourèd.
'Tis honour to deprive dishonour'd life;
The one will live, the other being dead:
So of shame's ashes shall my fame be bred;
  For in my death I murder shameful scorn:
  My shame so dead, mine honour is new-born.

"Dear lord of that dear jewel I have lost,
What legacy shall I bequeath to thee?
My resolution, love, shall be thy boast,
By whose example thou reveng'd mayst be.
How Tarquin must be us'd, read it in me:
  Myself, thy friend, will kill myself, thy foe,
  And, for my sake, serve thou false Tarquin so.

"This brief abridgment of my will I make: —
My soul and body to the skies and ground;
My resolution, husband, do thou take;

Mine honour be the knife's that makes my wound;
My shame be his that did my fame confound;
   And all my fame that lives disbursèd be
   To those that live, and think no shame of me.

"Thou, Collatine, shalt oversee this will;
How was I overseen that thou shalt see it!
My blood shall wash the slander of mine ill;
My life's foul deed, my life's fair end shall free it.
Faint not, faint heart, but stoutly say, 'So be it:'
   Yield to my hand; my hand shall conquer thee:
   Thou dead, both die, and both shall victors be."

This plot of death when sadly she had laid,
And wip'd the brinish pearl from her bright eyes,
With untun'd tongue she hoarsely calls her maid,
Whose swift obedience to her mistress hies;
For swift-wing'd duty with thought's feathers flies.
   Poor Lucrece' cheeks unto her maid seem so
   As winter meads when sun doth melt their snow.

Her mistress she doth give demure good-morrow,
With soft-slow tongue, true mark of modesty,
And sorts a sad look to her lady's sorrow,
For why her face wore sorrow's livery;
But durst not ask of her audaciously
   Why her two suns were cloud-eclipsèd so,
   Nor why her fair cheeks overwash'd with woe.

But as the earth doth weep, the sun being set,
Each flower moisten'd like a melting eye;
Even so the maid with swelling drops gan wet
Her circled eyne, enforc'd by sympathy
Of those fair suns set in her mistress' sky,
   Who in a salt-wav'd ocean quench their light,
   Which makes the maid weep like the dewy night.

A pretty while these pretty creatures stand,
Like ivory conduits coral cisterns filling:
One justly weeps; the other takes in hand

No cause, but company, of her drops spilling:
Their gentle sex to weep are often willing;
   Grieving themselves to guess at others' smarts,
   And then they drown their eyes, or break their hearts.

For men have marble, women waxen, minds,
And therefore are they form'd as marble will;
The weak oppress'd, th' impression of strange kinds
Is form'd in them by force, by fraud, or skill:
Then call them not the authors of their ill,
   No more than wax shall be accounted evil
   Wherein is stamp'd the semblance of a devil.

Their smoothness, like a goodly champaign plain,
Lays open all the little worms that creep;
In men, as in a rough-grown grove, remain
Cave-keeping evils that obscurely sleep:
Through crystal walls each little mote will peep:
   Though men can cover crimes with bold stern looks,
   Poor women's faces are their own faults' books.

No man inveigh against the wither'd flower,
But chide rough winter that the flower hath kill'd:
Not that devour'd, but that which doth devour,
Is worthy blame.   O, let it not be hild
Poor women's faults, that they are so fulfill'd
   With men's abuses: those proud lords, to blame,
   Make weak-made women tenants to their shame.

The precedent whereof in Lucrece view,
Assail'd by night with circumstances strong
Of present death, and shame that might ensue
By that her death, to do her husband wrong:
Such danger to resistance did belong,
   That dying fear through all her body spread;
   And who cannot abuse a body dead?

By this, mild patience bid fair Lucrece speak
To the poor counterfeit of her complaining:
"My girl," quoth she, "on what occasion break

Those tears from thee, that down thy cheeks are raining?
If thou dost weep for grief of my sustaining,
  Know, gentle wench, it small avails my mood:
  If tears could help, mine own would do me good.

"But tell me, girl, when went" — and there she stay'd
Till after a deep groan — "Tarquin from hence?"
"Madam, ere I was up," replied the maid,
"The more to blame my sluggard negligence:
Yet with the fault I thus far can dispense, —
  Myself was stirring ere the break of day,
  And, ere I rose, was Tarquin gone away.

"But, lady, if your maid may be so bold,
She would request to know your heaviness."
"O, peace!" quoth Lucrece: "if it should be told,
The repetition cannot make it less;
For more it is than 1 can well express:
  And that deep torture may be call'd a hell
  When more is felt than one hath power to tell.

"Go, get me hither paper, ink, and pen, —
Yet save that labour, for I have them here.
What should I say? — One of my husband's men
Bid thou be ready, by and by, to bear
A letter to my lord, my love, my dear:
  Bid him with speed prepare to carry it;
  The cause craves haste, and it will soon be writ."

Her maid is gone, and she prepares to write,
First hovering o'er the paper with her quill:
Conceit and grief an eager combat fight;
What wit sets down is blotted straight with will;
This is too curious-good, this blunt and ill:
  Much like a press of people at a door,
  Throng her inventions, which shall go before.

At last she thus begins: "Thou worthy lord
Of that unworthy wife that greeteth thee,
Health to thy person! next vouchsafe t' afford —

If ever, love, thy Lucrece thou wilt see —
Some present speed to come and visit me.
  So, I commend me from our house in grief:
  My woes are tedious, though my words are brief."

Here folds she up the tenour of her woe,
Her certain sorrow writ uncertainly.
By this short schedule Collatine may know
Her grief, but not her grief's true quality:
She dares not thereof make discovery,
  Lest he should hold it her own gross abuse,
  Ere she with blood had stain'd her stain'd excuse.

Besides, the life and feeling of her passion
She hoards, to spend when he is by to hear her;
When sighs and groans and tears may grace the fashion
Of her disgrace, the better so to clear her
From that suspicion which the world might bear her.
  To shun this blot, she would not blot the letter
  With words, till action might become them better.

To see sad sights moves more than hear them told;
For then the eye interprets to the ear
The heavy motion that it doth behold,
When every part a part of woe doth bear.
'Tis but a part of sorrow that we hear:
  Deep sounds make lesser noise than shallow fords,
  And sorrow ebbs, being blown with wind of words.

Her letter now is seal'd, and on it writ,
"At Ardea to my lord with more than haste."
The post attends, and she delivers it,
Charging the sour-fac'd groom to hie as fast   ·
As lagging fowls before the northern blast:
  Speed more than speed but dull and slow she deems:
  Extremity still urgeth such extremes.

The homely villain court'sies to her low;
And, blushing on her, with a steadfast eye
Receives the scroll without or yea or no,

And forth with bashful innocence doth hie.
But they whose guilt within their bosoms lie
  Imagine every eye beholds their blame;
  For Lucrece thought he blush'd to see her shame:

When, silly groom! God wot, it was defect
Of spirit, life, and bold audacity.
Such harmless creatures have a true respect
To talk in deeds, while others saucily
Promise more speed, but do it leisurely:
  Even so this pattern of the worn-out age
  Pawn'd honest looks, but laid no words to gage.

His kindled duty kindled her mistrust,
That two red fires in both their faces blaz'd;
She thought he blush'd, as knowing Tarquin's lust,
And, blushing with him, wistly on him gaz'd;
Her earnest eye did make him more amaz'd:
  The more she saw the blood his cheeks replenish,
  The more she thought he spied in her some blemish.

But long she thinks till he return again,
And yet the duteous vassal scarce is gone.
The weary time she cannot entertain,
For now 'tis stale to sigh, to weep, and groan:
So woe hath wearied woe, moan tirèd moan,
  That she her plaints a little while doth stay,
  Pausing for means to mourn some newer way.

At last she calls to mind where hangs a piece
Of skilful painting, made for Priam's Troy;
Before the which is drawn the power of Greece,
For Helen's rape the city to destroy,
Threatening cloud-kissing Ilion with annoy;
  Which the conceited painter drew so proud,
  As heaven, it seem'd, to kiss the turrets bow'd.

A thousand lamentable objects there,
In scorn of nature, art gave lifeless life:
Many a dry drop seem'd a weeping tear,

Shed for the slaughter'd husband by the wife:
The red blood reek'd, to show the painter's strife;
   And dying eyes gleam'd forth their ashy lights,
   Like dying coals burnt out in tedious nights.

There might you see the labouring pioner
Begrim'd with sweat, and smearèd all with dust;
And from the towers of Troy there would appear
The very eyes of men through loop-holes thrust,
Gazing upon the Greeks with little lust:
   Such sweet observance in this work was had,
   That one might see those far-off eyes look sad.

In great commanders grace and majesty
You might behold, triúmphing in their faces;
In youth, quick bearing and dexterity;
And here and there the painter interlaces
Pale cowards, marching on with trembling paces;
   Which heartless peasants did so well resemble,
   That one would swear he saw them quake and tremble.

In Ajax and Ulysses, O, what art
Of physiognomy might one behold!
The face of either cipher'd either's heart;
Their face their manners most expressly told:
In Ajax' eyes blunt rage and rigour roll'd;
   But the mild glance that sly Ulysses lent
   Show'd deep regard and smiling government.

There pleading might you see grave Nestor stand,
As 'twere encouraging the Greeks to fight:
Making such sober action with his hand,
That it beguil'd attention, charm'd the sight:
In speech, it seem'd, his beard, all silver white,
   Wagg'd up and down, and from his lips did fly
   Thin winding breath, which purl'd up to the sky.

About him were a press of gaping faces,
Which seem'd to swallow up his sound advice;
All jointly listening, but with several graces,

As if some mermaid did their cars entice,
Some high, some low, — the painter was so nice;
  The scalps of many, almost hid behind,
  To jump up higher seem'd, to mock the mind.

Here one man's hand lean'd on another's head,
His nose being shadow'd by his neighbour's car;
Here one, being throng'd, bears back, all boll'n and red;
Another, smother'd, seems to pelt and swear;
And in their rage such signs of rage they bear,
  As, but for loss of Nestor's golden words,
  It seem'd they would debate with angry swords.

For much imaginary work was there;
Conceit deceitful, so compact, so kind,
That for Achilles' image stood his spear,
Grip'd in an armèd hand; himself, behind,
Was left unseen, save to the eye of mind:
  A hand, a foot, a face, a leg, a head,
  Stood for the whole to be imaginèd.

And from the walls of strong-besiegèd Troy
When their brave hope, bold Hector, march'd to field,
Stood many Trojan mothers, sharing joy
To see their youthful sons bright weapons wield;
And to their hope they such odd action yield,
  That through their light joy seemèd to appear,
  Like bright things stain'd, a kind of heavy fear.

And from the strand of Dardan, where they fought,
To Simoïs' reedy banks the red blood ran,
Whose waves to imitate the battle sought
With swelling ridges; and their ranks began
To break upon the gallèd shore, and than
  Retire again, till, meeting greater ranks,
  They join, and shoot their foam at Simoïs' banks.

To this well-painted piece is Lucrece come,
To find a face where all distress is stell'd.
Many she sees where cares have carvèd some,

But none where all distress and dolour dwell'd,
Till she despairing Hecuba beheld,
  Staring on Priam's wounds with her old eyes,
  Which bleeding under Pyrrhus' proud foot lies.

In her the painter had anatomiz'd
Time's ruin, beauty's wreck, and grim care's reign:
Her cheeks with chaps and wrinkles were disguis'd;
Of what she was no semblance did remain:
Her blue blood chang'd to black in every vein,
  Wanting the spring that those shrunk pipes had fed,
  Show'd life imprison'd in a body dead.

On this sad shadow Lucrece spends her eyes,
And shapes her sorrow to the beldam's woes,
Who nothing wants to answer her but cries,
And bitter words to ban her cruel foes:
The painter was no god to lend her those;
  And therefore Lucrece swears he did her wrong,
  To give her so much grief, and not a tongue.

"Poor instrument," quoth she, "without a sound,
I'll tune thy woes with my lamenting tongue;
And drop sweet balm in Priam's painted wound,
And rail on Pyrrhus that hath done him wrong;
And with my tears quench Troy that burns so long;
  And with my knife scratch out the angry eyes
  Of all the Greeks that are thine enemies.

"Show me the strumpet that began this stir,
That with my nails her beauty I may tear.
Thy heat of lust, fond Paris, did incur
This load of wrath that burning Troy doth bear:
Thy eye kindled the fire that burneth here;
  And here in Troy, for trespass of thine eye,
  The sire, the son, the dame, and daughter die.

"Why should the private pleasure of some one
Become the public plague of many mo?
Let sin, alone committed, light alone

Upon his head that hath transgressèd so;
Let guiltless souls be freed from guilty woe:
  For one's offence why should so many fall,
  To plague a private sin in general?

"Lo, here weeps Hecuba, here Priam dies,
Here manly Hector faints, here Troilus swounds,
Here friend by friend in bloody channel lies,
And friend to friend gives unadvisèd wounds,
And one man's lust these many lives confounds:
  Had doting Priam check'd his son's desire,
  Troy had been bright with fame, and not with fire."

Here feelingly she weeps Troy's painted woes:
For sorrow, like a heavy-hanging bell,
Once set on ringing, with his own weight goes;
Then little strength rings out the doleful knell:
So Lucrece, set a-work, sad tales doth tell
  To pencill'd pensiveness and colour'd sorrow;
  She lends them words, and she their looks doth borrow.

She throws her eyes about the painting round,
And whom she finds forlorn she doth lament.
At last she sees a wretched image bound,
That piteous looks to Phrygian shepherds lent:
His face, though full of cares, yet show'd content;
  Onward to Troy with the blunt swains he goes,
  So mild, that Patience seem'd to scorn his woes.

In him the painter labour'd with his skill
To hide deceit, and give the harmless show
An humble gait, calm looks, eyes wailing still,
A brow unbent, that seem'd to welcome woe;
Cheeks neither red nor pale, but mingled so
  That blushing red no guilty instance gave,
  Nor ashy pale the fear that false hearts have.

But, like a constant and confirmèd devil,
He entertain'd a show so seeming just,
And therein so ensconc'd his secret evil,

That jealousy itself could not mistrust
False-creeping craft and perjury should thrust
  Into so bright a day such black-fac'd storms,
  Or blot with hell-born sin such saint-like forms.

The well-skill'd workman this mild image drew
For perjur'd Sinon, whose enchanting story
The credulous old Priam after slew;
Whose words, like wildfire, burnt the shining glory
Of rich-built Ilion, that the skies were sorry,
  And little stars shot from their fixèd places,
  When their glass fell wherein they view'd their faces.

This picture she advisedly perus'd,
And chid the painter for his wondrous skill,
Saying, some shape in Sinon's was abus'd;
So fair a form lodg'd not a mind so ill:
And still on him she gaz'd; and gazing still,
  Such signs of truth in his plain face she spied,
  That she concludes the picture was belied.

"It cannot be," quoth she, "that so much guile" —
She would have said "can lurk in such a look;"
But Tarquin's shape came in her mind the while,
And from her tongue "can lurk" from "cannot" took:
"It cannot be" she in that sense forsook,
  And turn'd it thus, "It cannot be, I find,
  But such a face should bear a wicked mind:

"For even as subtle Sinon here is painted,
So sober-sad, so weary, and so mild,
As if with grief or travail he had fainted,
To me came Tarquin armèd; so beguil'd
With outward honesty, but yet defil'd
  With inward vice: as Priam him did cherish,
  So did I Tarquin; so my Troy did perish.

"Look, look, how listening Priam wets his eyes,
To see those borrow'd tears that Sinon sheds!
Priam, why art thou old, and yet not wise?

For every tear he falls a Trojan bleeds:
His eye drops fire, no water thence proceeds;
  Those round clear pearls of his, that move thy pity,
  Are balls of quenchless fire to burn thy city.

"Such devils steal effects from lightless hell;
For Sinon in his fire doth quake with cold,
And in that cold hot-burning fire doth dwell;
These contraries such unity do hold,
Only to flatter fools, and make them bold:
  So Priam's trust false Sinon's tears doth flatter,
  That he finds means to burn his Troy with water."

Here, all enrag'd, such passion her assails,
That patience is quite beaten from her breast.
She tears the senseless Sinon with her nails,
Comparing him to that unhappy guest
Whose deed hath made herself herself detest:
  At last she smilingly with this gives o'er;
  "Fool, fool!" quoth she, "his wounds will not be sore."

Thus ebbs and flows the current of her sorrow,
And time doth weary time with her complaining.
She looks for night, and then she longs for morrow,
And both she thinks too long with her remaining:
Short time seems long in sorrow's sharp sustaining:
  Though woe be heavy, yet it seldom sleeps;
  And they that watch see time how slow it creeps.

Which all this time hath overslipp'd her thought,
That she with painted images hath spent;
Being from the feeling of her own grief brought
By deep surmise of others' detriment;
Losing her woes in shows of discontent.
  It easeth some, though none it ever cur'd,
  To think their dolour others have endur'd.

But now the mindful messenger, come back,
Brings home his lord and other company;
Who finds his Lucrece clad in mourning black;

And round about her tear-distainèd eye
Blue circles stream'd, like rainbows in the sky:
   These water-galls in her dim element
   Foretell new storms to those already spent.

Which when her sad-beholding husband saw,
Amazedly in her sad face he stares:
Her eyes, though sod in tears, look'd red and raw,
Her lively colour kill'd with deadly cares.
He hath no power to ask her how she fares:
   Both stood, like old acquaintance in a trance,
   Met far from home, wondering each other's chance.

At last he takes her by the bloodless hand,
And thus begins: "What uncouth ill event
Hath thee befall'n, that thou dost trembling stand?
Sweet love, what spite hath thy fair colour spent?
Why art thou thus attir'd in discontent?
   Unmask, dear dear, this moody heaviness,
   And tell thy grief, that we may give redress."

Three times with sighs she gives her sorrow fire,
Ere once she can discharge one word of woe:
At length address'd to answer his desire,
She modestly prepares to let them know
Her honour is ta'en prisoner by the foe;
   While Collatine and his consorted lords
   With sad attention long to hear her words.

And now this pale swan in her watery nest
Begins the sad dirge of her certain ending:
"Few words," quoth she, "shall fit the trespass best,
Where no excuse can give the fault amending:
In me more woes than words are now depending;
   And my laments would be drawn out too long,
   To tell them all with one poor tired tongue.

"Then be this all the task it hath to say:
Dear husband, in the interest of thy bed
A stranger came, and on that pillow lay

Where thou wast wont to rest thy weary head;
And what wrong else may be imaginèd
  By foul enforcement might be done to me,
  From that, alas, thy Lucrece is not free.

"For in the dreadful dead of dark midnight,
With shining falchion in my chamber came
A creeping creature, with a flaming light,
And softly cried, 'Awake, thou Roman dame,
And entertain my love; else lasting shame
  On thee and thine this night I will inflict,
  If thou my love's desire do contradict.

"'For some hard-favour'd groom of thine,' quoth he
'Unless thou yoke thy liking to my will,
I'll murder straight, and then I'll slaughter thee,
And swear I found you where you did fulfil
The loathsome act of lust, and so did kill
  The lechers in their deed: this act will be
  My fame, and thy perpetual infamy.'

"With this, I did begin to start and cry;
And then against my heart he set his sword,
Swearing, unless I took all patiently,
I should not live to speak another word;
So should my shame still rest upon record,
  And never be forgot in mighty Rome,
  Th' adulterate death of Lucrece and her groom.

"Mine enemy was strong, my poor self weak,
And far the weaker with so strong a fear:
My bloody judge forbade my tongue to speak;
No rightful plea might plead for justice there:
His scarlet lust came evidence to swear
  That my poor beauty had purloin'd his eyes;
  And when the judge is robb'd, the prisoner dies.

"O, teach me how to make mine own excuse!
Or, at the least, this refuge let me find, —
Though my gross blood be stain'd with this abuse,

24*

Immaculate and spotless is my mind;
That was not forc'd; that never was inclin'd
  To accessary yieldings, but still pure
  Doth in her poison'd closet yet endure."

Lo, here, the hopeless merchant of this loss,
With head declin'd, and voice damm'd up with woe,
With sad-set eyes, and wreathèd arms across,
From lips new-waxen pale begins to blow
The grief away that stops his answer so:
  But, wretched as he is, he strives in vain;
  What he breathes out his breath drinks up again.

As through an arch the violent-roaring tide
Outruns the eye that doth behold his haste,
Yet in the eddy boundeth in his pride
Back to the strait that forc'd him on so fast;
In rage sent out, recall'd in rage, being past:
  Even so his sighs, his sorrows, make a saw,
  To push grief on, and back the same grief draw.

Which speechless woe of his poor she attendeth,
And his untimely frenzy thus awaketh:
"Dear lord, thy sorrow to my sorrow lendeth
Another power; no flood by raining slaketh.
My woe too sensible thy passion maketh
  More feeling-painful: let it, then, suffice
  To drown one woe, one pair of weeping eyes.

"And for my sake, when I might charm thee so,
For she that was thy Lucrece, — now attend me:
Be suddenly revengèd on my foe,
Thine, mine, his own: suppose thou dost defend me
From what is past: the help that thou shalt lend me
  Comes all too late, yet let the traitor die;
  For sparing justice feeds iniquity.

"But ere I name him, you fair lords," quoth she,
Speaking to those that came with Collatine,
"Shall plight your honourable faiths to me,

With swift pursuit to venge this wrong of mine;
For 'tis a meritorious fair design
  To chase injustice with revengeful arms:
  Knights, by their oaths, should right poor ladies' harms."

At this request, with noble disposition
Each present lord began to promise aid,
As bound in knighthood to her imposition,
Longing to hear the hateful foe bewray'd.
But she, that yet her sad task hath not said,
  The protestation stops. "O, speak," quoth she,
  "How may this forcèd stain be wip'd from me?

"What is the quality of mine offence,
Being constrain'd with dreadful circumstance?
May my pure mind with the foul act dispense,
My low-declinèd honour to advance?
May any terms acquit me from this chance?
  The poison'd fountain clears itself again;
  And why not I from this compellèd stain?"

With this, they all at once began to say,
Her body's stain her mind untainted clears;
While with a joyless smile she turns away
The face, that map which deep impression bears
Of hard misfortune, carv'd in it with tears.
  "No, no," quoth she, "no dame, hereafter living,
  By my excuse shall claim excuse's giving."

Here with a sigh, as if her heart would break,
She throws forth Tarquin's name: "He, he," she says,
But more than "he" her poor tongue could not speak;
Till after many accents and delays,
Untimely breathings, sick and short assays,
  She utters this, "He, he, fair lords, 'tis he
  That guides this hand to give this wound to me."

Even here she sheathèd in her harmless breast
A harmful knife, that thence her soul unsheath'd:
That blow did bail it from the deep unrest

Of that polluted prison where it breath'd:
Her contrite sighs unto the clouds bequeath'd
   Her wingèd sprite, and through her wounds doth fly
   Life's lasting date from cancell'd destiny.

Stone-still, astonish'd with this deadly deed,
Stood Collatine and all his lordly crew;
Till Lucrece' father, that beholds her bleed,
Himself on her self-slaughter'd body threw;
And from the purple fountain Brutus drew
   The murderous knife, and, as it left the place,
   Her blood, in poor revenge, held it in chase;

And bubbling from her breast, it doth divide
In two slow rivers, that the crimson blood
Circles her body in on every side,
Who, like a late-sack'd island, vastly stood
Bare and unpeopled in this fearful flood.
   Some of her blood still pure and red remain'd,
   And some look'd black, and that false Tarquin stain'd.

About the mourning and congealèd face
Of that black blood a watery rigol goes,
Which seems to weep upon the tainted place:
And ever since, as pitying Lucrece' woes,
Corrupted blood some watery token shows;
   And blood untainted still doth red abide,
   Blushing at that which is so putrefied.

"Daughter, dear daughter," old Lucretius cries,
"That life was mine which thou hast here depriv'd.
If in the child the father's image lies,
Where shall I live now Lucrece is unliv'd?
Thou wast not to this end from me deriv'd.
   If children pre-decease progenitors,
   We are their offspring, and they none of ours.

"Poor broken glass, I often did behold
In thy sweet semblance my old age new born;
But now that fresh fair mirror, dim and old,

Shows me a bare-bon'd death by time outworn:
O, from thy cheeks my image thou hast torn,
   And shiver'd all the beauty of my glass,
   That I no more can see what once I was.

"O time, cease thou thy course, and last no longer,
If they surcease to be that should survive.
Shall rotten death make conquest of the stronger,
And leave the faltering feeble souls alive?
The old bees die, the young possess their hive:
   Then live, sweet Lucrece, live again, and see
   Thy father die, and not thy father thee."

By this, starts Collatine as from a dream,
And bids Lucretius give his sorrow place;
And then in key-cold Lucrece' bleeding stream
He falls, and bathes the pale fear in his face,
And counterfeits to die with her a space;
   Till manly shame bids him possess his breath,
   And live to be revengèd on her death.

The deep vexation of his inward soul
Hath serv'd a dumb arrest upon his tongue;
Who, mad that sorrow should his use control,
Or keep him from heart-easing words so long,
Begins to talk; but through his lips do throng
   Weak words, so thick come in his poor heart's aid,
   That no man could distinguish what he said.

Yet sometime "Tarquin" was pronouncèd plain,
But through his teeth, as if the name he tore.
This windy tempest, till it blow up rain,
Held back his sorrow's tide, to make it more;
At last it rains, and busy winds give o'er:
   Then son and father weep with equal strife
   Who should weep most, for daughter or for wife.

The one doth call her his, the other his,
Yet neither may possess the claim they lay.
The father says "She's mine." "O, mine she is,"

Replies her husband: "do not take away
My sorrow's interest; let no mourner say
 He weeps for her, for she was only mine,
 And only must be wail'd by Collatine."

"O," quoth Lucretius, "I did give that life
Which she too early and too late hath spill'd."
"Woe, woe," quoth Collatine, "she was my wife,
I ow'd her, and 'tis mine that she hath kill'd."
"My daughter" and "my wife" with clamours fill'd
 The dispers'd air, who, holding Lucrece' life,
 Answer'd their cries, "my daughter" and "my wife."

Brutus, who pluck'd the knife from Lucrece' side,
Seeing such emulation in their woe,
Began to clothe his wit in state and pride,
Burying in Lucrece' wound his folly's show.
He with the Romans was esteemèd so
 As silly-jeering idiots are with kings,
 For sportive words and uttering foolish things:

But now he throws that shallow habit by,
Wherein deep policy did him disguise;
And arm'd his long-hid wits advisedly,
To check the tears in Collatinus' eyes.
"Thou wrongèd lord of Rome," quoth he, "arise:
 Let my unsounded self, suppos'd a fool,
 Now set thy long-experienc'd wit to school.

"Why, Collatine, is woe the cure for woe?
Do wounds help wounds, or grief help grievous deeds?
Is it revenge to give thyself a blow
For his foul act by whom thy fair wife bleeds?
Such childish humour from weak minds proceeds:
 Thy wretched wife mistook the matter so,
 To slay herself, that should have slain her foe.

"Courageous Roman, do not steep thy heart
In such relenting dew of lamentations;
But kneel with me, and help to bear thy part,

To rouse our Roman gods with invocations,
That they will suffer these abominations,
  Since Rome herself in them doth stand disgrac'd,
  By our strong arms from forth her fair streets chas'd.

"Now, by the Capitol that we adore,
And by this chaste blood so unjustly stain'd,
By heaven's fair sun that breeds the fat earth's store,
By all our country rights in Rome maintain'd,
And by chaste Lucrece' soul that late complain'd
  Her wrongs to us, and by this bloody knife,
  We will revenge the death of this true wife."

This said, he struck his hand upon his breast,
And kiss'd the fatal knife, to end his vow;
And to his protestation urg'd the rest,
Who, wondering at him, did his words allow:
Then jointly to the ground their knees they bow;
  And that deep vow, which Brutus made before,
  He doth again repeat, and that they swore.

When they had sworn to this advisèd doom,
They did conclude to bear dead Lucrece thence,
To show her bleeding body thorough Rome,
And so to publish Tarquin's foul offence:
Which being done with speedy diligence,
  The Romans plausibly did give consent
  To Tarquin's everlasting banishment.

SONNETS.

I.

FROM fairest creatures we desire increase,
That thereby beauty's rose might never die,
But as the riper should by time decease,
His tender heir might bear his memory:
But thou, contracted to thine own bright eyes,
Feed'st thy light's flame with self-substantial fuel,
Making a famine where abundance lies,
Thyself thy foe, to thy sweet self too cruel.
Thou that art now the world's fresh ornament,
And only herald to the gaudy spring,
Within thine own bud buriest thy content,
And, tender churl, mak'st waste in niggarding.
  Pity the world, or else this glutton be,
  To eat the world's due, by the grave and thee.

II.

When forty winters shall besiege thy brow,
And dig deep trenches in thy beauty's field,
Thy youth's proud livery, so gaz'd on now,
Will be a tatter'd weed, of small worth held:
Then being ask'd where all thy beauty lies,
Where all the treasure of thy lusty days, —
To say, within thine own deep-sunken eyes,
Were an all-eating shame and thriftless praise.
How much more praise deserv'd thy beauty's use,
If thou couldst answer — "This fair child of mine
Shall sum my count, and make my old excuse," —
Proving his beauty by succession thine!

This were to be new made when thou art old,
And see thy blood warm when thou feel'st it cold.

III.

Look in thy glass, and tell the face thou viewest
Now is the time that face should form another;
Whose fresh repair if now thou not renewest,
Thou dost beguile the world, unbless some mother.
For where is she so fair whose unear'd womb
Disdains the tillage of thy husbandry?
Or who is he so fond will be the tomb
Of his self-love, to stop posterity?
Thou art thy mother's glass, and she in thee
Calls back the lovely April of her prime:
So thou through windows of thine age shalt see,
Despite of wrinkles, this thy golden time.
  But if thou live, remember'd not to be,
  Die single, and thine image dies with thee.

IV.

Unthrifty loveliness, why dost thou spend
Upon thyself thy beauty's legacy?
Nature's bequest gives nothing, but doth lend;
And, being frank, she lends to those are free.
Then, beauteous niggard, why dost thou abuse
The bounteous largess given thee to give?
Profitless usurer, why dost thou use
So great a sum of sums, yet canst not live?
For having traffic with thyself alone,
Thou of thyself thy sweet self dost deceive.
Then how, when nature calls thee to be gone,
What acceptable audit canst thou leave?
  Thy unus'd beauty must be tomb'd with thee,
  Which, usèd, lives th' executor to be.

V.

Those hours, that with gentle work did frame
The lovely gaze where every eye doth dwell,

Will play the tyrants to the very same,
And that unfair which fairly doth excel;
For never-resting time leads summer on
To hideous winter and confounds him there;
Sap check'd with frost, and lusty leaves quite gone,
Beauty o'ersnow'd, and bareness every where:
Then, were not summer's distillation left,
A liquid prisoner pent in walls of glass,
Beauty's effect with beauty were bereft,
Nor it, nor no remembrance what it was:
   But flowers distill'd, though they with winter meet,
   Leese but their show; their substance still lives sweet.

VI.

Then let not winter's ragged hand deface
In thee thy summer, ere thou be distill'd:
Make sweet some vial; treasure thou some place
With beauty's treasure, ere it be self-kill'd.
That use is not forbidden usury,
Which happies those that pay the willing loan;
That's for thyself to breed another thee,
Or ten times happier, be it ten for one;
Ten times thyself were happier than thou art,
If ten of thine ten times refigur'd thee:
Then what could death do, if thou shouldst depart,
Leaving thee living in posterity?
   Be not self-will'd, for thou art much too fair
   To be death's conquest, and make worms thine heir

VII.

Lo, in the orient when the gracious light
Lifts up his burning head, each under eye
Doth homage to his new-appearing sight,
Serving with looks his sacred majesty;
And having climb'd the steep-up heavenly hill,
Resembling strong youth in his middle age,
Yet mortal looks adore his beauty still,
Attending on his golden pilgrimage;

But when from highmost pitch, with weary car,
Like feeble age, he reeleth from the day,
The eyes, fore duteous, now converted are
From his low tract, and look another way:
  So thou, thyself outgoing in thy noon,
  Unlook'd on diest, unless thou get a son.

VIII.

Music to hear, why hear'st thou music sadly?
Sweets with sweets war not, joy delights in joy.
Why lov'st thou that which thou receiv'st not gladly,
Or else receiv'st with pleasure thine annoy?
If the true concord of well-tunèd sounds,
By unions married, do offend thine ear,
They do but sweetly chide thee, who confounds
In singleness the parts that thou shouldst bear.
Mark how one string, sweet husband to another,
Strikes each in each by mutual ordering;
Resembling sire and child and happy mother,
Who, all in one, one pleasing note do sing:
  Whose speechless song, being many, seeming one,
  Sings this to thee, "thou single wilt prove none"

IX.

Is it for fear to wet a widow's eye
That thou consum'st thyself in single life?
Ah! if thou issueless shalt hap to die,
The world will wail thee, like a makeless wife;
The world will be thy widow, and still weep
That thou no form of thee hast left behind,
When every private widow well may keep,
By children's eyes, her husband's shape in mind.
Look, what an unthrift in the world doth spend
Shifts but his place, for still the world enjoys it;
But beauty's waste hath in the world an end,
And kept unus'd, the user so destroys it.
  No love toward others in that bosom sits
  That on himself such murderous shame commits.

X.

For shame! deny that thou bear'st love to any,
Who for thyself art so unprovident.
Grant, if thou wilt, thou art belov'd of many,
But that thou none lov'st is most evident;
For thou art so possess'd with murderous hate,
That 'gainst thyself thou stick'st not to conspire,
Seeking that beauteous roof to ruinate,
Which to repair should be thy chief desire.
O, change thy thought, that I may change my mind!
Shall hate be fairer lodg'd than gentle love?
Be, as thy presence is, gracious and kind,
Or to thyself, at least, kind-hearted prove:
  Make thee another self, for love of me,
  That beauty still may live in thine or thee.

XI.

As fast as thou shalt wane, so fast thou growest
In one of thine, from that which thou departest;
And that fresh blood which youngly thou bestowest
Thou mayst call thine when thou from youth convertest.
Herein lives wisdom, beauty, and increase;
Without this, folly, age, and cold decay:
If all were minded so, the times should cease,
And threescore year would make the world away.
Let those whom Nature hath not made for store,
Harsh, featureless, and rude, barrenly perish:
Look, whom she best endow'd she gave the more;
Which bounteous gift thou shouldst in bounty cherish:
  She carv'd thee for her seal, and meant thereby
  Thou shouldst print more, not let that copy die.

XII.

When I do count the clock that tells the time,
And see the brave day sunk in hideous night;
When I behold the violet past prime,
And sable curls all silver'd o'er with white;

When lofty trees I see barren of leaves,
Which erst from heat did canopy the herd,
And summer's green, all girded up in sheaves,
Borne on the bier with white and bristly beard;
Then of thy beauty do I question make,
That thou among the wastes of time must go,
Since sweets and beauties do themselves forsake,
And die as fast as they see others grow;
  And nothing 'gainst Time's scythe can make defence
  Save breed, to brave him when he takes thee hence.

XIII.

O, that you were yourself! but, love, you are
No longer yours than you yourself here live:
Against this coming end you should prepare,
And your sweet semblance to some other give.
So should that beauty which you hold in lease
Find no determination; then you were
Yourself again, after yourself's decease,
When your sweet issue your sweet form should bear.
Who lets so fair a house fall to decay,
Which husbandry in honour might uphold
Against the stormy gusts of winter's day,
And barren rage of death's eternal cold?
  O, none but unthrifts: — dear my love, you know
  You had a father; let your son say so.

XIV.

Not from the stars do I my judgment pluck;
And yet methinks I have astronomy,
But not to tell of good or evil luck,
Of plagues, of dearths, or seasons' quality;
Nor can I fortune to brief minutes tell,
Pointing to each his thunder, rain, and wind,
Or say with princes if it shall go well,
By oft predict that I in heaven find:
But from thine eyes my knowledge I derive,
And, constant stars, in them I read such art,

As truth and beauty shall together thrive,
If from thyself to store thou wouldst convert;
  Or else of thee this I prognosticate,—
  Thy end is truth's and beauty's doom and date.

XV.

When I consider every thing that grows'
Holds in perfection but a little moment,
That this huge stage presenteth naught but shows
Whereon the stars in secret influence comment;
When I perceive that men as plants increase,
Cheerèd and check'd even by the self-same sky,
Vaunt in their youthful sap, at height decrease,
And wear their brave state out of memory;
Then the conceit of this inconstant stay
Sets you most rich in youth before my sight,
Where wasteful Time debateth with Decay,
To change your day of youth to sullied night;
  And, all in war with Time, for love of you,
  As he takes from you, I engraft you new.

XVI.

But wherefore do not you a mightier way
Make war upon this bloody tyrant, Time?
And fortify yourself in your decay
With means more blessèd than my barren rhyme?
Now stand you on the top of happy hours;
And many maiden gardens, yet unset,
With virtuous wish would bear your living flowers,
Much liker than your painted counterfeit:
So should the lines of life that life repair,
Which this, Time's pencil, or my pupil pen,
Neither in inward worth nor outward fair,
Can make you live yourself in eyes of men.
  To give away yourself keeps yourself still;
  And you must live, drawn by your own sweet skill.

XVII.

Who will believe my verse in time to come,
If it were fill'd with your most high deserts?
Though yet, heaven knows, it is but as a tomb
Which hides your life, and shows not half your parts.
If I could write the beauty of your eyes,
And in fresh numbers number all your graces,
The age to come would say, "This poet lies,
Such heavenly touches ne'er touch'd earthly faces."
So should my papers, yellow'd with their age,
Be scorn'd, like old men of less truth than tongue;
And your true rights be term'd a poet's rage,
And stretchèd metre of an antique song:
    But were some child of yours alive that time,
    You should live twice, — in it, and in my rhyme.

XVIII.

Shall I compare thee to a summer's day?
Thou art more lovely and more temperate:
Rough winds do shake the darling buds of May,
And summer's lease hath all too short a date:
Sometime too hot the eye of heaven shines,
And often is his gold complexion dimm'd;
And every fair from fair sometime declines,
By chance, or nature's changing course, untrimm'd;
But thy eternal summer shall not fade,
Nor lose possession of that fair thou owest;
Nor shall Death brag thou wander'st in his shade,
When in eternal lines to time thou growest:
    So long as men can breathe, or eyes can see,
    So long lives this, and this gives life to thee.

XIX.

Devouring Time, blunt thou the lion's paws,
And make the earth devour her own sweet brood;
Pluck the keen teeth from the fierce tiger's jaws,
And burn the long-liv'd phœnix in her blood;

Make glad and sorry seasons as thou fleets,
And do whate'er thou wilt, swift-footed Time,
To the wide world and all her fading sweets;
But I forbid thee one most heinous crime:
O, carve not with thy hours my love's fair brow,
Nor draw no lines there with thine antique pen;
Him in thy course untainted do allow
For beauty's pattern to succeeding men.
 Yet, do thy worst, old Time: despite thy wrong,
 My love shall in my verse ever live young.

XX.

A woman's face, with Nature's own hand painted,
Hast thou, the master-mistress of my passion;
A woman's gentle heart, but not acquainted
With shifting change, as is false women's fashion;
An eye more bright than theirs, less false in rolling,
Gilding the object whereupon it gazeth;
A man in hue all hues in his controlling,
Which steals men's eyes, and women's souls amazeth.
And for a woman wert thou first created;
Till Nature, as she wrought thee, fell a-doting,
And by addition me of thee defeated,
By adding one thing to my purpose nothing.
 But since she prick'd thee out for women's pleasure,
 Mine be thy love, and thy love's use their treasure.

XXI.

So is it not with me as with that Muse
Stirr'd by a painted beauty to his verse,
Who heaven itself for ornament doth use,
And every fair with his fair doth rehearse;
Making a couplement of proud compare,
With sun and moon, with earth and sea's rich gems,
With April's first-born flowers, and all things rare
That heaven's air in this huge rondure hems.
O, let me, true in love, but truly write,
And then believe me, my love is as fair

As any mother's child, though not so bright
As those gold candles fix'd in heaven's air:
  Let them say more that like of hearsay well;
  I will not praise that purpose not to sell.

XXII.

My glass shall not persuade me I am old,
So long as youth and thou are of one date;
But when in thee time's furrows I behold,
Then look I death my days should expiate.
For all that beauty that doth cover thee
Is but the seemly raiment of my heart,
Which in thy breast doth live, as thine in me:
How can I, then, be elder than thou art?
O, therefore, love, be of thyself so wary
As I, not for myself, but for thee will;
Bearing thy heart, which I will keep so chary
As tender nurse her babe from faring ill.
  Presume not on thy heart when mine is slain;
  Thou gav'st me thine, not to give back again.

XXIII.

As an unperfect actor on the stage,
Who, with his fear is put besides his part,
Or some fierce thing replete with too much rage,
Whose strength's abundance weakens his own heart;
So I, for fear of trust, forget to say
The perfect ceremony of love's rite,
And in mine own love's strength seem to decay,
O'ercharg'd with burden of mine own love's might.
O, let my books be, then, the eloquence,
And dumb presagers of my speaking breast;
Who plead for love, and look for recompense,
More than that tongue that more hath more express'd.
  O, learn to read what silent love hath writ:
  To hear with eyes belongs to love's fine wit.

25*

XXIV.

Mine eye hath play'd the painter, and hath stell'd
Thy beauty's form in table of my heart;
My body is the frame wherein 'tis held,
And perspective it is best painter's art.
For through the painter must you see his skill,
To find where your true image pictur'd lies;
Which in my bosom's shop is hanging still,
That hath his windows glazèd with thine eyes.
Now see what good turns eyes for eyes have done:
Mine eyes have drawn thy shape, and thine for me
Are windows to my breast, where-through the sun
Delights to peep, to gaze therein on thee;
   Yet eyes this cunning want to grace their art,
   They draw but what they see, know not the heart.

XXV.

Let those who are in favour with their stars
Of public honour and proud titles boast,
Whilst I, whom fortune of such triumph bars,
Unlook'd for joy in that I honour most.
Great princes' favourites their fair leaves spread
But as the marigold at the sun's eye;
And in themselves their pride lies burièd,
For at a frown they in their glory die.
The painful warrior famousèd for fight,
After a thousand victories once foil'd,
Is from the book of honour razèd quite,
And all the rest forgot for which he toil'd:
   Then happy I, that love and am belov'd
   Where I may not remove nor be remov'd.

XXVI.

Lord of my love, to whom in vassalage
Thy merit hath my duty strongly knit,
To thee I send this written embassage,
To witness duty, not to show my wit:

Duty so great, which wit so poor as mine
May make seem bare, in wanting words to show it,
But that I hope some good conceit of thine
In thy soul's thought, all naked, will bestow it;
Till whatsoever star that guides my moving,
Points on me graciously with fair aspéct,
And puts apparel on my tatter'd loving,
To show me worthy of thy sweet respect:
   Then may I dare to boast how I do love thee;
   Till then not show my head where thou mayst prove me.

XXVII.

Weary with toil, I haste me to my bed,
The dear repose for limbs with travel tir'd;
But then begins a journey in my head,
To work my mind, when body's work 's expir'd:
For then my thoughts, from far where I abide,
Intend a zealous pilgrimage to thee,
And keep my drooping eyelids open wide,
Looking on darkness which the blind do see:
Save that my soul's imaginary sight
Presents thy shadow to my sightless view,
Which, like a jewel hung in ghastly night,
Makes black night beauteous, and her old face new.
   Lo, thus, by day my limbs, by night my mind,
   For thee and for myself no quiet find.

XXVIII.

How can I, then, return in happy plight,
That am debarr'd the benefit of rest?
When day's oppression is not eas'd by night,
But day by night, and night by day, oppress'd?
And each, though enemies to either's reign,
Do in consent shake hands to torture me;
The one by toil, the other to complain
How far I toil, still farther off from thee.
I tell the day, to please him, thou art bright,
And dost him grace when clouds do blot the heaven:

So flatter I the swart-complexion'd night;
When sparkling stars twire not, thou gild'st the even.
 But day doth daily draw my sorrows longer,
  And night doth nightly make grief's strength seem
   stronger.

XXIX.

When, in disgrace with fortune and men's eyes,
I all alone beweep my outcast state,
And trouble deaf heaven with my bootless cries,
And look upon myself, and curse my fate,
Wishing me like to one more rich in hope,
Featur'd like him, like him with friends possess'd,
Desiring this man's art, and that man's scope,
With what I most enjoy contented least;
Yet in these thoughts myself almost despising,
Haply I think on thee, — and then my state,
Like to the lark at break of day arising
From sullen earth, sings hymns at heaven's gate;
 For thy sweet love remember'd such wealth brings,
  That then I scorn to change my state with kings.

XXX.

When to the sessions of sweet silent thought
I summon up remembrance of things past,
I sigh the lack of many a thing I sought,
And with old woes new wail my dear time's waste:
Then can I drown an eye, unus'd to flow,
For precious friends hid in death's dateless night,
And weep afresh love's long-since-cancell'd woe,
And moan th' expense of many a vanish'd sight:
Then can I grieve at grievances foregone,
And heavily from woe to woe tell o'er
The sad account of fore-bemoanèd moan,
Which I new pay as if not paid before.
 But if the while I think on thee, dear friend,
  All losses are restor'd, and sorrows end.

XXXI.

Thy bosom is endearèd with all hearts,
Which I by lacking have supposèd dead;
And there reigns love, and all love's loving parts,
And all those friends which I thought burièd.
How many a holy and obsequious tear
Hath dear-religious love stol'n from mine eye,
As interest of the dead, which now appear
But things remov'd, that hidden in thee lie!
Thou art the grave where buried love doth live,
Hung with the trophies of my lovers gone,
Who all their parts of me to thee did give;
That due of many now is thine alone:
  Their images I lov'd I view in thee,
  And thou, all they, hast all the all of me.

XXXII.

If thou survive my well-contented day,
When that churl Death my bones with dust shall cover,
And shalt by fortune once more re-survey
These poor rude lines of thy deceasèd lover, —
Compare them with the bettering of the time,
And though they be outstripp'd by every pen,
Reserve them for my love, not for their rhyme,
Exceeded by the height of happier men. •
O, then vouchsafe me but this loving thought, —
"Had my friend's Muse grown with this growing age,
A dearer birth than this his love had brought,
To march in ranks of better equipage:
  But since he died, and poets better prove,
  Theirs for their style I'll read, his for his love."

XXXIII.

Full many a glorious morning have I seen
Flatter the mountain-tops with sovereign eye,
Kissing with golden face the meadows green,
Gilding pale streams with heavenly alchemy;

Anon permit the basest clouds to ride
With ugly rack on his celestial face,
And from the forlorn world his visage hide,
Stealing unseen to west with this disgrace:
Even so my sun one early morn did shine
With all-triumphant splendour on my brow;
But, out, alack! he was but one hour mine,
The region cloud hath mask'd him from me now.
  Yet him for this my love no whit disdaineth;
  Suns of the world may stain when heaven's sun staineth.

XXXIV.

Why didst thou promise such a beauteous day,
And make me travel forth without my cloak,
To let base clouds o'ertake me in my way,
Hiding thy bravery in their rotten smoke?
'Tis not enough that through the cloud thou break,
To dry the rain on my storm-beaten face,
For no man well of such a salve can speak
That heals the wound, and cures not the disgrace:
Nor can thy shame give physic to my grief;
Though thou repent, yet I have still the loss:
Th' offender's sorrow lends but weak relief
To him that bears the strong offence's cross.
  Ah, but those tears are pearl which thy love sheds,
  And they are rich, and ransom all ill deeds.

XXXV.

No more be griev'd at that which thou hast done:
Roses have thorns, and silver fountains mud;
Clouds and eclipses stain both moon and sun,
And loathsome canker lives in sweetest bud.
All men make faults, and even I in this,
Authórizing thy trespass with compare,
Myself corrupting, salving thy amiss,
Excusing thy sins more than thy sins are;
For to thy sensual fault I bring in sense, —
Thy adverse party is thy advocate, —

And 'gainst myself a lawful plea commence:
Such civil war is in my love and hate,
 That I an accessary needs must be
 To that sweet thief which sourly robs from me.

XXXVI.

Let me confess that we two must be twain,
Although our undivided loves are one:
So shall those blots that do with me remain,
Without thy help, by me be borne alone.
In our two loves there is but one respect,
Though in our lives a separable spite,
Which though it alter not love's sole effect,
Yet doth it steal sweet hours from love's delight.
I may not evermore acknowledge thee,
Lest my bewailèd guilt should do thee shame;
Nor thou with public kindness honour me,
Unless thou take that honour from thy name:
 But do not so; I love thee in such sort,
 As, thou being mine, mine is thy good report.

XXXVII.

As a decrepit father takes delight
To see his active child do deeds of youth,
So I, made lame by fortune's dearest spite,
Take all my comfort of thy worth and truth;
For whether beauty, birth, or wealth, or wit,
Or any of these all, or all, or more,
Entitled in thy parts do crownèd sit,
I make my love engrafted to this store:
So then I am not lame, poor, nor despis'd,
Whilst that this shadow doth such substance give,
That I in thy abundance am suffic'd,
And by a part of all thy glory live.
 Look, what is best, that best I wish in thee:
 This wish I have; then ten times happy me!

XXXVIII.

How can my Muse want subject to invent,
While thou dost breathe, that pour'st into my verse
Thine own sweet argument, too excellent
For every vulgar paper to rehearse?
O, give thyself the thanks, if aught in me
Worthy perusal stand against thy sight;
For who's so dumb that cannot write to thee,
When thou thyself dost give invention light?
Be thou the tenth Muse, ten times more in worth
Than those old nine which rhymers invocate;
And he that calls on thee, let him bring forth
Eternal numbers to outlive long date.
   If my slight Muse do please these curious days,
   The pain be mine, but thine shall be the praise.

XXXIX.

O, how thy worth with manners may I sing,
When thou art all the better part of me?
What can mine own praise to mine own self bring?
And what is 't but mine own when I praise thee?
Even for this let us divided live,
And our dear love lose name of single one,
That by this separation I may give
That due to thee which thou deserv'st alone.
O absence, what a torment wouldst thou prove,
Were it not thy sour leisure gave sweet leave
To entertain the time with thoughts of love, —
Which time and thoughts so sweetly doth deceive, —
   And that thou teachest how to make one twain,
   By praising him here who doth hence remain!

XL.

Take all my loves, my love, yea, take them all;
What hast thou then more than thou hadst before?
No love, my love, that thou mayst true love call;
All mine was thine before thou hadst this more

Then, if for my love thou my love receivest,
I cannot blame thee for my love thou usest;
But yet be blam'd, if thou thyself deceivest
By wilful taste of what thyself refusest.
I do forgive thy robbery, gentle thief,
Although thou steal thee all my poverty;
And yet, love knows, it is a greater grief
To bear love's wrong than hate's known injury.
  Lascivious grace, in whom all ill well shows,
  Kill me with spites; yet we must not be foes.

XLI.

Those pretty wrongs that liberty commits,
When I am sometime absent from thy heart,
Thy beauty and thy years full well befits,
For still temptation follows where thou art.
Gentle thou art, and therefore to be won,
Beauteous thou art, therefore to be assail'd;
And when a woman woos, what woman's son
Will sourly leave her till she have prevail'd?
Ay me! but yet thou mightst my seat forbear,
And chide thy beauty and thy straying youth,
Who lead thee in their riot even there
Where thou art forc'd to break a twofold truth,—
  Hers, by thy beauty tempting her to thee,
  Thine, by thy beauty being false to me.

XLII.

That thou hast her, it is not all my grief,
And yet it may be said I lov'd her dearly;
That she hath thee, is of my wailing chief,
A loss in love that touches me more nearly.
Loving offenders, thus I will excuse ye: —
Thou dost love her, because thou know'st I love her;
And for my sake even so doth she abuse me,
Suffering my friend for my sake to approve her.
If I lose thee, my loss is my love's gain,
And losing her, my friend hath found that loss;

Both find each other, and I lose both twain,
And both for my sake lay on me this cross:
   But here's the joy, — my friend and I are one;
   Sweet flattery! — then she loves but me alone.

XLIII.

When most I wink, then do mine eyes best see,
For all the day they view things unrespected;
But when I sleep, in dreams they look on thee,
And, darkly bright, are bright in dark directed.
Then thou, whose shadow shadows doth make bright,
How would thy shadow's form form happy show
To the clear day with thy much clearer light,
When to unseeing eyes thy shade shines so!
How would, I say, mine eyes be blessèd made
By looking on thee in the living day,
When in dead night thy fair-imperfect shade
Through heavy sleep on sightless eyes doth stay!
   All days are nights to see till I see thee,
   And nights bright days when dreams do show thee me.

XLIV.

If the dull substance of my flesh were thought,
Injurious distance should not stop my way;
For then, despite of space, I would be brought,
From limits far remote, where thou dost stay.
No matter then although my foot did stand
Upon the farthest earth remov'd from thee;
For nimble thought can jump both sea and land,
As soon as think the place where he would be.
But, ah, thought kills me, that I am not thought,
To leap large lengths of miles when thou art gone,
But that, so much of earth and water wrought,
I must attend time's leisure with my moan;
   Receiving naught by elements so slow
   But heavy tears, badges of either's woe:

XLV.

The other two, slight air and purging fire,
Are both with thee, wherever I abide;
The first my thought, the other my desire,
These present-absent with swift motion slide.
For when these quicker elements are gone
In tender embassy of love to thee,
My life, being made of four, with two alone
Sinks down to death, oppress'd with melancholy;
Until life's composition be recur'd
By those swift messengers return'd from thee,
Who even but now come back again, assur'd
Of thy fair health, recounting it to me:
  This told, I joy; but then no longer glad,
  I send them back again, and straight grow sad.

XLVI.

Mine eye and heart are at a mortal war,
How to divide the conquest of thy sight;
Mine eye my heart thy picture's sight would bar,
My heart mine eye the freedom of that right.
My heart doth plead that thou in him dost lie, —
A closet never pierc'd with crystal eyes, —
But the defendant doth that plea deny,
And says in him thy fair appearance lies.
To 'cide this title is impannelèd
A quest of thoughts, all tenants to the heart;
And by their verdict is determinèd
The clear eye's moiety and the dear heart's part:
  As thus, — mine eye's due is thy outward part,
  And my heart's right thy inward love of heart.

XLVII.

Betwixt mine eye and heart a league is took,
And each doth good turns now unto the other:
When that mine eye is famish'd for a look,
Or heart in love with sighs himself doth smother,

With my love's picture then my eye doth feast,
And to the painted banquet bids my heart;
Another time mine eye is my heart's guest,
And in his thoughts of love doth share a part:
So, either by thy picture or my love,
Thyself away art present still with me;
For thou not farther than my thoughts canst move,
And I am still with them, and they with thee;
  Or, if they sleep, thy picture in my sight
  Awakes my heart to heart's and eye's delight.

XLVIII.

How careful was I, when I took my way,
Each trifle under truest bars to thrust,
That to my use it might unusèd stay
From hands of falsehood, in sure wards of trust!
But thou, to whom my jewels trifles are,
Most worthy comfort, now my greatest grief,
Thou, best of dearest, and mine only care,
Art left the prey of every vulgar thief.
Thee have I not lock'd up in any chest,
Save where thou art not, though I feel thou art,
Within the gentle closure of my breast,
From whence at pleasure thou mayst come and part;
  And even thence thou wilt be stol'n, I fear,
  For truth proves thievish for a prize so dear.

XLIX.

Against that time, if ever that time come,
When I shall see thee frown on my defects,
Whenas thy love hath cast his utmost sum,
Call'd to that audit by advis'd respects;
Against that time when thou shalt strangely pass,
And scarcely greet me with that sun, thine eye,
When love, converted from the thing it was,
Shall reasons find of settled gravity, —
Against that time do I ensconce me here
Within the knowledge of mine own desert,

And this my hand against myself uprear,
To guard the lawful reasons on thy part:
  To leave poor me thou hast the strength of laws,
  Since why to love I can allege no cause.

L.

How heavy do I journey on the way,
When what I seek — my weary travel's end —
Doth teach that ease and that repose to say,
"Thus far the miles are measur'd from thy friend!"
The beast that bears me, tirèd with my woe,
Plods dully on, to bear that weight in me,
As if by some instinct the wretch did know
His rider lov'd not speed, being made from thee:
The bloody spur cannot provoke him on
That sometimes anger thrusts into his hide;
Which heavily he answers with a groan,
More sharp to me than spurring to his side;
  For that same groan doth put this in my mind, —
  My grief lies onward, and my joy behind.

LI.

Thus can my love excuse the slow offence
Of my dull bearer when from thee I speed:
From where thou art why should I haste me thence?
Till I return, of posting is no need.
O, what excuse will my poor beast then find,
When swift extremity can seem but slow?
Then should I spur, though mounted on the wind,
In wingèd speed no motion shall I know:
Then can no horse with my desire keep pace;
Therefore desire, of perfect'st love being made,
Shall neigh — no dull flesh — in his fiery race;
But love, for love, thus shall excuse my jade, —
  Since from thee going he went wilful-slow,
  Towards thee I'll run, and give him leave to go.

LII.

So am I as the rich, whose blessèd key
Can bring him to his sweet up-lockèd treasure,
The which he will not every hour survey,
For blunting the fine point of seldom pleasure. .
Therefore are feasts so solemn and so rare,
Since, seldom coming, in the long year set,
Like stones of worth they thinly placèd are,
Or captain jewels in the carcanet.
So is the time that keeps you, as my chest,
Or as the wardrobe which the robe doth hide,
To make some special instant special-blest,
By new unfolding his imprison'd pride.
  Blessèd are you, whose worthiness gives scope,
  Being had, to triumph, being lack'd, to hope.

LIII.

What is your substance, whereof are you made,
That millions of strange shadows on you tend?
Since every one hath, every one, one shade,
And you, but one, can every shadow lend.
Describe Adonis, and the counterfeit
Is poorly imitated after you;
On Helen's cheek all art of beauty set,
And you in Grecian tires are painted new:
Speak of the spring, and foison of the year;
The one doth shadow of your beauty show,
The other as your bounty doth appear;
And you in every blessèd shape we know.
  In all external grace you have some part,
  But you like none, none you, for constant heart.

LIV.

O, how much more doth beauty beauteous seem
By that sweet ornament which truth doth give!
The rose looks fair, but fairer we it deem
For that sweet odour which doth in it live.

The canker-blooms have full as deep a dye
As the perfumèd tincture of the roses,
Hang on such thorns, and play as wantonly
When summer's breath their maskèd buds discloses:
But, for their virtue only is their show,
They live unwoo'd, and unrespected fade;
Die to themselves. Sweet roses do not so;
Of their sweet deaths are sweetest odours made:
 And so of you, beauteous and lovely youth,
 When that shall vade, by verse distills your truth.

<h2 style="text-align:center">LV. ✕</h2>

Not marble, nor the gilded monuments
Of princes, shall outlive this powerful rhyme;
But you shall shine more bright in these contents
Than unswept stone, besmear'd with sluttish time.
When wasteful war shall statues overturn,
And broils root out the work of masonry,
Nor Mars his sword nor war's quick fire shall burn
The living record of your memory.
'Gainst death and all-oblivious enmity
Shall you pace forth; your praise shall still find room
Even in the eyes of all posterity
That wear this world out to the ending doom.
 So, till the judgment that yourself arise,
 You live in this, and dwell in lovers' eyes.

<h2 style="text-align:center">LVI.</h2>

Sweet love, renew thy force; be it not said
Thy edge should blunter be than appetite,
Which but to-day by feeding is allay'd,
To-morrow sharpen'd in his former might:
So, love, be thou; although to-day thou fill
Thy hungry eyes even till they wink with fullness,
To-morrow see again, and do not kill
The spirit of love with a perpetual dullness.
Let this sad interim like the ocean be
Which parts the shore, where two contracted new

Come daily to the banks, that, when they see
Return of love, more blest may be the view;
   Or call it winter, which, being full of care,
   Makes summer's welcome thrice more wish'd, more rare.

LVII.

Being your slave, what should I do but tend
Upon the hours and times of your desire?
I have no precious time at all to spend,
Nor services to do, till you require.
Nor dare I chide the world-without-end hour
Whilst I, my sovereign, watch the clock for you,
Nor think the bitterness of àbsence sour
When you have bid your servant once adieu;
Nor dare I question with my jealous thought
Where you may be, or your affairs suppose,
But, like a sad slave, stay and think of nought
Save, where you are how happy you make those.
   So true a fool is love, that in your will,
   Though you do any thing, he thinks no ill.

LVIII.

That god forbid that made me first your slave,
I should in thought control your times of pleasure,
Or at your hand th' account of hours to crave,
Being your vassal, bound to stay your leisure!
O, let me suffer, being at your beck,
Th' imprison'd absence of your liberty;
And patience, tame to sufferance, bide each check,
Without accusing you of injury.
Be where you list, your charter is so strong,
That you yourself may privilege your time
To what you will; to you it doth belong
Yourself to pardon of self-doing crime.
   I am to wait, though waiting so be hell;
   Not blame your pleasure, be it ill or well.

LIX.

If there be nothing new, but that which is
Hath been before, how are our brains beguil'd,
Which, labouring for invention, bear amiss
The second burden of a former child!
O, that record could with a backward look,
Even of five hundred courses of the sun,
Show me your image in some antique book,
Since mind at first in character was done!
That I might see what the old world could say
To this composèd wonder of your frame;
Whether we're mended, or whêr better they,
Or whether revolution be the same.
  O, sure I am, the wits of former days
  To subjects worse have given admiring praise.

LX.

Like as the waves make towards the pebbled shore,
So do our minutes hasten to their end;
Each changing place with that which goes before,
In sequent toil all forwards do contend.
Nativity, once in the main of light,
Crawls to maturity, wherewith being crown'd,
Crookèd eclipses 'gainst his glory fight,
And Time that gave doth now his gift confound.
Time doth transfix the flourish set on youth,
And delves the parallels in beauty's brow;
Feeds on the rarities of nature's truth,
And nothing stands but for his scythe to mow:
  And yet, to times in hope my verse shall stand,
  Praising thy worth, despite his cruel hand.

LXI.

Is it thy will thy image should keep open
My heavy eyelids to the weary night?
Dost thou desire my slumbers should be broken,
While shadows like to thee do mock my sight?

26 *

Is it thy spirit that thou send'st from thee
So far from home into my deeds to pry,
To find out shames and idle hours in me,
The scope and tenour of thy jealousy?
O, no! thy love, though much, is not so great:
It is my love that keeps mine eye awake;
Mine own true love that doth my rest defeat,
To play the watchman ever for thy sake:
　　For thee watch I whilst thou dost wake elsewhere,
　　From me far off, with others all too near.

LXII.

Sin of self-love possesseth all mine eye,
And all my soul, and all my every part;
And for this sin there is no remedy,
It is so grounded inward in my heart.
Methinks no face so gracious is as mine,
No shape so true, no truth of such account;
And for myself mine own worth do define,
As I all other in all worths surmount.
But when my glass shows me myself indeed,
Beated and chapp'd with tann'd antiquity,
Mine own self-love quite contrary I read;
Self so self-loving were iniquity.
　　'Tis thee myself that for myself I praise,
　　Painting my age with beauty of thy days.

LXIII.

Against my love shall be, as I am now,
With Time's injurious hand crush'd and o'erworn;
When hours have drain'd his blood, and fill'd his brow
With lines and wrinkles; when his youthful morn
Hath travell'd on to age's steepy night;
And all those beauties whereof now he's king
Are vanishing or vanish'd out of sight,
Stealing away the treasure of his spring;
For such a time do I now fortify
Against confounding age's cruel knife,

That he shall never cut from memory
My sweet love's beauty, though my lover's life:
   His beauty shall in these black lines be seen,
   And they shall live, and he in them still green.

LXIV.

When I have seen by Time's fell hand defac'd
The rich proud cost of outworn buried age;
When sometime lofty towers I see down-raz'd,
And brass eternal slave to mortal rage;
When I have seen the hungry ocean gain
Advantage on the kingdom of the shore,
And the firm soil win of the watery main,
Increasing store with loss, and loss with store;
When I have seen such interchange of state,
Or state itself confounded to decay;
Ruin hath taught me thus to ruminate, —
That Time will come and take my love away.
   This thought is as a death, which cannot choose
   But weep to have that which it fears to lose.

LXV.

Since brass, nor stone, nor earth, nor boundless sea,
But sad mortality o'ersways their power,
How with this rage shall beauty hold a plea,
Whose action is no stronger than a flower?
O, how shall summer's honey-breath hold out
Against the wreckful siege of battering days,
When rocks impregnable are not so stout,
Nor gates of steel so strong, but Time decays?
O fearful meditation! where, alack,
Shall Time's best jewel from Time's chest lie hid?
Or what strong hand can hold his swift foot back?
Or who his spoil of beauty can forbid?
   O, none, unless this miracle have might,
   That in black ink my love may still shine bright.

LXVI.

Tir'd with all these, for restful death I cry, ·—
As, to behold desert a beggar born,
And needy nothing trimm'd in jollity,
And purest faith unhappily forsworn,
And gilded honour shamefully misplac'd,
And maiden virtue rudely strumpeted,
And right perfection wrongfully disgrac'd,
And strength by limping sway disabled,
And art made tongue-tied by authority,
And folly, doctor-like, controlling skill,
And simple truth miscall'd simplicity,
And captive good attending captain ill: —
   Tir'd with all these, from these would I be gone,
   Save that, to die, I leave my love alone.

LXVII.

Ah, wherefore with infection should he live,
And with his presence grace impiety,
That sin by him advantage should achieve,
And lace itself with his society?
Why should false painting imitate his cheek,
And steal dead seeing of his living hue?
Why should poor beauty indirectly seek
Roses of shadow, since his rose is true?
Why should he live, now Nature bankrupt is,
Beggar'd of blood to blush through lively veins?
For she hath no exchequer now but his,
And, proud of many, lives upon his gains.
   O, him she stores, to show what wealth she had
   In days long since, before these last so bad.

LXVIII.

Thus is his cheek the map of days outworn,
When beauty liv'd and died as flowers do now,
Before these bastard signs of fair were born,
Or durst inhabit on a living brow;

Before the golden tresses of the dead,
The right of sepulchres, were shorn away,
To live a second life on second head;
Ere beauty's dead fleece made another gay:
In him those holy antique hours are seen,
Without all ornament, itself, and true,
Making no summer of another's green,
Robbing no old to dress his beauty new;
  And him as for a map doth Nature store,
  To show false Art what beauty was of yore.

LXIX.

Those parts of thee that the world's eye doth view
Want nothing that the thought of hearts can mend;
All tongues, the voice of souls, give thee that due,
Uttering bare truth, even so as foes commend.
Thy outward thus with outward praise is crown'd;
But those same tongues, that give thee so thine own,
In other accents do this praise confound
By seeing farther than the eye hath shown.
They look into the beauty of thy mind,
And that, in guess, they measure by thy deeds;
Then, churls, their thoughts, although their eyes were kind,
To thy fair flower add the rank smell of weeds:
  But why thy odour matcheth not thy show,
  The solve is this, — that thou dost common grow.

LXX.

That thou art blam'd shall not be thy defect,
For slander's mark was ever yet the fair;
The ornament of beauty is suspect,
A crow that flies in heaven's sweetest air.
So thou be good, slander doth but approve
Thy worth the greater, being woo'd of time;
For canker vice the sweetest buds doth love,
And thou present'st a pure unstainèd prime.
Thou hast pass'd by the ambush of young days,
Either not assail'd, or victor being charg'd;

Yet this thy praise can not be so thy praise,
To tie up envy evermore enlarg'd:
  If some suspect of ill mask'd not thy show,
  Then thou alone kingdoms of hearts shouldst owe.

LXXI.

No longer mourn for me when I am dead
Than you shall hear the surly sullen bell
Give warning to the world that I am fled
From this vile world, with vilest worms to dwell:
Nay, if you read this line, remember not
The hand that writ it; for I love you so,
That I in your sweet thoughts would be forgot,
If thinking on me then should make you woe.
O, if, I say, you look upon this verse
When I perhaps compounded am with clay,
Do not so much as my poor name rehearse;
But let your love even with my life decay;
  Lest the wise world should look into your moan,
  And mock you with me after I am gone.

LXXII.

O, lest the world should task you to recite
What merit liv'd in me, that you should love
After my death, — dear love, forget me quite,
For you in me can nothing worthy prove;
Unless you would devise some virtuous lie,
To do more for me than mine own desert,
And hang more praise upon deceased I
Than niggard truth would willingly impart:
O, lest your true love may seem false in this,
That you for love speak well of me untrue,
My name be buried where my body is,
And live no more to shame nor me nor you.
  For I am sham'd by that which I bring forth,
  And so should you, to love things nothing worth.

LXXIII.

That time of year thou mayst in me behold
When yellow leaves, or none, or few, do hang
Upon those boughs which shake against the cold,
Bare ruin'd choirs, where late the sweet birds sang.
In me thou see'st the twilight of such day
As after sunset fadeth in the west;
Which by and by black night doth take away,
Death's second self, that seals up all in rest.
In me thou see'st the glowing of such fire,
That on the ashes of his youth doth lie,
As the death-bed whereon it must expire,
Consum'd with that which it was nourish'd by.
  This thou perceiv'st, which makes thy love more strong,
  To love that well which thou must leave ere long:

LXXIV.

But be contented: when that fell arrest
Without all bail shall carry me away,
My life hath in this line some interest,
Which for memorial still with thee shall stay.
When thou reviewest this, thou dost review
The very part was consecrate to thee:
The earth can have but earth, which is his due;
My spirit is thine, the better part of me:
So, then, thou hast but lost the dregs of life,
The prey of worms, my body being dead;
The coward conquest of a wretch's knife,
Too base of thee to be rememberèd.
  The worth of that is that which it contains,
  And that is this, and this with thee remains.

LXXV.

So are you to my thoughts as food to life,
Or as sweet-season'd showers are to the ground;
And for the peace of you I hold such strife
As 'twixt a miser and his wealth is found;

Now proud as an enjoyer, and anon
Doubting the filching age will steal his treasure;
Now counting best to be with you alone,
Then better'd that the world may see my pleasure:
Sometime all full with feasting on your sight,
And by and by clean starvèd for a look;
Possessing or pursuing no delight,
Save what is had or must from you be took.
　Thus do I pine and surfeit day by day,
　　Or gluttoning on all, or all away.

LXXVI.

Why is my verse so barren of new pride,
So far from variation or quick change?
Why, with the time, do I not glance aside
To new-found methods and to compounds strange?
Why write I still all one, ever the same,
And keep invention in a noted weed,
That every word doth almost tell my name,
Showing their birth, and where they did proceed?
O, know, sweet love, I always write of you,
And you and love are still my argument;
So all my best is dressing old words new,
Spending again what is already spent:
　For as the sun is daily new and old,
　　So is my love still telling what is told.

LXXVII.

Thy glass will show thee how thy beauties wear,
Thy dial how thy precious minutes waste;
The vacant leaves thy mind's imprint will bear,
And of this book this learning mayst thou taste.
The wrinkles which thy glass will truly show,
Of mouthèd graves will give thee memory;
Thou by thy dial's shady stealth mayst know
Time's thievish progress to eternity.
Look, what thy memory can not contain,
Commit to these waste blanks, and thou shalt find

Those children nurs'd, deliver'd from thy brain,
To take a new acquaintance of thy mind.
  These offices, so oft as thou wilt look,
  Shall profit thee, and much enrich thy book.

LXXVIII.

So oft have I invok'd thee for my Muse,
And found such fair assistance in my verse,
As every alien pen hath got my use,
And under thee their poesy disperse.
Thine eyes, that taught the dumb on high to sing,
And heavy ignorance aloft to fly,
Have added feathers to the learned's wing,
And given grace a double majesty.
Yet be most proud of that which I compile,
Whose influence is thine, and born of thee:
In others' works thou dost but mend the style,
And arts with thy sweet graces gracèd be;
  But thou art all my art, and dost advance
  As high as learning my rude ignorance.

LXXIX.

Whilst I alone did call upon thy aid,
My verse alone had all thy gentle grace;
But now my gracious numbers are decay'd,
And my sick Muse doth give another place.
I grant, sweet love, thy lovely argument
Deserves the travail of a worthier pen;
Yet what of thee thy poet doth invent   ·
He robs thee of, and pays it thee again.
He lends thee virtue, and he stole that word
From thy behaviour; beauty doth he give,
And found it in thy cheek; he can afford
No praise to thee but what in thee doth live.
  Then thank him not for that which he doth say,
  Since what he owes thee thou thyself dost pay.

LXXX.

O, how I faint when I of you do write,
Knowing a better spirit doth use your name,
And in the praise thereof spends all his might,
To make me tongue-tied, speaking of your fame!
But since your worth, wide as the ocean is,
The humble as the proudest sail doth bear,
My saucy bark, inferior far to his,
On your broad main doth wilfully appear.
Your shallowest help will hold me up afloat,
While he upon your soundless deep doth ride;
Or, being wreck'd, I am a worthless boat,
He of tall building and of goodly pride:
    Then if he thrive, and I be cast away,
    The worst was this, — my love was my decay.

LXXXI.

Or I shall live your epitaph to make,
Or you survive when I in earth am rotten;
From hence your memory death cannot take,
Although in me each part will be forgotten.
Your name from hence immortal life shall have,
Though I, once gone, to all the world must die:
The earth can yield me but a common grave,
When you entombèd in men's eyes shall lie.
Your monument shall be my gentle verse,
Which eyes not yet created shall o'er-read;
And tongues to be your being shall rehearse,
When all the breathers of this world are dead;
    You still shall live, — such virtue hath my pen, —
    Where breath most breathes — even in the mouths of men.

LXXXII.

I grant thou wert not married to my Muse,
And therefore mayst without attaint o'erlook
The dedicated words which writers use
Of their fair subject, blessing every book.

Thou art as fair in knowledge as in hue,
Finding thy worth a limit past my praise;
And therefore art enforc'd to seek anew
Some fresher stamp of the time-bettering days.
And do so, love; yet when they have devis'd
What strainèd touches rhetoric can lend,
Thou truly fair wert truly sympathiz'd
In true-plain words by thy true-telling friend;
   And their gross painting might be better us'd
   Where cheeks need blood, — in thee it is abus'd.

LXXXIII.

I never saw that you did painting need,
And therefore to your fair no painting set;
I found, or thought I found, you did exceed
The barren tender of a poet's debt:
And therefore have I slept in your report,
That you yourself, being extant, well might show
How far a modern quill doth come too short,
Speaking of worth, what worth in you doth grow.
This silence for my sin you did impute,
Which shall be most my glory, being dumb;
For I impair not beauty, being mute,
When others would give life, and bring a tomb.
   There lives more life in one of your fair eyes
   Than both your poets can in praise devise.

LXXXIV.

Who is it that says most? which can say more
Than this rich praise — that you alone are you?
In whose cónfine immurèd is the store
Which should example where your equal grew.
Lean penury within that pen doth dwell
That to his subject lends not some small glory;
But he that writes of you, if he can tell
That you are you, so dignifies his story:
Let him but copy what in you is writ,
Not making worse what nature made so clear,

And such a counterpart shall fame his wit,
Making his style admirèd every where.
  You to your beauteous blessings add a curse,
  Being fond on praise, which makes your praises worse.

LXXXV.

My tongue-tied Muse in manners holds her still,
While comments of your praise, richly compil'd,
Reserve their character with golden quill,
And precious phrase by all the Muses fil'd.
I think good thoughts, whilst other write good words,
And, like unletter'd clerk, still cry "Amen"
To every hymn that able spirit affords,
In polish'd form of well-refinèd pen.
Hearing you prais'd, I say "'Tis so, 'tis true,"
And to the most of praise add something more;
But that is in my thought, whose love to you,
Though words come hindmost, holds his rank before.
  Then others for the breath of words respect, —
  Me for my dumb thoughts, speaking in effect.

LXXXVI.

Was it the proud full sail of his great verse,
Bound for the prize of all-too-precious you,
That did my ripe thoughts in my brain inhearse,
Making their tomb the womb wherein they grew?
Was it his spirit, by spirits taught to write
Above a mortal pitch, that struck me dead?
No, neither he, nor his compeers by night
Giving him aid, my verse astonishèd.
He, nor that affable familiar ghost
Which nightly gulls him with intelligence,
As victors, of my silence cannot boast;
I was not sick of any fear from thence:
  But when your countenance fil'd up his line,
  Then lack'd I matter; that enfeebled mine.

LXXXVII.

Farewell! thou art too dear for my possessing,
And like enough thou know'st thy estimate:
The charter of thy worth gives thee releasing;
My bonds in thee are all determinate.
For how do I hold thee but by thy granting?
And for that riches where is my deserving?
The cause of this fair gift in me is wanting,
And so my patent back again is swerving.
Thyself thou gav'st, thy own worth then not knowing,
Or me, to whom thou gav'st it, else mistaking;
So thy great gift, upon misprision growing,
Comes home again, on better judgment making.
   Thus have I had thee, as a dream doth flatter,
   In sleep a king, but waking no such matter.

LXXXVIII.

When thou shalt be dispos'd to set me light,
And place my merit in the eye of scorn,
Upon thy side against myself I'll fight,
And prove thee virtuous, though thou art forsworn.
With mine own weakness being best acquainted,
Upon thy part I can set down a story
Of faults conceal'd, wherein I am attainted;
That thou, in losing me, shalt win much glory:
And I by this will be a gainer too;
For bending all my loving thoughts on thee,
The injuries that to myself I do,
Doing thee vantage, double-vantage me.
   Such is my love, to thee I so belong,
   That for thy right myself will bear all wrong.

LXXXIX.

Say that thou didst forsake me for some fault,
And I will comment upon that offence:
Speak of my lameness, and I straight will halt,
Against thy reasons making no defence.

Thou canst not, love, disgrace me half so ill,
To set a form upon desirèd change,
As I'll myself disgrace: knowing thy will,
I will acquaintance strangle, and look strange;
Be absent from thy walks; and in my tongue
Thy sweet-belovèd name no more shall dwell,
Lest I, too much profane, should do it wrong,
And haply of our old acquaintance tell.
    For thee, against myself I'll vow debate,
    For I must ne'er love him whom thou dost hate.

XC.

Then hate me when thou wilt; if ever, now;
Now, while the world is bent my deeds to cross,
Join with the spite of fortune, make me bow,
And do not drop in for an after-loss:
Ah, do not, when my heart hath scap'd this sorrow,
Come in the rearward of a conquer'd woe;
Give not a windy night a rainy morrow,
To linger out a purpos'd overthrow.
If thou wilt leave me, do not leave me last,
When other petty griefs have done their spite,
But in the onset come: so shall·I taste
At first the very worst of fortune's might;
    And other strains of woe, which now seem woe,
    Compar'd with loss of thee will not seem so.

XCI.

Some glory in their birth, some in their skill,
Some in their wealth, some in their bodies' force;
Some in their garments, though new-fangled ill;
Some in their hawks and hounds, some in their horse;
And every humour hath his adjunct pleasure,
Wherein it finds a joy above the rest:
But these particulars are not my measure;
All these I better in one general best.
Thy love is better than high birth to me,
Richer than wealth, prouder than garments' cost,

Of more delight than hawks or horses be;
And having thee, of all men's pride I boast:
   Wretched in this alone, that thou mayst take
   All this away, and me most wretched make.

XCII.

But do thy worst to steal thyself away,
For term of life thou art assurèd mine;
And life no longer than thy love will stay,
For it depends upon that love of thine.
Then need I not to fear the worst of wrongs,
When in the least of them my life hath end.
I see a better state to me belongs
Than that which on thy humour doth depend:
Thou canst not vex me with inconstant mind,
Since that my life on thy revolt doth lie.
O, what a happy title do I find,
Happy to have thy love, happy to die!
   But what's so blessèd-fair that fears no blot?
   Thou mayst be false, and yet I know it not:

XCIII.

So shall I live, supposing thou art true,
Like a deceivèd husband; so love's face
May still seem love to me, though alter'd new;
Thy looks with me, thy heart in other place:
For there can live no hatred in thine eye,
Therefore in that I cannot know thy change.
In many's looks the false heart's history
Is writ in moods and frowns and wrinkles strange;
But heaven in thy creation did decree
That in thy face sweet love should ever dwell;
Whate'er thy thoughts or thy heart's workings be,
Thy looks should nothing thence but sweetness tell.
   How like Eve's apple doth thy beauty grow,
   If thy sweet virtue answer not thy show!

XCIV.

They that have power to hurt and will do none,
That do not do the thing they most do show,
Who, moving others, are themselves as stone,
Unmovèd, cold, and to temptation slow;
They rightly do inherit heaven's graces,
And husband nature's riches from expense;
They are the lords and owners of their faces,
Others but stewards of their excellence.
The summer's flower is to the summer sweet,
Though to itself it only live and die;
But if that flower with base infection meet,
The basest weed outbraves his dignity:
  For sweetest things turn sourest by their deeds
  Lilies that fester smell far worse than weeds.

XCV.

How sweet and lovely dost thou make the shame
Which, like a canker in the fragrant rose,
Doth spot the beauty of thy budding name!
O, in what sweets dost thou thy sins enclose!
That tongue that tells the story of thy days,
Making lascivious comments on thy sport,
Cannot dispraise but in a kind of praise;
Naming thy name blesses an ill report.
O, what a mansion have those vices got
Which for their habitation chose out thee,
Where beauty's veil doth cover every blot,
And all things turn to fair that eyes can see!
  Take heed, dear heart, of this large privilege;
  The hardest knife ill-us'd doth lose his edge.

XCVI.

Some say, thy fault is youth, some wantonness;
Some say, thy grace is youth and gentle sport;
Both grace and faults are lov'd of more and less:
Thou mak'st faults graces that to thee resort.

As on the finger of a thronèd queen
The basest jewel will be well esteem'd,
So are those errors that in thee are seen
To truths translated, and for true things deem'd.
How many lambs might the stern wolf betray,
If like a lamb he could his looks translate!
How many gazers mightst thou lead away,
If thou wouldst use the strength of all thy state!
　But do not so; I love thee in such sort,
　As thou being mine, mine is thy good report.

XCVII.

How like a winter hath my absence been
From thee, the pleasure of the fleeting year!
What freezings have I felt, what dark days seen!
What old December's bareness every where!
And yet this time remov'd was summer's time;
The teeming autumn, big with rich increase,
Bearing the wanton burden of the prime,
Like widow'd wombs after their lords' decease:
Yet this abundant issue seem'd to me
But hope of orphans and unfather'd fruit;
For summer and his pleasures wait on thee,
And, thou away, the very birds are mute;
　Or, if they sing, 'tis with so dull a cheer,
　That leaves look pale, dreading the winter's near.

XCVIII.

From you have I been absent in the spring,
When proud-pied April, dress'd in all his trim,
Hath put a spirit of youth in every thing,
That heavy Saturn laugh'd and leap'd with him.
Yet nor the lays of birds, nor the sweet smell
Of different flowers in odour and in hue,
Could make me any summer's story tell,
Or from their proud lap pluck them where they grew:
Nor did I wonder at the lily's white,
Nor praise the deep vermilion in the rose;

27*

They were but sweet, but figures of delight,
Drawn after you, — you pattern of all those.
 Yet seem'd it winter still, and, you away,
 As with your shadow I with these did play:

XCIX.

The forward violet thus did I chide: —
Sweet thief, whence didst thou steal thy sweet that smells,
If not from my love's breath? The purple pride
Which on thy soft cheek for complexion dwells
In my love's veins thou hast too grossly dy'd.
The lily I condemnèd for thy hand;
And buds of marjoram had stol'n thy hair:
The roses fearfully on thorns did stand,
One blushing shame, another white despair;
A third, nor red nor white, had stol'n of both,
And to his robbery had annex'd thy breath;
But, for his theft, in pride of all his growth
A vengeful canker eat him up to death.
 More flowers I noted, yet I none could see
 But sweet or colour it had stol'n from thee.

C.

Where art thou, Muse, that thou forgett'st so long
To speak of that which gives thee all thy might?
Spend'st thou thy fury on some worthless song,
Darkening thy power to lend base subjects light?
Return, forgetful Muse, and straight redeem
In gentle numbers time so idly spent;
Sing to the ear that doth thy lays esteem,
And gives thy pen both skill and argument.
Rise, resty Muse, my love's sweet face survey,
If Time have any wrinkle graven there;
If any, be a satire to decay,
And make Time's spoils despisèd every where.
 Give my love fame faster than Time wastes life;
 So thou prevent'st his scythe and crookèd knife.

CI.

O truant Muse, what shall be thy amends
For thy neglect of truth in beauty dy'd?
Both truth and beauty on my love depends;
So dost thou too, and therein dignified.
Make answer, Muse: wilt thou not haply say,
"Truth needs no colour, with his colour fix'd;
Beauty no pencil, beauty's truth to lay;
But best is best, if never intermix'd"?
Because he needs no praise, wilt thou be dumb?
Excuse not silence so: for 't lies in thee
To make him much outlive a gilded tomb,
And to be prais'd of ages yet to be.
 Then do thy office, Muse; I teach thee how
 To make him seem long hence as he shows now.

CII.

My love is strengthen'd, though more weak in seeming;
I love not less, though less the show appear:
That love is merchandiz'd whose rich esteeming
The owner's tongue doth publish every where.
Our love was new, and then but in the spring,
When I was wont to greet it with my lays;
As Philomel in summer's front doth sing,
And stops her pipe in growth of riper days:
Not that the summer is less pleasant now
Than when her mournful hymns did hush the night,
But that wild music burdens every bough,
And sweets grown common lose their dear delight.
 Therefore, like her, I sometime hold my tongue,
 Because I would not dull you with my song.

CIII.

Alack, what poverty my Muse brings forth,
That having such a scope to show her pride,
The argument, all bare, is of more worth
Than when it hath my added praise beside!

O, blame me not, if I no more can write!
Look in your glass, and there appears a face
That overgoes my blunt invention quite,
Dulling my lines, and doing me disgrace.
Were it not sinful, then, striving to mend,
To mar the subject that before was well?
For to no other pass my verses tend
Than of your graces and your gifts to tell;
　　And more, much more, than in my verse can sit,
　　Your own glass shows you when you look in it.

CIV.

To me, fair friend, you never can be old,
For as you were when first your eye I ey'd,
Such seems your beauty still.　Three winters' cold
Have from the forests shook three summers' pride,
Three beauteous springs to yellow autumn turn'd
In process of the seasons have I seen,
Three April perfumes in three hot Junes burn'd,
Since first I saw you fresh, which yet are green.
Ah, yet doth beauty, like a dial-hand,
Steal from his figure, and no pace perceiv'd;
So your sweet hue, which methinks still doth stand,
Hath motion, and mine eye may be deceiv'd:
　　For fear of which, hear this, thou age unbred, —
　　Ere you were born was beauty's summer dead.

CV.

Let not my love be call'd idolatry,
Nor my belovèd as an idol show,
Since all alike my songs and praises be
To one, of one, still such, and ever so.
Kind is my love to-day, to-morrow kind,
Still constant in a wondrous excellence;
Therefore my verse to constancy confin'd,
One thing expressing, leaves out difference.
Fair, kind, and true, is all my argument, —
Fair, kind, and true, varying to other words;

And in this change is my invention spent,
Three themes in one, which wondrous scope affords.
  Fair, kind, and true, have often liv'd alone,
  Which three till now never kept seat in one.

CVI.

When in the chronicle of wasted time
I see descriptions of the fairest wights,
And beauty making beautiful old rhyme
In praise of ladies dead and lovely knights,
Then, in the blazon of sweet beauty's best,
Of hand, of foot, of lip, of eye, of brow,
I see their antique pen would have express'd
Even such a beauty as you master now.
So all their praises are but prophecies
Of this our time, all you prefiguring;
And, for they look'd but with divining eyes,
They had not skill enough your worth to sing:
  For we, which now behold these present days,
  Have eyes to wonder, but lack tongues to praise.

CVII.

Not mine own fears, nor the prophetic soul
Of the wide world dreaming on things to come,
Can yet the lease of my true love control,
Suppos'd as forfeit to a cónfin'd doom.
The mortal moon hath her eclipse endur'd,
And the sad augurs mock their owu presage;
Incertainties now crown themselves assur'd,
And peace proclaims olives of endless age.
Now with the drops of this most balmy time
My love looks fresh, and Death to me subscribes,
Since, spite of him, I'll live in this poor rhyme,
While he insults o'er dull and speechless tribes:
  And thou in this shalt find thy monument,
  When tyrants' crests and tombs of brass are spent.

CVIII.

What's in the brain, that ink may character,
Which hath not figur'd to thee my true spirit?
What's new to speak, what new to register,
That may express my love, or thy dear merit?
Nothing, sweet boy; but yet, like prayers divine,
I must each day say o'er the very same;
Counting no old thing old, thou mine, I thine,
Even as when first I hallow'd thy fair name.
So that eternal love in love's fresh case
Weighs not the dust and injury of age,
Nor gives to necessary wrinkles place,
But makes antiquity for aye his page;
     Finding the first conceit of love there bred,
     Where time and outward form would show it dead.

CIX.

O, never say that I was false of heart,
Though absence seem'd my flame to qualify.
As easy might I from myself depart
As from my soul, which in thy breast doth lie:
That is my home of love: if I have rang'd,
Like him that travels, I return again;
Just to the time, not with the time exchang'd, —
So that myself bring water for my stain.
Never believe, though in my nature reign'd
All frailties that besiege all kinds of blood,
That it could so preposterously be stain'd,
To leave for nothing all thy sum of good; .
     For nothing this wide universe I call,
     Save thou, my rose; in it thou art my all.

CX.

Alas, 'tis true I have gone here and there,
And made myself a motley to the view,
Gor'd mine own thoughts, sold cheap what is most dear,
Made old offences of affections new;

Most true it is that I have look'd on truth
Askance and strangely: but, by all above,
These blenches gave my heart another youth,
And worse essays prov'd thee my best of love.
Now all is done, have what shall have no end:
Mine appetite I never more will grind
On newer proof, to try an older friend,
A god in love, to whom I am confin'd.
  Then give me welcome, next my heaven the best,
  Even to thy pure and most most loving breast.

CXI.

O, for my sake do you with Fortune chide,
The guilty goddess of my harmful deeds,
That did not better for my life' provide
Than public means which public manners breeds.
Thence comes it that my name receives a brand;
And almost thence my nature is subdu'd
To what it works in, like the dyer's hand:
Pity me, then, and wish I were renew'd;
Whilst, like a willing patient, I will drink
Potions of eisel 'gainst my strong infection;
No bitterness that I will bitter think,
Nor double penance, to correct correction.
  Pity me, then, dear friend, and I assure ye
  Even that your pity is enough to cure me.

CXII.

Your love and pity doth th' impression fill
Which vulgar scandal stamp'd upon my brow;
For what care I who calls me well or ill,
So you o'er-green my bad, my good allow?
You are my all-the-world, and I must strive
To know my shames and praises from your tongue;
None else to me, nor I to none alive,
That my steel'd sense' or changes right or wrong.
In so profound abysm I throw all care
Of others' voices, that my adder's sense'

To critic and to flatterer stoppèd are.
Mark how with my neglect I do dispense: —
   You are so strongly in my purpose bred,
   That all the world besides methinks they're dead.

CXIII.

Since I left you, mine eye is in my mind;
And that which governs me to go about
Doth part his function, and is partly blind,
Seems seeing, but effectually is out;
For it no form delivers to the heart
Of bird, of flower, or shape, which it doth latch:
Of his quick objects hath the mind no part,
Nor his own vision holds what it doth catch;
For if it see the rud'st or gentlest sight,
The most sweet favour or deformed'st creature,
The mountain or the sea, the day or night,
The crow or dove, it shapes them to your feature:
   Incapable of more, replete with you,
   My most true mind thus maketh mine untrue.

CXIV.

Or whether doth my mind, being crown'd with you,
Drink up the monarch's plague, this flattery?
Or whether shall I say, mine eye saith true,
And that your love taught it this alchemy,
To make of monsters and things indigest
Such cherubins as your sweet self resemble,
Creating every bad a perfect best,
As fast as objects to his beams assemble?
O, 'tis the first; 'tis flattery in my seeing,
And my great mind most kingly drinks it up:
Mine eye well knows what with his gust is greeing,
And to his palate doth prepare the cup:
   If it be poison'd, 'tis the lesser sin
   That mine eye loves it, and doth first begin.

CXV.

Those lines that I before have writ do lie,
Even those that said I could not love you dearer:
Yet then my judgment knew no reason why
My most full flame should afterwards burn clearer.
But reckoning Time, whose million'd accidents
Creep in 'twixt vows, and change decrees of kings,
Tan sacred beauty, blunt the sharp'st intents,
Divert strong minds to the course of altering things;
Alas, why, fearing of Time's tyranny,
Might I not then say, "Now I love you best,"
When I was certain o'er incertainty,
Crowning the present, doubting of the rest?
  Love is a babe; then might I not say so,
  To give full growth to that which still doth grow?

CXVI.

Let me not to the marriage of true minds
Admit impediments.   Love is not love
Which alters when it alteration finds,
Or bends with the remover to remove:
O, no! it is an ever-fixèd mark,
That looks on tempests, and is never shaken;
It is the star to every wandering bark,
Whose worth's unknown, although his height be taken.
Love's not Time's fool, though rosy lips and cheeks
Within his bending sickle's compass come;
Love alters not with his brief hours and weeks,
But bears it out even to the edge of doom.
  If this be error, and upon me prov'd,
  I never writ, nor no man ever lov'd.

CXVII.

Accuse me thus: — that I have scanted all
Wherein I should your great deserts repay;
Forgot upon your dearest love to call,
Whereto all bonds do tie me day by day;

That I have frequent been with unknown minds,
And given to time your own dear-purchas'd right;
That 1 have hoisted sail to all the winds
Which should transport me farthest from your sight.
Book both my wilfulness and errors down
And on just proof surmise accumulate;
Bring me within the level of your frown,
But shoot not at me in your waken'd hate;
   Since my appeal says I did strive to prove
   The constancy and virtue of your love.

CXVIII.

Like as, to make our appetites more keen,
With eager compounds we our palate urge;
As, to prevent our maladies unseen,
We sicken to shun sickness when we purge;
Even so, being full of your ne'er-cloying sweetness,
To bitter sauces did I frame my feeding;
And, sick of welfare, found a kind of meetness
To be diseas'd, ere that there was true needing.
Thus policy in love, t' anticipate
The ills that were not, grew to faults assur'd,
And brought to medicine a healthful state,
Which, rank of goodness, would by ill be cur'd:
   But thence I learn, and find the lesson true,
   Drugs poison him that so fell sick of you.

CXIX.

What potions have I drunk of Siren tears,
Distill'd from limbecks foul as hell within,
Applying fears to hopes, and hopes to fears,
Still losing when I saw myself to win!
What wretched errors hath my heart committed,
Whilst it hath thought itself so blessèd never!
How have mine eyes out of their spheres been fitted,
In the distraction of this madding fever!
O benefit of ill! now I find true
That better is by evil still made better;

And ruin'd love, when it is built anew,
Grows fairer than at first, more strong, far greater.
  So I return rebuk'd to my content,
  And gain by ill thrice more than I have spent.

CXX.

That you were once unkind befriends me now,
And for that sorrow which I then did feel
Needs must I under my transgression bow,
Unless my nerves were brass or hammer'd steel.
For if you were by my unkindness shaken,
As I by yours, you've pass'd a hell of time;
And I, a tyrant, have no leisure taken
To weigh how once I suffer'd in your crime.
O, that our night of woe might have remember'd
My deepest sense, how hard true sorrow hits,
And soon to you, as you to me then, tender'd
The humble salve which wounded bosoms fits!
  But that your trespass now becomes a fee;
  Mine ransoms yours, and yours must ransom me.

CXXI.

'Tis better to be vile than vile-esteem'd,
When not to be receives reproach of being;
And the just pleasure lost, which is so deem'd
Not by our feeling, but by others' seeing:
For why should others' false-adulterate eyes
Give salutation to my sportive blood?
Or on my frailties why are frailer spies,
Which in their wills count bad what I think good?
No, — I am that I am; and they that level
At my abuses reckon up their own:
I may be straight, though they themselves be bevel;
By their rank thoughts my deeds must not be shown;
  Unless this general evil they maintain, —
  All men are bad, and in their badness reign.

CXXII.

Thy gift, thy tables, are within my brain
Full character'd with lasting memory,
Which shall above that idle rank remain,
Beyond all date, even to eternity:
Or, at the least, so long as brain and heart
Have faculty by nature to subsist;
Till each to raz'd oblivion yield his part
Of thee, thy record never can be miss'd.
That poor retention could not so much hold,
Nor need I tallies thy dear love to score;
Therefore to give them from me was I bold,
To trust those tables that receive thee more:
   To keep an adjunct to remember thee
   Were to import forgetfulness in me.

CXXIII.

No, Time, thou shalt not boast that I do change:
Thy pyramids built up with newer might
To me are nothing novel, nothing strange;
They are but dressings of a former sight.
Our dates are brief, and therefore we admire
What thou dost foist upon us that is old;
And rather make them born to our desire
Than think that we before have heard them told.
Thy registers and thee I both defy,
Not wondering at the present nor the past;
For thy records and what we see do lie,
Made more or less by thy continual haste.
   This I do vow, and this shall ever be,
   I will be true, despite thy scythe and thee.

CXXIV.

If my dear love were but the child of state,
It might for Fortune's bastard be unfather'd,
As subject to Time's love or to Time's hate,
Weeds among weeds, or flowers with flowers gather'd.

No, it was builded far from accident;
It suffers not in smiling pomp, nor falls
Under the blow of thrallèd discontent,
Whereto th' inviting time our fashion calls:
It fears not policy, that heretic,
Which works on leases of short-number'd hours,
But all alone stands hugely politic,
That it nor grows with heat nor drowns with showers.
  To this I witness call the fools of time,
  Which die for goodness, who have liv'd for crime.

CXXV.

Were 't aught to me I bore the canopy,
With my extern the outward honouring,
Or laid great bases for eternity,
Which prove more short than waste or ruining?
Have I not seen dwellers on form and favour
Lose all, and more, by paying too much rent,
For compound sweet forgoing simple savour,
Pitiful thrivers, in their gazing spent?
No, let me be obsequious in thy heart,
And take thou my oblation, poor but free,
Which is not mix'd with seconds, knows no art,
But mutual render, only me for thee.
  Hence, thou suborn'd informer! a true soul
  When most impeach'd stands least in thy control.

CXXVI.

O thou, my lovely boy, who in thy power
Dost hold Time's fickle glass, his sickle, hour;
Who hast by waning grown, and therein show'st
Thy lovers withering, as thy sweet self grow'st;
If Nature, sovereign mistress over wrack,
As thou goest onwards, still will pluck thee back,
She keeps thee to this purpose, that her skill
May time disgrace, and wretched minutes kill.

Yet fear her, O thou minion of her pleasure!
She may detain, but not still keep, her treasure:
Her audit, though delay'd, answer'd must be,
And her quietus is to render thee.

CXXVII.

In the old age black was not counted fair,
Or if it were, it bore not beauty's name;
But now is black beauty's successive heir,
And beauty slander'd with a bastard shame:
For since each hand hath put on nature's power,
Fairing the foul with art's false-borrow'd face,
Sweet beauty hath no name, no holy bower,
But is profan'd, if not lives in disgrace.
Therefore my mistress' eyes are raven black;
Her eyes so suited, as they mourners seem
At such who, not born fair, no beauty lack,
Slandering creation with a false esteem:
   Yet so they mourn, becoming of their woe,
   That every tongue says beauty should look so.

CXXVIII.

How oft, when thou, my music, music play'st,
Upon that blessèd wood whose motion sounds
With thy sweet fingers, when thou gently sway'st
The wiry concord that mine ear confounds,
Do I envy those jacks that nimble leap
To kiss the tender inward of thy hand,
Whilst my poor lips, which should that harvest reap,
At the wood's boldness by thee blushing stand!
To be so tickled, they would change their state
And situation with those dancing chips,
O'er whom thy fingers walk with gentle gait,
Making dead wood more bless'd than living lips.
   Since saucy jacks so happy are in this,
   Give them thy fingers, me thy lips to kiss.

CXXIX.

Th' expense of spirit in a waste of shame
Is lust in action; and till action, lust
Is perjur'd, murderous, bloody, full of blame,
Savage, extreme, rude, cruel, not to trust;
Enjoy'd no sooner but despisèd straight;
Past reason hunted; and no sooner had,
Past reason hated, as a swallow'd bait,
On purpose laid to make the taker mad:
Mad in pursuit, and in possession so;
Had, having, and in quest to have, extreme;
A bliss in proof, — and prov'd, a very woe;
Before, a joy propos'd; behind, a dream.
  All this the world well knows; yet none knows well
  To shun the heaven that leads men to this hell.

CXXX.

My mistress' eyes are nothing like the sun;
Coral is far more red than her lips' red:
If snow be white, why then her breasts are dun;
If hairs be wires, black wires grow on her head.
I have seen roses damask'd, red and white,
But no such roses see I in her cheeks;
And in some perfumes is there more delight
Than in the breath that from my mistress reeks.
I love to hear her speak, — yet well I know
That music hath a far more pleasing sound:
I grant I never saw a goddess go, —
My mistress, when she walks, treads on the ground.
  And yet, by heaven, I think my love as rare
  As any she belied with false compare.

CXXXI.

Thou art as tyrannous, so as thou art,
As those whose beauties proudly make them cruel;
For well thou know'st to my dear-doting heart
Thou art the fairest and most precious jewel.

Yet, in good faith, some say that thee behold,
Thy face hath not the power to make love groan:
To say they err I dare not be so bold,
Although I swear it to myself alone.
And, to be sure that is not false I swear,
A thousand groans, but thinking on thy face,
One on another's neck, do witness bear
Thy black is fairest in my judgment's place.
  In nothing art thou black save in thy deeds,
  And thence this slander, as I think, proceeds.

CXXXII.

Thine eyes I love, and they, as pitying me,
Knowing thy heart torments me with disdain,
Have put on black, and loving mourners be,
Looking with pretty ruth upon my pain.
And truly not the morning sun of heaven
Better becomes the gray cheeks of the east,
Nor that full star that ushers in the even
Doth half that glory to the sober west,
As those two mourning eyes become thy face:
O, let it, then, as well beseem thy heart
To mourn for me, since mourning doth thee grace,
And suit thy pity like in every part.
  Then will I swear beauty herself is black,
  And all they foul that thy complexion lack.

CXXXIII.

Beshrew that heart that makes my heart to groan
For that deep wound it gives my friend and me!
Is 't not enough to torture me alone,
But slave to slavery my sweet'st friend must be?
Me from myself thy cruel eye hath taken,
And my next self thou harder hast engross'd:
Of him, myself, and thee, I am forsaken;
A torment thrice threefold thus to be cross'd.
Prison my heart in thy steel bosom's ward,
But then my friend's heart let my poor heart bail;

Whoe'er keeps me, let my heart be his guard;
Thou canst not then use rigour in my gaol:
  And yet thou wilt; for I, being pent in thee,
  Perforce am thine, and all that is in me.

CXXXIV.

So, now I have confess'd that he is thine,
And I myself am mortgag'd to thy will,
Myself I'll forfeit, so that other mine
Thou wilt restore, to be my comfort still:
But thou wilt not, nor he will not be free,
For thou art covetous, and he is kind;
He learn'd but, surety-like, to write for me,
Under that bond that him as fast doth bind.
The statute of thy beauty thou wilt take,
Thou usurer, that putt'st forth all to use,
And sue a friend came debtor for my sake;
So him I lose through my unkind abuse.
  Him have I lost; thou hast both him and me:
  He pays the whole, and yet am I not free.

CXXXV.

Whoever hath her wish, thou hast thy *Will*,
And *Will* to boot, and *Will* in overplus;
More than enough am I that vex thee still,
To thy sweet will making addition thus.
Wilt thou, whose will is large and spacious,
Not once vouchsafe to hide my will in thine?
Shall will in others seem right gracious,
And in my will no fair acceptance shine?
The sea, all water, yet receives rain still,
And in abundance addeth to his store;
So thou, being rich in *Will*, add to thy *Will*
One will of mine, to make thy large *Will* more.
  Let no unkind, no fair beseechers kill;
  Think all but one, and me in that one *Will*.

CXXXVI.

If thy soul check thee that I come so near,
Swear to thy blind soul that I was thy *Will*,
And will, thy soul knows, is admitted there;
Thus far for love my love-suit, sweet, fulfil.
Will will fulfil the treasure of thy love,
Ay, fill it full with wills, and my will one.
In things of great receipt with ease we prove
Among a number one is reckon'd none:
Then in the number let me pass untold,
Though in thy stores' account I one must be;
For nothing hold me, so it please thee hold
That nothing me, a something, sweet, to thee:
    Make but my name thy love, and love that still,
    And then thou lov'st me, — for my name is *Will*.

CXXXVII.

Thou blind fool, Love, what dost thou to mine eyes,
That they behold, and see not what they see?
They know what beauty is, see where it lies,
Yet what the best is take the worst to be.
If eyes, corrupt by over-partial looks,
Be anchor'd in the bay where all men ride,
Why of eyes' falsehood hast thou forgèd hooks,
Whereto the judgment of my heart is tied?
Why should my heart think that a several plot
Which my heart knows the wide world's common place?
Or mine eyes seeing this, say this is not,
To put fair truth upon so foul a face?
    In things right-true my heart and eyes have err'd,
    And to this false plague are they now transferr'd.

CXXXVIII.

When my love swears that she is made of truth,
I do believe her, though I know she lies,
That she might think me some untutor'd youth,
Unlearnèd in the world's false subtleties.

Thus vainly thinking that she thinks me young,
Although she knows my days are past the best,
Simply I credit her false-speaking tongue:
On both sides thus is simple truth supprest.
But wherefore says she not she is unjust?
And wherefore say not I that I am old?
O, love's best habit is in seeming trust,
And age in love loves not to have years told:
 Therefore I lie with her and she with me,
 And in our faults by lies we flatter'd be.

CXXXIX.

O, call not me to justify the wrong
That thy unkindness lays upon my heart;
Wound me not with thine eye, but with thy tongue;
Use power with power, and slay me not by art.
Tell me thou lov'st elsewhere; but in my sight,
Dear heart, forbear to glance thine eye aside:
What need'st thou wound with cunning, when thy might
Is more than my o'erpress'd defence can bide?
Let me excuse thee: ah, my love well knows
Her pretty looks have been mine enemies;
And therefore from my face she turns my foes,
That they elsewhere might dart their injuries:
 Yet do not so; but since I am near slain,
 Kill me outright with looks, and rid my pain.

CXL.

Be wise as thou art cruel; do not press
My tongue-tied patience with too much disdain;
Lest sorrow lend me words, and words express
The manner of my pity-wanting pain.
If I might teach thee wit, better it were,
Though not to love, yet, love, to tell me so; —
As testy sick men, when their deaths be near,
No news but health from their physicians know; —
For, if I should despair, I should grow mad,
And in my madness might speak ill of thee:

Now this ill-wresting world is grown so bad,
Mad slanderers by mad ears believèd be:
  That I may not be so, nor thou belied,
  Bear thine eyes straight, though thy proud heart go wide.

CXLI.

In faith, I do not love thee with mine eyes,
For they in thee a thousand errors note;
But 'tis my heart that loves what they despise,
Who, in despite of view, is pleas'd to dote;
Nor are mine ears with thy tongue's tune delighted;
Nor tender feeling, to base touches prone,
Nor taste, nor smell, desire to be invited
To any sensual feast with thee alone:
But my five wits nor my five senses can
Dissuade one foolish heart from serving thee,
Who leaves unsway'd the likeness of a man,
Thy proud heart's slave and vassal wretch to be:
  Only my plague thus far I count my gain,
  That she that makes me sin awards me pain.

CXLII.

Love is my sin, and thy dear virtue hate,
Hate of my sin, grounded on sinful loving:
O, but with mine compare thou thine own state,
And thou shalt find it merits not reproving;
Or, if it do, not from those lips of thine,
That have profan'd their scarlet ornaments
And seal'd false bonds of love as oft as mine,
Robb'd others' beds' revenues of their rents.
Be 't lawful I love thee, as thou lov'st those
Whom thine eyes woo as mine impórtune thee:
Root pity in thy heart, that, when it grows,
Thy pity may deserve to pitied be.
  If thou dost seek to have what thou dost hide,
  By self-example mayst thou be denied!

CXLIII.

Lo, as a careful housewife runs to catch
One of her feather'd creatures broke away,
Sets down her babe, and makes all swift dispatch
In pursuit of the thing she would have stay;
Whilst her neglected child holds her in chase,
Cries to catch her whose busy care is bent
To follow that which flies before her face,
Not prizing her poor infant's discontent:
So runn'st thou after that which flies from thee,
Whilst I thy babe chase thee afar behind;
But if thou catch thy hope, turn back to me,
And play the mother's part, kiss me, be kind:
  So will I pray that thou mayst have thy *Will*,
  If thou turn back, and my loud crying still.

CXLIV.

Two loves I have of comfort and despair,
Which like two spirits do suggest me still:
The better angel is a man right fair,
The worser spirit a woman colour'd ill.
To win me soon to hell, my female evil
Tempteth my better angel from my side,
And would corrupt my saint to be a devil,
Wooing his purity with her foul pride.
And whether that my angel be turn'd fiend
Suspect I may, yet not directly tell;
But being both from me, both to each friend,
I guess one angel in another's hell:
  Yet this shall I ne'er know, but live in doubt,
  Till my bad angel fire my good one out.

CXLV.

Those lips that Love's own hand did make
Breath'd forth the sound that said "I hate"
To me that languish'd for her sake:
But when she saw my woful state,

Straight in her heart did mercy come,
Chiding that tongue that ever sweet
Was us'd in giving gentle doom;
And taught it thus anew to greet;
"I hate" she alter'd with an end,
That follow'd it as gentle day
Doth follow night, who, like a fiend,
From heaven to hell is flown away;
   "I hate" from hate away she threw,
   And sav'd my life, saying — "Not you."

CXLVI.

Poor soul, the centre of my sinful earth,
Fool'd by these rebel powers that thee array,
Why dost thou pine within and suffer dearth,
Painting thy outward walls so costly gay?
Why so large cost, having so short a lease,
Dost thou upon thy fading mansion spend?
Shall worms, inheritors of this excess,
Eat up thy charge? is this thy body's end?
Then, soul, live thou upon thy servant's loss,
And let that pine to aggravate thy store;
Buy terms divine in selling hours of dross;
Within be fed, without be rich no more:
   So shalt thou feed on Death, that feeds on men,
   And Death once dead, there's no more dying then.

CXLVII.

My love is as a fever, longing still
For that which longer nurseth the disease;
Feeding on that which doth preserve the ill,
Th' uncertain-sickly appetite to please.
My reason, the physician to my love,
Angry that his prescriptions are not kept,
Hath left me, and I desperate now approve
Desire is death, which physic did except.
Past cure I am, now reason is past care,
And frantic-mad with evermore unrest;

My thoughts and my discourse as madmen's are,
At random from the truth vainly express'd;
  For I have sworn thee fair, and thought thee bright,
  Who art as black as hell, as dark as night.

CXLVIII.

O me, what eyes hath Love put in my head,
Which have no correspondence with true sight!
Or, if they have, where is my judgment fled,
That censures falsely what they see aright?
If that be fair whereon my false eyes dote,
What means the world to say it is not so?
If it be not, then love doth well denote
Love's eye is not so true as all men's no.
How can it? O, how can Love's eye be true,
That is so vex'd with watching and with tears?
No marvel, then, though I mistake my view;
The sun itself sees not till heaven clears.
  O cunning Love! with tears thou keep'st me blind,
  Lest eyes well-seeing thy foul faults should find.

CXLIX.

Canst thou, O cruel! say I love thee not,
When I, against myself, with thee partake?
Do I not think on thee, when I forgot
Am of myself, all tyrant, for thy sake?
Who hateth thee that I do call my friend?
On whom frown'st thou that I do fawn upon?
Nay, if thou lour'st on me, do I not spend
Revenge upon myself with present moan?
What merit do I in myself respect,
That is so proud thy service to despise,
When all my best doth worship thy defect,
Commanded by the motion of thine eyes?
  But, love, hate on, for now I know thy mind;
  Those that can see thou lov'st, and I am blind.

CL.

O, from what power hast thou this powerful might
With insufficiency my heart to sway?

To make me give the lie to my true sight,
And swear that brightness doth not grace the day?
Whence hast thou this becoming of things ill,
That in the very refuse of thy deeds.
There is such strength and warrantise of skill,
That, in my mind, thy worst all best exceeds?
Who taught thee how to make me love thee more,
The more I hear and see just cause of hate?
O, though I love what others do abhor,
With others thou shouldst not abhor my state:
　If thy unworthiness rais'd love in me,
　More worthy I to be belov'd of thee.

CLI.

Love is too young to know what conscience is;
Yet who knows not conscience is born of love?
Then, gentle cheater, urge not my amiss,
Lest guilty of my faults thy sweet self prove:
For, thou betraying me, I do betray
My nobler part to my gross body's treason;
My soul doth tell my body that he may
Triumph in love; flesh stays no farther reason;
But, rising at thy name, doth point out thee
As his triumphant prize.　Proud of this pride,
He is contented thy poor drudge to be,
To stand in thy affairs, fall by thy side.
　No want of conscience hold it that I call
　Her "love" for whose dear love I rise and fall.

CLII.

In loving thee thou know'st I am forsworn,
But thou art twice forsworn, to me love swearing;
In act thy bed-vow broke, and new faith torn,
In vowing new hate after new love bearing.
But why of two oaths' breach do I accuse thee,
When I break twenty? I am perjur'd most;
For all my vows are oaths but to misuse thee,
And all my honest faith in thee is lost:

For I have sworn deep oaths of thy deep kindness,
Oaths of thy love, thy truth, thy constancy;
And, to enlighten thee, gave eyes to blindness,
Or made them swear against the thing they see;
    For I have sworn thee fair, — more perjur'd I,
    To swear, against the truth, so foul a lie!

CLIII.

Cupid laid by his brand, and fell asleep:
A maid of Dian's this advantage found,
And his love-kindling fire did quickly steep
In a cold valley-fountain of that ground;
Which borrow'd from this holy fire of Love
A dateless-lively heat, still to endure,
And grew a seething bath, which yet men prove
Against strange maladies a sovereign cure.
But at my mistress' eye Love's brand new-fir'd,
The boy for trial needs would touch my breast;
I, sick withal, the help of bath desir'd,
And thither hied, a sad distemper'd guest,
    But found no cure: the bath for my help lies
    Where Cupid got new fire, — my mistress' eyes.

CLIV.

The little Love-god lying once asleep
Laid by his side his heart-inflaming brand,
Whilst many nymphs that vow'd chaste life to keep
Came tripping by; but in her maiden hand
The fairest votary took up that fire
Which many legions of true hearts had warm'd;
And so the general of hot desire
Was sleeping by a virgin hand disarm'd.
This brand she quenchèd in a cool well by,
Which from Love's fire took heat perpetual,
Growing a bath and healthful remedy
For men diseas'd; but I, my mistress' thrall,
    Came there for cure, and this by that I prove,
    Love's fire heats water, water cools not love.

A LOVER'S COMPLAINT.

From off a hill whose concave womb re-worded
A plaintful story from a sistering vale,
My spirits t'attend this double voice accorded,
And down I laid to list the sad-tun'd tale;
Ere long espied a fickle maid full pale,
Tearing of papers, breaking rings a-twain,
Storming her world with sorrow's wind and rain.

Upon her head a platted hive of straw,
Which fortified her visage from the sun,
Whereon the thought might think sometime it saw
The carcass of a beauty spent and done:
Time had not scythèd all that youth begun,
Nor youth all quit; but, spite of heaven's fell rage,
Some beauty peep'd through lattice of sear'd age.

Oft did she heave her napkin to her eyne,
Which on it had conceited characters,
Laundering the silken figures in the brine
That season'd woe had pelleted in tears,
And often reading what contents it bears;
As often shrieking undistinguish'd woe,
In clamours of all size, both high and low.

Sometimes her levell'd eyes their carriage ride,
As they did battery to the spheres intend;
Sometimes diverted their poor balls are tied
To th' orbèd earth; sometimes they do extend
Their view right on; anon their gazes lend
To every place at once, and, nowhere fix'd,
The mind and sight distractedly commix'd.

Her hair, nor loose nor tied in formal plat,
Proclaim'd in her a careless hand of pride;

For some, untuck'd, descended her sheav'd hat,
Hanging her pale and pinèd cheek beside;
Some in her threaden fillet still did bide,
And, true to bondage, would not break from thence,
Though slackly braided in loose negligence.

A thousand favours from a maund she drew
Of amber, crystal, and of beaded jet,
Which one by one she in a river threw,
Upon whose weeping margent she was set;
Like usury, applying wet to wet,
Or monarch's hands that let not bounty fall
Where want cries some, but where excess begs all.

Of folded schedules had she many a one,
Which she perus'd, sigh'd, tore, and gave the flood;
Crack'd many a ring of posied gold and bone,
Bidding them find their sepulchres in mud;
Found yet more letters sadly penn'd in blood,
With sleided silk feat and affectedly
Enswath'd, and seal'd to curious secrecy.

These often bath'd she in her fluxive eyes,
And often kiss'd, and often gan to tear;
Cried, "O false blood, thou register of lies,
What unapprovèd witness dost thou bear!
Ink would have seem'd more black and damnèd here!"
This said, in top of rage the lines she rents,
Big discontent so breaking their contents.

A reverend man that graz'd his cattle nigh —
Sometime a blusterer, that the ruffle knew
Of court, of city, and had let go by
The swiftest hours, observèd as they flew —
Towards this afflicted fancy fastly drew,
And, privileg'd by age, desires to know
In brief the grounds and motives of her woe.

So slides he down upon his grainèd bat,
And comely-distant sits he by her side;

When he again desires her, being sat,
Her grievance with his hearing to divide:
If that from him there may be aught applied
Which may her suffering ecstasy assuage,
'Tis promis'd in the charity of age.

"Father," she says, "though in me you behold
The injury of many a blasting hour,
Let it not tell your judgment I am old;
Not age, but sorrow, over me hath power:
I might as yet have been a spreading flower,
Fresh to myself, if I had self-applied
Love to myself, and to no love beside.

"But, woe is me! too early I attended
A youthful suit — it was to gain my grace —
Of one by nature's outwards so commended,
That maidens' eyes stuck over all his face:
Love lack'd a dwelling, and made him her place;
And when in his fair parts she did abide,
She was new lodg'd, and newly deified.

"His browny locks did hang in crookèd curls;
And every light occasion of the wind
Upon his lips their silken parcels hurls.
What's sweet to do, to do will aptly find:
Each eye that saw him did enchant the mind;
For on his visage was in little drawn
What largeness thinks in Paradise was sawn.

"Small show of man was yet upon his chin;
His phœnix down began but to appear,
Like unshorn velvet, on that termless skin,
Whose bare out-bragg'd the web it seem'd to wear:
Yet show'd his visage by that cost more dear;
And nice affections wavering stood in doubt
If best were as it was, or best without.

"His qualities were beauteous as his form,
For maiden-tongu'd he was, and thereof free;

Yet, if men mov'd him, was he such a storm
As oft 'twixt May and April is to see,
When winds breathe sweet, unruly though they be.
His rudeness so with his authóriz'd youth
Did livery falseness in a pride of truth.

"Well could he ride, and often men would say,
'That horse his mettle from his rider takes:
Proud of subjection, noble by the sway,
What rounds, what bounds, what course, what stop he makes!'
And controversy hence a question takes,
Whether the horse by him became his deed,
Or he his manage by the well-doing steed.

"But quickly on this side the verdict went:
His real habitude gave life and grace
To appertainings and to ornament,
Accomplish'd in himself, not in his case:
All aids, themselves made fairer by their place,
Came for additions; yet their purpos'd trim
Piec'd not his grace, but were all grac'd by him.

"So on the tip of his subduing tongue
All kind of arguments and question deep,
All replication prompt, and reason strong,
For his advantage still did wake and sleep:
To make the weeper laugh, the laugher weep,
He had the dialect and different skill,
Catching all passions in his craft of will:

"That he did in the general bosom reign
Of young, of old; and sexes both enchanted,
To dwell with him in thoughts, or to remain
In personal duty, following where he haunted:
Consents bewitch'd, ere he desire, have granted;
And dialogu'd for him what he would say,
Ask'd their own wills, and made their wills obey.

"Many there were that did his picture get,
To serve their eyes, and in it put their mind;

Like fools that in th' imagination set
The goodly objects which abroad they find
Of lands and mansions, theirs in thought assign'd;
And labouring in more pleasures to bestow them
Than the true gouty landlord which doth owe them:

"So many have, that never touch'd his hand,
Sweetly suppos'd them mistress' of his heart.
My woful self, that did in freedom stand,
And was my own fee-simple, not in part,
What with his art in youth, and youth in art,
Threw my affections in his charmèd power,
Reserv'd the stalk, and gave him all my flower.

"Yet did I not, as some my equals did,
Demand of him, nor being desir'd yielded;
Finding myself in honour so forbid,
With safest distance I mine honour shielded:
Experience for me many bulwarks builded
Of proofs new-bleeding, which remain'd the foil
Of this false jewel, and his amorous spoil.

"But, ah, who ever shunn'd by precedent
The destin'd ill she must herself assay?
Or forc'd examples, 'gainst her own content,
To put the by-pass'd perils in her way?
Counsel may stop awhile what will not stay;
For when we rage, advice is often seen
By blunting us to make our wits more keen.

"Nor gives it satisfaction to our blood,
That we must curb it upon others' proof;
To be forbod the sweets that seem so good,
For fear of harms that preach in our behoof.
O appetite, from judgment stand aloof!
The one a palate hath that needs will taste,
Though Reason weep, and cry, 'It is thy last.'

"For further I could say, 'This man's untrue,'
And knew the patterns of his foul beguiling;

Heard where his plants in others' orchards grew,
Saw how deceits were gilded in his smiling;
Knew vows were ever brokers to defiling;
Thought characters and words merely but art,
And bastards of his foul-adulterate heart.

"And long upon these terms I held my city,
Till thus he gan besiege me: 'Gentle maid,
Have of my suffering youth some feeling pity,
And be not of my holy vows afraid:
That's to ye sworn to none was ever said;
For feasts of love I have been call'd unto,
Till now did ne'er invite, nor never woo.

"'All my offences that abroad you see
Are errors of the blood, none of the mind;
Love made them not: with acture they may be,
Where neither party is nor true nor kind:
They sought their shame that so their shame did find;
And so much less of shame in me remains,
By how much of me their reproach contains.

"'Among the many that mine eyes have seen,
Not one whose flame my heart so much as warm'd,
Or my affection put to the smallest teen,
Or any of my leisures ever charm'd:
Harm have I done to them, but ne'er was harm'd;
Kept hearts in liveries, but mine own was free,
And reign'd, commanding in his monarchy.

"'Look here, what tributes wounded fancies sent me,
Of paled pearls and rubies red as blood;
Figuring that they their passions likewise lent me
Of grief and blushes, aptly understood
In bloodless white and the encrimson'd mood;
Effects of terror and dear modesty,
Encamp'd in hearts, but fighting outwardly.

"'And, lo, behold these talents of their hair,
With twisted metal amorously impleach'd,

Shakespeare. VII.   29

I have receiv'd from many a several fair, —
Their kind acceptance weepingly beseech'd, —
With the annexions of fair gems enrich'd,
And deep-brain'd sonnets that did amplify
Each stone's dear nature, worth, and quality.

" 'The diamond, — why, 'twas beautiful and hard,
Whereto his invis'd properties did tend;
The deep-green emerald, in whose fresh regard
Weak sights their sickly radiance do amend;
The heaven-hu'd sapphire, and the opal blend
With objects manifold: each several stone,
With wit well blazon'd, smil'd or made some moan.

" 'Lo', all these trophies of affections hot,
Of pensiv'd and subdu'd desires the tender,
Nature hath charg'd me that I hoard them not,
But yield them up where I myself must render,
That is, to you, my origin and ender;
For these, of force, must your oblations be,
Since I their altar, you enpatron me.

" 'O, then, advance of yours that phraseless hand,
Whose white weighs down the airy scale of praise;
Take all these similes to your own command,
Hallow'd with sighs that burning lungs did raise;
What me your minister, for you obeys,
Works under you; and to your audit comes
Their distract parcels in combinèd sums.

" 'Lo, this device was sent me from a nun,
A sister sanctified, of holiest note;
Which late her noble suit in court did shun,
Whose rarest havings made the blossoms dote;
For she was sought by spirits of richest coat,
But kept cold distance, and did thence remove,
To spend her living in eternal love.

" 'But, O my sweet, what labour is't to leave
The thing we have not, mastering what not strives, —

Paling the place which did no form receive,
Playing patient sports in unconstrainèd gyves?
She that her fame so to herself contrives,
The scars of battle scapeth by the flight,
And makes her absence valiant, not her might.

" 'O, pardon me, in that my boast is true:
The accident which brought me to her eye
Upon the moment did her force subdue,
And now she would the cagèd cloister fly:
Religious love put out Religion's eye:
Not to be tempted, would she be immur'd,
And now, to tempt all, liberty procur'd.

" 'How mighty, then, you are, O, hear me tell!
The broken bosoms that to me belong
Have emptied all their fountains in my well,
And mine I pour your ocean all among:
I strong o'er them, and you o'er me being strong,
Must for your victory us all congest,
As compound love to physic your cold breast.

" 'My parts had power to charm a sacred nun,
Who, disciplin'd, ay, dieted in grace,
Believ'd her eyes when they t' assail begun,
All vows and consecrations giving place:
O most potential love! vow, bond, nor space,
In thee hath neither sting, knot, nor confine,
For thou art all, and all things else are thine.

" 'When thou impressest, what are precepts worth
Of stale example? When thou wilt inflame,
How coldly those impediments stand forth
Of wealth, of filial fear, law, kindred, fame!
Love's arms are peace, 'gainst rule, 'gainst sense, 'gainst shame;
And sweetens, in the suffering pangs it bears,
The aloes of all forces, shocks, and fears.

" 'Now all these hearts that do on mine depend,
Feeling it break, with bleeding groans they pine;

29*

And supplicant their sighs to you extend,
To leave the battery that you make 'gainst mine,
Lending soft audience to my sweet design,
And credent soul to that strong-bonded oath
That shall prefer and undertake my troth.'

"This said, his watery eyes he did dismount,
Whose sights till then were levell'd on my face;
Each cheek a river running from a fount
With brinish current downward flow'd apace:
O, how the channel to the stream gave grace!
Who glaz'd with crystal gate the glowing roses
That flame through water which their hue encloses.

"O father, what a hell of witchcraft lies
In the small orb of one particular tear!
But with the inundation of the eyes
What rocky heart to water will not wear?
What breast so cold that is not warmèd here?
O cleft effect! cold modesty, hot wrath,
Both fire from hence and chill extincture hath.

"For, lo, his passion, but an art of craft,
Even there resolv'd my reason into tears;
There my white stole of chastity I daff'd,
Shook off my sober guards and civil fears;
Appear to him, as he to me appears,
All melting; though our drops this difference bore,
His poison'd me, and mine did him restore.

"In him a plenitude of subtle matter,
Applied to cautels, all strange forms receives,
Of burning blushes, or of weeping water,
Or swooning paleness; and he takes and leaves,
In either's aptness, as it best deceives,
To blush at speeches rank, to weep at woes,
Or to turn white and swoon at tragic shows:

"That not a heart which in his level came
Could scape the hail of his all-hurting aim,

Showing fair nature is both kind and tame;
And, veil'd in them, did win whom he would maim:
Against the thing he sought he would exclaim;
When he most burn'd in heart-wish'd luxury,
He preach'd pure maid, and prais'd cold chastity.

"Thus merely with the garment of a Grace
The naked and concealèd fiend he cover'd;
That th' unexperient gave the tempter place,
Which, like a cherubin, above them hover'd.
Who, young and simple, would not be so lover'd?
Ay me! I fell; and yet do question make
What I should do again for such a sake.

"O, that infected moisture of his eye,
O, that false fire which in his cheek so glow'd,
O, that forc'd thunder from his heart did fly,
O, that sad breath his spongy lungs bestow'd,
O, all that borrow'd motion seeming ow'd,
Would yet again betray the fore-betray'd,
And new pervert a reconcilèd maid!"

THE PASSIONATE PILGRIM.

I.

Sweet Cytherea, sitting by a brook
With young Adonis, lovely, fresh, and green,
Did court the lad with many a lovely look, —
Such looks as none could look but beauty's queen.
She told him stories to delight his ear;
She show'd him favours to allure his eye;
To win his heart, she touch'd him here and there, —
Touches so soft still conquer chastity.
But whether unripe years did want conceit,
Or he refus'd to take her figur'd proffer,
The tender nibbler would not touch the bait,
But smile and jest at every gentle offer:
    Then fell she on her back, fair queen, and toward:
    He rose and ran away, — ah, fool too froward!

II.

Scarce had the sun dried up the dewy morn,
And scarce the herd gone to the hedge for shade,
When Cytherea, all in love forlorn,
A longing tarriance for Adonis made
Under an osier growing by a brook,
A brook where Adon us'd to cool his spleen:
Hot was the day; she hotter that did look
For his approach, that often there had been.
Anon he comes, and throws his mantle by,
And stood stark naked on the brook's green brim:
The sun look'd on the world with glorious eye,
Yet not so wistly as this queen on him.

He, spying her, bounc'd in, whereas he stood:
"O Jove," quoth she, "why was not I a flood!"

III.

Fair was the morn when the fair queen of love,

* * * * * * *

Paler for sorrow than her milk-white dove,
For Adon's sake, a youngster proud and wild;
Her stand she takes upon a steep-up hill:
Anon Adonis comes with horn and hounds;
She, silly queen, with more than love's good will,
Forbade the boy he should not pass those grounds:
"Once," quoth she, "did I see a fair sweet youth
Here in these brakes deep-wounded with a boar,
Deep in the thigh, a spectacle of ruth!
See, in my thigh," quoth she, "here was the sore."
　She showèd hers: he saw more wounds than one,
　And blushing fled, and left her all alone.

IV.

Venus, with young Adonis sitting by her
Under a myrtle shade, began to woo him:
She told the youngling how god Mars did try her,
And as he fell to her, so fell she to him.
"Even thus," quoth she, "the warlike god embrac'd me,"
And then she clipp'd Adonis in her arms;
"Even thus," quoth she, "the warlike god unlac'd me,"
As if the boy should use like loving charms;
"Even thus," quoth she, "he seizèd on my lips,"
And with her lips on his did act the seizure:
But as she fetchèd breath, away he skips,
And would not take her meaning nor her pleasure.
　Ah, that I had my lady at this bay,
　To kiss and clip me till I run away!

V.

Fair is my love, but not so fair as fickle;
Mild as a dove, but neither true nor trusty;
Brighter than glass, and yet, as glass is, brittle;
Softer than wax, and yet, as iron, rusty:

A lily pale, with damask dye to grace her,
None fairer, nor none falser to deface her.

Her lips to mine how often hath she join'd,
Between each kiss her oaths of true love swearing!
How many tales to please me hath she coin'd,
Dreading my love, the loss thereof still fearing!
Yet in the midst of all her pure protestings,
Her faith, her oaths, her tears, and all were jestings.

She burn'd with love, as straw with fire flameth;
She burn'd out love, as soon as straw out-burneth;
She fram'd the love, and yet she foil'd the framing;
She bade love last, and yet she fell a-turning.
Was this a lover, or a lecher whether?
Bad in the best, though excellent in neither.

VI.

If music and sweet poetry agree,
As they must needs, the sister and the brother,
Then must the love be great twixt thee and me,
Because thou lov'st the one, and I the other.
Dowland to thee is dear, whose heavenly touch
Upon the lute doth ravish human sense;
Spenser to me, whose deep conceit is such
As, passing all conceit, needs no defence.
Thou lov'st to hear the sweet melodious sound
That Phœbus' lute, the queen of music, makes;
And I in deep delight am chiefly drown'd
Whenas himself to singing he betakes.
One god is god of both, as poets feign;
One knight loves both, and both in thee remain.

VII.

Sweet rose, fair flower, untimely pluck'd, soon vaded,
Plucked in the bud, and vaded in the spring!
Bright orient pearl, alack, too timely shaded!
Fair creature, kill'd too soon by death's sharp sting!
Like a green plum that hangs upon a tree,
And falls, through wind, before the fall should be.

I weep for thee, and yet no cause I have;
For why thou left'st me nothing in thy will:
And yet thou left'st me more than I did crave;
For why I cravèd nothing of thee still:
  O yes, dear friend, I pardon crave of thee, —
  Thy discontent thou didst bequeath to me.

VIII.

  Crabbèd age and youth
    Cannot live together:
  Youth is full of pleasance,
    Age is full of care;
  Youth like summer morn,
    Age like winter weather;
  Youth like summer brave,
    Age like winter bare.
  Youth is full of sport,
  Age's breath is short;
    Youth is nimble, age is lame;
  Youth is hot and bold,
  Age is weak and cold;
    Youth is wild, and age is tame.
  Age, I do abhor thee,
  Youth, I do adore thee;
    O, my love, my love is young!
  Age, I do defy thee: —
  O, sweet shepherd, hie thee,
    For methinks thou stay'st too long.

IX.

Beauty is but a vain and doubtful good;
A shining gloss that vadeth suddenly;
A flower that dies when first it gins to bud;
A brittle glass that's broken presently:
  A doubtful good, a gloss, a glass, a flower,
  Lost, vaded, broken, dead within an hour.

And as goods lost are seld or never found,
As vaded gloss no rubbing will refresh,

As flowers dead lie wither'd on the ground,
As broken glass no cement can redress, —
   So beauty blemish'd once for ever's lost,
   In spite of physic, painting, pain, and cost.

X.

Good night, good rest. Ah, neither be my share:
She bade good night that kept my rest away;
And daff'd me to a cabin hang'd with care,
To descant on the doubts of my decay.
   "Farewell," quoth she, "and come again to-morrow:"
   Fare well I could not, for I supp'd with sorrow.

Yet at my parting sweetly did she smile,
In scorn or friendship, nill I construe whether:
'T may be, she joy'd to jest at my exile,
'T may be, again to make me wander thither:
   "Wander," a word for shadows like myself,
   As take the pain, but cannot pluck the pelf.

XI.

Lord, how mine eyes throw gazes to the east!
My heart doth charge the watch; the morning rise
Doth cite each moving sense from idle rest.
Not daring trust the office of mine eyes,
   While Philomela sits and sings, I sit and mark,
   And wish her lays were tunèd like the lark;

For she doth welcome daylight with her ditty,
And drives away dark dismal-dreaming night:
The night so pack'd, I post unto my pretty;
Heart hath his hope, and eyes their wishèd sight;
   Sorrow chang'd to solace, solace mix'd with sorrow;
   For why she sigh'd, and bade me come to-morrow.

Were I with her, the night would post too soon;
But now are minutes added to the hours;
To spite me now, each minute seems a moon;
Yet not for me, shine sun to succour flowers!
   Pack night, peep day; good day, of night now borrow:
   Show, night, to-night, and length thyself to-morrow.

XII.

It was a lording's daughter, the fairest one of three,
That likèd of her master as well as well might be,
Till looking on an Englishman, the fair'st that eye could see,
  Her fancy fell a-turning.
Long was the combat doubtful that love with love did fight,
To leave the master loveless, or kill the gallant knight:
To put in practice either, alas, it was a spite
  Unto the silly damsel!
But one must be refusèd; more mickle was the pain
That nothing could be usèd to turn them both to gain,
For of the two the trusty knight was wounded with disdain:
  Alas, she could not help it!
Thus art with arms contending was victor of the day,
Which by a gift of learning did bear the maid away:
Then, lullaby, the learnèd man hath got the lady gay;
  For now my song is ended.

XIII.

My flocks feed not,
My ewes breed not,
My rams speed not,
  All is amiss:
Love's denying,
Faith's defying,
Heart's renying,
  Causer of this.
All my merry jigs are quite forgot,
All my lady's love is lost, God wot:
Where her faith was firmly fix'd in love,
There a nay is plac'd without remove.
One silly cross
Wrought all my loss;
  O frowning Fortune, cursèd, fickle dame!
For now I see
Inconstancy
  More in women than in men remain.

In black mourn I,
All fears scorn I,
Love hath forlorn me,
  Living in thrall:
Heart is bleeding,
All help needing, —
O cruel speeding,
  Fraughted with gall!
My shepherd's pipe can sound no deal;
My wether's bell rings doleful knell;
My curtal dog, that wont t' have play'd,
Plays not at all, but seems afraid;
My sighs so deep
Procure to weep,
  In howling wise, to see my doleful plight.
How sighs resound
Through heartless ground,
  Like a thousand vanquish'd men in bloody fight!

Clear wells spring not,
Sweet birds sing not,
Green plants bring not
  Forth their dye;
Herds stand weeping,
Flocks all sleeping,
Nymphs back peeping
  Fearfully:
All our pleasure known to us poor swains,
All our merry meetings on the plains,
All our evening sport from us is fled,
All our love is lost, for Love is dead.
Farewell, sweet lass,
Thy like ne'er was
  For a sweet content, the cause of all my moan:
Poor Corydon
Must live alone;
  Other help for him I see that there is none.

XIV.

Whenas thine eye hath chose the dame,
And stall'd the deer that thou shouldst strike, •
Let reason rule things worthy blame,
As well as partial fancy like:
 Take counsel of some wiser head,
 Neither too young nor yet unwed.

And when thou com'st thy tale to tell,'
Smooth not thy tongue with filèd talk,
Lest she some subtle practice smell, —
A cripple soon can find a halt; —
 But plainly say thou lov'st her well,
 And set thy person forth to sell.

What though her frowning brows be bent,
Her cloudy looks will clear ere night:
And then too late she will repent
That thus dissembled her delight;
 And twice desire, ere it be day,
 That which with scorn she put away.

What though she strive to try her strength,
And ban and brawl, and say thee nay,
Her feeble force will yield at length,
When craft hath taught her thus to say, —
 "Had women been so strong as men,
 In faith, you had not had it then."

And to her will frame all thy ways;
Spare not to spend, — and chiefly there
Where thy desert may merit praise,
By ringing in thy lady's ear:
 The strongest castle, tower, and town,
 The golden bullet beats it down.

Serve always with assurèd trust,
And in thy suit be humble-true;
Unless thy lady prove unjust,
Press never thou to choose anew:

When time shall serve, be thou not slack
To proffer, though she put thee back.

The wiles and guiles that women work,
Dissembled with an outward show,
The tricks and toys that in them lurk,
The cock that treads them shall not know.
   Have you not heard it said full oft,
   A woman's nay doth stand for naught?

Think women still to strive with men,
To sin, and never for to saint:
Here is no heaven; they holy then
When time with age shall them attaint.
   Were kisses all the joys in bed,
   One woman would another wed.

But, soft! enough, — too much, I fear;
For if my mistress hear my song,
She will not stick to warm my ear,
To teach my tongue to be so long:
   Yet will she blush, here be it said,
   To hear her secrets so bewray'd.

XV.

   As it fell upon a day
   In the merry month of May,
   Sitting in a pleasant shade
   Which a grove of myrtles made,
   Beasts did leap, and birds did sing,
   Trees did grow, and plants did spring;
   Every thing did banish moan,
   Save the nightingale alone:
   She, poor bird, as all forlorn,
   Lean'd her breast up-till a thorn,
   And there sung the dolefull'st ditty,
   That to hear it was great pity:
   "Fie, fie, fie," now would she cry;
   "Tereu, tereu," by and by;

That to hear her so complain,
Scarce I could from tears refrain;
For her griefs, so lively shown,
Made me think upon mine own.
Ah, thought I, thou mourn'st in vain! -
None takes pity on thy pain:
Senseless trees they cannot hear thee;
Ruthless beasts they will not cheer thee:
King Pandion he is dead;
All thy friends are lapp'd in lead;
All thy fellow birds do sing,
Careless of thy sorrowing.
Even so, poor bird, like thee,
None alive will pity me.
Whilst as fickle Fortune smil'd,
Thou and I were both beguil'd.
   Every one that flatters thee
Is no friend in misery.
Words are easy, like the wind;
Faithful friends are hard to find:
Every man will be thy friend
Whilst thou hast wherewith to spend;
But if store of crowns be scant,
No man will supply thy want.
If that one be prodigal,
Bountiful they will him call,
And with such-like flattering,
"Pity but he were a king;"
If he be addict to vice,
Quickly him they will entice;
If to women he be bent,
They have him at commandment:
But if Fortune once do frown,
Then farewell his great renown;
They that fawn'd on him before
Use his company no more.
He that is thy friend indeed,

He will help thee in thy need:
If thou sorrow, he will weep;
If thou wake, he cannot sleep;
Thus of every grief in heart
He with thee doth bear a part.
These are certain signs to know
Faithful friend from flattering foe.

THE PHŒNIX AND TURTLE.

Let the bird of loudest lay,
On the sole Arabian tree,
Herald sad and trumpet be,
To whose sound chaste wings obey.

But thou shrieking harbinger,
Foul precurrer of the fiend,
Augur of the fever's end,
To this troop come thou not near!

From this session interdict
Every fowl of tyrant wing,
Save the eagle, feather'd king:
Keep the obsequy so strict.

Let the priest in surplice white,
That defunctive music can,
Be the death-divining swan,
Lest the requiem lack his right.

And thou treble-dated crow,
That thy sable gender mak'st
With the breath thou giv'st and tak'st,
'Mongst our mourners shalt thou go.

Here the anthem doth commence: —
Love and constancy is dead;
Phœnix and the turtle fled
In a mutual flame from hence.

So they lov'd, as love in twain
Had the essence but in one;
Two distincts, division none:
Number there in love was slain.

Hearts remote, yet not asunder;
Distance, and no space was seen
'Twixt this turtle and his queen:
But in them it were a wonder.

So between them love did shine,
That the turtle saw his right
Flaming in the phœnix' sight;
Either was the other's mine.

Property was thus appall'd,
That the self was not the same;
Single nature's double name
Neither two nor one was call'd.

Reason, in itself confounded,
Saw division grow together,
To themselves yet either neither,
Simple were so well compounded;

That it cried, How true a twain
Seemeth this concordant one!
Love hath reason, reason none,
If what parts can so remain.

Whereupon it made this threne
To the phœnix and the dove,
Co-supremes and stars of love,
As chorus to their tragic scene.

THRENOS.

Beauty, truth, and rarity,
Grace in all simplicity,
Here enclos'd in cinders lie.

Death is now the phœnix' nest;
And the turtle's loyal breast
To eternity doth rest;

Leaving no posterity: —
'Twas not their infirmity,
It was married chastity.

Truth may seem, but cannot be;
Beauty brag, but 'tis not she;
Truth and beauty buried be.

To this urn let those repair
That are either true or fair;
For these dead birds sigh a prayer.

THE LIFE

OF

WILLIAM SHAKESPEARE.

On the 23d April 1564 occurred the most important event, perhaps, in the literary history of the world — the birth of the great English dramatist — of the immortal Shakespeare. He was born in the pleasant town of Stratford-upon-Avon in Warwickshire. His father, by trade a glover, and not, as has been erroneously asserted, either a dealer in wool, or a butcher, (the absurd fiction related by Aubrey that our dramatist himself exercised the latter trade scarcely merits allusion,) was born near Stratford about the year 1530: and is supposed to have been the son of Richard Shakespeare, farmer, who tenanted a house and land belonging to Robert Arden, a small, but respectable land-proprietor of Wilmecote in the parish of Aston Cantlowe, not far from Stratford. To Mary, seventh daughter of the above Robert Arden, John Shakespeare was married. She inherited from her father, besides a sum in money, a small estate in fee, in the parish of Aston Cantlowe, called Asbyes, consisting of a messuage, fifty acres of arable land, six acres of meadow and pasture, and a right of common for all kinds of cattle. This simple pair, become in our times so interesting when we are contemplating the almost miraculous genius, and wide-spread fame of their illustrious offspring, were married in the year 1557; and we are justified in thinking that the bridegroom's affairs were sufficiently prosperous to warrant his union with the youngest of seven co-heiresses. The Ardens were an ancient and considerable family in Warwickshire, who derived their name from the forest of Arden in or near which they had possessions. One

30*

of them Sir John Arden, the brother of Mary's great-grand-
father, had been esquire of the body to Henry VII., who had
bountifully rewarded his services and fidelity. Many Shakespeares were resident at an early date in different parts of
Warwickshire, as well as in some of the adjoining counties;
the name however was very differently written: we find Shakspere, Shakespere, Shakespeyre, Shaxper, Chacsper, Shakespeare and Shakspeare; the first was written by the great
dramatist himself in a volume of a translation of Montaigne's
essays known to have belonged to him, and now in the British
Museum; the last is the manner in which he signed his final
testament.

The first fruit of the union of John Shakespeare and Mary
Arden was a daughter, baptized by the name of Joan, on the
15th Sept. 1558. She died in early infancy. The second child
Margaret, was baptized on the 2d Dec. 1562, and died in the
following April. Our great dramatist was born therefore a
year after, and the memorandum of his baptism in the church
register is precisely in the following form: —

"1564 April 26. Gulielmus filius Johannes[sic]Shakspere."
So that whoever kept the book either committed a common
clerical error or was no great proficient in the rules of gram-
mar. He was baptized therefore three days after he was born,
for it was at that period the custom to carry infants very early
to the font. A house is still pointed out in Henley-street, as
that in which William Shakespeare first saw the light, and in
this street, his father was owner of a copyhold dwelling. His
two sisters having died before his birth, William became the
eldest child of his parents, and in the course of time his mother
bore to her husband five more children. Gilbert born in 1566.
Joan in 1569. Anne in 1571, who died at an early age, being
buried in 1579. Richard in 1573 and Edmund born in the
spring of 1580. While William Shakespeare was yet in extreme
infancy, a malignant fever denominated the plague, broke out
at Stratford, he was but two months old when it made its appearance; it does not appear to have reached any member of
John Shakespeare's family, we mention it therefore merely to

notice that on this calamitous visitation he contributed one shilling to the relief of the poor, showing that at this date he was in moderate and probably comfortable, though not in affluent circumstances, and we are warranted in concluding that he was then an industrious and thriving tradesman. At the time of his marriage he was probably a member of the corporation of Stratford; in 1558 he was appointed one of the four constables, and soon after he was chosen one of four persons, called affeerors, whose duty it was to impose fines on their fellow-townsmen for offences against the bye-laws of the borough. He continued to advance in rank and importance in the corporation, and was elected one of the fourteen aldermen of Stratford on the 4th July 1565, and rather more than three years afterwards the father of our poet was chosen bailiff, when his son William was four years and a half old. This was the highest distinction in the power of his fellow-townsmen to bestow, yet although he had risen to a station so respectable, and was at the same time a magistrate, his name being in the commission of the peace, he was not able to write. There was however nothing remarkable in this inability, for in 1565 when one John Wheler was called by nineteen aldermen and burgesses to undertake the duties of bailiff, John Shakespeare was among twelve other marksmen, including the then bailiff, and the "head alderman." The simple Mary Arden too could not boast of a more accomplished education than her husband, for it is recorded that she also was unable to pen her name.

In 1570 when William Shakespeare was in his seventh year, his father rented a meadow two miles from Stratford; the annual payment was £ 8, a considerable sum, certainly, for that time; and in 1575 he bought two freehold houses, with orchards and gardens, in Henley-street for £ 40. To one of these he is supposed to have removed his family; but for aught we know he had lived from the time of his marriage and continued to live in 1574 in the copyhold in Henley-street, which had been alienated to him eighteen years before.

It is indisputable, we apprehend, that soon after this date the tide of John Shakespeare's affairs began to turn, and that he experienced disappointments and losses which seriously affected his pecuniary circumstances. At a borough hall on the 29th Jan. 1577-8 it was ordered that every alderman in Stratford should pay 6 s. 8 d., and every burgess 3 s. 4 d. towards "the furniture of three pikemen, two billmen, and one archer." Now although John Shakespeare was not only an alderman, but had been chosen "head alderman" in 1571, he was allowed to contribute only 3 s. 4 d., as if he had been merely a burgess. In November, 1578, when every alderman was required to "pay weekly to the relief of the poor 4 d.," John Shakespeare and another were excepted. Other proofs might be added to these. In the same year he mortgaged his wife's estate, called Asbyes, for £ 40. But the most striking confirmation of his embarrassments about this date is that he parted with his wife's interest in two tenements in Snitterfield for the small sum of £ 4. Another point worthy of notice in this newly-discovered document — the deed of sale of his wife's property, is, that he is termed "yeoman," and not *glover:* perhaps in 1579, although he continued to occupy a house in Stratford, he had relinquished his original trade, and having embarked in agricultural pursuits, to which he had not been educated, had been unsuccessful. This may appear not an unnatural mode of accounting for some of his difficulties.

At the period of the sale of their Snitterfield property by his father and mother, William Shakespeare was in his sixteenth year, and in what way he had been educated is mere matter of conjecture. It is highly probable that he was at the free-school of Stratford, founded in the reign of Edward IV., and subsequently chartered by Edward VI. We know nothing of the time when he might first have been sent thither; but if so sent between 1570 and 1578, Walter Roche, Thomas Hunt, and Thomas Jenkins, were successively masters, and from them he must have derived the rudiments of his Latin and Greek. That his father and mother could give him no instruction of the kind is quite certain from the proof we have adduced that neither of them could write; but this very deficiency might render them more desirous that their eldest son, at least, if not their children in general, should receive the best education circumstances would allow. The free grammar-school of Stratford afforded an opportunity of which, it is not unlikely, the parents of William Shakespeare availed themselves.

As we are ignorant of the time when he went to school, we are also in the dark as to the period when he left it. Rowe, indeed, has told us that the poverty of John Shakespeare, and the necessity of employing his son profitably at home, induced him to withdraw him, at an early age, from the place of instruction. But the education of the son of a member of the corporation would cost nothing; so that, if the boy were removed from school at the period of his father's embarrassments, the expense of continuing his studies there could not have entered into the calculation: he must have been taken away, as Rowe states, to aid his father in the maintenance of his family; and we are without the power of confirming or contradicting his statement.

Aubrey has asserted positively, that "in his younger years Shakespeare had been a schoolmaster in the country;" and the truth may be, that being a young man of abilities, and rapid in the acquisition of knowledge, he had been employed by Jenkins (the master of the school from 1577 to 1580) to aid him in the instruction of the junior boys.

We decidedly concur with Malone in thinking, that after Shakespeare quitted the free-school, he was employed in the office of an attorney. Proofs of something like a legal education are to be found in many of his plays; they do not occur anything like so frequently in the dramatic productions of his contemporaries. We doubt if, in the whole works of Marlowe, Greene, Peele, Jonson, Heywood, Chapman, Marston, Dekker, and Webster, so many law terms and allusions are to be found, as in only six or eight plays by Shakespeare; and these applied with much technical exactness and propriety. We may presume that, if so employed, he was paid something for his services; for, if he were to earn nothing, his father could have had no motive for taking him from school. Supposing him to have ceased to receive instruction from Jenkins in 1579, when his father's distresses were apparently most severe, we may easily imagine that he was, for the next year or two, in the office of one of the seven attorneys of Stratford. That he wrote a good hand we are perfectly sure, not only from the extant specimens of his signature, when in health, but from the ridicule which, in "Hamlet," (Act V. sc. II) he throws upon such as affected to write illegibly

"I once did hold it, as our statists do,
A baseness to write fair."

In truth, many of his dramatic contemporaries wrote excellently; Ben Jonson's penmanship was beautiful.

It is certain also that Shakespeare wrote with great facility, and that his compositions required little correction. This fact we have on the indubitable assertion of Ben Jonson, who thus speaks in his "Discoveries," written in old age, when as he tells us, his memory began to fail, and printed in 1641: — "I remember the players have often mentioned it as an honour to Shakespeare, that in his writing (whatsoever he penned) he never blotted out line. My answer hath been, Would he had blotted a thousand! which they thought a malevolent speech. I had not told posterity this, but for their ignorance, who chuse that circumstance to commend their friend by, wherein he most faulted; and so justify mine own candour, for I loved the man, and do honour his memory (on this side idolatry) as much as any. He was indeed honest, and of an open and free nature; had an excellent fancy, brave notions, and gentle expressions, wherein he flowed with that facility, that sometimes it was necessary he should be stopped. His wit was in his own power, would the use of it had been so too! But he redeemed his vices with his virtues: there was ever more in him to be praised than to be pardoned."

Excepting from mere tradition, we hear not a syllable regarding William Shakespeare from the time of his birth until he had considerably passed his eighteenth year, and then we suddenly come to one of the most important events of his life, established on irrefragable testimony: we allude to his marriage with Anne Hathaway, which could not have taken place before the 28th Nov. 1582, because on that day two persons, entered into a preliminary bond, in the penalty of £40 to be forfeited to the bishop of the diocese of Worcester, if it were thereafter found that there existed any lawful impediment to the solemnization of matrimony between William Shakespeare and Anne Hathaway, of Stratford. The object was to obtain such a dispensation from the bishop of Worcester as would authorise a clergyman to unite the bride and groom after only a single publication of the banns; and it is not to be concealed, or denied, that the whole proceeding seems to indicate haste and secrecy. The seal used when the bond was executed, has upon it the initials R. H., as if it had belonged to R. Hathaway, the father of the bride, who had thus it would seem given his consent to the union, and who, Rowe tells us, was "said to have been a substantial yeoman." It is not known at what church the ceremony was performed, but certainly not a Stratford-upon-Avon, to which both the parties belonged, and where it would have been registered. A recent search in the registers of several of the churches in the neighbourhood of Stratford has not been attended with any success.

Considering all the circumstances, there might be good reasons why the father of Anne Hathaway should concur in the alliance. The first child of William and Anne Shakespeare was christened Susanna on the 26th May, 1583, and the baptismal register stands thus: —

"1583. May 26. Susanna daughter to William Shakspere."

Anne was between seven and eight years older than her young husband, and several passages in Shakespeare's plays seem to point directly at the evils resulting from unions in which the parties were "misgraffed in respect of years." The most remarkable of these is the well-known speech of the Duke to Viola, in "Twelfth Night," (Act II. sc. IV) where he says,

> "Let still the woman take
> An elder than herself; so wears she to him,
> So sways she level in her husband's heart:
> For, boy, however we do praise ourselves,
> Our fancies are more giddy and unfirm,

> More longing, wavering, sooner lost and won,
> Than women's are."

Afterwards the Duke adds,

> "Then, let thy love be younger than thyself,
> Or thy affection cannot hold the bent."

Whether these lines did or did not originate in the author's reflections on his own marriage, they are so applicable to his own case, that it seems impossible he should have written them without recalling the circumstances attending his hasty union, and the disparity of years between himself and his wife. It is incident to our nature that youths, just advancing to manhood, should feel with peculiar strength the attraction of women whose charms have reached the full-blown summer of beauty; but we cannot think it so necessary a consequence as some have supposed, that Anne Hathaway should have possessed peculiar personal advantages. It may be remarked that poets have often appeared comparatively indifferent to the features and persons of their mistresses, since in proportion to the strength of their imaginative faculty, they have been able to supply all physical deficiences.

The balance of such imperfect information as remains to us, leads us to the opinion that Shakespeare was not a very happy married man. The disparity of age between himself and his wife was such, that she could not "sway level in her husband's heart;" a difference which would become more apparent as they advanced in years. To this may be added the fact, that Shakespeare quitted his home at Stratford a very few years after he had become a husband and a father, and that although he revisited his native town frequently, and ultimately settled there with his family, there is no proof that his wife ever returned with him to London, or resided with him during any of his lengthened sojourns in the metropolis: yet it is very possible, nay very probable, that she may have done so; for in 1609 he certainly paid a weekly poor-rate to an amount that would indicate that he occupied a house in Southwark capable of receiving his family, but we are, here, as on many other points, compelled to deplore the absence of distinct testimony. The doubtful and ambig-

uous indications to be gleaned from his Sonnets contain little
to show that he was of a domestic turn, or that he found any
great enjoyment in the society of his wife. That such may
have been the fact we do not pretend to deny, and we believe
that much favourable evidence upon the point has been lost:
all we venture to advance on a question of so much difficulty
and delicacy is, that what remains to us is not, as far as it
goes, perfectly satisfactory.

In the beginning of 1585 Shakespeare's wife produced him
twins — a boy and a girl — and they were baptized at Stratford Church on the 2d Feb. in that year. The registration is,
of course, dated 2d Feb. 1584, as the year 1585 did not at that
date begin until after 25th March: it runs thus: —

> "1584. Feb. 2. Hamnet & Judeth sonne & daughter to
> Williā Shakspere."

It is a fact not altogether unimportant, with relation to the
terms of affection between Shakespeare and his wife in the
subsequent part of his career, that she brought him no more
children, although in 1585 she was only thirty years old.
Nevertheless, according to the Rev. Mr. Dyce, it is unfair
to conclude from certain passages in our author's plays, —
each of which passages more or less grows out of the in-
cidents of the play, — that he had cause to complain of
domestic unhappiness: indeed, without taking into account
the tradition of his regular visits to Stratford, we have strong
presumptive evidence to the contrary in the fact, that the
wife of his youth was the companion of his latest years,
when he had raised himself to opulence and to the position of
a gentleman.

That Shakespeare quitted his home and his family not long
afterwards has not been disputed, but no ground for this step
has ever been derived from domestic disagreements. It has
been alleged that he was obliged to leave Stratford on account
of a scrape in which he had involved himself by stealing, or
assisting in stealing, deer from the grounds of Charlecote, the
property of Sir Thomas Lucy, about five miles from the
borough. As Rowe is the oldest authority in print for this

story, we give it in his own words:—"He had, by a misfortune
common enough to young fellows, fallen into ill company; and
among them some, that made a frequent practice of deer-
stealing, engaged him more than once in robbing the park that
belonged to Sir Thomas Lucy of Charlecote, near Stratford.
For this he was prosecuted by that gentleman, as he thought,
somewhat too severely; and in order to revenge that ill-usage,
he made a ballad upon him. And though this, probably the
first essay of his poetry, be lost, yet it is said to have been so
very bitter, that it redoubled the prosecution against him to
that degree, that he was obliged to leave his business and
family in Warwickshire for some time, and shelter himself in
London." Malone produced a manuscript of uncertain date,
added by the Rev. R. Davies, who died in 1707, to the papers
of Fulman, which gives the incident a slight confirmation,
though the account is obviously exaggerated and distorted.
The terms are these:—"He (Shakespeare) was much given to
all unluckiness in stealing venison and rabbits, particularly
from Sir Lucy, who had him oft whipped and sometimes im-
prisoned, and at last made him fly his native country, to his
great advancement. But his revenge was so great that he is
his Justice Clodpate, and calls him a great man, and that, in
allusion to his name, bore three louses rampant for his arms."
Here we see that Davies calls Sir Thomas Lucy only "Sir
Lucy," as if he did not know his Christian name, and he was
ignorant that such a character as Justice Clodpate is not to be
found in any of Shakespeare's plays. According to Oldys:—
"A gentleman of the name of Jones, of Turbich in Worcester-
shire, died in 1703, at the age of ninety, and he remembered
to have heard, from several old people of Stratford, the story
of Shakespeare's robbing Sir Thomas Lucy's park; and they
added that the ballad had been affixed on the park-gate, as
an additional exasperation to the knight." Oldys preserved
a stanza of this satirical effusion, which he had received from
a relation of old Mr. Jones: it runs thus:—

> "A parliemente member, a justice of peace,
>   At home a poor scare-crowe, at London an asse;

If lowsie is Lucy, as some volke miscalle it,
Then Lucy is lowsie whatever befall it:
    He thinks himself greate,
    Yet an asse in his state
We allowe by his ears but with asses to mate.
    If Lucy is lowsie, as some volke miscalle it,
    Sing lewsie Lucy, whatever befall it."

What is called a "complete copy of the verses," contained in "Malone's Shakspeare, by Boswell," is evidently not genuine.

In reflecting upon the general probability or improbability of this important incident in Shakespeare's life, it is not to be forgotten, that deer-stealing, at the period referred to, was by no means an uncommon offence. Neither was it considered to include any moral stain, but was often committed by young men, by way of frolic, for the purpose of furnishing a feast, and not with any view to sale or emolument. If Shakespeare even ran into such an indiscretion, (and we own, that we cannot entirely discredit the story) he did no more than many of his contemporaries; and one of the ablest, most learned, and bitterest enemies of theatrical performances, Dr. John Rainolds, who wrote just before the close of the sixteenth century, expressly mentions deer-stealing as a venial crime of which unruly and misguided youth was sometimes guilty, and he couples it merely with carousing in taverns and robbing orchards. It is very possible, therefore, that the main offence against Sir Thomas Lucy was, not stealing his deer, but writing the ballad, and sticking it on his gate. Sir Thomas Lucy died in 1600, and the mention of deer-stealing, and of the "dozen white luces" by Slender, and of the "dozen white louses" by Sir Hugh Evans, in the opening of "The Merry Wives of Windsor," seems too obvious to be mistaken. True it is, that the coat of arms of Sir Thomas Lucy contained only "three luces (pike-fishes) hariant, argent;" but it is easy to imagine, that while Shakespeare would wish the ridicule to be understood and felt by the knight and his friends, he might not desire that it should be too generally intelligible, and therefore multiplied the luces to "a dozen." We believe that "The Merry Wives of Windsor" was written before the demise

of the Sir Thomas Lucy, whose indignation Shakespeare had
incurred, among other reasons, because we are convinced that
our great dramatist was too generous in his nature to have
carried his resentment beyond the grave, and to have cast
ridicule upon a dead adversary, whatever might have been
his sufferings while he was a living one.

The question whether he did or did not quit Stratford for
the metropolis on this account, is one of much importance in
the poet's history, but it is one also upon which we shall, in
all probability, never arrive at certainty. The traditions may
be founded upon an actual occurrence, but it is very possible
that that alone did not determine Shakespeare's line of conduct. His residence in Stratford may have been rendered in-
convenient by the near neighbourhood of such a hostile and
powerful magistrate, but perhaps he would nevertheless not
have quitted the town, had not other circumstances combined
to produce such a decision. What those circumstances might
be we proceed now to consider.

Aubrey, who was a very curious and minute investigator,
although undeniably too credulous, mentions not a word about
deer-stealing, but he tells us that Shakespeare was "inclined
naturally to poetry and acting," and to this inclination he
attributes his journey to London at an early age. That this
youthful propensity existed there can be no dispute, and it is
easy to trace how it may have been promoted and streng-
thened. The corporation of Stratford seem to have given
great encouragement to companies of players arriving there.
We know that when itinerant actors came to any considerable
town, it was their custom to wait upon the mayor, bailiff, or
other head of the corporation, in order to ask permission to
perform, either in the town-hall, or if that could not be granted
to them, elsewhere. It so happens that the earliest record of
the representation of any plays in Stratford-upon-Avon, is
dated in 1569, the year John Shakespeare was bailiff, when
the "Queen's Players" received 9 s. out of the corporate funds.
It is to be remarked also, that several of the players with
whom Shakespeare was afterwards connected, appear to have

come originally from Stratford or its neighbourhood. We may mention the names of Burbage, Slye, Heminge, and Thomas Greene, the last indisputably of Stratford; these names are familiar to all who are acquainted with the detailed history of our stage at that period.

The frequent performances of various associations of actors in Stratford and elsewhere, and the taste for theatricals thereby produced, may have had the effect of drawing not a few young men in Warwickshire from their homes, to follow the attractive and profitable profession; and such may have been the case with Shakespeare, without supposing that domestic differences arising out of disparity of age or any other cause, influenced his determination, or that he was driven away by the terrors of Sir Thomas Lucy. Moreover the sudden increase a year or two before to his little family may have stimulated his youthful and ardent mind with the desire of augmenting the means of sustaining objects so dear to him, and thus induced him to seek to transfer to a more enlarged field, and to an ampler stage those talents and that genius of which he must surely at this time have been in some degree conscious. May not some too of the great actors of the day in these their occasional visits to his native town, themselves men of consummate skill and nice discrimination, may not *they* have discovered, appreciated and aroused the embryo wit and dramatist, even though he remained himself unconscious of his dormant powers. Such a presumption seems justified by and naturally to arise from the consideration of all the circumstances, and enables us without seeking other less probable causes, to account simply and rationally for Shakespeare's first visit to London.

It has been matter of speculation, whether Shakespeare visited Kenilworth Castle, when Queen Elizabeth was entertained there by the Earl of Leicester in 1575, and whether the pomp and pageantry he then witnessed did not give a colour to his mind and a direction to his pursuits. Considering that he was then only in his eleventh year, we own, that we cannot believe he found his way into that gorgeous and august as-

sembly. Kenilworth was fourteen miles distant: John Shakespeare, although he had been bailiff, and was still head-alder-
man of Stratford, was not a man of sufficient rank and importance to be there in any official capacity; and he probably
had not means to equip himself and his son for such an expedition. It may be very well as a matter of fancy to indulge
such a notion, but as it seems to us, every reasonable probability is against it. That Shakespeare heard of the extensive
preparations, and of the magnificent entertainment, there can
be no doubt: it was an event calculated to create a strong
sensation in the whole of that part of the country; and if the
celebrated passage in "A Midsummer Night's Dream" (Act II.
sc. 1), had any reference to it, it did not require that Shakespeare should have been present in order to have written it,
especially, when, if necessary, he had Gascoyne's "Princely
Pleasures of Kenilworth" and Laneham's "Letter" to assist
his memory.

In reference to the period when our great dramatist aban-
doned his native town for London, we think that sufficient
attention has not been paid to an important incident in the
life of his father. From the tenor of an entry in the records
of the borough, it seems quite evident that John Shakespeare
was deprived of his gown as Alderman of Stratford in the
autumn of 1586. On the 6th Sept. of that year the following
memorandum was made in the register by the town clerk: —

"At thys halle William Smythe and Richard Courte are
chosen to be aldermen in the places of John Wheler and John
Shaxpere; for that Mr. Wheler dothe desyre to be put owt of
the companye, and Mr. Shaxpere dothe not come to the halles
when they be warned, nor hathe not done of longe tyme."

We must presume, that John Shakespeare was not a con-
senting, or at all events, not a willing, party to this proceeding;
for, had he desired his removal, we should no doubt have been
told so. Malone ascertained from an inspection of the ancient
books of the borough, that he had ceased to attend the halls
when "warned" from the year 1579 downwards. That is the
same year when being so distressed for money, he disposed

of his wife's small property in Snitterfield. It will not fail,
therefore, to be remarked that the two events, Shakespeare's
departure for London, and his father's removal from the office
of alderman seem to have been coincident. Malone "supposed" that our great poet left Stratford "about the year 1586
or 1587," but it seems to us more likely that the event hap-
pened in the former year. His twins, Hamnet and Judith
were baptized in February 1585, and his father did not cease
to be an alderman until a year and seven months afterwards.
The fact, that his son had become a player, may have had
something to do with the lower rank his brethren of the bench
thought he ought to hold in the corporation; or the resolution
of the son to abandon his home may have arisen out of the
degradation of the father in his native town; but we cannot
help thinking that the two circumstances were in some way
connected, and that the period of the departure of William
Shakespeare to seek his fortune in a company of players in
the metropolis, may be fixed in the latter end of 1586.

Nevertheless, we do not hear of him in London until three
years afterwards, when we find him a sharer in the Blackfriars
theatre. It had been constructed upon the site of the dissolved
monastery, beyond the jurisdiction of the lord mayor and corporation of London, who had always evinced decided hostility
to dramatic representations. The undertaking seems to have
been prosperous from the beginning; and in 1589 no fewer
than sixteen performers were sharers in it, including, besides
Shakespeare and Burbage, Thomas Greene of Stratford-upon-
Avon, and Nicholas Tooley, also a Warwickshire man. In
1589 some general complaints were made, that improper
matters had been introduced into plays; one company having
brought Martin Marprelate upon the stage in a manner to
give offence to the Puritans; so that two bodies of players
were ordered to desist from all performances. The silencing
of other associations was probably beneficial to that exhibiting
at Blackfriars, and if no proceeding of any kind had been
instituted against James Burbage and his partners, we may
presume that they would have continued quietly to reap their

augmented harvest. We are led to infer, however, that they
also apprehended, and experienced, some measure of restraint,
and feeling conscious that they had given no just ground of
offence, they transmitted to the privy council a sort of certificate of their good conduct, asserting that they had never
introduced into their representations matters of state or religion, and that no complaint of that kind had ever been pre-
ferred against them. This certificate passed into the hands
of Lord Ellesmere, then attorney-general, and it has been
preserved among his papers. Here we see that Shakespeare's name stands twelfth in the enumeration of the
members of the company; but we do not rest much on the
succession in which they are inserted, because among the
four names which follow that of our great dramatist are
certainly two performers, one of them of the highest reputation, and the other of long standing in the profession.
In this document too we see the important fact, as regards
the biography of Shakespeare, that in 1589 he was, not only
an actor but a sharer in the undertaking at Blackfriars. The
position of his name in the list may seem to show that, even
in 1589, he was a person of considerable importance in relation to the success of the sharers in Blackfriars. In November,
1589, he was in the middle of his twenty-sixth year, and in
the full strength, if not in the highest maturity, of his mental
and bodily powers.

We can have no hesitation in believing that he originally
came to London, in order to obtain his livelihood by the stage,
and with no other view. Aubrey tells us that he was "inclined
naturally to poetry and acting;" and the poverty of his father,
and the difficulty of obtaining profitable employment in the
country for the maintenance of his family, without other
motives, may have induced him readily to give way to that
inclination. Aubrey, who had probably taken due means to
inform himself, adds, that "he did act exceedingly well;" and
we are convinced that the opinion, founded chiefly upon a
statement by Rowe, that Shakespeare was a very moderate
performer, is erroneous. It seems likely that for two or three

years he employed himself chiefly in the more active duties of the profession he had chosen; for, at that time, Peele, a very practised and popular play-wright, was a member of the company; but there is reason to think that Peele did not continue one of the Lord Chamberlain's players after 1590. While Peele remained a member of the company, Shakespeare's services as a dramatist may not materially have interfered with his exertions as an actor; but afterwards when Peele had joined a rival establishment, he may have been much more frequently called upon to employ his pen, and then his value in that department becoming clearly understood, he was less frequently a performer. He was, doubtless, soon busily and profitably engaged as a dramatist; and this remark on the rareness of his appearance on the stage will of course apply more strongly in his after-life, when he produced one or more dramas every year.

"His name is printed, as the custom was in those times, amongst those of the other players, before some old plays, but without any particular account of what sort of parts he used to play; and though I have inquired, I never could meet with any further account of him this way, than that the top of his performance was the Ghost in his own 'Hamlet.' " — Rowe's Life. Shakespeare's name stands first among the players of "Every Man in his Humour," and fifth among those of "Sejanus."

His instructions to the players in "Hamlet" have often been noticed as establishing that he was admirably acquainted with the theory of the art; and if, as Rowe asserts, he only took the short part of the Ghost in this tragedy, we are to recollect that even if he had considered himself competent to it, the study of such a character as Hamlet (the longest on the stage as it is now acted, and still longer as originally written) must have consumed more time than he could well afford to bestow upon it, especially when we call to mind that there was a member of the company who had hitherto represented most of the heroes, and whose excellence was as undoubted, as his popularity was extraordinary. To Richard Burbage was therefore assigned the arduous character of the Prince, while the author took the brief, but important part of the Ghost, which required person, deportment, judgment, and voice, with a delivery distinct, solemn, and impressive; and if this part is badly represented, the whole drama, based upon the terrible, irresistible truth of this vision, falls to the ground. We may affirm, therefore, that all the elements of a good and great actor are needed for the due performance of "the buried majesty of Denmark."

It is impossible to determine, almost impossible to guess what Shakespeare had or had not written in 1589. That he had chiefly employed his pen in the revival, alteration, and improvement of existing dramas we are strongly disposed to believe, but that he had not ventured upon original composition it would be much too bold to assert. We have every reason to think that some of the plays, upon which he was employed, were not by any means entirely his own, we allude to the three parts of "Henry VI." The "Comedy of Errors" we take to be one of the pieces, which, having been first written by an inferior dramatist, was heightened and amended by Shakespeare, perhaps about the date of which we are now speaking, and "Love's Labour's Lost," or "The Two Gentlemen of Verona," may have been original compositions brought upon the stage prior to 1590. We also consider it more than probable that "Titus Andronicus" belongs even to an earlier period; but we feel convinced, that although Shakespeare had by this time given indications of powers superior to those of any of his rivals he could not have written any of his greater works until some years afterwards. With regard to productions unconnected with the stage, there are several pieces among his scattered poems, and some of his sonnets, that indisputably belong to an early part of his life. Francis Meres tells us in 1598 that "Shakespeare's sugar'd sonnets were handed about among his private friends, many years before they were printed." A young man, so gifted, would not, and could not, wait until he was five or six and twenty before he made considerable and most successful attempts at poetical composition; and we feel morally certain that "Venus and Adonis" was in being anterior to Shakespeare's quitting Stratford. It bears all the marks of youthful vigour, of strong passion, of luxuriant imagination, together with a force and originality of expression which betoken the first efforts of a great mind, not always well regulated in its taste: it seems to have been written in the open air of a fine country like Warwickshire, possessing all the freshness of the recent impression of natural objects; and we will go so far as to say, that we do not think even Shakespeare himself could have produced it, in the form it bears, after he had reached the age of forty. It was quite new in its class, being founded upon no model, either ancient or modern: nothing like it had been attempted before, and nothing comparable to it was produced afterwards. Thus in 1593 he might call it, in the dedication to Lord Southampton, "the first heir of his invention" in a double sense, not merely because it was the first printed, but because it was the first written of his productions.

The information we now possess enables us at once to reject the story, that Shakespeare's earliest employment at a theatre was holding the horses of noblemen and gentlemen who visited it, and that he had under him a number of lads who were known as "Shakespeare's boys." Shiels in his "Lives of the Poets" was the first to give currency to this idle invention: it was repeated by Dr. Johnson, and has often been reiterated since; and we should hardly have thought it worth notice now, if it had not found a place in many modern accounts of our great dramatist. The company to which he attached himself had not unfrequently performed in Stratford; some of the chief members of it had come from his own part of the country, and even from the very town in which he was born; and he was not in a station of life, nor so destitute of means and friends, as to have been reduced to such an extremity.

Besides having written "Venus and Adonis" before he came to London, Shakespeare may also have composed its counterpart, "Lucrece", which first appeared in print in 1594.

It is in a different stanza, and in some respects in a different
style; and after he joined the Blackfriars company, the author
may possibly have added parts, (such, for instance, as the
long and minute description of the siege of Troy in the
tapestry) which indicate a closer acquaintance with the modes
and habits of society; but even here no knowledge is displayed that might not have been acquired in Warwickshire.
As he had exhibited the wantonness of lawless passion in
"Venus and Adonis," he followed it up by the exaltation of
matronlike chastity in "Lucrece;" and there is, we think,
nothing in the latter poem which a young man of one or two
and twenty, so endowed, might not have written. Neither
is it at all impossible that he had done something in connexion.
with the stage while he was yet a resident in his native town,
and before he had made up his mind to quit it. He may have
contributed temporary prologues or epilogues; he may have
inserted speeches and occasional passages in older plays: he
may even have assisted some of the companies in getting up,
and performing the dramas they represented in or near Stratford. We own that this conjecture appears at least plausible,
and the Lord Chamberlain's servants (known as the Earl of
Leicester's players until 1587) may have experienced his
utility in both departments, and may have held out strong in-
ducements to so promising a novice to continue his assistance
by accompanying them to London. Although in 1586 only
one company performed in Stratford, in the very next year
(that in which we have supposed Shakespeare to have become
a regular actor) five companies were entertained in the
borough: one of these consisted of the players of the Earl of
Leicester, to whom the Blackfriars theatre belonged; and it
is very possible that Shakespeare at that date exhibited before
his fellow-townsmen in his new professional capacity. Before
this time his performances may have been merely of an
amateur description. What we have here said seems a natural
and an easy way of accounting for Shakespeare's station as a
sharer at the Blackfriars theatre in 1589, about three years
after we suppose him to have finally adopted the profession

of an actor, and to have come to London for the purpose of pursuing it.

We come now to the earliest known allusion to Shakespeare as a dramatist; and although his surname is not given, we apprehend there can be no hesitation in applying what is said to him: it is contained in Spenser's "Tears of the Muses," a poem printed in 1591. The application of the passage to Shakespeare has been much contested, but the difficulty in our mind is, how the lines are to be explained by reference to any other dramatist of the time, even supposing, as we believe, that our great poet was at this period only rising into notice as a writer for the stage. The lines are these: —

> "And he, the man whom Nature selfe had made
> To mock herselfe, and truth to imitate
> With kindly counter under mimick shade,
> Our pleasant Willy, ah! is dead of late:
> With whom all joy and jolly meriment
> Is also deaded and in dolour drent.
>
> "In stead thereof, scoffing scurrilitie,
> And scornfull follie, with contempt, is crept,
> Rolling in rymes of shameles ribaudrie,
> Without regard or due decorum kept:
> Each idle wit at will presumes to make,
> And doth the learned's taske vpon him take.
>
> "But that same gentle spirit, from whose pen
> Large streames of honnie and sweete nectar flowe,
> Scorning the boldnes of such base-borne men,
> Which dare their follies forth so rashlie throwe,
> Doth rather choose to sit in idle cell
> Than so himselfe to mockerie to sell."

The most striking of these lines, with reference to our present inquiry, is the first: Willy was "dead" as far as regarded the admirable dramatic talents he had already displayed, which had enabled him, even before 1591, to outstrip all living rivalry, and to afford the most certain indications of the still greater things Spenser saw he would accomplish: he was "dead," because he

> "Doth rather choose to sit in idle cell
> Than so himselfe to mockerie to sell."

It is to be borne in mind that these stanzas are put into
the mouth of Thalia, whose lamentation on the degeneracy
of the stage, especially in comedy, follows those of Calliope
and Melpomene. We are persuaded that Shakespeare, early
in his theatrical life, must have written much, in the way
of revivals, alterations, or joint productions with other
poets, which has been for ever lost. We believe that he
was concerned in "The Yorkshire Tragedy," and that he
may have contributed some parts of "Arden of Feversham;"
but we do not think he aided Fletcher in writing "The Two
Noble Kinsmen," and there is not a single passage in "The
Birth of Merlin" worthy of his most careless moments. "The
first part of Sir John Oldcastle," and several other supposi-
tious dramas in the folio of 1664, which would have done little
credit to Shakespeare, have been ascertained to be the works
of other dramatists. We conclude, that none of his greatest
original dramatic productions had yet come from his pen; but
if in 1591 he had only brought out "The Two Gentlemen of
Verona" and "Love's Labour's Lost," they are so infinitely
superior to the best works of his predecessors, that the justice
of the tribute paid by Spenser to his genius would at once be
admitted. If before 1591 he had not accomplished all he was
capable of, he had given the clearest indications of high
genius, abundantly sufficient to justify the anticipation of
Spenser that he was a man

> — "whom Nature selfe had made
> To mock herselfe, and truth to imitate: "

a passage which in itself admirably comprises, and compresses
nearly all the excellences of which dramatic poetry is susceptible — the mockery of nature, and the imitation of truth.

Another point is, that Spenser, if not a Warwickshire man,
was at one time a resident in that county, and later in life
may have become acquainted with Shakespeare, who was
eleven years younger; and the author of "The Tears of the
Muses," at the age of thirty-seven, may have paid a merited
tribute to his young friend of twenty-six, and we may be for-

given for clinging to the conjecture that the greatest romantic poet of this country was on terms of friendship with the greatest dramatist of the world. This circumstance may appear to give new point, and a more certain application to the well-remembered lines in "A Midsummer Night's Dream," (Act V. sc. 1) in which Shakespeare has been supposed to refer to the death of Spenser, and which may have been a subsequent insertion, for the sake of repaying by one poet a debt of gratitude to the other.

The silence of Shakespeare referred to by Spenser may have been caused by the general inhibition of theatrical performances about this time. In the autumn of 1592 the plague broke out in London, and the players were thus prevented from acting in the metropolis. It was at this juncture, probably, if indeed he ever were in that country, that Shakespeare visited Italy. External evidence there is none, not even a tradition of such a journey has descended to us. The internal evidence, in our estimation, is by no means strong, and we think that if he had travelled to Venice, Verona, or Florence, we should have had more distinct and positive testimony of the fact in his works than can be adduced from them. Although we do not believe he ever was in Italy, we admit we are without evidence to prove a negative; he may have gone there without having left behind him any distinct record of the fact.

During the prevalence of the infectious malady of 1592, died one of the most notorious and distinguished of the literary men of the time, — Robert Greene. He left behind him a work, published a few months afterwards by Chettle, a fellow dramatist, under the title of "A Groatsworth of Wit, bought with a Million of Repentance," and preceded by an address "To those who spend their wits in making plays." Here we meet with the second notice of Shakespeare, and it is necessary to observe that Greene is urging the play-writers to break off all connexion with the players: — Base-minded men, if by my misery ye be not warned; for unto none of you, like me, sought those burs to cleave; those puppets, I mean, that speak from our mouths, those anticks garnished in our colours. Yes, trust them not; for there is an upstart crow, beautified with our feathers, that with his *Tiger's heart wrapp'd in a player's hide*, supposes he is as well able to bombast out a blank-verse, as the best of you: and being an absolute *Johannes Fac-totum*, is, in his own conceit, the only Shake-scene in a country. Let these apes imitate your past excellence, and never more acquaint them with your admired inventions.

Hence it is evident that Shakespeare, in 1592, had established such a reputation, and was so important a rival of the dramatists, who, until he came forward, had kept undisputed possession of the stage, as to excite their envy and enmity. It also proves that our great poet possessed such variety of talent, that, for the purposes of the company of which he was a member, he could do anything he was called on to perform; he was an actor, a writer of original plays, an adopter and improver of those already in existence, and no doubt contributed prologues or epilogues, and inserted scenes, speeches, or passages on any temporary emergency. Shakespeare took offence at this gross and public attack, and Chettle offered all the amends in his power — an apology. "The other (Shakespeare) whom I did not so much spare as since I wish I had, for I might have used my own discretion (the author being dead), that I did not I am as sorry as if the original fault had been my fault; because myself have seen his demeanour no less civil, than he is excellent in the quality he professes: besides, divers of worship have reported his uprightness of dealing, which argues his honesty, and his facetious grace in writing, that approves his art." In this apology one of the most noticeable points, is the tribute paid to our great dramatist's abilities as an actor, the word "quality" was applied, at that date, peculiarly and technically to acting; and the amends made for this envious assault shows most decisively the high opinion entertained of him, towards the close of 1592, as an actor, an author, and a man.

More than ten years afterwards, Chettle paid another tribute to our great dramatist, in his "England's Mourning Garment," where after reproaching the leading poets of the day, for not writing in honour of Queen Elizabeth, who was just dead, he thus addresses Shakespeare: —

> "Nor doth the silver-tongèd Melicert
> Drop from his honied Muse one sable teare
> To mourne her death that gracèd his desert,
> And to his laies opend her royall earo.
> Shepheard, remember our Elizabeth,
> And sing her Rape done by that Tarquin, Death."

This passage is important, with reference to the royal encouragement given to Shakespeare, and the approbation of his plays at Court: Elizabeth had "graced his desert," and "open'd her royal ear" to "his lays."

Spenser in 1594 gave another proof of his admiration of our poet in "Colin Clout" in which he addresses him by the name of Ætion: —

> "And there, though last not least, is Ætion;
> A gentler shepheard may no where be found;
> Whose Muse, full of high thoughts' invention,
> Doth, like himselfe, heroically sound."

The epithet "gentle," at a later date, almost always accompanied the name of our great and amiable dramatist. The words "heroically sound" show that Shakespeare had somewhat changed the character of his compositions; Spenser before had applauded him for unrivalled talents in comedy: by the year 1594 our dramatist must have given some great and remarkable proofs of his genius, in a loftier strain of poetry than belongs to comedy; — he had, no doubt, produced one or more of his great historical plays, his "Richard II." and "Richard III.," both of which, however, together with "Romeo and Juliet," came first from the press in 1597.

A document has been lately discovered in the State Paper Office, being a return of the names of some inhabitants of Stratford-upon-Avon, and among them that of John Shakespeare "presented for not cominge monethlie to the church, according to her Majesties lawes." Hence it has been doubted whether John Shakespeare may not have been a Roman Catholic. Whether he were, or were not a member of the protestant reformed Church, it is not to be disputed that his children were all baptized at the ordinary and established place of wor-

ship in the parish. That his son William was educated, lived,
and died a protestant we have no doubt. In "Henry VIII."
(Act V. sc. IV) a reference seems evidently made to the completion of the Reformation under our maiden queen in five
expressive words: —

> "In her days . . . .
> *God shall be truly known."*

We have already stated our distinct and deliberate opinion
that "Venus and Adonis" was written before its author left
his home in Warwickshire. He kept it by him for some years,
and it came first from the press in 1593, preceded by a dedication to the Earl of Southampton. Its popularity was great
and instantaneous, for a new edition was called for in 1594,
a third in 1596, a fourth in 1600, and a fifth in 1602, and there
were probably intervening impressions, which have disap-
peared among the popular and destroyed literature of the
time. We may conclude that this admirable and unequalled
production first introduced its author to the notice of Lord
Southampton; and it is evident from the opening of the dedication, that Shakespeare had not taken the precaution of
ascertaining, beforehand, the wishes of the young nobleman,
who was nine years his junior. We may be sure that this dedication was acceptable, and our poet followed it up by inscri-
bing to the same peer, but in a much more confident strain,
his "Lucrece" in the succeeding year. About the year 1600
the Earl of Southampton bestowed a most extraordinary proof
of his high-munificence on our author. It was not unusual,
at that time, for noblemen, to whom works were dedicated, to
make presents of money to the writers; but there is no instance upon record of such generous bounty, on an occasion
of the kind, as that of which we are now to speak. The Lord
Chamberlain's servants had entered upon the project of building the Globe theatre not very far to the west of the Southwark end of London Bridge. The building was completed
towards the spring of 1595 about the same time that, or soon
after "Lucrece" came out; and there is good reason to believe that the young and bountiful nobleman, having heard of

this enterprise from the peculiar interest he is known to have taken in all matters relating to the stage, and incited by warm admiration of the two poems, in the forefront of which he rejoiced to see his own name, presented Shakespeare with £1000., to enable him to make good the money he was to produce, as his proportion, for the completion of the Globe. We do not mean to say that our great dramatist needed the money, or that he could not have deposited it, as well as the other sharers in the Blackfriars; but Lord Southampton may not have thought it necessary to inquire, whether he did or did not want it. Although Shakespeare had not yet reached the climax of his excellence, he knew him to be the greatest dramatist this country had yet produced, and in the exercise of his bounty he measured the poet by his desert, and bestowed on him a sum worthy of his own title and character.

The Globe theatre was a round wooden building, open to the sky, while the stage was protected from the weather by an overhanging roof of thatch. At this period of our stage-history the performances usually began at three o'clock in the afternoon; for the citizens transacted their business and dined early. We may feel assured that the opening of a new theatre, larger than any in the town, was celebrated by the production of a new play. Considering his station and duties in the company and his popularity as a dramatist, we may be confident also that the new play was written by Shakespeare; but we are not, we frankly own, able to offer an opinion as to which play this was. In this theatre the performances were continued during the spring, summer, and autumn, while in the winter the company returned to the Blackfriars, which was enclosed, lighted from within, and comparatively warm. In consequence no doubt of their increased popularity, owing, we may readily imagine, in a great degree to the success of Shakespeare's plays, the company found the Blackfriars theatre too small for their audiences, and wished to repair and enlarge it. A remonstrance of certain of the inhabitants of the precinct was made against this enlargement; to which an answer was put in on the part of the actors. This answer is

a very valuable relic, as it gives the names of the players who
were proprietors of the theatre, and Shakespeare's name now,
in 1596, is fifth in a list of eight, while in 1589 it stood twelfth
in a list of sixteen.

Where Shakespeare had resided from the time when he
first came to London, until the period of which we are now
speaking, we have no information; but in July, 1596, he was
living in Southwark, perhaps to be close to the scene of action,
and to superintend the performances at the Globe, which were
continued through at least seven months of the year.

We have already mentioned that in 1578 John Shakespeare
and his wife, in order to relieve themselves from pecuniary
embarrassment, mortgaged the little estate of the latter, called
Asbyes, for £40. As it consisted of sixty acres of land, with
a dwelling-house, it must have been worth three times the
sum advanced; the mortgagers were again to be put in possession, if they repaid the money borrowed on or before
Michaelmas-day 1580. They tendered the £40., on the day
appointed, but it was refused, unless other monies, which they
owed to the mortgagee Edmund Lambert, were repaid at the
same time. He therefore died in possession of Asbyes, in
1586; and it descended to his eldest son; who held it still
in 1597. In order to recover this property John and Mary
Shakespeare, filed a bill in chancery, on the 24th Nov. 1597.
No trace of any decree having been pronounced has been preserved in the records of the Court of Chancery; the inference,
therefore, is that the suit was settled without coming to this
extremity. We can have little doubt that the bill had been
filed with the concurrence, and at the instance, of our great
dramatist, who at this date was rapidly acquiring wealth. He
knew that, during the last seventeen years, his father and
mother had been deprived of their right to Asbyes, and in all
probability his money was employed in order to commence
and prosecute the suit in chancery; we think, therefore, we
may conclude, that the heir John Lambert, finding he had no
chance of success, relinquished his claim, on payment of the
£40., and the other sums due to him. It seems too that the

Shakespeares did not again let it, but cultivated it themselves; for we have some new documentary evidence to produce, leading to the belief that our poet was at this time a land-owner, or at all events, a land-occupier, to some extent in the neighbourhood of Stratford-upon-Avon.

Aubrey informs us, that Shakespeare was "wont to go to his native country once a year." Nothing is more natural or probable, and that when he had acquired sufficient property he would be anxious to settle his family comfortably and independently in Stratford. We must suppose that his father and mother were mainly dependent upon him, notwithstanding the recovery of the little estate of Asbyes; and he may have employed his brother Gilbert, who was two years and a half younger than himself, and perhaps accustomed to agricultural pursuits, to look after his farming concerns in the country, while he himself was absent superintending his highly profitable theatrical undertakings in London. In 1597 our poet must have been in receipt of a considerable and increasing income: he was part proprietor of the Globe and Blackfriars theatres, both excellent speculations; he was an actor doubtless earning a good salary, and he was the most popular and applauded dramatic writer of the day. In the summer he might find leisure to visit his native town, and we may be tolerably sure that he was there in August, 1596, when he had the misfortune to lose his only son Hamnet, one of the twins born in the spring of 1585; the boy completed his eleventh year in February, 1596, so that his death must have been a very severe trial for his parents. The form of the entry of the burial in the register of the church of Stratford is as follows:—

"1596. August 11. Hamnet filius William Shakspere."

The dearth of provisions in England in the years 1596 and 1597 was so great, that the price of the bushel of wheat rose to thirteen shillings. The townspeople of Stratford "groaned with the wants they felt through the dearness of corn," and the malcontents went in great numbers to Sir Thomas Lucy to complain of the maltsters for engrossing it. Connected with this dearth, the Shakespeare society is in possession of a document of much value as regards the biography of our poet. It is thus headed: — "The noate of corne and malte, taken the 4th of February, in the 40th year of the raigne of our most gracious Soveraigne Ladie, Queen Elizabeth, &c." and in the margin opposite the title are the words "Stratforde Burroughe, Warwicke." It was prepared in order to ascertain how much corn and malt there really was in the town. The names and residences of the Townsmen are all given, so that we are enabled to prove in what part of Stratford the family of our great poet then dwelt; it was in Chapel-street Ward, and it appears that at this date William Shakespeare had ten quarters of corn in his possession. The name of John Shakespeare is not mentioned, so that the two old people, with some of their children, were probably living in the house of their son William. Ten quarters does not seem much more than would be needed for his own consumption; but it affords some proof of his means and substance at this date, that only two persons in Chapel-street Ward had a larger quantity in their hands. We are led to infer from this that our great dramatist was a cultivator of land, and that the wheat in his granary was grown on his mother's estate of Asbyes.

We must now return to London to advert to a passage in the life of Shakespeare, relating to the commencement of the connexion between him and Ben Jonson, which began with a remarkable piece of humanity and good-nature. Jonson, at that time altogether unknown to the world had offered one of his plays to the players, to have it acted, and they, into whose hands it was put, after having turned it carelessly and superciliously over, were just upon returning it to him with an ill-natured answer, that it would be of no service to their company, when Shakespeare, luckily, cast his eye upon it, and found something so well in it, as to engage him first to read it through, and afterwards to recommend it and its author to the public. Shakespeare was at this time thirty-four, and nothing could be more consistent with his amiable and generous character, than that he should have interested himself in favour of a writer, who was ten years his junior, and who gave such undoubted proofs of genius as are displayed in "Every Man in his Humour." Our great dramatist, established in public favour by such comedies as "The Merchant of Venice" and "A Midsummer Night's Dream," by such a tragedy as "Romeo and Juliet," and by such histories as "King John," "Richard II.," and "Richard III.," must have felt himself above all rivalry, and could well afford this act of "humanity and good-nature," on behalf of a young, needy, and meritorious author. The earliest enumeration of Shakespeare's dramas appeared in 1598 in a work by Francis Meres, in which we find these interesting passages : —

"As the soule of Euphorbus was thought to live in Pythagoras, so the sweete wittie soule of Ovid lives in mellifluous and hony-tongued Shakespeare; witnes his *Venus and Adonis*, his *Lucrece*, his sugred Sonnets among his private friends, &c."

"As *Plautus* and *Seneca* are accounted the best for comedy and tragedy among the Latines, so Shakespeare among the English is the most excellent in both kinds for the stage; for comedy, witnes his *Gentlemen of Verona*, his *Errors*, his *Love Labors Lost*, his *Love Labours Wonne*, his *Midsummers Night Dreame*, and his *Merchant of Venice*; for tragedy, his *Richard the 2., Richard the 3., Henry the 4., King John, Titus Andronicus*, and his *Romeo and Juliet*."

"As Epius Stolo said that the Muses would speake with Plautus tongue, if they would speak Latin, so I say that the Muses would speak with Shakespeares fine-filed phrase, if they would speak English."

It is a remarkable circumstance, evincing how completely the companies of actors were able to keep popular pieces from the press, that until Shakespeare had been a writer for his company eleven years, not a single play was by him published, and then the four first were printed without his name, as if the bookseller considered the omission would not affect the sale; and it is our conviction, after the most minute and patient examination of every old impression, that Shakespeare in no instance authorized the publication of his plays; he allowed mangled and deformed copies of his greatest works to be circulated for many years, and did not think it worth his while to expose the fraud, which remained, in many cases, undetected, until the appearance of the folio of 1623.

In the document we have produced, relating to the quantity of corn in Stratford, it is stated that Shakespeare's residence was in Chapel-street Ward: it was called "the great house," or "New Place." We thus find him, in the beginning of 1598, occupying one of the best houses, in one of the best parts of Stratford. He who had quitted his native town about twelve years before, poor and comparatively friendless, was able, by the profits of his own exertions, and the exercise of his own talents to return to it, and establish his family in more comfort and opulence, than they had ever before enjoyed. In this house tradition says Shakespeare planted a mulberry-tree, about the year 1609. This tree was in existence up to the year 1755; in the spring of 1742, Garrick was entertained under it by Sir Hugh Clopton. New Place remained in possession of Shakespeare's successors until the Restoration; it was then repurchased by the Clopton family: about 1752 it was sold to a clergyman of the name of Gastrell, who, on some offence taken at the authorities of the borough of Stratford on the subject of rating the house, pulled it down, and cut down the mulberry-tree.

The father of our great poet died in 1601, and was buried at Stratford-upon-Avon. Of the eight children which his wife, Mary Arden, had brought him, the following were then alive, William, Gilbert, Joan, Richard, and Edmund. The later years of John Shakespeare (who, it is supposed, was in his seventy-first year), were doubtless easy and comfortable, and the prosperity of his eldest son must have placed him beyond the reach of pecuniary difficulties.

Elizabeth, from the commencement of her reign, seems to have extended her personal patronage to the drama; scarcely a Christmas or Shrovetide passed, during the forty-five years she occupied the throne, when there were not dramatic entertainments at one of her palaces. The latest visit she paid to any of her nobility was to the Lord Keeper, Sir Thomas

Egerton, at Harefield, only nine or ten months before her death, and upon this occasion "Othello" (having been got up for her amusement) was represented before her, in August 1602. Burbage played the Moor of Venice. It is uncertain whether Shakespeare himself appeared in the piece. The proofs appear to be tolerably conclusive, that "Henry V.," "Twelfth Night," and "Hamlet" were written respectively in 1599, 1600, and 1601.

Ten days after James I. reached London he took the Lord Chamberlain's players into his pay and patronage, calling them "the King's servants," a title they always afterwards enjoyed. He issued a warrant, under the privy seal, for making out a patent under the great seal, authorizing them to perform in any part of the kingdom. In the list of nine actors named, Shakespeare's name now stands second; so that his progress upward in connexion with the profession had been gradual and uniform.

Having established his family in "New Place" in 1597, he seems to have contemplated considerable additions to his property there. In May 1602, he laid out £ 320 upon 107 acres of land, and attached it to his dwelling; in the autumn of the same year he became owner of a copyhold tenement, in Stratford, in 1603 he bought a messuage for £ 60, and in 1605 the lease of the great tithes for £ 440.

On the 5th June, 1607, his eldest daughter, Susanna, being then twenty-four years old, was married to Mr. John Hall of Stratford, physician. She died in 1649, aged 66. Elizabeth Hall, her daughter by Dr. Hall, and grand-daughter to our poet, was married in 1626, to Mr. Thomas Nash (who died in 1647), and in 1649, to Mr. John Bernard, of Abingdon, who was knighted after the Restoration. Lady Bernard died childless in 1670. She was the last of the lineal descendants of William Shakespeare.

In December 1607, six months after his daughter Susanna's marriage, he lost his brother Edmund, aged twenty-eight; and eight months later in September, 1608, his mother was borne to the tomb. It is most probable that he was present at his

mother's funeral, as we know him to have been in Stratford in
the following month. His brother Richard died in 1612. His
daughter Judith married in 1616 a Mr. Thomas Quiney, by
whom she had three sons, who all died unmarried.

The last time we hear of Shakespeare as an actor is in
1603 when he performed in Ben Jonson's Sejanus, soon after
which he retired from the stage, perhaps in 1604. In 1608
however he was still a sharer in the two theatres. In 1609, we
find from a document which has come down to us, that Shakespeare held four shares in the Blackfriars theatre valued at
that time at £ 133 6 s. 8 d. per annum: besides this he was
proprietor of the wardrobe valued at £ 500, this we may
presume he lent to the company for a certain consideration,
and ten per cent. seems a very low rate of payment; if taken
however at that sum, it would add £ 50 a year to the £ 133
6 s. 8 d. already mentioned, making £ 183 6 s. 8 d. a year, besides what our great dramatist gained by the profits of his pen.
Without including any thing on this account, and supposing
the Globe to have been as profitable as the Blackfriars, it is
evident that Shakespeare's income could hardly have been
less (taking every known source of emolument into view), than
£ 400 a year, a sum equal to £ 2000 a year at the present
time. From this period until 1612 we hear very little of our
dramatist, when it is probable that he retired permanently to
Stratford, having previously disposed of his theatrical property in London. Here, in his native town, he passed the rest
of his days in tranquil retirement, and in the enjoyment of
the society of his friends, whether residing in the country or
occasionally visiting him from the metropolis. "The latter
part of his life," says Rowe, "was spent, as all men of sense
will wish theirs may be, in ease, retirement, and the society of
his friends;" and he adds what cannot be doubted, that "his
pleasurable wit and good-nature engaged him in the acquaintance, and entitled him to the friendship of the gentlemen of
the neighbourhood." He must have been of a lively and com-
panionable disposition; and his long residence in London,
amid the bustling and varied scenes connected with his public

life, independently of his natural powers of conversation, could not fail to render his society most agreeable and desirable.

In 1616 he was seized with his last and fatal illness, what this was we have no satisfactory means of knowing, but it was probably not of long duration; for if when he subscribed his will he had really been in health, we are persuaded that at the age of only fifty-two he would have signed his name with greater steadiness and distinctness. All three signatures are more or less infirm and illegible, but he seems to have made an effort to write his best when he affixed both his names at length at the end. "By me William Shakspeare." In regard to his will the request which has attracted most attention is an interlineation in the following words, "Item, I gyve unto my wief my second best bed with the furniture." Upon this passage has been founded a charge against Shakespeare that he only remembered his wife as an afterthought, and then merely gave her an "old bed." Our dramatist has of late years been relieved from the stigma, thus attempted to be thrown upon him, by the mere remark, that his property being principally freehold, the widow by the ordinary operation of the law of England would be entitled to, what is legally known by the term dower.

A monument was erected to Shakespeare in Stratford church, and on a tablet below his bust are placed the following inscriptions: —

> "Jvdicio Pylivm, genio Socratem, arte Maronem,
> Tvrra tegit, popvlvs mæret, Olympvs habet.
>
> Stay, passenger, why goest thov by so fast?
> Read, if thov canst, whom enviovs Death hath plast
> Within this monvment, Shakspeare; with whome
> Quick natvre dide; whose name doth deck ys tombe
> Far more then cost; sieh [sith] all yᵗ he hath writt
> Leaves living art bvt page to serve his witt.
> Obiit Año Doi 1616
> Ætatis 53, die 23 Ap."

On a flat grave-stone in front of the monument, we read these lines, and tradition says, that they were written by Shakespeare himself: —

"Good frend, for Jesvs sake forbeare
To digg the dvst encloased heare:
Bleste be ye man yᵗ spares thes stones,
And cvrst be he yᵗ movos my bonos."

We have thus brought into a consecutive narrative the particulars respecting the life of the "myriad-minded Shakespeare" which we have been able, during a long series of years, to collect. Yet, after all, we cannot but be aware how little has been accomplished. "Of William Shakespeare," says Hallam, "whom, through the mouths of those whom he has inspired to body forth the modifications of his immense mind, we seem to know better than any human writer, it may be truly said that we scarcely know anything. We see him, so far as we do see him, not in himself, but in a reflex image from the objectivity in which he is manifested: he is Falstaff, and Mercutio, and Malvolio, and Jacques, and Portia, and Imogen, and Lear, and Othello; but to us he is scarcely a determined person, a substantial reality of past time, the man Shakespeare. The name of Shakespeare is the greatest in our literature, — it is the greatest in all literature. No man ever came near to him in the creative powers of the mind; no man had ever such strength at once, and such variety of imagination."

If the details of his life be imperfect, the history of his mind is complete; and we leave the reader to turn from the contemplation of "the man Shakespeare" to THE POET SHAKESPEARE.

GLOSSARY.

Abhominable, *abominable.*

Abide, *to sojourn, to tarry awhile; to answer for, to be accountable for, to stand the consequences of.*

Abodements, *forebodements, omens.*

Aby, *the same as to abide (see its second sense).*

Acture, *action.*

Adamant, *the magnet, the loadstone.*

Addiction, *inclination; the being addicted or given to.*

Addition, *title, mark of distinction; exaggeration.*

Address, *to prepare, to make ready.*

Admittance, *fashion.*

Affection, *affectation; imagination; sympathy.*

Affectioned, *affected.*

Affeer'd, *confirmed, established.*

Affin'd, *joined by affinity.*

Affront, *a meeting face to face, a hostile encounter.*

Affront, *to meet, to encounter.*

Affy, *to betroth; to trust, to confide.*

Aglet-baby, *a small image or head cut on the tag of a point or lace.*

Agnize, *to acknowledge, to avow.*

Aim, *guess, conjecture; — to cry aim, to encourage; to give aim, to direct; — to aim, to aim at; to guess, to conjecture.*

Alderliefest, *dearest of all.*

Ale, *alehouse.*

Aleven, *eleven.*

All-hallown summer, *late summer.*

Allow, *to approve; to license, to privilege.*

Amaimon, *the name of a demon.*

Ames-ace, *both aces, — the lowest throw upon the dice.*

Amiss, *misfortune; fault.*

Amort (All), *dejected, dispirited.*

Anchor, *an anchorite, hermit.*

Ancient, *a standard; a standard-bearer, an ensign-bearer.*

Angel (An ancient), *an old worthy.*

Apparent, *heir-apparent, next claimant.*

Apperil, *peril.*

Apple-John, *a shrivelled and withered apple.*

Approbation, *proof; probation, novitiate.*

Approof, *approbation; proof.*

Approve, *to prove; to ratify, to confirm; to recommend to approbation.*

Aquilon, *the North Wind.*

Arabian bird, *the phœnix.*

Arch, *chief, leader.*

Argier, *the old name for Algiers.*

Argo, *a vulgar corruption of the Latin word ergo.*

Argosy, *a ship of great bulk and burden, fit either for merchandise or war.*

Argument, *conversation, discourse; subject, matter.*

Articulate, *to enter into articles; to exhibit in articles.*

Aspersion, *sprinkling.*

As's, *a quibble between as the conditional particle, and ass the beast of burden.*

Assinego, *a silly, a stupid fellow.*

Atomies, *atoms.*

Atomy, *a corruption of anatomy, a skeleton.*

Atone, *to agree, to unite; to reconcile.*

Attask'd, *taxed, blamed.*

Attorney, *an advocate, a pleader; a substitute, a deputy.*

Aunt, *a good old dame; a cant term for a loose woman.*

Awkward, *distorted; adverse.*

Baccare, *a cant exclamation, signifying "Go back."*

Baffle, *to treat ignominiously, to use contemptuously.*

Bajazet's mute; *the allusion in this passage (where the original reads mule) has not yet been explained.*

Baldrick, *a belt.*

Bale, *sorrow, evil.*

Balk'd, *piled up in balks or ridges.*

Ballast, *the contracted form of* ballased *or* ballaced, *ballasted.*

Balm, *the oil of consecration.*

Ban, *a curse; to curse.*

Band, *a bond.*

Ban-dogs, *properly* band-dogs, *so called because on account of their fierceness they required to be bound or chained.*

Banquet, *dessert.*

Barbason, *the name of a demon.*

Barbed steeds, *steeds equipped with military trappings and ornaments.*

Baring, *shaving.*

Barm, *yeast.*

Barson, *a corruption of* Barston, *a village in Warwickshire.*

Base, *a rustic game.*

Basilisk, *an imaginary creature (called also* cockatrice*), supposed to kill by its very look; a huge piece of ordnance, carrying a ball of very great weight.*

Basta, *enough.*

Bastard, *a sweetish wine.*

Bate, *strife, contention.*

Bate, *to flutter, to flap the wings; to abate, to diminish, to lessen; to grow less; to except; to blunt.*

Batlet, *a bat for beating clothes in washing.*

Batten, *to grow fat.*

Bavin, *a faggot of brushwood.*

Bavin wits, *flashing wits.*

Beadsman, *one who prays for the welfare of another.*

Bear in hand, *to keep in expectation, to flatter one's hopes, to amuse with false pretences.*

Beautified, *beautiful.*

Become, *to adorn, to set-off, to grace.*

Be-mete, *to be-measure.*

Benison, *blessing.*

Besmirch, *to be-smut.*

Besort, *attendance, train.*

Besort, *to suit, to befit, to become.*

Bestow, *to stow, to lodge, to place; to carry, to show.*

Bestraught, *distraught, mad.*

Beteem, *to give in streaming abundance; to suffer, to permit.*

Bewray, *to discover.*

Bid, *to invite.*

Bid, *endured.*

Bilbo, *a sword.*

Bilboes, *a bar of iron with fetters annexed to it.*

Bill, *a sort of pike or halbert, or rather a kind of battle-axe affixed to a long staff; a forest-bill, an implement carried by foresters; a placard posted by public challengers; a billet, a note.*

Bin, *been.*

Bird-bolt, *a short thick arrow with a blunted extremity, for killing birds without piercing them.*

Birthdom, *birthright.*

Bisson, *blind; blinding.*

Blench, *to start off, to fly off, to shrink, to flinch.*

Blenches, *starts, or aberrations from rectitude.*

Blent, *blended.*

Block, *the shape or fashion of a hat, — properly the mould on which felt hats were formed; the hat itself.*

Blood, *disposition, inclination, temperament, impulse; to be in blood, to be in good condition, to be vigorous.*

Blue-coats, *the common dress of serving-men in Shakespeare's time.*

Bob, *a taunt, a scoff.*

Bob, *to cheat.*

Bodg'd, *botch'd.*

Bodkin, *a small dagger.*

Bollen, *swollen.*

Bolted, *sifted.*

Bombard, *a large leathern vessel for distributing liquor.*

Bombast, *material for stuffing out dresses.*

Book, *one's studies, learning; a writing, a paper.*

Boot, *profit, gain, something added; — booty; — to benefit, to enrich; to put on boots.*

Bosky, *woody.*

Bosom, *wish, desire.*

Bots, *worms that breed in the entrails of horses.*

Bottom, *a low ground, a valley; a ball of thread.*

Bottom it on me, *wind it on me, make me the bottom or centre on which it is wound.*

Bought and sold, *see:* buy and sell.

Bourn, *a limit, a boundary; a brook, a rivulet.*

Brabbler, *a clamorous quarrelsome*

person, a *wrangler; the name of a
hound.*

Brace, *armour for the arm; state of
defence.*

Brach, *a scenting dog: a lurcher, or
beagle; or any fine-nosed hound.*

Braid, *crafty, deceitful; — to upbraid,
to reproach.*

Brain, *to comprehend, to understand.*

Brave, *a boast, a vaunt, a defiance; —
to make fine or splendid; to defy, to
bluster.*

Bravery, *finery, sumptuous apparel,
magnificence; bravado.*

Brawl (A French), *a dance.*

Break up, *to break open; to carve.*

Break with, *to open a subject to; to
break an engagement with.*

Breast, *voice.*

Breathe, *to utter, to speak; to take
exercise.*

Breese, *the gad-fly.*

Bribed buck, *a buck given away in
presents.*

Brief, *a short writing, an abstract; a
contract of espousals, a license of marriage; a letter.*

Brock, *a badger.*

Brogues (Clouted), *nailed coarse shoes.*

Broker, *a pander, a procuress, a go-
between.*

Brooch, *ornament.*

Bruit, *to report loudly.*

Buck-basket, *a basket in which linen
was carried to be bucked.*

Buckle, *to bend, to bow; to join in close
fight, to engage with, to encounter.*

Bug, *bugbear.*

Bulk, *a kind of stall, board, or ledge
outside a house, on which articles were
set for sale.*

Burgonet, *a close-fitting helmet.*

Burst, *broke, broken.*

Buss, *to kiss.*

But, *unless, except.*

Butt-shaft, *a kind of arrow, used for
shooting at butts.*

Buy and sell, *to dispose of utterly, to
over-reach, to betray.*

Buzzard, *a common and inferior kind
of hawk; a beetle (so named from its
buzzing).*

'by, *an abbreviation of aby (which see).*

By 'r lakin, *by our ladykin, by our
little Lady.*

Cain-coloured beard (A), *a beard resembling in colour (sandy-red) that
with which Cain was commonly represented in tapestries and pictures.*

Caliban, *a metathesis from Cannibal.*

Caliver, *hand-gun.*

Callet, *a drab, a trull, a jade.*

Canary, *a wine brought from the Canary
Islands; a blunder of Mrs. Quickly for
Quandary; a quick and lively dance.*

Candied, *sugared, flattering, glozing;
congealed.*

Candle-wasters, *revellers, who, sitting
up all night, waste many candles.*

Canker, *the dog-rose; a caterpillar.*

Cantle, *a corner, an angle, a piece, a
portion, a parcel.*

Cantons, *cantos, songs.*

Canvas-climber, *one who climbs the
mast, to furl, or unfurl, the canvas or
sails.*

Capable, *intelligent, able to understand,
quick of apprehension; susceptible,
impressible, sensible; qualified as heir,
capable of inheriting; capacious, com-
prehensive.*

Capitulate, *to draw up heads or articles.*

Capocchio, *a simpleton.*

Captions, *capable of receiving.*

Carack, *a galleon, a large ship of burden.*

Carbonado, *a piece of meat cut cross-
wise for broiling.*

Carcanet, *necklace.*

Carded, *mixed, debased by mixing.*

Carduus benedictus, *blessed thistle.*

Carl, *churl, rustic, pleasant, boor.*

Carpet-mongers, *equivalent to Carpet-
knights, effeminate persons.*

Carry coals, *to put up with insults, to
submit to any degradation.*

Carry out a side, *to win the game.*

Case, *skin; a pair, a couple.*

Cassocks, *loose outward military coats.*

Cast, *to dismiss; to empty; to cast up,
to compute; also used with a quibble
between its two senses "to throw" and
"to vomit"; cast water, to find out
diseases by inspecting the urine.*

Castilian, *cant term.*

Castiliano volto, *grave solemn looks.*

Castle, *a close helmet.*

Catalan, *a cant term for a thief or
sharper.*

Cat-o'-mountain, *a wild-cat.*

Cease, *to cause to cease, to stop; to decease, to die.*

Censure, *opinion, judgment; judicial sentence.*

Censure, *to pass judgment or opinion on; to pass sentence judicially.*

'cerns, *concerns.*

Cess (Out of all), *out of all measure.*

Cesse, *to cease.*

Chamberers, *men of intrigue.*

Chambers, *small pieces of ordnance.*

Champain, *open country.*

Chape, *the hook or loop at the top of a scabbard.*

Chapmen, *sellers; buyers.*

Chaps, *jaws; clefts, breaks in the continuity of the skin.*

Character, *hand-writing, writing.*

Character, *to inscribe, to infix strongly.*

Characts, *inscriptions, marks.*

Chare, *a turn or bout of work, a job or task-work.*

Charge-house, *a common school in distinction to a free one.*

Chariest, *most cautious, scrupulous.*

Charm, *to bewitch; to compel to be silent.*

Charneco, *a Portuguese wine.*

Chaudron, *part of the entrails of an animal.*

Cheater, *an escheator.*

Check, *a term in falconry, applied to a hawk when she forsakes her proper game, and follows some other of inferior kind that crosses her in her flight; a reproof, a rebuke.*

Cherry-pit, *a game.*

Cheveril, *kid-leather.*

Che vor you, *I warn you (Somersetshire dialect).*

Chide, *to sound, to resound, to echo; — with, to quarrel.*

Childing, *teeming, fruitful.*

Chopine, *a high shoe.*

Choris, *chorus (for the sake of a rhyme).*

Cinque-pace, *a dance.*

Circle, *Circuit, a diadem.*

Cital, *recital, account.*

Civil, *sober, grave, decent, solemn.*

Clamour, *to curb, to restrain.*

Clean, *quite, entirely.*

Clepe, *to call.*

Close, *secret; secretly, by stealth; — to close with, or in with, to come to an agreement with, to comply with, to unite with.*

Clout, *the nail or pin of the target.*

Clubs, *a popular cry to part the combatants.*

Cock, *a weather-cock; a cock-boat (small boat); — a corruption of, or euphemism for God.*

Cockatrice, *see: Basilisk.*

Cog, *to cheat, to wheedle, to load a die.*

Coign, *a corner-stone at the exterior angle of a building.*

Coistrel, *a paltry groom, one only fit to carry arms, but not to use them.*

Collied, *smutted, blackened, darkened.*

Collier, *a term of the highest reproach.*

Colours, *specious appearances, deceits.*

Colt, *to fool, to trick, to gull; to horse.*

Co-mart, *a joint bargain.*

Combinate, *contracted.*

Comfortable, *susceptible of comfort, cheerful; ready to give comfort.*

Comforting, *encouraging, abetting.*

Commodity, *profit, advantage.*

Compact, *compacted, composed; confederated, leagued.*

Companion, *a term of contempt, equivalent to „fellow."*

Compassed window, *a bow-window.*

Competitor, *a coadjutor, a partner, a confederate.*

Comply, *to compliment.*

Composition, *a compact, an agreement; consistency.*

Composture, *a compost.*

Composure, *a combination.*

Compt, *account, reckoning.*

Comptible, *impressible, susceptible, sensitive.*

Con, *to know.*

Conceit, *conception, thought, imagination, fancy; a fanciful gewgaw; — to conceive, to imagine.*

Concolinel, *perhaps the (corrupted) title or beginning or burden of some Italian song.*

Condition, *disposition, temper, quality; an art, a profession; place; — instead of on condition.*

Confect, *see: Count confect.*

Confound, *to consume (applied to the spending of time); to destroy.*

Congest, *to heap together.*

Congreeing, *agreeing together.*

Congreeted, *saluted reciprocally.*

Conjecture, *suspicion.*

Consort, *a company, a band, of musicians, — a concert; — a fellowship, a fraternity.*

Consort, *to accompany.*

Contain, *to retain; to restrain.*

Con thanks, *to give thanks (the French sçavoir gré; the Germ. Dank wissen).*

Continent, *that which contains any thing; that which is contained in any thing.*

Contraction, *contract.*

Contrive, *to wear out, to pass away, to spend.*

Convent, *to summon, to cite; to assemble, to collect; to serve, to agree, to be convenient.*

Convey, *to steal; to manage secretly and artfully.*

Conveyance, *dexterity; juggling artifice, secret management.*

Convince, *to conquer, to overcome; to convict.*

Convive, *to feast together.*

Cony-catch, *to deceive, to cheat, to impose upon, to sharp.*

Cony-catching, *a jocular deceiving.*

Cope, *the canopy of heaven; — to cope, to pay, to reward; to encounter.*

Copy, *a main subject, a theme.*

Coranto, *a very lively and rapid dance.*

Corky, *dry, withered.*

Corrigible, *corrective, having the power to correct.*

Cosiers, *cobblers, botchers.*

Costard, *head.*

Coted, *overtook, overpassed.*

Cot-quean, *a man who busies himself too much in female affairs.*

Counsel, *secrecy.*

Count confect, *a nobleman made out of sugar.*

Countenance, *specious appearance, hypocrisy; entertainment, treatment; patronage; — to receive, to entertain.*

Counter, *the wrong way in the chace and a prison in London; a piece of false coin.*

Counterfeit, *portrait, likeness, picture; a piece of false money; — counterfeit presentment, mimic representation.*

Counter-gate, *the gate of the Counter-prison in London.*

Counterpoints, *counterpanes of arras.*

Court-cupboard, *a sort of movable sideboard.*

Court holy-water, *flattery, fine speeches without deeds.*

Cowl-staff, *a staff (or pole), used for carrying a large tub or basket, with two handles (held on the shoulders of two persons).*

Coy, *to stroke, to caress, to fondle; to make difficulty, to condescend unwillingly.*

Crab, *a wild-apple.*

Crack, *an arch, lively boy; — to brag, to boast.*

Cracked within the ring, *uncurrent gold.*

Crants, *crown, chaplet, garland.*

Crare, *a small vessel.*

Credent, *inforcing credit; credible; easy of belief.*

Credit, *credible avouch; account, information; belief. (Tw. N. IV. 3.)*

Cresset, *a cresset light.*

Critic, *a cynic.*

Critical, *cynical, censorious.*

Crone, *an old worn-out woman.*

Crona, *a piece of money, so called because coin was formerly stamped with a cross.*

Crow-keeper, *a person (a boy generally) employed to scare the crows from the corn-fields, &c., and armed with a bow and arrows.*

Crush a cup, *a drinking term.*

Cunning, *knowledge, skill; — knowing, skilful.*

Curb, *to bend, to cringe.*

Curiosity, *an over-nice scrupulousness in manners, dress, &c.*

'currents, *occurrences.*

Cursorary, *cursory.*

Curst, *shrewish, cross-grained, ill-tempered, fierce, irascible, angry; froward, perverse.*

Curtle-axe, *a cutlass.*

Customer, *a cant term for a loose woman; an accustomed visitor.*

Cut, *a common horse.*

Cyprus, *cipres or cypress, a fine transparent stuff, similar to crape, either white or black, but more commonly the latter.*

Daff, *to doff, to do off, to put off.*

Danger, *debt.*

Dare, *a defiance, a challenge; — to terrify.*

Darraign, *to prepare, to arrange.*
Daub, *to disguise.*
Day-bed, *a couch, a sofa.*
Day-woman, *dairy-woman.*
Deal, *part, portion.*
Dear, *dire: — that which has to do with the affections; — piteous; — important.*
Deceivable, *deceptious.*
Deck, *a pack of cards.*
Deck, *to sprinkle.*
Decline, *to lean, to incline; to run through from first to last.*
Defeat, *an undoing, a destruction; — to undo, to alter, to disguise.*
Deftly, *dexterously, adroitly.*
Defy, *to refuse, to reject, to renounce.*
Demerits, *merits.*
Den, *see: god-den and good den.*
Denay, *denial.*
Denay, *to deny.*
Denier, *the twelfth part of a French sous, used to signify a very trifling sum.*
Deny, *to refuse, to reject, to renounce.*
Depart with, *to part with.*
Depose, *to cause to make solemn deposition; to give witness, to attest, to declare upon oath.*
Dern, *lonely, dreary.*
Derogate, *to degrade one's self; — degraded.*
Derogately, *with derogation.*
Descant, *a variation upon a melody, hence, metaphorically, a comment on a given theme.*
Design, *to mark out, to show.*
Desperate, *bold, venturous, confident.*
Detect, *to display, to discover.*
Detected, *suspected, accused, charged.*
Dich, *optative mood, perhaps corrupted of "do it."*
Diet, *food regulated by the rules of medicine; — to diet, to have one's food regulated by th. r. of med.*
Diffuse, *to disorder.*
Diffused, *wild, irregular, extravagant.*
Dild, *see: God dild you.*
Diminutives, *very small pieces of money.*
Disable, *to detract from, to disparage, to undervalue; to impair.*
Disappointed, *unprepared.*
Disclose, *the peeping of young birds through the shell; — to disclose, to hatch; to open.*
Dishabited, *dislodged.*

Dishonesty, *inchastity.*
Dislike, *to express dislike of a thing; to displease.*
Dislimns, *unpaints, obliterates what was before limned.*
Dismes, *tenths.*
Disnatur'd, *devoid of natural affection.*
Dispose, *disposition; disposal.*
Disputable, *inclined to dispute, disputatious.*
Dispute, *to reason upon.*
Dis-seat, *to unseat, to dethrone.*
Distain, *to sully by contrast, to throw into shade.*
Division, *variations in music.*
Doff, *to do off, to put off.*
Do him dead, *kill him.*
Dole, *dolour, grieve; dealing, allotment, distribution.*
Don, *to do on, to put on.*
Done, *destroyed, consumed.*
Double, *deceitful (with a quibble).*
Doubt, *fear; — to fear.*
Doucets, *the testes of a deer.*
Dout, *to do out, to put out, to extinguish.*
Dowle, *particle of down in a feather.*
Down-gyved, *hanging down like the loose cincture which confines the fetters round the ancles.*
Drabbing, *following loose women.*
Draff, *to refuse of any sort of food.*
Drollery, *a puppet-show; a picture or sketch of some scene of low humour.*
Drumble, *to be slow and sluggish, to go lazily or awkwardly about a thing.*
Dudgeon, *haft or handle of a dagger.*
Duke, *a leader, a general, a commander.*
Dump, *formerly the received term for a melancholy strain in music; appears to have been also a kind of dance.*
Dup, *to do up, to open.*

Eager, *sour, sharp, keen.*
Eaning time, *time of bringing forth young.*
Eanlings, *young lambs just dropped.*
Ear, *to plough, to till.*
Eche, *to eke out, to lengthen out.*
Ecstasy, *alienation of mind.*
Effects, *intended deeds.*
Eftest, *quickest, readiest.*
Eisel, *vinegar.*
Eld, *old age.*

Element, *initiation, rudimentary knowledge; the heaven, the sky.*

Elf, *to entangle, to mat together, as if the work of elfs or fairies.*

Elvish-mark'd, *marked by the elves or fairies.*

Embarquements, *embargoes, impediments.*

Embossed, *foaming at the mouth from fatigue; swollen, protuberant.*

Empory, *sovereign command, dominion; a kingdom.*

Enactures, *actions, effects.*

Enfeoff'd, *granted out as a feoff or estate, gave up.*

Engiue, *an instrument of torture, the rack; a military implement, an engine of war.*

Engross, *to make gross, to fatten; to gather together, to heap up, to amass.*

Ensconce, *to protect or cover with a sconce or fort; to hide.*

Enseamed, *greasy, filthy.*

Entertain, *entertainment; — to receive into service.*

Entreat, *to treat; to entertain.*

Envious, *malicious.*

Envoy, *see:* L'envoy.

Envy, *malice, hatred, ill-will; — to bear malice, hatred, or ill-will to.*

Escoted, *paid.*

Esperance, *hope (used as a war-cry).*

Ever, *see: not ever.*

Everlasting, *a kind of stuff for dress.*

Excrement, *beard, hair.*

Exempt, *taken away, separated, parted.*

Exercise, *a religious lecture, a sermon.*

Exhibition, *an allowance, a pension.*

Exigent, *an exigence; extremity, end.*

Exion, *blunder for* action.

Expedience, *expedition, haste, dispatch; an enterprise, an undertaking.*

Expedient, *expeditious, immediate.*

Explate, *fully completed and ended.*

Extend, *to extend the praise of a person; to seize (a law-term).*

Eyases, *young nestling hawks.*

Eyas-musket, *a young male sparrow-hawk.*

Eye of green, *a slight tint of green.*

Eyne, *eyes.*

Face, *to carry a false appearance, to play the hypocrite; to oppose with im-*

pudence, *to bully; to turn up with facings; to patch, to mend with a different colour.*

Fadge, *to suit, to fit, to agree.*

Fading, *the burden of a popular Irish song and the name of a dance.*

Fair, *fairness, beauty.*

Fall, *to let fall; to fall away, to shrink.*

Fancy, *love; — to love.*

Fangled, *gaudy, vainly decorated.*

Fantastical, *imaginary.*

Fap, *fuddled, drunk.*

Far', *farther.*

Farce, *to stuff.*

Fardel, *a burden, a bundle, a pack.*

Fashions, *the farcy, a disease in horses.*

Fast, *fasted; — settled, fixed.*

Fast and loose, *a cheating game.*

Favour, *countenance, aspect, appearance; a love-token.*

Fear, *to terrify, to frighten.*

Feat, *dexterous, ready, neat, trim.*

Feature, *form, person in general.*

Fedary, *a colleague, associate, or confederate.*

Fee-farm, *for ever.*

Fell of hair, *skin covered with hair, hairy scalp.*

Fellow, *a companion; an equal.*

Fere, *a companion, a mate (husband or wife).*

Festinately, *speedily, quickly.*

Festival terms, *holiday language, fine phraseology.*

Fot, *fetched.*

Fetch of warrant, *a warranted, sanctioned, or approved artifice or device.*

File, *a number, a list; — to polish; to defile; to keep equal pace.*

Fine, *a conclusion, an end; — to end; to refine, to embellish.*

Firago, *for virago.*

Fire-drake, *a fiery dragon, a meteor; a sort of fire-work.*

Fishmonger, *a cant term for a wencher.*

Fives, *an inflammation of the parotid glands in horses.*

Fixure, *fixture, fixedness.*

Flap-jacks, *pancakes.*

Flaw, *gust, a sudden and violent blast of wind; a tempestuous uproar; a sudden commotion of mind.*

Flecked, *spotted, dappled.*

Fleet, *to float; to make to pass.*

Flew'd, *having large hanging flews or chaps.*

Flote, *flood, wave, sea.*

Foin, *to push, to thrust (in fencing).*

Foison, *plenty, store.*

Fond, *foolish, simple, silly; — to dote.*

Foot, *to seize with the foot; to strike w. th. f., to kick, to spurn; to tread, to walk; to move with measured steps, to dance; to fix or set foot in, or to set foot on.*

For, *for that, because; because of.*

For and, *equivalent to and also.*

Force, *to regard, to care for, to heed; to enforce; to stuff; to strengthen.*

Force (Of), *of necessity, necessarily.*

Fordo, *to undo, to destroy.*

Formal, *regular; retaining its proper and essential characteristic.*

Forslow, *to delay, to loiter.*

Forspoke, *spoke against, gainsaid.*

For why, *because, for this reason that.*

Fox, *the broad-sword.*

Frampal, *frampold, peevish, froward; uneasy, unquiet.*

Frank, *to sty.*

Frets, *the stops of instruments of the lute or guitar kind.*

Frippery, *a shop for the sale of second-hand apparel.*

From, *a way from, departing from.*

Front, *a beginning; — to oppose, to affront.*

Frontier, *an outwork in fortification.*

Frush, *to bruise, to break to pieces.*

Fullam, *a loaded die.*

Gad, *a point.*

Gage, *a pledge; — to pledge.*

Gain-giving, *misgiving.*

Gait, *way; proceeding.*

Galliard, *a quick and lively dance.*

Gallow, *to scare, to frighten.*

Gallowglasses, *heavy-armed foot-soldiers of Ireland.*

Gamester, *a frolicksome, adventurous person; a facetious fellow, a wag; a prostitute.*

Garboils, *tumults, uproars, commotions.*

Gaskins, *loose hose or breeches.*

Gaudy-night, *a night of festivity and rejoicing.*

Gear, *dress; matter in hand, business; stuff.*

Geck, *a fool, a bubble; a subject of ridicule, a jest.*

General, *the people, the multitude.*

Germane, *or german, related, akin.*

Germens, *germs, seeds.*

Gest, *a resting-place; a period.*

Gib-cat, *an old male cat.*

Gilt, *gilding, golden show, display of gold; money.*

Gimmal-bit, *double-bit.*

Gin, *to begin.*

Ging, *a gang.*

Gird, *a sarcasm, a gibe; — to gibe, to taunt.*

Gis, *a corruption of Jesus.*

Gleek, *joke, jeer, scoff; — to joke, to jeer, to scoff.*

Gloze, *to expound, to comment; to flatter, to wheedle, to cajole.*

Godded, *deified.*

God-den, *good e'en.*

God dild you, *a variation of God ild (yield, requite) you.*

Good, *good friend, good fellow; of substance, rich.*

Good den, *good e'en.*

Good-jer, *good-year, a corruption of goujeer (which see).*

Good masters, *patrons.*

Gorbellied, *swag-bellied, paunchy.*

Go to the world, *to be married, to commence housekeeper.*

Goujeers, *the venereal disease.*

Gourd, *a false die.*

Gouts, *drops.*

Grace, *physical virtue; — to favour, to honour, to bless.*

Grained, *ingrained; furrowed, rough.*

Gramercy, *great thanks.*

Gratulate, *to congratulate; to be rejoiced at, worthy of gratulation.*

Gree, *to agree.*

Green, *sickly.*

Grime, *dirt, sullying blackness; — to dirt, to sully deeply.*

Gripe, *griffin, vulture.*

Grise, *step.*

Groundlings, *spectators who stood on the ground in that part of the theatre which answered to the pit in a modern playhouse.*

Grow, *to accrue; — to a point, proceed to a conclusion, to business.*

Guard, *to face, to trim, to ornament.*

Guards, *facings, trimmings.*

Guerdon, *reward, recompense.*
Gust, *to taste, to perceive.*

Haggard, *wild hawk; — wild, wanton, libertine.*
Halidom, *holiness, faith, sanctity.*
Hand-fast, *a contract, a bethrothal, a marriage-engagement.*
Handsaw, *for heronshaw.*
Hangman, *an executioner; — rascally.*
Hard, *unpleasant.*
Haught, *haughty.*
Hefts, *heavings, retchings.*
Henchman, *a page.*
Hent, *a hold, an opportunity to be seized; — to seize, to take possession of, to take hold of.*
Herb of grace, *rue.*
Hest, *command.*
Hide fox and all after, *a sport among children.*
High men and low men, *two kinds of false dice.*
Hight, *called, named.*
Hild, *a form of* held, *used for the sake of the rhyme.*
Hilding, *a low, degenerate wretch.*
Hint, *suggestion.*
Hobby-horse, *a silly fellow; a loose woman.*
Holding, *burden of a song; — consistency, fitness.*
Honesty, *chastity; decency; liberality, generosity.*
Hoodman-blind, *the game which we now call blind-man's-buff.*
Hot-house, *a bagnio (which was often a brothel).*
Hoxes, *houghs, ham-strings.*
Hugger-mugger (In), *secretly.*
Hulk, *a heavy or large ship.*
Hull, *to float, to swim, as borne along or driven by wind or water.*
Humorous, *perverse, capricious; humid, damp.*
Hunt-counter, *a dog that runs the wrong way.*
Hunt's-up, *a morning song.*
Hurlyburly, *an uproar, a tumult.*
Husbandry, *economical government, thrift, economical prudence.*

Idle, *trifling; vain, weak; useless, infertile, unfruitful, barren.*

I'fecks, *most probably a corruption of* in faith.
Iguomy, *ignominy.*
Ild, *a corruption of* yield.
Imbare, *to lay bare.*
Imp, *a shoot, a graft; an offspring; — to graft, to splice a falcon's broken feathers.*
Impartial, *neutral.*
Impeachment, *an imputation, a reproach; an obstruction, a hindrance.*
Imponed, *impawned.*
Importance, *importunity, the thing imported or implied; the import.*
Important, *importunate.*
Impose, *an imposition, an injunction; — to enjoin, to command.*
Incense, *to incite, to instigate, to set on; to kindle.*
Inclips, *embraces, encircles.*
Include, *to shut in, restrain; to close, to conclude.*
Incony, *fine, delicate, pretty.*
Indent, *an indentation, a bending inwards; — to bargain, to contract, to compound.*
Index, *a prelude, any thing preparatory to another.*
Indifferency, *impartiality; moderation, ordinary size.*
Indifferent, *impartial; ordinary; indifferently, tolerably.*
Indigest, *a thing indigested, an unformed mass; — indigested, unformed, shapeless.*
Indirection, *crooked conduct, dishonest practice; oblique means.*
Induction, *a beginning; introduction.*
Indurance, *confinement.*
Informal, *deranged, insane.*
Ingener, *an ingenious person, a deviser, an artist, a painter.*
Ingenious, *ingenuous, acute, lively.*
Inhabitable, *uninhabitable.*
Inhibit, *to prohibit, to forbid.*
Inkhorn mate, *a bookish man, or a bookman.*
Inkle, *a kind of inferior tape.*
Inland-bred, *brought up among civilised persons.*
Inn, *a house or habitation.*
Innocent, *an idiot, a natural fool, a simpleton.*
Insane root, *the root which causes insanity, perhaps hemlock.*

Instance, *motive, inducement, cause, ground; symptom, prognostic; information, assurance; proof, example, indication.*

Intend, *to pretend; to set forth, to make to appear.*

Intrinse, *intricate.*

Invis'd, *invisible, unseen.*

Inward, *intimate, confidential.*

Jack, *the small bowl aimed at in the game of bowling; a common term of contempt and reproach; an automaton that in public clocks struck the bell on the outside.*

Jacks, *the keys of the virginal.*

Jade, *to ride, to over-sway, to over-master; to drive harassed and dispirited; to subject to harassing and mean offices.*

Jar o' the clock, *tick of the clock.*

Jet, *to strut; — upon, to encroach upon.*

Jig, *a theatrical entertainment.*

Jovial, *like Jove.*

Jump, *a hazard, a chance.*

Jump, *to agree; to risk, to hazard.*

Jump, *exactly, coincident with.*

Justicer, *a justice.*

Kam, *crooked; clean kam, quite crooked, quite wrong.*

Keech, *a lump of fat.*

Keel, *to cool.*

Keep, *care; — to live, to dwell; to restrain.*

Ken, *a view, a reach of sight; — to know; to descry.*

Kern, *a foot soldier, armed with a dart or a skean; a boor.*

Kind, *nature; — natural; possessed of natural affection.*

Kindle, *to incite; to bring forth.*

Kindly, *naturally, in a natural manner; aptly, pertinently.*

King and Beggar, *a ballad.*

King'd, *ruled; raised to royalty, made a king.*

Kirtle (A full), *a jacket and petticoat; a half-kirtle, either the one or the other.*

Kissing-comfits, *sugar-plums perfumed, to sweeten the breath.*

Knapped, *snapped, broke off short; rapped, struck.*

Laced mutton, *a dressed courtesan; a richly-attired piece of woman's flesh.*

Lag, *the last or lowest part or class; — late, tardy, coming short of.*

Lantern, *a spacious round or octagonal turret full of windows, by means of which cathedrals, and sometimes halls, are illuminated.*

Large, *free, coarse, licentious.*

Latch, *to lay hold of, to catch; to lick over, to anoint.*

Laugh-and-lie-down, *a game at cards.*

Lavolt, Lavolta, *a dance for two persons, consisting much in high bounds and whirls.*

Lay, *a wager; — to waylay.*

Leaguer, *camp.*

Leasing, *lying.*

Leather-coats, *the apples generally known as golden russetings.*

Leave, *licentiousness; — to part with; to leave off, to desist.*

Leer, *complexion, colour.*

Leese, *to lose.*

'leges, *alleges.*

Leiger, Lieger, *a resident ambassador at a foreign court.*

Leman, *a paramour, a lover; a mistress, a sweetheart.*

Lenten, *spare.*

L'envoy, *a sort of postscript; a farewell or moral at the end of a tale or poem.*

Let, *a hindrance; — to hinder; to detain; to forbear.*

Lewd, *wicked, base, vile.*

Liberty, *libertinism, licentiousness.*

Lie, *to reside, to sojourn.*

Liefest, *dearest.*

Lieutenantry, *proxy, deputation.*

Lifter, *thief.*

Light o' Love, *a tune.*

Lightly, *easily, readily; commonly, usually.*

Like, *to make like, to liken; to please.*

Likelihood, *similitude; semblance, appearance.*

Liking, *condition of body.*

Limbo, *hell; a cant term for "a prison, confinement."*

Line, *to strengthen; to delineate.*

List, *desire, inclination; limit, boundary; — to like, to please, to choose.*

Livelihood, *liveliness, appearance of life, animation.*

Liver, *anciently supposed to be the inspirer of amorous passion and the seat of love.*

Loach, *a fish.*

Lockram, *a sort of cheap linen, made of different degrees of fineness.*

Loggats, *the game called nine-pins.*

Long, *to belong.*

Longly, *longingly.*

Loof'd, *brought close to the wind (a sea-term).*

Look, *to look for, to look out; — upon, to look on, to be a looker-on.*

Lordings, *little lords; sirs, masters (an ancient form of address).*

Losel, *a worthless fellow, a scoundrel.*

Love-in-idleness, *one of the several names of the viola tricolor (pansy, heart's ease).*

Lover, *a mistress; a male friend.*

Loves (Of all), *for love's sake, by all means.*

Luce, *a pike fish.*

Lunes, *fits of lunacy, mad freaks.*

Lurch o' the garland, *to gain the victory.*

Lust, *pleasure, inclination, liking.*

Lustic, *lusty, healthy, cheerful.*

Lym, *a lime-hound, a sporting dog.*

Mace, *a sceptre; a club of metal.*

Maculate, *stained, impure.*

Made, *see: make.*

Mail'd up in shame, *wrapped up in shame.*

Make, *to make the fortune of; to fasten, to bar; to do; to make up, to raise as profit.*

Make dainty, *to hold out, or refuse, affecting to be delicate or dainty.*

Make forth, *to go forth? to advance?*

Make nice, *to be scrupulous.*

Make strange, *to affect coyness, coldness, indifference.*

Male, *a male parent.*

Malkin, *the diminutive of Mal (Mary), a contemptuous term for a coarse wench.*

Malt-horse, *a dull heavy horse, like a brewer's horse.*

Malt-worms, *tipplers of ale.*

Manage, *management, administration, conduct; a course, a running in the lists; the training of a horse how to obey the hand and voice; the management or government of a horse.*

Mandragora, *mandrake, often mentioned as a powerful soporific.*

Mankind, *masculine, violent, termagant.*

Man of salt, *a man of tears.*

Man of wax, *a man as perfectly formed as if he had been modelled in wax.*

Many, *a multitude.*

Marchpane, *a sort of sweet biscuit.*

Mare (Rides the wild), *plays at see-saw.*

Mart, *to traffic.*

Mary-buds, *marigold-buds.*

Match, *compact; — to set a match, to make an appointment.*

Mate, *to confound, to bewilder; to match, to equal; to marry.*

Maugre, *in spite of.*

Maund, *basket.*

Meacock wretch, *a spiritless, dastardly wretch.*

Meal'd, *mingled, compounded.*

Mean, *instrument used to promote an end; the intermediate part between the tenor and treble (in music); opportunity, power.*

Measles, *lepers, scurvy fellows.*

Measure, *a dance.*

Meddle, *to mingle, to mix.*

Meed, *merit, desert.*

Meet with, *to counteract; — to be meet with, to be even with.*

Meiny, *household attendants, retinue.*

Mell with, *to meddle with.*

Mephostophilus, *the evil spirit in the popular History of Faustus, and in Marlowe's play of the same name.*

Merchant, *a familiar and contemptuous term, equivalent to "chap, fellow;" a merchantman, a ship of trade.*

Mere, *absolute, entire.*

Mess, *a small portion; a party of four.*

Mete-yard, *a measuring-yard.*

Micher, *a truant.*

Middle-earth, *our earth or world.*

Mince, *to walk in affected manner, mincing, or making small, the steps.*

Mind, *to intend, to be disposed; to remind; to call to remembrance.*

Miser, *a miserable creature, a wretch.*

Misprise, *to undervalue; to mistake.*

Miss, *misbehaviour; loss, want; — to do without, to dispense with.*

Mo, *more.*

Shakespeare. VII.

Mobled, *muffled or covered up about the head.*

Modern, *trite, ordinary, common.*

Moiety, *a portion, a share.*

Momentary, *lasting for a moment, momentary.*

Montanto, *a fencing term.*

Moon-calf, *a false conception, or a foetus imperfectly formed, in consequence, as was supposed, of the influence of the moon, a monster.*

Morisco, *a morris-dancer.*

Mortal, *deadly, murderous; — exceeding, very.*

Mortified, *dead to the world, ascetic.*

Mortise, *a hole cut in one piece of wood fitted to receive the tenon or correspondent portion of another piece.*

Mort of the deer, *death of the deer.*

Mot, *a motto, a word, a sentence.*

Motion, *a puppet-show; a puppet.*

Motley, *the particoloured dress worn by domestic fools or jesters.*

Mouse, *a term of endearment; — to tear in pieces, to devour; to hunt for mice.*

Mouse-hunt, *stoat, a sort of weasel.*

Mow, *a wry mouth, a distorted face; — to make mouths.*

Much, *an ironical expression of contempt and denial.*

Muset, *a muse (of a hare), an opening in a fence or thicket.*

Mutine, *to mutiny.*

Mutines, *mutineers.*

Mutton, *a cant term for a courtesan.*

Mystery, *an art, a calling.*

Napkin, *a handkerchief.*

Nayword, *a watch-word; a by-word, a laughing-stock.*

Neif, *a fist.*

Nether-stocks, *lower stocks, stockings.*

Nice, *scrupulous, precise, squeamish; trifling, unimportant, petty; particular (?).*

Nicholas' clerks (Saint), *a cant term for highwaymen and robbers.*

Nick (Out of all), *beyond all reckoning.*

Night-rule, *night-revel, night-sport.*

Nill, *will not.*

Nine-men's-morris, *a place set apart for a Moorish dance by nine men.*

Noble, *a gold coin.*

Nobless, *nobleness.*

Noddy, *a simpleton, a fool.*

Noise (Sneak's), *means a company of musicians or a concert.*

Nonce (For the), *for the once, for the occasion.*

Not, *not only.*

Not ever, *not always.*

Nousle, *to nurse.*

Novem, *or Novum, a game at dice, played by five or six persons.*

Nowl, *head.*

Nuncle, *a contraction of mine uncle (and the usual address, it appears, of the domestic fool to his superiors).*

O, *any thing circular.*

Oathable, *capable of having an oath administered.*

Ob, *the abbreviation of obolum.*

Obsequious, *careful of obsequies or of funeral rites; belonging to obsequies, funereal.*

Obstacle, *obstinate.*

Occupation, *mechanics; a man of any –, a mechanic.*

'Ods pittikins, *God's pity, diminutively used by the addition of ,,kin."*

Oeilliards, *amorous glances, ogles.*

O'ercrows, *crows over, triumphs over, overpowers.*

O'erlooked, *bewitched.*

O'er-raught, *over-reached, cheated; overtook, overpassed.*

Of, *on.*

Omen, *a portentous event.*

On, *of.*

Once, *sometime, at one time or other; once for all.*

Opal, *a gem which varies its appearance (colours) as it is viewed in different lights.*

Opinion, *credit, reputation; self-opinion, conceit.*

Opposite, *an adversary; — adverse, hostile.*

Orb, *the orbit, the path of a planet; the circle in a field, known by the name of fairy-ring.*

Ordinant, *ordaining, decreeing, swaying.*

Ort, *a scrap, a leaving.*

Ostent, *a show, a display.*

Ouphs, *elves, goblins.*

Overscutched, *over-whipped.*

Owe, *to own, to have, to possess.*

Pack, *to practise unlawful confederacy or collusion.*

Paction, *a compact, a contract, an alliance.*

Paddock, *toad; a familiar spirit, in the shape of a toad.*

Paid, *see: Pay.*

Pajock, *certainly means peacock.*

Palabras, *words.*

Pale, *paleness; — to make pale; to enclose as with a pale, to encompass, to encircle.*

Pall, *to cloak, to wrap.*

Palled fortunes, *decayed, waned, impaired fortunes.*

Palter, *to shuffle, to equivocate, to act or speak unsteadily or dubiously with the intention to deceive.*

Pantler, *the servant who took care of the pantry or of the bread.*

Parcel-gilt, *partly-gilt.*

Parish-garden, *a vulgarism for Paris-garden, the famous bear-garden in Southwark.*

Paritor, *an officer of the Bishop's Court.*

Parle, *a parley; — to parley.*

Parlous, *perilous.*

Part, *partly; — a party; — to depart.*

Partake, *to take part; to extend participation of.*

Parted, *endowed with parts.*

Pash, *head.*

Pass, *to surpass, to exceed limits, to pass belief; to die; to pass sentence; to care for, to regard; to assure, to convey.*

Passable, *that may be passed through; sufficient to procure a pass or admission.*

Passado, *a pass or motion forwards (a fencing term).*

Passage, *the moving to and fro, the crossing, of passengers; a passing away.*

Passion, *sorrow, emotion; — to express sorrow or emotion.*

Passionate, *sorrowful; — to express passionately.*

Pastry, *a room where pastry is made.*

Patch, *a domestic fool.*

Patchery, *roguery.*

Pattern, *an instance, an example.*

Pauca (*a cant expression*), *the abbreviation of* pauca verba.

Pavin, *a grave and stately dance.*

Pay, *to beat; to punish, to dispatch, to settle; to requite, to hit.*

Peak, *to become emaciated; to mope, to be spiritless.*

Peat, *pet, fondling, darling.*

Pedant, *a teacher of languages, a schoolmaster.*

Peevish, *silly, foolish, trifling.*

Peg-a-Ramsey, *a tune.*

Peise, *to weigh down, to oppress; to poise, to balance.*

Pelleted, *formed into small balls (globules, drops); consisting of small balls (hail-stones).*

Pelting, *paltry, contemptible.*

Penner, *a case for holding pens.*

Perdy, *verily (par Dieu).*

Perfect, *certain, well assured, well informed; — to instruct fully.*

Perforce, *by violence; of necessity.*

Periapts, *amulets, charms worn as preservatives against diseases or mischief.*

Period, *an end, a conclusion; — to put an end to.*

Perjure, *perjurer; — to taint with perjury, to corrupt.*

Pertly, *alertly, quickly; saucily.*

Pew-fellow, *companion, partner.*

Pheeze, *to beat, to chastise, to humble.*

Phisnomy, *physiognomy.*

Pick, *to pitch.*

Pied, *parti-coloured.*

Pight, *pitched; fixed, settled.*

Pilcher, *scabbard, sheath.*

Pill, *to pillage, to spoil, to rob.*

Pin-and-web, *cataract in the eye.*

Pinked, *worked in eyelet-holes.*

Pitch and pay, *a proverbial expression equivalent to pay down at once, pay on delivery.*

Place, *a seat, a mansion, a residence; a term in falconry, meaning "the greatest elevation which a bird of prey attains in its flight;" precedence; an office of honour, preferment; in place, present.*

Plague, *a punishment; — to punish.*

Plain, *to complain; to make plain.*

Planched, *boarded, planked,*

Plash, *a pool.*

Plates, *pieces of silver money.*

Platforms, *plans, schemes.*

Plausibly, *by acclamation.*

Plausive, *pleasing, taking; specious, plausible.*

33*

Pleached, *interwoven*, *intertwined*.

Please-man, *an officious parasite*.

Point, *a lace furnished with a tag by which the breeches were held up*.

Point-device, *finically-exact*, *minutely-exact*.

Poking-sticks, *instruments for setting the plaits of ruffs*.

Polled, *shorn*, *bald-headed*; *bared*, *cleared*.

Pomander, *a ball of perfume*.

Pomewater, *a species of apple*.

Poor-John, *hake salted and dried*.

Porpentine, *a porcupine*.

Port, *external pomp of appearance, state; a gate;* — *to bring into port*.

Possess, *to inform precisely; to have power over, as an unclean spirit, to render insane*.

Potato, *formerly regarded as a strong provocative*.

Pottle, *a measure of two quarts*.

Pouncet-box, *perfume-box*.

Powder, *to salt*.

Practice, *contrivance, artifice, stratagem, treachery, conspiracy*.

Practisants, *confederates in stratagem*.

'praise, *to appraise*.

Prank, *to deck out, to dress up, to adorn*.

Precedent, *the original draft of a writing: a prognostic, an indication*.

Preceptial, *consisting of precepts*.

Pregnant, *ready and knowing; apprehensive, ready to understand; full of force or conviction, or full of proof in itself; dexterous, ready*.

Presence, *person; the presence-chamber in a palace*.

Press, *an impress, a commission to force persons into military service; a crowd, a throng*.

Prest, *ready*.

Pretence, *intention, design*.

Pretend, *to intend, to design; to hold out? to portend?*

Prevent, *to anticipate*.

Prick, *a point on the dial; the point in the centre of the butts; a prickle; a skewer;* — *to nominate by a puncture or mark*.

Pricket, *a buck of the second year.*

Prime, *first, principal; eager;* — *the spring*.

Primero, *a game at cards*.

Princox, *a pert youth*.

Print (in), *with great exactness, with precision*.

Private, *privacy; private and confidential intelligence*.

Prize, *privilege*.

Prodigious, *portentous, unnatural, monstrous;* — *son, Launce's blunder for prodigal son*.

Proface, *much good may it do you.*

Proin, *to prune*.

Prone, *prompt, ready, significant, expressive; forward, headstrong*.

Proof, *firm temper, impenetrability*.

Proper, *one's own, what belongs to an individual; well-looking, handsome*.

Property, *a thing quite at our disposal, and to be treated as we please;* — *to appropriate, to make a property of; to endow with properties or qualities*.

Propose, *conversation;* — *to discourse, to hold forth; to converse; to image to oneself*.

Prorogue, *to lengthen out, to prolong; to put off, to delay*.

Provand, *provender*.

Pugging, *prigging, thieving*.

Pulpiter, *a preacher*.

Pun, *to pound, to beat*.

Punto, *a thrust, a stroke*.

Purchase, *a cant term for stolen goods, booty*.

Put on, *to instigate*.

Puttock, *a kite*.

Quail, *to overpower; to faint, to sink into dejection; to slacken; to relax*.

Quaint, *ingenious, clever, artful; neat, elegant, well-fancied*.

Quality, *(used technically to signify) the profession of an actor; a profession, a calling, an occupation*.

Quarrel, *square-headed arrow*.

Quarry, *a heap of dead game*.

Quarter, *an allotted post or station*.

Quat, *a pimple*.

Queasy, *squeamish, fastidious; delicate, unsettled, what requires to be handled nicely; nauseated, disgusted*.

Quell, *murder, assassination;* — *to kill*.

Quern, *a hand-mill for grinding corn*.

Quest, *a search, an inquiry; an inquest, an impannelled jury; an inquisition*.

Question, *conversation; a point, a topic; — to converse.*

Quick, *living, alive; lively; inventive, quick-witted; pregnant.*

Quip, *a sharp retort, a taunt, a repartee.*

Quire, *a company, an assembly; — to sing in concert.*

Quit, *to acquit; to requite, to retaliate, to avenge; to set free, to release.*

Quittance, *an acquittance, a release, a discharge; a requital; — to requite.*

Quiver, *nimble, agile, active.*

Quoif, *a cap.*

Quote, *to note, to mark.*

Rabbit-sucker, *a sucking rabbit.*

Rabble, *a band of inferior spirits.*

Rack, *a mass of vapoury clouds; — to move like vapour; to exaggerate.*

Ragged, *broken, unequal, rough; beggarly, base, ignominious.*

Rank, *a row; — exuberant, grown to great height; gross.*

Rapture, *a violent seizure; a fit.*

Rascal, *a deer lean and out of season.*

Rash, *quick, hasty, sudden, violent.*

Raught, *reached; snatched away.*

Ravin, *to devour eagerly; — ravening, devouring.*

Rayed, *berayed, befouled.*

Read, *advice, counsel.*

Ready, *dressed.*

Reason, *to converse, to talk.*

Rebate, *to make obtuse, to dull.*

Recheat, *a point of the chase to call back the hounds.*

Reck, *to care for.*

Recorder, *a sort of flute or flageolet.*

Reechy, *smoky; sweaty, greasy, filthy.*

Regard, *respect, consideration; a look; a view, a prospect.*

Regiment, *government, sway, rule.*

Regreet, *an exchange of (and simply a) salutation; — to re-salute, to salute.*

Reguerdon (In), *in recompense, in return.*

Remember, *to remind; to mention.*

Remorseful, *compassionate, full of pity.*

Remorseless, *pitiless, relentless.*

Render, *an account, an avowal, a confession; — to describe, to represent, to give an account, to state.*

Renege, *to deny; to renounce.*

Repeal, *a recall; — to recall.*

Replication, *a repercussion, a reverberation; a reply.*

Repured, *purified.*

Resolve, *to satisfy, to inform, to remove perplexity or uncertainty, to convince, to solve; to make up one's mind fully; to dissolve.*

Respect, *regard, consideration.*

Respective, *respectful, formal; mindful, considerate; worthy of regard or respect, respectable; regardful.*

Rest (To set up one's), *meaning that the speaker is perfectly determined on a thing, is a metaphor taken from play, where the highest stake the parties were disposed to venture was called the rest.*

Retire, *a retreat; — to withdraw, to draw back.*

Re-word, *to repeat in the same words; to re-echo.*

Rid, *to dispatch, to get rid of; to destroy.*

Riding the mare, *being hanged.*

Rigol, *a circle, a round.*

Rim, *entrails.*

Ring-time, *time for marriage.*

Rivage, *a back, a shore.*

Rivals, *partners, associates.*

Rivo, *a Bacchanalian exclamation.*

Road, *a roadstead, a haven; a journey; an inroad.*

Romage, *tumultuous hurry, or movement.*

Ronyon, *a mangy, scabby creature.*

Rook'd, *squatted down, lodged, roosted.*

Rother, *a horned beast.*

Round, *a dance in a circle with joined hands; a diadem; — plain-spoken, unceremonious, without reserve; — to surround; to grow round; to whisper.*

Rouse, *a large draught, a bumper, a carouse.*

Rout, *a company, a multitude, a tumultuous crowd, a rabble; a tumult, a brawl.*

Roynish, *mangy, scabby.*

Ruddock, *red breast.*

Sad, *serious, grave.*

Safe, *to make safe.*

Sag, *to hang down heavily, to droop, to flag.*

Said, *see: well-said.*

Sain, *said.*

Sallet, *a close-fitting headpiece.*

Saltiers, *satyrs.*

Samingo, *a corruption or abbreviation of, or intended blunder for, San Domingo, and used as the burden to a drinking-song.*

Sand-blind, *very dim-sighted, purblind.*

Sans, *without.*

Sauce, *to treat insolently, to abuse; (in vulgar language) to serve out.*

Savagery, *barbarity, cruelty; wild growth.*

Saw, *a saying, a maxim, a discourse.*

Say, *an assay, a sample, a taste.*

Scamble, *to scramble.*

Scape, *a sally, an irregularity, a freak; an act of lewdness.*

Scarf, *to put on loosely like a scarf; to cover as with a bandage; to adorn with flags and streamers.*

Scathe, *hurt, damage; — to hurt, to injure.*

Sconce, *a round fortification; a head; — to ensconce, to hide.*

Scotch, *to make incisions, to score or cut slightly.*

Scroyles, *scabby fellows.*

Sculls, *shoals.*

Scut, *a tail.*

Seam, *grease, lard.*

Season, *to confirm, to establish; (in a culinary sense) to preserve by salting; to temper.*

Sect, *sex; a cutting.*

Seel, *to close up the eyes, to blind.*

Seeming, *specious; — fair appearance; — seemly, becomingly.*

Seethe, *to boil.*

Seld, *seldom.*

Self-bounty, *inherent generosity.*

Semblable, *a resemblance, a likeness; — like, resembling, similar.*

Sennet, *a particular set of notes on the trumpet or cornet.*

Serpigo, *a sort of tetter or dry eruption on the skin.*

Servant, *lover.*

Setter, *one who watches, and points out to his comrades, the persons to be plundered.*

Shales, *shells the outer coats of fruits.*

Shards, *fragments of broken pottery, of pots, of tiles, etc.*

Shearman, *one who shears woollen cloth.*

Sheen, *brightness, splendour; — shining, bright.*

Sheep-biter, *a cant term for a thief.*

Sheep-biting, *thievish, thieve-like.*

Shend, *to chide, to rate, to scold.*

Shent, *treated roughly, ruined, undone.*

Ship-tire, *a sort of head-dress.*

Shoon, *shoes.*

Shove-groat, *a game.*

Shrive, *to confess as a priest does a penitent.*

Sib, *akin, related to.*

Side sleeves, *long sleeves.*

Siege, *seat; place, rank; stool.*

Sightless, *unsightly; invisible.*

Sign, *to show, to denote, to mark.*

Silly, *harmless, inoffensive; plain, simple.*

Simular, *a simulator; — counterfeited.*

Single, *weak, feeble; simple, void of guile.*

Sink-a-pace, *a corruption of* cinque-pace *(a dance).*

Sir, *a gentleman; a gallant, a courtier; a title formerly applied to priests and curates in general; used by a speaker in soliloquy.*

Sire, *to beget, to produce.*

Sirrah, *used not as a word of disrespect, but as a familiar address; an address to a woman.*

Sizes, *allowances.*

Skills not, *it matters not, it makes no difference.*

Skinker, *drawer.*

Skipper, *a youngster.*

Skirr, *to move rapidly, to scour.*

Sleavesilk, *soft floss silk.*

Sledded, *borne or mounted on a sled.*

Sleided silk, *untwisted silk.*

'slight, *a contraction of by this light, or by his (God's) light.*

Slip, *a piece of false money, synonymous with counterfeit; the noose by which greyhounds were held before they were allowed to start for the game; — to loose the hounds from the slip.*

Sliver, *a slip, a slice, a portion cut or broken off; — to cleave, to split, to cut off, to tear off.*

Slop, *large loose trousers or breeches.*

Slubber, *to do carelessly or imperfectly; to obscure, to soil.*

Smirch, *to smut, to soil, to obscure.*

Smooth, *to stroke, to caress, to fondle, to flatter.*

Snatches, *shuffling, quibbling answers; fragments, scraps.*

Sneak-cup, *one who sneaks from his cup, balks his cup.*

Sneap, *a check, a rebuke, a snubbing; — to check, to nip.*

Snick-up, *an exclamation of contempt, equivalent to " Go and hang yourself !"*

Snuff, *an object of contempt; snuffs, angers, offence-takings.*

Solace, *to render mirthful, to amuse; to be mirthful, to take pleasure.*

Solve, *solution.*

Sometime, *sometimes; formerly, in other times.*

Sonties (By God's), *by God's saints? or by God's sanctity? or by God's santé (i. e. health)?*

Sooth, *truth; sweetness, softness.*

Sort, *a set, a company, a crew; rank, quality; a lot; — to class, to rank; to choose, to select; to suit, to accord, to fit: to adapt, to frame; to associate, to consort; to bring to a good issue (or simply to an issue); to fall out, to happen in the issue.*

Sorts, *classes or orders of persons; different degrees; portions or companies.*

Sowl, *to lug, to seize.*

Speak thick, *or fast, to crowd one word on another, without proper intervals of articulation.*

Speak within door, *do not clamour so as to be heard beyond the house.*

Sperr, *to shut, to bar, to make fast.*

Spill, *to destroy.*

Spleen, *humour, caprice, and inconstancy; haste in excess; violent mirth.*

Sprag, *or sprack, ready, quick, alert.*

Spring, *a young shoot of a tree; a beginning.*

Square, *equitable, fair; quadrate, suitable; — to quarrel.*

Squash, *an unripe peascod.*

Squire, *a square, a rule.*

Stage, *to exhibit publicly, to represent on the stage.*

Staggers, *a kind of apoplexy which attacks horses.*

Stain, *tincture; disgrace.*

Stale, *a decoy, bail; a stalking-horse, a pretence, a mask; a cant term for a prostitute; laughing stock, harlot; —*

to render stale, *to make cheap or common.*

Stall, *to dwell; to keep as in a stall; to install, to invest.*

Staniel, *another name for the kestrel or windhover.*

Star, *sphere.*

Starkly, *stiffly.*

State, *an estate; a raised chair, with a canopy over it, a chair of state; a person of high rank.*

Station, *a mode of standing, an attitude; the act of standing, the state of repose.*

Statist, *a statesman.*

Stell'd, *fixed.*

Stickler, *an arbitrator in combats.*

Stigmatic, *a deformed person.*

Stint, *to cease; to stop, to cause to stop.*

Stithy, *a smithy, a forge.*

Stoccado, stoccata, *a thrust in fencing.*

Stock, *a stocking; an abbreviation of stoccado: — to put in the stocks.*

Stomach, *stubborn resolution, courage; anger, resentment: pride, arrogance; — to resent, to bear an angry remembrance of.*

Stone-bow, *a cross-bow for shooting stones, or rather bullets.*

Stoop, *or stoup, a cup.*

Stover, *fodder.*

Strain, *a turn, a tendency, an inborn disposition; a stock, a race, a lineage.*

Strange, *coy, shy, reserved; foreign, a stranger.*

Strappado, *a kind of military punishment.*

Strike, *(a naval term) to lower the sails; to blast or affect by sudden and secret influence; to tap.*

Stuck, *a thrust in fencing.*

Stuff, *luggage, movables.*

Subscribe, *to agree to; to yield, to give way, to surrender.*

Sugar mixed with wine, *in Shakespeare's time it was a common custom in England to mix sugar with wine.*

Suggest, *to tempt, to incite, to seduce.*

Suggestion, *temptation, seduction.*

Suit, *a court-solicitation, a petition or request made to a prince or statesman; a love-suit; suit-service, service due to a superior lord; — to clothe, to dress.*

Sumpter, *a horse or mule to carry necessaries on a journey.*

Suppose, *supposition.*

Surcease, *a cessation*; — *to cease.*

Swart, *black, dark, dusky.*

Swath, *a line or row of grass as left by the scythe; a linen bandage for a new-born child; infancy.*

Sweet-and-twenty, *twenty times sweet.*

Sweeting, *a kind of sweet apple.*

Sweet mouth, *sweet tooth.*

Sworder, *a swordsman, a cutthroat, a gladiator.*

Table, *a board, a pannel, the surface on which a picture is painted; the whole collection of lines on the skin within the hand; a memorandum-book.*

Tabor, *a sort of small drum.*

Tabourines, *small drums.*

Tag (The), *the common people, the rabble; the tag-rag people.*

Take, *to captivate, to delight; to bewitch, to affect with malignant influence; to strike (with disease); to leap; to take refuge.*

Take in, *to conquer, to subdue.*

Take me with you, *let me understand you.*

Take on, *to grieve; to simulate, to pretend.*

Take order, *to adopt measures, to make necessary dispositions.*

Take out, *to copy.*

Take peace with, *to forgive, to pardon.*

Take scorn, *to disdain.*

Take the head, *to act without restraint, to take undue liberties; to take away or omit the sovereign's chief and usual title.*

Take thought, *to turn melancholy.*

Take truce and take a truce, *to make peace.*

Take up, *to settle, to make up; to levy; to obtain goods on credit, to take commodities upon trust.*

Tall, *able, bold, stout.*

Tang, *a twang, a ringing bell-like sound; — to twang, to ring out.*

Tarre, *to provoke, to incite, to set on, to encourage in an attack.*

Task, *to keep busy, to occupy; to challenge; to tax.*

Taste, *a trial; — to try, to prove.*

Tawdry-lace, *a sort of ornament worn by women, generally round the neck.*

Tawney coats, *a bishop's livery.*

Teen, *grief, trouble, vexation.*

Temper, *temperament, constitution; — to mould, to work, to fashion; to compound, to form by mixture; to work together to a proper consistence.*

Ten bones (By these), *by these fingers.*

Ten commandments (My), *the nails of my fingers.*

Tent, *to search a wound.*

Tercel, *male goss-hawk.*

Tester, *a coin, the value of which in Shakespeare's days was sixpence.*

Thews, *muscular strength, bodily vigour.*

Thou 'rt, *thou wert.*

Thrasonical, *boastful.*

Three-pile, *three-piled velvet, velvet of the richest and costliest kind.*

Throw, *a throw of the dice and time.*

Tickle-brain, *a species of strong liquor.*

Tick-tack, *properly, a game at tables, a sort of backgammon.*

Tilly-vally, *an interjection of contempt.*

Timeless, *untimely.*

Timely, *early.*

Time-pleaser, *one who complies with prevailing opinions whatever they be.*

Tinct, *colour, dye, stain; tincture, the grand elixir of the alchemists.*

Tire, *to pull, to tear, to seize eagerly, to feed ravenously; to attire.*

Toge, *a gown, a robe.*

Top, *to rise above, to surpass; to prune.*

Topple, *to tumble, to fall down; to make to tumble, to throw down.*

Touch, *touchstone; true metal, tried qualities; a feat; a perception; a trait; exact performance of agreement.*

Touse, *to pull, to pluck, to tear, to draw.*

Toy, *a trifle; a fancy, a freak of imagination.*

Trash, *a worthless person; — to check, as a huntsman his hounds.*

Traverse, *(a term in fencing) to use a posture of opposition, or to oppose a movement; (a military term) to march, to march up and down.*

Tray-trip, *a game at cards.*

Treachers, *traitors.*

Trick, *a peculiarity; a course, a manner, a habit; knack, faculty; a toy, a puppet.*

Troll-my-dames, *the name of a game, also called pigeon-holes.*

Trot, *an old woman.*

True-penny, *a mining term; hearty old fellow; staunch and trusty; true to his purpose or pledge.*

Tuck, *rapier.*

Tucket, *a flourish on the trumpet.*

Turk (To turn), *to change completely condition or opinion.*

Turn, *to change, to alter; to return.*

Twire, *to peep out, to gleam or appear at intervals.*

Type, *a distinguishing mark.*

Unanel'd, *without extreme unction.*

Unavoided, *unavoidable, inevitable.*

Unbated, *unblunted, without a button on the point; undiminished.*

Unbolted, *unsifted, gross, utter.*

Unbookish, *ignorant.*

Uncape, *to unearth, to dig out the fox when earthed.*

Uncouth, *unusual, strange; wild.*

Undergo, *to undertake; to be subject to; to sustain, to support; to endure with firmness.*

Under-wrought, *underworked, undermined.*

Unear'd, *unploughed, untilled.*

Uneath, *scarcely, hardly.*

Unexpressive, *inexpressible, ineffable.*

Unhappy, *mischievous.*

Unhatch'd practice, *treason not brought to light, undisclosed.*

Unhousell'd, *not having received the Sacrament.*

Unimprov'd, *unreproved, uncensured, unimpeached.*

Union, *a pearl of the finest kind.*

Unmann'd, *untamed, applied to a hawk.*

Unpregnant, *unready, inapt, unable.*

Unrespective, *inconsiderate, unthinking; unregarded, unvalued: unrespective sieve, a common voider.*

Unresting, *never at rest.*

Unsmirched, *unsmutted, undefiled.*

Unstate, *to deprive of state, to degrade.*

Urchin, *a particular sort of fairy.*

Urchin-snouted, *with a snout like that of a hedgehog.*

Use, *usance, interest of money; present possession; profit, benefit; custom, common occurrence; — to continue, to make a practice of.*

Utis, *or utas, the eight day, or the space of eight days, after any festival.*

Utter, *to sell; to expel, to put forth.*

Utterance, *extremity.*

Vail, *to lower, to let fall.*

Validity, *worth, value.*

Vanity, *a magical show or illusion.*

Vantbrace, *armour for the fore arm.*

Varlet, *a servant to a knight or warrior.*

Vaward, *advanced guard of an army.*

Venue *or* veney, *(a fencing term) a thrust.*

Via, *away! an interjection of exultation or encouragement.*

Vice, *a character in old plays.*

Vie, *to hazard, to put down, a certain sum upon a hand of cards.*

Vinewed'st, *most mouldy.*

Viol-de-gamboys, *a base-viol or viol da gamba.*

Violenteth, *becomes violent, acts with violence, rages.*

Virtue, *essence; valour.*

Voice, *to nominate, to vote; to rumour, to report, to proclaim.*

Waft, *to beckon; to turn, to direct; — wafted.*

Wage, *to pay wages to, to remunerate; to stake in wager; to be opposed as equal stakes in a wager; to prosecute, to continue to encounter; to contend, to strive.*

Wann'd, *turned pale.*

Wanton, *a childish, feeble, effeminate person.*

Ward, *custody, confinement; a guard in fencing, a posture of defence; — to defend, to protect.*

Warn, *to summon.*

Water-work, *painting is distemper.*

Web and pin, *cataract in the eye.*

Weet, *to wit, to know.*

Weird Sisters, *the Fates.*

Wolkin eye, *a sky-coloured, a sky-blue eye.*

Well said, *equivalent to well done.*

Wesand, *the throat.*

Westward-ho! *one of the exclamations of the watermen who plied on the Thames.*

Wher, *whether.*

Where, *where that, whereas.*

Whiffler, *fifer.*
While, whiles, *until.*
Whilo-ere, *ere-while, some time before.*
White (To hit tho), *to hit the mark.*
Whoobub, *a hubbub.*
Wilderness, *wildness, wild growth.*
Wimpled, *hooded, veiled, blindfolded.*
Wincot, *the usual corruption of Wilmecote, a village near Stratford-upon-Avon.*
Window'd, *placed in a window; broken into openings.*
Wis (I), *I ween.*
Wise gentleman, *equivalent to wise-acre, witling.*
Wish, *to recommend.*
Wist, *knew.*
Wit, *the mental power, wisdom, sense; contrivance, stratagem; — to know.*
Woe, *woful, sorry.*
Wood, *mad, wild.*
Woodcock, *a cant term for a simpleton.*
Wooden thing, *awkward business.*
Woodman, *a forester, a huntsman; one who hunts female game, a wencher.*

Woo't, *or* wo't, *for wilt.*
Workings, *labours of thought; acts.*
World, *see:* Go to the world.
Worm, *a serpent; also used in the sense of creature, as a term of commiseration, sometimes of contempt.*
Worts, *all kinds of pot-herbs.*
Wreak, *revenge; — to revenge.*
Wrest, *a tuning-key for drawing up the strings of musical instruments.*
Wroth, *calamity, misfortune.*

Yare, *ready, brisk, active, nimble, handy.*
Ycleped, yclipod, *called, named.*
Yearn, *to grieve, to vex.*
Yield, *to requite.*
You're, *you were.*

Zany, *a buffoon, a merry-andrew, a mimic.*
Zenith, *(in an astrological sense) the highest point of one's fortune.*

PRINTING OFFICE OF THE PUBLISHER.